P9-DNU-330

PRAISE FOR INTERNATIONAL BESTSELLING AUTHOR EMELIE SCHEPP

ON *MARKED FOR LIFE*

"A stellar first in a crime trilogy.... Schepp couples an insightful look at the personal and professional lives of her characters with an unflinching multi-layered plot loaded with surprises."
—*Publishers Weekly*, starred review

"A fast-paced thriller with a good blend of police procedural, the draw of a ninja-strong female lead, and enough adrenaline to make a good night's sleep a near impossibility."
—*Booklist*

"Move over, Jo Nesbø."
—*Fort Worth Star-Telegram*

"Intriguing.... The challenging, multi-layered heroine makes it worth the read."
—*Kirkus Reviews*

"An exceptional novel.... The author has done a great job with the characters, and readers will want to continue reading this trilogy to see how these cliff-hangers are going to play out."
—*Suspense Magazine*

"One mind-blowing thriller.... It will keep readers guessing and thirsty for more."
—*Manhattan Book Review*

ON *MARKED FOR REVENGE*

"In Swedish author Schepp's outstanding second novel, [she] sure-handedly brings her characters to unhappy life in a police procedural that lays bare the most sordid aspects of immigrant-related crime."
—*Publishers Weekly*, starred review

"Emelie Schepp is rapidly securing her place as the master of the ensemble police procedural.... Make time to read *Marked for Revenge* in one sitting. The pages just fly by."
—*Bookreporter*

Also by Emelie Schepp

MARKED FOR LIFE
MARKED FOR REVENGE

EMELIE SCHEPP

SLOWLY WE DIE

NEW HANOVER COUNTY
PUBLIC LIBRARY
201 CHESTNUT STREET
WILMINGTON, NC 28401

If you purchased this book without a cover you should be aware
that this book is stolen property. It was reported as "unsold and
destroyed" to the publisher, and neither the author nor the
publisher has received any payment for this "stripped book."

mira

Recycling programs
for this product may
not exist in your area.

ISBN-13: 978-0-7783-1966-5

Slowly We Die

Swedish Edition © 2016 by Emelie Schepp

English Edition © 2018 by Emelie Schepp

Published by arrangement with Grand Agency

Translation by Suzanne Martin Cheadle

All rights reserved. Except for use in any review, the reproduction or utilization of this work
in whole or in part in any form by any electronic, mechanical or other means, now known or
hereafter invented, including xerography, photocopying and recording, or in any information
storage or retrieval system, is forbidden without the written permission of the publisher,
MIRA Books, 22 Adelaide St. West, 40th Floor, Toronto, Ontario M5H 4E3, Canada.

This is a work of fiction. Names, characters, places and incidents are either the product
of the author's imagination or are used fictitiously, and any resemblance to actual persons,
living or dead, business establishments, events or locales is entirely coincidental.

® and TM are trademarks of Harlequin Enterprises Limited or its corporate affiliates.
Trademarks indicated with ® are registered in the United States Patent and Trademark Office,
the Canadian Intellectual Property Office and in other countries.

For questions and comments about the quality of this book, please contact us at
CustomerService@Harlequin.com.

BookClubbish.com

Printed in U.S.A.

To Dad

SLOWLY
WE
DIE

PROLOGUE

THE WOMAN OPENED HER EYES AND LOOKED straight up at me. Her hands began clawing desperately at the air, as if she'd just realized what was about to happen.

I could see her surprise, her confusion, and I whispered to her that there was no alternative, that it was too late, she had already seen too much in the back of the ambulance.

She should have kept her eyes closed, shouldn't have looked around with her meddling gaze, shouldn't have seen me take the ring.

"I'm sorry," I said, pressing my hands against her nose and mouth, "but what would you do if you were me?"

She didn't answer. How could she?

She struggled again to pull her face away from me, making one last desperate attempt. Her thin body thrashed up and down on the stretcher. She tried to grab my hands, but instead her fingers just pulled at my arms with increasing panic. Her nails tore at my skin, but I didn't stop. I pressed harder. Harder.

She tried to scream, and I heard a gurgling sound. She couldn't keep it up any longer; her strength began to wane, and she blinked a few times without any tears falling.

And then, finally, it came. The awareness. This was the end. Her brain let go of all other thoughts, taking in the reality—crystal clear and horrifying.

There was no sound, only a tiny gasp as she surrendered, as her body finally relaxed and became completely still.

I took my hand away from her mouth and listened to the silence. I smiled. It felt so simple, so undeniable, so complete.

This was a deviation from the plan, yes, but nevertheless it was a beginning. I was filled with excited anticipation, with revenge.

CHAPTER
ONE

Wednesday

PHILIP ENGSTRÖM LEANED AGAINST THE BLACK
kitchen counter at the ambulance station in Norrköping. Cool
spring air wafted in through an open window. He reached for
the cup in the coffee machine, wrapped his fingers around it
and enjoyed its warmth. Then he walked through the room,
sank down onto one of the sofas and took a couple of sips before putting the cup on the nearby coffee table.

He had one hour left before his overnight ambulance shift
ended. He had to fight a strong desire to close his eyes and
drift off, if only for a few minutes.

He knew that he shouldn't give in to his exhaustion; he
needed to pull himself together after the shift's stressful events,
but he couldn't help himself. He nodded off and was dragged
down into sleep where he dreamed of a whirling, rushing

waterfall. Then he heard someone yell, and he jerked himself awake, his hands fumbling over the table and knocking over his coffee cup.

"Philip!"

"Hi, Sandra," he said, drowsily.

Sandra Gustafsson stood six feet from him, one hand on her hip. Her hair was blond and her eyes the same green as their work clothes. She was the newest paramedic, the most recent in a series of recruits. She was in her early twenties, competent, worked hard and seemed to care about her colleagues.

"Still tired?" she asked.

"Not one bit," Philip said, getting up and wiping the coffee from the table with a wad of paper towels before sitting back down on the couch.

She looked at him as he attempted to stifle a yawn, then went to the coffee machine, picked up two cups and filled them.

He couldn't resist smiling when she held one out to him. He took a quick sip and glanced at his watch.

"Time to go home soon," she said.

"Yep," he said.

"Do you want to talk before you go?"

She sat in the armchair across from him. Her body was trim and fit.

"About what?"

"About the patient who died."

"No. Why would I want to do that?" he said, taking another sip of coffee, still feeling drowsy and thinking that he really should start taking better care of himself. The nature of his work meant his sleep was often broken, and as a result he didn't sleep enough. He knew he needed more than an hour or so here or there.

"It was an unusual situation," she said.

"It was your everyday heart attack. What is there to talk about?"

"The patient could have survived."

"But she didn't, okay?" Philip listened to the hum from the coffee machine as he thought about the woman who had died on his shift. He noticed his hands trembling.

"I'm just wondering how you feel about it all," she said.

"Sandra," he said, putting his mug on the table. "I know you're just trying to be supportive, but that psychology nonsense doesn't work on me."

"So you don't want to talk?"

"No. I already said so."

"I just thought…"

"What did you think? That we would sit in a circle and hug each other? Should we all put on our comfiest pajamas, too?"

"According to protocol…"

"Let it go. I've worked as an ambulance nurse here for five years. I know exactly what the protocol is."

"Then you also know it's not okay to fall asleep on a call."

Silence filled the room.

"Just think if someone found out?" she whispered.

"No one will find out," he said. "As far as I'm concerned, it falls under work confidentiality."

"What?"

He looked around, checking that no one was within earshot.

"You heard what I said."

"What the hell, it can't be like that!" she said.

Philip met her gaze. "Why not?"

"You're not sane," she said. "You're completely…"

"I know it sounds strange."

"Strange? It sounds wrong…"

He looked at the door and thought about how much he

wanted to leave work right this very moment. He wanted to feel the calm, hear the silence, above all be rid of Sandra.

"I'm sorry, Philip. I can't let it go. You're the one who messed up, not me."

"I never mess up, just so you know. And that's not why the patient died."

"Do you really believe that?"

Philip stared at her as he raked his hand through his hair and took a deep breath to calm himself.

"Okay," he said after a long moment. "This is what we'll do. If, contrary to my expectations, anyone finds out that I happened to fall asleep briefly on a call, I promise I'll report myself."

"What about me, if that happens?"

"You can blame everything on me. Claim you were afraid to say anything because you were new on the job and all of that. Make it all my fault."

She just looked at him.

"Do we have a deal?" he said.

"Yes, this one time," she said, quietly. "But you should really get a handle on things. One more incident and I'll report you."

"Thanks," he said, leaning forward and laying a hand on her shoulder.

"I'm serious," she said.

"I know," he said, getting up.

Prosecutor Jana Berzelius sat on one of the chairs in the broadcast studio with her legs crossed. She was waiting for her turn to be interviewed by Richard Hansen, the host of the morning program for Channel P4 Östergötland on Swedish Radio.

When she saw Hansen's signal, she walked silently to the

seat opposite him and put a pair of headphones on. She listened as Hansen smoothly changed topics and announced that next up was Norrköping lead prosecutor Jana Berzelius, here to talk about a rise in criminal gang activity.

"Extortion, robbery and violent attacks with hammers, knives and automatic weapons. Gang violence continues to increase. Jana Berzelius, you've been the lead investigator in many cases of serious organized crime here in Norrköping for many years. What do you think is the reason for the increased violence we're seeing?"

Jana cleared her throat. "First of all, we have to remember that we're talking about the number of *reported* crimes, that an increase in crime, statistically speaking, isn't the same thing as an *actual* increase in crime..."

"You're saying that the numbers lie?"

"What we can see is that gang violence all over Sweden is increasing, at the same time as violence in society in general is decreasing."

"And what is causing the increased gang violence?"

"There are a number of possible explanations," she said.

"Name a few."

She leaned forward. "You already named the most important ones in your introduction, and I can only agree that increased access to firearms along with an increase in social and economic segregation are contributing factors in this context."

"As you know, we've been tracking the criminal gangs in Norrköping," Hansen said, looking down at the papers in front of him. "Our stories about gang activities regarding the illegal trafficking of weapons, narcotics and people are our most-followed stories. It has been a year since that coverage originally appeared, and there's hardly been any improvement in this area. Very few jail sentences have been handed down, few cases have even ended up at trial and many people are saying that the Swedish legal system is failing. Should we be concerned?"

"There is always a risk of error in the criminal justice system, which in unfortunate cases can lead to wrongful convictions or even a failure to convict."

"Can a biased prosecutor pose such a risk?"

"Yes, just as much as manipulated police reports, misleading expert witnesses or false testimony. No one, not even a prosecutor such as myself, can deny that these are the dangers that sometimes result in wrongful convictions," Jana said.

"And what do you think about those voices calling for harsher sentencing for violent crimes, for example?"

"We can't prove that harsher sentencing results in fewer crimes. However..."

"In the United States, they have prioritized stricter sentencing, and it has resulted in—" Hansen said.

"But we're talking about Sweden. Norrköping, specifically," Jana clarified.

Hansen looked down at his papers again. "Stricter sentencing is an important objective of the opposition's legal policy."

"The foremost duty of criminal policy should be to work for increased opportunities for crime prevention."

Hansen looked up at her and said, "In so-called Policegate, police brass and businessmen have been accused of interfering with justice, accepting bribes and smuggling narcotics, and they will very likely receive long prison sentences, if convicted."

"That's correct."

"From what I understand, Policegate is both complicated and unusual. Besides the obviously reckless elements of violent crime, this is also about a state-appointed official of the highest level who abused his authority, and very gravely so."

"You're referring to National Police Commissioner Anders

Wester," Jana said. "But we don't have the whole story yet, and not all of the suspects have been questioned..."

"That's true, but you can't deny that harsh sentences are needed in such a unique circumstance, to set a precedent for how seriously our society views this type of crime, can you? This is about our trust in the police force."

"I can't comment on that case," Jana said.

"But don't you agree that the penal system is a way for society to see how seriously different offenses are taken?" Hansen said.

"Yes, but as I said, there is no proof that harsher sentences result in fewer crimes, in the short term at least."

"If I understand you correctly, you think that, instead, we should invest more resources in policies that focus on prevention, and this is the only way to lower crime?"

"Yes. Of course."

"And what has led you to this conclusion?"

Jana looked him straight in the eye.

"Experience."

Nurse Mattias Bohed was walking through Ward 11 at Vrinnevi Hospital with his colleague Sofia Olsson. Outside Room 38 sat a high-security guard named Andreas Hedberg, his back straight and hands folded. As the two nurses approached, Hedberg smiled shyly in Sofia's direction and stood to unlock the door.

Once they had entered the room, Hedberg closed the door behind them and locked them in.

Murder suspect Danilo Peña had been receiving care in this private room, with a security guard stationed outside the door around the clock. Mattias didn't know much more about the patient than what he had read online—that the guy was a criminal who had been mixed up in what had come to be called Policegate. He was suspected of having killed several Thai girls caught up in drug trafficking. The nursing staff that had been handpicked to take care of him had received a strict warning: absolutely no one was allowed to be alone with the patient in the room.

"Did someone forget to turn off the light?" Sofia asked when she saw that the lamp near the bed was on.

"No," Mattias said. "I don't think so."

The private room was small and, aside from the usual medical equipment and monitors, contained only a bed, a nightstand and a chair.

Sofia took out a small glass bottle and swirled it carefully before drawing the fluid into a syringe.

"Oh, by the way, you heard that the patient woke up yesterday, right?" she asked.

"You're kidding."

"Yes, I am," she said, smiling.

"Are you trying to scare me?"

"No, I just want you to be careful."

The patient lay quietly in the bed, except for the rhythmic motion of his chest as it rose and fell with every breath. He was flat on his back with his eyes closed, a heart monitor attached to his chest and arms tucked under the blanket.

Mattias kept his distance even though he knew that the patient was in a drug-induced sleep.

"What's up with you? I was just joking," Sofia said, noticing Mattias's nervousness. "He's never shown the slightest sign of waking up when I've been here. He's hardly even moved— he's been lying just like this every single time I've come in."

"But theoretically he could wake up if the medicine isn't strong enough."

"Oh, just relax," she said.

"But, really, what would happen if he did?"

"He's not going to wake up," she said. She walked over to the bed and spoke to the patient in a calm voice telling him that it was time for his shot.

"Why are you talking to him if he can't hear you?"

"Force of habit, maybe?"

She held the syringe full of sedative in her left hand and lifted the blanket up with her right.

"Could you give me a hand?" she asked.

Mattias went over and stood beside her, then reached over and wiped the skin of the patient's upper arm with an alcohol swab. Danilo Peña's body looked thin, he thought. He had probably lost a lot of muscle mass while lying in that hospital bed.

Mattias walked around the bed and tossed the swab into the wastebasket as he watched Sofia move the syringe closer to Peña's upper arm.

"Sweet dreams," she said.

Just then, Peña's hand twitched and his eyes opened. Sofia jumped back and dropped the syringe on the floor. It rolled under the bed.

"Is he awake?" asked Mattias, who had backed up several steps toward the door.

"No. Look, his eyes are cloudy, unfocused. He's still unconscious. But I wasn't prepared for him to… I mean, I was just so surprised."

She leaned over to pick up the syringe, stretching her arm under the bed, but it had rolled out of reach.

"It's on your side. Could you pick it up while I prepare a new one?"

Mattias looked nervously at the patient before kneeling down on the floor. He could see Sofia's feet and legs as he searched under the bed.

The syringe lay far back against the wall; his name tag and

the pens in his chest pocket scraped against his chest as he wriggled in to reach it.

Just then, he heard a thud above him. He looked around but couldn't see Sofia's legs anymore.

"Sofia?" he said, getting up quickly, his hand gripping the syringe.

His body flooded with adrenaline when he saw that the blanket had been cast off and the bed was now empty.

Draped across the chair next to the bed was Sofia, her arms hanging limply and her eyes closed.

Mattias stared at her, his heart pounding so hard that it thundered in his ears. Not until then did he realize that he should press the alarm button and call for help, or call for the guard. But his body refused to obey him.

He took a step back, turned slowly and discovered the patient standing completely still behind him, just two steps away, his fists clenched and his eyes dark.

Mattias gripped the syringe harder and raised it, as if to defend himself.

"Don't even think about it," Peña said hoarsely, stepping toward the nurse.

Mattias tried to jab the syringe into Peña, but his arm movement was too predictable. Peña caught his arm instead and twisted it, causing a sharp pain to shoot through Mattias's body.

"What do you want?" Mattias whimpered. "Just tell me what you want, I can help you…"

The pain in his arm rendered him unable to say anything more. He couldn't stand it any longer, and the syringe slipped from his hand and fell to the floor.

"Take off your clothes."

"What?"

"Take off your clothes. Now!"

"Okay, okay," Mattias said, but remained standing. He felt paralyzed, as if he were completely incapable of moving.

Only when Peña repeated the words a third time did he finally understand. As he pulled his white shirt over his head and dropped it to the floor, he noticed Peña's monitor wires came loose and dropped to the floor.

"Pants, too."

Mattias glanced toward the door.

"Are you stupid? Hurry up."

The blow to his face came so quickly, Mattias didn't have time to react. He touched his mouth gingerly and felt warm blood between his fingers.

Peña leaned over and picked up the syringe.

"Please," Mattias said, "I'll do whatever you want…"

"Your pants."

Mattias quickly undid the drawstring on his white pants, pulling them down past his knees. He tried to pull one leg out, but his white gym shoe got caught in the fabric. He lost his balance and fell sideways. He felt a sharp pain in his hip as he landed on the floor but continued tugging on his pants leg.

He finally got his shoes and pants off and noticed the goose bumps covering his skin. He thought about his son, Vincent, who always got undressed so slowly. He always had to nag the boy when it was time to take a bath or go to bed. Now he promised himself that he would never nag him again. Never again, he thought, feeling a lump forming in his throat.

"You forgot your socks. Come on!"

Mattias pulled off his socks, and looked at Peña.

"I have a family, a son…"

"Get up," Danilo said. "And get into the bed."

Mattias stumbled forward, lacking nearly all physical control, but he managed to stay on his feet and climb up onto the sheets. He waited, panting and trembling.

"Now what?"

"Lie down," Peña said.

"Here? In the bed?"

"In the bed."

Mattias noticed the sheets were still warm as he laid his head on the pillow. He was uncomfortable but didn't dare move. Next to the bed he noticed a heart monitor machine and IV fluid pole.

Peña bent over and attached the heart monitor clip to Mattias, then picked up the shirt and pants from the floor, and put them on. The pants hung loosely from his waist. Then he turned back toward Mattias, pushed aside the sheet and held the original syringe over the nurse's naked chest, a half-inch above his heart.

"It's time for your shot," he said with a sneer.

Mattias saw the needle pierce his skin. Then everything happened so quickly he didn't have time to react as a coldness spread through his veins.

A red dot appeared from the puncture wound and soaked into the white sheet.

He should have felt scared, but he didn't feel anything. All he could do was observe and register.

Peña said something, but the words echoed as if they had been uttered in a tunnel. Mattias saw him adjust the white shirt, pick up the pen that had fallen on the floor, put it in his breast pocket and look at himself in the mirror. He smoothed both hands over his dark hair before turning again toward Mattias.

"Sweet dreams," he said.

He walked toward the door. Mattias heard it unlock, open and close again.

"This can't be happening," was his last thought.

Then he felt it come. The silence.

Followed by the chill. It began in his feet and hands, spreading slowly from his legs, arms and head in toward his heart.

And finally, darkness.

CHAPTER
TWO

Unknown caller.

JANA BERZELIUS SIGHED, IGNORED THE CALL AND turned her cell phone facedown on the desk. She seldom, almost never, answered if the number was unlisted, and for the moment didn't want to be disturbed.

She had left the Swedish Radio offices on foot, walked down the hill and across Järnbron, picked up her briefcase from her apartment, then drove to her office in the Public Prosecution Building. Once at her desk, she cast a glance at the computer screen and began typing.

Her cell phone rang again.

This time she picked her phone up and looked at the display, which again read *Unknown caller.*

Just then she heard a knock on the glass door. She looked

up and saw her colleague Per Åström standing there with a wide grin. He waved hello with his whole hand.

She had come to enjoy Per, and now and then they had dinner together. Per was, practically speaking, the only social company she allowed herself. She didn't like socializing in general, and felt no need to hang out with other people just for the sake of it. To her, conversation was meant almost exclusively for the purposes of work. When she was in the courtroom, she had no problem making long statements in order to present facts, but personal conversations were a challenge—a challenge she wasn't interested in taking on. She wanted to keep her private life private.

Per knocked again, miming: *Can I come in?*

She looked at her ringing cell phone again, then at Per standing outside the door. If she let him in, she could count on wasting more precious work time—after already having lost a whole morning at the radio studio. Per rarely kept to the short version of stories, and even if he saw her look at her watch, he wouldn't take the hint that she had other things to do besides listening to him.

The decision was simple.

She shook her head at Per as if to say "not now," which only seemed to confuse him. So she spun her chair a half turn away from him, put her phone to her ear and answered the call. "Hello, have I reached Jana Berzelius? This is chief physician Alexander Eliasson." The voice was remarkably calm. "Is this a good time to talk?"

She frowned.

"What is this regarding, Dr. Eliasson?" she asked.

"I'm sorry to call like this, but...I would like you to come down to the hospital."

"Why?"

"Early this morning an ambulance was called to your parents' house in Lindö and…"

"How is he?"

"I'm afraid that…"

"My father, how is he?"

"I'm not calling about your father."

"I'm sorry, I thought that…"

She took a deep breath.

"I've been trying to reach him all morning," the doctor said. "Your father and I have been friends for a long time, you see."

"My father has difficulty communicating these days," she said.

"Yes, I know, and I'm so sorry about what happened to him."

"It was self-inflicted."

She looked out the window, watching birds soar high over the rooftops.

"So what is it you're calling about?"

"I'm afraid the ambulance didn't arrive at the hospital in time."

A few seconds passed as she tried to collect her thoughts.

"Are you talking about my mother?" she said quietly.

"Yes, I am," the doctor said. "And I'm truly sorry, but your mother…Margaretha…has passed away."

The sun peeked through the thick blanket of clouds, and the bare trees cast thin shadows over the asphalt. Detective Chief Inspector Henrik Levin pulled into a parking spot next to a Volvo and sat for a moment with his hands on the wheel. He looked at the police cruisers and knew that the forensic techs were already there.

Officers had searched the area and collected footage from

the traffic cameras. The search for Danilo Peña, who had apparently escaped from the hospital, was in full force.

"Hello? Are you going to sit there all day?" Mia Bolander had opened the passenger door and was giving Henrik a tired look. He turned off the ignition, stepped out of the car and walked with Mia toward the main entrance.

As they walked, Henrik surveyed the area. He saw the people's curious looks and the uniformed officers standing with their legs shoulder-width apart on either side of the rotating doors. Then he let his gaze wander over the large parking lot to the little grove of trees and stones and back to the hospital buildings.

"He's probably long gone," Mia said, registering his searching gaze. "But it's fucking bold of him to walk straight out through the main entrance."

"If that's what he did," Henrik said. "Four buses have left the area, twenty-odd civilian cars and two ambulances, but no one saw him."

"Have we closed off the hospital exits?" she asked.

"Yes," he replied.

"And monitored the buses?"

"We've checked them. Nothing."

"Paratransit services?"

"Nothing there, either."

"And taxis?"

"We've checked with all companies, but we got nothing."

"So how are we going to get him *this* time?" she asked with a sigh.

"The BOLO has already gone out. But he could just as easily still be somewhere on the hospital campus."

"I hardly think so," Mia said, wrinkling her nose. "And the guard?"

"He's still missing. Danilo probably took him with him."

With a practiced motion, Henrik lifted the plastic police tape. He held it up for Mia before he ducked under it himself and walked with heavy steps toward Ward 11.

He squinted at the bright spotlight shining from Room 38 and saw forensic technician Anneli Lindgren crouching down in the middle of the hospital room. Her white protective coverall rustled as she stood up. She pulled off her mask and nodded toward them.

Henrik stepped inside, then Mia followed. Both looked around. The air was warm, and a red handprint was visible on the floor.

"We've lifted footprints from Danilo Peña, so we know he got out of bed here—" Anneli gestured to the right side of the bed "—attacked the female nurse here, knocking her unconscious. She fell onto the chair, where we found her."

"And the other nurse?" Mia asked.

"He was passed out in the bed when we came."

"In the bed?"

Anneli nodded.

"Naked," she added.

Henrik shoved his hands into his pockets and turned his gaze toward the door.

"So Danilo Peña forces Mattias Bohed to take off his clothes and lie in bed, then Peña dresses in Mattias's scrubs, asks the guard to unlock the door and leaves the room."

Henrik walked slowly to the door.

"So when Peña leaves the room…" he repeated, stepping into the hallway. "He attacks the guard, but doesn't leave him here."

"Probably takes him with him because he wants to use him as a hostage," Anneli said. "But no one has seen either of them. Not yet, anyway."

Henrik looked up at the ceiling and stroked his hand over his chin.

"So he leaves the ward with the guard's help, but doesn't go to the main entrance…"

"No, he likely goes down this fire exit over here," Anneli said, pointing to the end of the hallway.

"Show me."

They walked through the ward past a series of rooms and stopped outside the door that was the fire exit.

"We haven't had time to go through all the elevators yet," Anneli said, "but look at this." She pointed to a bloody fingerprint on the doorframe. "But I have to get back now," she said.

"Okay," Henrik said. He listened to her footsteps become fainter as he stayed and examined the fingerprint. Then he carefully opened the fire exit door, walked slowly down the staircase to the next level and stood in front of that stairwell door, which he examined just as carefully. As he was about to turn the door handle, he noticed another bloody fingerprint. He slowly opened the door to Ward 9. Down the hallway, a television was blaring an interior decorating show. Henrik heard the show's music along with the voice of the host, who apparently was teaching viewers how to build a stepladder. Henrik headed in that direction. As he passed the room, he saw an older woman in floral pants sitting on a couch, her gaze fixed on the TV set.

He walked by a number of other rooms, their doors all closed.

At the end of the hallway, he noticed that the door to a storage closet was ajar.

As he surveyed the area, he could still hear hammering coming from the TV as he tried to count how many civilians might be in the vicinity. Suddenly he heard a moan from the storage closet.

He drew his weapon and held his breath for a moment. Then he pushed the door all the way open with his left hand, his weapon pointed straight into the darkness.

"Police!" he yelled, but then lowered his weapon, his heart still pounding when he saw it wasn't Danilo Peña in the closet.

It was the guard.

Jana Berzelius didn't bother waiting for the stoplight to turn green before crossing Albrektsvägen and speeding along Gamla Övägen. As she drove, she mentally replayed the call she had just gotten from chief physician Alexander Eliasson that said her mother was dead.

A dreamlike feeling spread through her body, and she became increasingly surprised at her reaction. Her mother—not her birth mother, but the woman who had adopted her—had been one of the few people with whom she'd had something resembling a relationship.

But had she loved her?

No, maybe not.

When she had first received the news about Margaretha, she wanted to scream at the top of her lungs, smash something to pieces. Why couldn't anyone in her life stay safe! But instead she had stood in her office, quiet and still, as if not to let the pain in, not to grant it space within her. Then, without a word to anyone, she had left her office, gone down the stairs, taken a deep breath of spring air and gotten into her car.

At the main entrance to Vrinnevi Hospital, where the ambulance had taken her mother, Jana noticed a heavy police presence. But she didn't think much of it as she stepped through the emergency room doors.

A man with a high forehead and a silvery gray beard put his hand out and greeted her kindly.

"Hi, I'm Dr. Alexander Eliasson. We spoke on the phone."

She introduced herself.

"I'm anxious to know the cause of death," she said.

"Yes, I understand," Alexander said in a calm and friendly voice. "Your mother, Margaretha, died of a heart attack. And although the ambulance arrived quickly, the paramedics couldn't save her life. As I'm sure you know, heart attack is the most common cause of death in Sweden."

Jana nodded.

"What do you think?" he said. "Should we go…see her?"

Jana nodded again.

They walked down a hallway. She was in no hurry to face what awaited her, but at the same time wanted to get the identification behind her. She walked a few paces behind the doctor. He looked back now and then and tried to smile at her, but she avoided his gaze.

"It's hard, I know," he said. "But at the same time, it's an important part of the grieving process. I've heard many people say that seeing their loved one a last time gave them a sense of relief, a release."

She didn't answer.

"But certainly, there are many ways to feel, think and act when we're confronted with the fate that awaits us all. Especially when we're dealing with a parent. Were you close, you and your mom?"

He made one more attempt at small talk, but gave up after a while when he realized that she wasn't interested.

Her concentration was fixed on her footsteps; she thought about how each step sent small, imperceptible waves through her body.

"I imagine in your profession you are accustomed to seeing the deceased. But it can affect you differently when it is someone you are close to," the doctor said when they arrived at the room.

She remained silent, and he mumbled something as he reached his hand forward and pushed the door handle.

The door to the small room opened slowly. He let her go in first, and she felt his searching gaze on her. What was he expecting? Sorrow and nervousness? Or desperation, screaming, pleading?

Instead of meeting his gaze, she stood in the middle of the room without moving a muscle.

The entire room was yellow. The linoleum floor, the walls, the ventilation shaft. There were a table and two chairs, and a print on the wall depicting a blue sky over a valley. Otherwise the room was void of personality.

A room for death.

Her mother, Margaretha Berzelius, lay on a gurney with a white sheet covering her body. Her small, pale hands lay by her side atop the sheet. The tendons were visible under the skin. Her thin-rimmed glasses were missing. Her eyes were closed, but her mouth was gaping open. Jana noticed the slight bruise marks on her mother's nostrils and thought it must have come from CPR.

"I am terribly, terribly sorry," the chief physician said, pulling a chair forward. Jana shook her head.

"Are we done?" she asked.

"There's no hurry," he said. "Take your time."

Jana felt her jaw muscles tighten.

"Thank you," she said. "But I would like to leave now."

Philip Engström unlocked the door of his single-story house in Skarphagen, stepped inside, flicked on the light and stood there as the door swung shut behind him with a thud.

From the silence, he could tell that his wife, Lina, wasn't home. Did she have a lecture? Or was she at the library work-

ing on her thesis? He couldn't remember what she had told
him when he left for work the day before.

He yawned as he took off his shoes and jacket. He continued into the bathroom and took a pill from a blister pack of
Imovane—a sleep aid—and swallowed it with a sip of water.
Then he popped another sedative, Sobril, into his mouth and
pushed it far back on his tongue to avoid its terrible taste. He
swallowed that, too.

He'd been having trouble sleeping for at least ten years now.
But he was able to get by as long as he took the pills that his
doctor prescribed for him. He could only sleep when medi-
cated, and so his sleep was never really deep or refreshing.
But at least he slept.

As he dried his hands on a towel, he realized that his ring
finger felt naked. He held up his hand and saw his wedding ring was missing. Where had he had it last? In the crew
lounge? In the ambulance? In the locker room? He hadn't the
faintest idea.

Damn it!

Philip went into the bedroom and lay down, pulling the
comforter over himself and closing his eyes. He tried to relax
but couldn't. He tossed and turned, kicked off the comforter,
then quickly pulled it back over his body again.

Shit!

The conversation with his colleague Sandra hadn't exactly
made him feel calmer. He knew that she meant well, but it
unnerved him. If she hadn't become a close friend of Lina's,
he would never put up with her intrusiveness.

Sure, sometimes you might want to process something by
talking it through. But in this case, what was there to talk
about? Nothing. Absolutely nothing. A patient died on the
way to the hospital. Period. No one's fault. It happens. Not
everyone survives a heart attack.

Truth be told, there was only one person he could really talk to these days. Not about his feelings, of course, but about everything else. His colleague Katarina Vinston, who was six years older than him and who was not only incredibly supportive, but also a skilled paramedic and ambulance driver.

He and Katarina had spent a lot of time together on the job. They had long conversations in the rig, and often ate and even exercised together in between calls. Their professional relationship had gradually spilled over into a more personal one. Katarina was the only person he could fully confide in. She was his best friend.

Philip reached for his pants on the floor, and although he knew the pills would take effect any minute, he pulled his cell phone from his pocket and called Katarina on FaceTime. When she answered, he immediately wrinkled his forehead in worry. The beautiful, dark-haired woman he knew was now pale-faced, her cheeks sunken in.

"It seems as if you've been out sick a long time," he said.

"Only a week," she said softly, "not *that* long."

"You don't look like yourself," he said, "but I'm still glad to see you."

She laughed out loud.

"I take it I should ask how you're feeling," he said.

"I'm better," she said.

"Better, meaning healthy?"

"Yes. I'll be there for our workout tomorrow."

"Are you sure?"

She laughed again, louder this time, and Philip saw her eyes glitter.

"But I would've liked to stay at home a bit longer," she said.

"Why? Aren't you feeling well enough?"

"Oh, that's not it. I'm just getting tired of working, of the routine. Aren't you?"

"No, actually. I could work forever as long as the job stays interesting."

"And you think it is?"

"Yes, I do. I like my colleagues, and enjoy being with them and they…well…"

"They like being with you?"

"Yes. At least I think so."

"And that's important to you?"

"What can I say?" Philip said, his voice steady, meeting her thoughtful gaze. "I'm reliable. Without me, the whole place would fall apart."

"What about Richard Nilsson?" she asked suddenly.

"What about him?"

"I was asked to take his shift tonight, but I said no. Is he sick, too?"

"No idea. Either he has a bad cold, or he's sitting at home with his old lady and kids. Doesn't matter to me."

"So did you take the shift, Philip?"

"Yes. I clock in again at eight tonight."

"And that's the start of a twenty-four-hour shift?"

"It's not against the rules."

She held her pale blue eyes on him for a long time before saying: "I don't understand how you can do it. Don't you get exhausted?"

"Not really," he said, and now it was his turn to smile. He grinned widely but not convincingly enough.

She shook her head. "It's never a problem for you, is it?" she said.

"Nope. I like to keep busy and I like my job."

"Well, I'm going to have a problem with you if you don't go to sleep now."

"Why? What do you mean?"

"I mean that I want to work alongside a well-rested colleague at eight o'clock tomorrow morning. Especially if you've already been working the previous twelve hours. So go to sleep now."

"It's hard to sleep when it's still light out."

"Try anyway."

"Yeah, yeah," he said. "See you in the morning, then, Katarina."

And then she was gone.

Philip put the phone down on his stomach and observed the numbness starting to flow through his body from the pills. He looked at the potted plant on the windowsill, watched the leaves swaying back and forth, and relaxed, relieved that the pills had started to take effect.

Jana Berzelius had seen death up close many times. But seeing her mother's body at the hospital was another thing altogether. It was too close, and she hadn't been prepared for it. Now her body would be sent to the morgue, lying there until the funeral took place.

Jana didn't care that a heart attack was the most common cause of death in Sweden. The only thing she could think about was how sad she felt now that her mother was really gone—forever. And that the sadness surprised her.

She rested her elbow on the inside of the car door and decided there was no reason to get all emotional. Her mother was dead, and she might as well just notify her father immediately. He should know.

She started to drive, passed a small truck, swung through a roundabout and continued on Lindövägen. She darted around a bus marked with orange-and-red circles that was about to swing out from its stop. The driver honked the horn loudly with annoyance several times at her.

When she stopped in front of the large white house in the

wealthy Lindö neighborhood, she realized that her palms were damp. Her keys jingled as she unlocked the front door to her childhood home.

In the hallway, she was met by a musty odor that repulsed her. She felt a fleeting panic in her chest and fought the impulse to leave, to escape the rotten, sickly sweet smell of illness.

But she had no choice.

She had to tell her father.

Her palms were still sweating as she unbuttoned her coat and hung it on the brass hook.

Jana glanced down the hallway lined with rooms, then walked toward the kitchen. The house was unlit, but sunlight peeked in through the curtains of the living room and was reflected on the ceiling as she passed through.

She could hear a strange rolling sound coming from the kitchen.

She stood still, listening.

It was almost three months ago that her father tried to commit suicide when she confronted him about his involvement in Policegate. She alone knew that he had been corrupt throughout his career as a prosecutor. And she had made a promise to him to never reveal it.

She heard it again. A heavy, swinging sound, as if a person was slowly wheeling himself across a wooden floor.

As she entered the kitchen, she saw the wheelchair and stood observing for a long time.

There he sat.

Old. Gray. Miserable. Incapacitated.

"Hello, Father," she said.

Lead investigator Gunnar Öhrn opened a can of Coca-Cola and drank it quickly, as if he were worried it would go flat.

Henrik and Mia stood next to him near the window. It was afternoon, and the staff kitchen was otherwise empty.

"It feels shitty to be hunting Danilo Peña again," Mia said, slurping her coffee.

"The boathouse where you caught him, might he have gone back there?" asked Henrik.

"Hardly," Mia said. "He's definitely fucking disturbed, but he's not that crazy. Arkösund has to be the last place he'd go."

Mia thought of the boathouse, and she could almost feel the cold whirling flakes as she watched the ambulance helicopter take off into the sky above her. They had managed to rescue a Thai girl from drowning, a girl who had been used as a mule in the Policegate drug ring. Close to the boathouse they had also found Danilo, the man who was holding the Thai girl captive in the boathouse and who had tried to kill her.

Gunnar sighed.

"But how could he be in a medically induced coma and then just suddenly stand up, plan his escape and just walk away? The doctors at Vrinnevi must not have been monitoring his condition very closely," he said. "Why was he in the hospital for so long, anyway?"

"I talked with one of the doctors," Henrik said. "There'd been a complication after the various surgeries he underwent for his injuries. Something had started leaking after the last of the operations when they stitched up his intestines. It caused an infection, if I understood the doctor correctly," Henrik said. "Danilo was on a number of medications as he recovered, including Stesolid, which is a muscle relaxant and a sedative…"

"And which put Mattias right to sleep," Mia said.

"Yes, Stesolid makes you drowsy. But if you stick a needle full directly into your chest, you risk hitting the heart or lungs. You can die if you don't get care immediately."

"So Mattias Bohed got lucky," Gunnar said. "Have we

gotten any information from the guard who was beaten and locked in the closet?"

"Nothing worthwhile," Henrik said.

Anneli Lindgren came into the staff kitchen and nodded at them, her eyebrows raised.

"Are you having a meeting in here?" she asked.

"Only of the more informal variety," Henrik replied.

She took a mug from the cupboard and filled it with hot water. Gunnar tried to ignore Anneli, pretending that his former live-in partner and the mother of his child hadn't entered the room.

"Was his name Anders, the guard?" he asked.

"Andreas," Henrik said.

"Sorry, I…"

Gunnar took three long, slow gulps of his Coke as he waited for Anneli to leave the room with her cup of tea.

"So. Where were we?" he said once the sound of her footsteps had disappeared down the hallway.

"The guard's name is Andreas Hedberg, and he's twenty-four years old," Henrik said. "Worked as a guard for a year or so."

"And he probably won't stay after this," Mia said.

"Why did they have a relative rookie outside the door? I thought we insisted on only the most experienced," Gunnar said. "Have we checked him out thoroughly? He didn't help Peña, did he?"

"And received a beating as thanks, you mean?" Mia said.

"Probably not," Henrik said. "But we're questioning him this afternoon."

"Should we put Danilo's name out there?" Gunnar asked. "I assume the media has already snapped up the news. You don't cordon off the entrance to Vrinnevi without good reason."

Henrik furrowed his brow.

"What do you mean?"

"I mean that Danilo Peña is a dangerous criminal."

"But we've already issued a BOLO for him once, in connection with Policegate," Henrik said, looking resolute. "Won't it make us look completely ridiculous if we put his name and picture out there again?"

"Yes, but do we have a choice?" Mia said. "How long can we hide that Peña has escaped from his guarded room at the hospital? If something happens while he's AWOL, it will only mean that we have to deal with a whole new mess of shit. Haven't we already had enough to deal with?"

"You have a point there, Mia," Gunnar said, setting his empty can on the table. "But I agree with Henrik, that it's probably better to work quietly for a bit longer."

"Good," Henrik said. "We have to focus on finding him before the media even knows that he has escaped and prove that our new organization actually works."

Gunnar grinned.

"Okay, then," he said. "Collect all of the information we have on Danilo."

"What do you want to know?" Henrik asked.

"I want to know everything. Again."

CHAPTER
THREE

PHILIP ENGSTRÖM STARED AT THE CEILING LIGHT, thinking about the strange dream he'd just woken up from. He had been in a museum, looking at a man dressed all in white who was standing completely still in a glass case. The disturbing part was that the man looked exactly like him.

He reached across the bed, grabbed his cell phone to check the time and saw that it was already five in the afternoon. He also saw a text from Lina, read it quickly and got out of bed.

He put on his pants and pulled a shirt over his head as he left the bedroom and walked into the kitchen. As usual, the refrigerator door refused to open until he jerked the handle with both hands. He surveyed its contents: butter packets, ketchup bottle, jar of pickles.

Just as he picked up the milk carton to check the expiration date, he heard Lina's voice from the entranceway.

"Hello? Sweetie, are you home?"

"Yes, I'm here," he answered. He heard the front door close as he took a mouthful of milk from the carton and put it back in the fridge. When she came into the kitchen, he was standing quietly by the kitchen table.

"Great that you're already up," she said. "Did you sleep well?"

"Yeah," he mumbled.

She caressed his arm, gave him a light kiss on the cheek and set a white plastic bag on the table.

"I got takeout."

"Oh, nice."

"Red curry."

"Are we celebrating something?" he asked

"No, I just didn't want to waste time cooking dinner. I thought we could use the time for something better."

Philip felt her hand slip around his arm, and he looked at her. The text message she'd sent earlier had been just three words: *Snuggle time tonight.*

It meant that she wanted to have sex at least once if not more in the next few hours before he had to leave for work. Their wedding three years ago had marked the beginning of a long struggle with infertility. He was now in his thirties, and she was only twenty-five, and it felt as if they already had tried everything. Their specialist could not find any medical reason why they couldn't get pregnant on their own; they were told they probably just needed to relax.

Lina eventually devised the current plan, a schedule to have sex as often as possible around when she was ovulating,

Today happened to be three days before, and so they should have sex. Not necessarily because they wanted to—just because that was how their life was now.

"We have to," she said.

"I know, I know," he said. But he didn't want to think

about routines and schedules. Not today, and especially not now. He hoped the stiffness of his smile wouldn't give him away, but it did.

"Don't you want to?"

"Of course I do."

"Are you sure?"

"Yes!" he said, much more emphatically than he'd intended.

She jerked away and refused to look at him, instead staring into the bag at the aluminum containers with their steaming lids.

Philip didn't know what to say. He hated the goddamn plan. Hated to have sex on schedule like a stupid robot.

One day several years ago he had been told by his own father that he was a coward, a loser, for choosing to be an ambulance nurse. He hadn't spoken to his father since that day, but what if he had? What would his father say to him if he found out that his son wasn't even capable of getting his wife, the love of his life, pregnant? Would he call him a double loser? Or something even worse?

Fortunately he would never know. He made a promise to himself never to speak with his father again. But even so, his father's words had affected him. He actually felt like a loser all the time, but he tried not to show it or speak of it. Not even with Lina. He didn't want to let her in that close. Didn't want her to think of him as both inadequate and weak.

"Look…" he said. "I'm sorry."

"It's okay," she said, shrugging her shoulders in disappointment and pulling one of the containers out of the bag.

Suddenly he felt dizzy and closed his eyes when he realized he was seeing double. When he opened them again, she was looking at him questioningly.

"Maybe we should just eat," she said curtly, taking out the other container.

Now it was his turn to stop her.

"Come on, now…" he said.

She shook her head so forcefully that her light brown hair fell into her face. He went over to her, lifted her chin and kissed her softly on the mouth. Then he let his hand travel over her cheek and around the back of her neck. He looked at her with a smile in his eyes and knew there was only one way to make her happy.

He pressed his lips against hers again, and this time, she responded in kind. His hands found the small of her back and her skin underneath her clothes, her soft breasts, her panties.

They might just as well make love right there on the table, or standing against the wall, or on the kitchen floor. He didn't care, and he knew she didn't, either. Nothing else mattered as long as they had sex.

Now he felt her eager hands pulling at his shirt. Her breath quickened as he pressed her against the wall, felt her body trembling in excitement. He kissed her again.

"Come with me," he said, holding out his hand.

"Aren't we going to eat?" she said, taking it.

"Yes, but let's start with dessert."

Jana Berzelius watched as her father held his fork clumsily, bringing it to his mouth with great concentration. But his hand seemed to have a mind of its own and the food ended up on his cheek and chin. She was sitting with him and his nurse in the kitchen in Lindö.

Her mother had told her that meals took time and that her father had finally begun to eat by himself, but Jana had never imagined that she would see him eating like a child, undignified, a bib around his neck and food around his mouth.

He dropped the food again, then lowered his fork to scoop up another bite when the nurse stopped him. She smiled, took the fork from him and picked up a small mound of mashed potatoes.

"Open your mouth," she said softly.

But he refused, turning his head away and pressing his lips together like a defiant child. She bumped the mashed potatoes against his mouth.

"Come now, open your mouth now, Karl."

Jana had no desire to sit there any longer and watch him struggle with his meal. She left the kitchen soundlessly.

She went up the stairs and through the hallway, opening the door to her father's office. From the doorway, she surveyed the shelves, desk and paintings on the walls.

It had all happened in this room.

Jana had tried to stop him that day from shooting himself with the pistol. The bullet had traveled diagonally, injuring the left side of his brain, which meant that he couldn't walk or move his body properly.

She stepped into the room now and walked around the desk. She saw the mess of papers and thought how nothing was like the old days. Her father's strict order was gone, the sense of control that had been his signature all these years.

She paged slowly through bills for water, electricity, trash collection. Various dates, all out of order. Dozens of papers in no organization whatsoever.

She had just begun straightening them into a neat stack when she heard someone clear their throat behind her. She looked up and saw the caretaker standing in the doorway.

"Yes?" Jana said curtly, irritated at the woman's curious gaze.

"You're the daughter, Jana, right?" she asked. "I didn't have the chance to greet you properly in the kitchen. I'm Elin Ronander."

"I didn't want to disturb him while he was eating," Jana said.

"And I'm sorry to bother you now, but I'm just wondering where Margaretha is…?" Elin said. "She always leaves a note on the kitchen table if she is going somewhere. When we came home early this morning from the overnight stay at the rehabilitation center in Örebro early, she wasn't here. I was surprised and there wasn't a note. I called her cell, but…"

Jana looked at her. "How long have you been taking care of my father?"

"Since he came home from the hospital. Your mother hired me because she was feeling overwhelmed. I work twenty-four-hour days."

"So how well do you know Karl?"

"Well, I take care of his physical needs," she said. "But I don't know much beyond that."

"I want your objective opinion. I need to know exactly how he's doing and what his prognosis is."

Multiple wrinkles appeared on Elin's forehead as she took off her glasses and polished them on her knitted cardigan.

"Karl has made considerable progress in recent weeks," she said.

"And what about the future?"

"That I can't say. You'd of course have to ask his doctors."

Jana picked up the stack of papers, tapping it twice against the desk.

"But do you think he might make a full recovery?"

Elin sighed and put her glasses back on.

"I imagine it's going to be a long and difficult rehabilitation for him, but I'm seeing distinct improvements all the time. Just a week ago, he couldn't get out of his wheelchair without help. This morning he not only got out of it, but took a few steps all by himself."

"So the answer is yes?"

"Look, it's very difficult to say for sure, but if everything

goes well, he should eventually be able to walk in the garden here."

"And his speech?"

"He will need to work on that regularly, too. Every day. He
needs that stimulation in order to learn to speak again," she
said. "And it's important that family members help as much
as they can."

"I can't come here that often," Jana said.

She walked around the desk, past Elin.

"Then your mother will have to bear a heavy load. My
contract is only for two more months."

Jana froze.

"I'll renew the contract if you will take full responsibility
for his rehabilitation. Is that acceptable?"

Elin nodded yes.

"Good," Jana said. "And one more thing."

"Yes?"

"Tell Father that his wife is dead."

Anneli Lindgren stood on the staircase landing and raised
her hand to knock. It felt odd standing there like a stranger
outside her own front door. She unzipped her jacket as she
waited and ran her hand down over her shirt in an attempt
to smooth out any wrinkles that had formed over the course
of the day.

Gunnar opened the door but wouldn't look directly at her.
He hadn't last time, either.

"It's all in the bedroom," he said, leaving the door ajar as
he walked back into the kitchen.

She noticed the odor of fried food and saw an empty fry-
ing pan on the stove. A jar of lingonberry jam and two empty
plates sat on the kitchen table.

"Don't you use the hood vent?" she asked.

"There are six boxes," he said, ignoring her question and putting the lid back on the jam jar. "They're right by the door."

"Does Adam know I'm here?"

"Adam!" Gunnar yelled at the top of his lungs.

"Well, he certainly does now!" Anneli said, smiling in an attempt to lighten the tense atmosphere.

But Gunnar didn't smile. He didn't say anything. She felt her cheeks begin to flush, and she shifted uncomfortably.

"I guess I'd better get started," she said.

"Yes, do," he said.

As she went toward the bedroom, she noticed how unkempt the apartment was. The bathroom faucet was dripping. In the living room, the remote control had been tossed onto the floor, with the batteries alongside.

The boxes were stacked up next to the closet. Four in one stack, two in another. The first box hardly weighed anything; it was probably only light clothes. The second was heavier, and she was panting by the time she got it to the car.

She didn't want these boxes, actually. She didn't need what was in them and felt annoyed that neither Gunnar nor their son, Adam, offered to carry them to the car for her.

She stopped to catch her breath and rested her hand against the cold car window. Closing her eyes, she felt the chill spread through her fingers.

A voice inside her blamed herself: *It was your fault! All of it was your fault!*

She knew it was. If only she hadn't given in to Anders that time.

It was still her own damn fault. She had been cheating on Gunnar, and now she had to move out of his condo. It wasn't the first time she and Gunnar had lived apart. Actually, she couldn't count how many times they had separated and then gotten back together again. The one thing she could be sure of was that they had been together on and off for twenty years. The other thing she could be sure of was that she had screwed up big-time.

She had thought it would be easy to find a new place to live, but the housing market had heated up. Condos were hard to come by, and rentals were in high demand. It had never been so difficult just to rent a place.

She hadn't dreamed she would have to call her mother and ask if she could live with her, even temporarily. Sure, she'd done this before—but that was when she was twenty years old, maybe twenty-two.

Now she was fifty-four.

Her son, Adam, was waiting for her in the hallway after she stuffed the last box in the car.

His skin was broken out in acne, and his bangs were combed to the side, covering his entire right eye. A white headphone cord hung around his neck, his cell phone in his right hand.

"Are you ready?" she asked.

"Yeah," he said wearily and walked past her.

"Bye!" she called into the apartment, but all she received in response was silence.

She walked down two steps but then stopped, thinking she should go back and say something, explain to Gunnar that it wasn't really fair, that this was her home, too. She should be able to stay.

She wanted to stay, to start over, forget her misstep and move on from it.

"Mom?" Adam's voice echoed in the stairwell. He was standing a few steps below her and was holding one headphone out from his ear, looking at her questioningly.

"Are you coming?"

"I'm coming."

She sighed, cast one last glance at what was no longer her front door and continued down the stairs.

Jana Berzelius crossed the street and continued on to the narrow lanes of the Knäppingsborg shopping district. The shop windows displayed a crowded jumble of hand towels, pillows and cookware decorated with branches and leaves, featuring every imaginable shade of blue and green.

Upon entering her apartment, she took her phone out of her coat pocket, hung up the coat and went into the bedroom. She noticed that Per Åström had called, but she didn't bother listening to his message. She was sure he was wondering why she'd left the office so hastily today, and she had no desire to explain it to him. Her mother's death was a private affair. She had all she could handle just thinking about having to make the funeral arrangements.

She tossed the phone on the bed, stripped down to her underwear and wrapped herself in her bathrobe. She had intended to heat up some tomato soup for dinner, but now she didn't have any appetite. Instead, she took out a bottle of white Bordeaux from the refrigerator and poured herself a glass of wine.

After two sips, she held the cold glass against her forehead. She wanted to cool herself down, repress the thoughts that had again begun running through her head. She was filled with rage, a rage that usually made her feel invincible and strong, but right now was making her feel weak—because her mother's death made her think about the death of a different woman. The woman who had actually given birth to her.

Jana took the glass from her forehead and gazed into it, at the concentric circles created on the surface by the vibration of her trembling hand. She took another sip of wine and tried to push her thoughts away, knowing that if she didn't stop them, they would take her to the painful memory of her real mother.

Her biological mom. The one who was murdered so many years ago.

She didn't want to think about her real mother. She hadn't in many years. But now she couldn't stop where her mind was racing.

She raised the glass to her lips but hardly noticed as she swallowed. She had already been dragged down into her memories and found herself back in that tight, stuffy metal shipping container as it made its way across the Atlantic. She sat huddled up next to her mother, kept asking her over and over if they would be there soon. Her dad had told her to be quiet like everyone else packed into that airless space.

They had been on their way to a new land, to Sweden, to the promise of a new and better life.

She remembered how her heart had been pounding as the shipping container was eventually opened. Three men stood outside. With weapons in hand, they selected seven children. She was one of them. She could still feel the harsh grip on her arm as she was yanked out into the light, away from the mother and father she loved and who had protected her.

That was the last time she saw her birth parents alive.

The men pointed their weapons directly into that tight, stuffy space. She would never forget the deafening sound of shots being fired. But the worst part came when everything had fallen silent and the men took a step back to admire their work.

Jana swallowed hard and rubbed the back of her neck. She drew her fingers over the welted letters that were carved there long ago, K-E-R.

Maybe it had been a mistake to start digging up her past. Maybe it would have been better to just let it be once she escaped and was adopted by Karl and Margaretha. Once she was educated and had a safe new life—even if she had no clear memory of what had come before.

But she was haunted by those carved letters K-E-R—and was determined to discover what they stood for. So she set out to collect information over the years, filling journal after journal, writing and drawing her memories from dreams and nightmares. And from all of these notes, a terrifying picture of her childhood had formed.

She had been forced to train with the other trafficked orphans as a child soldier, a mercenary whose only purpose was to kill.

Her adoptive mother, Margaretha, had never known any of this. But her adoptive father, Karl, knew *everything*. As it turns out, he had been a part of it. To protect himself, her father found out where she had hidden her boxes that contained all of her journals and notes, and he had stolen them from her, had put them in his own secret hiding place. But now he was incapacitated. She needed to find out where those boxes were stored. Was anyone guarding them? Making sure they didn't fall into the wrong hands?

Who? Jana thought, raising her glass to her mouth again.

Henrik Levin carefully closed the front door behind him. He left his shoes in the hallway, hung up his jacket, then stepped into the kitchen. He could hear his infant son, Vilgot, screaming and his wife, Emma, talking softly to him in the bedroom upstairs. She was shushing him gently, saying it was time to go to sleep.

Henrik smiled to himself and walked up the stairs, peeking quietly into the bedroom and seeing Emma standing there with Vilgot in her arms. Her delicate face was pale, and her hair, which was almost always in a large topknot, hung loose. He nodded to her quietly, then continued silently to his son

Felix's room, stroked his hair and whispered good-night. Then he went to his daughter Vilma's room, where he accidentally stepped squarely on a Lego.

"Shit!" he said.

"Daddy, you swore."

"Why aren't you asleep?" he asked, leaning over the bed and meeting Vilma's large, blinking eyes.

"You said 'shit,'" she said.

"Don't say that word."

"But *you* just did."

"We shouldn't say ugly words."

"Why did you do it, then?"

"Because I hurt my foot."

"Don't we say 'ow' then?"

"Yes, but sometimes we say ugly words when we hurt ourselves or when we're angry or tired."

"Why?"

"Because. Now, my curious little monkey, it's time for you to sleep."

Henrik pulled the covers up to her chin and kissed her on the forehead. He closed the door quietly.

Emma turned toward him as he returned to their bedroom. They hugged with Vilgot between them.

"Hi," Henrik said. "You look beautiful."

"Thanks," Emma whispered.

Henrik laid his hand gently on Vilgot's little head.

"Did you have a good day today?"

"No. Vilgot's not sleeping enough. I remember both Felix and Vilma could sleep a few hours in a row by this point. Vilgot hardly sleeps more than fifteen minutes at a time, it seems. I don't get anything done during the day. I have no idea how I'm going to be able to plan this move."

"Don't worry about it. The movers are coming a week from

Friday, and the cleaners come the weekend after that. All we have to do is pack."

"It's a little more than 'all we have to do,'" she said, rocking the baby in her arms. "I feel so stressed. When I walk around the house, all I see is all the stuff that needs to be done. You don't see it day in and day out."

"I know," he said. "But I have a few other things to think about right now. A man accused of murder escaped from the hospital today."

"From the hospital?" Emma asked, looking at him. "Who?"

"Do you remember Danilo Peña?"

"Yes, of course. He escaped?"

"Yes."

"Oh dear," she said. "And you're searching for him, I assume."

"Yes, everywhere."

"Around the clock?"

Henrik met her gaze.

"Yes."

"So I'm going to have to take care of the move myself," she said.

"Not necessarily."

Henrik let his eyes drift to the floor, seeing the scene before him again. The ambushed male nurse with the syringe stuck in his chest, the bloody fingerprints, the guard beaten and tied up in the closet. A violent criminal on the loose.

Vilgot whimpered, bringing Henrik back to reality.

"Let me take him now," he said to Emma.

"Are you sure?"

"You need to eat."

"What about you?"

"I'll eat after you do."

Emma padded out of the bedroom.

Henrik shifted Vilgot in his arms and rocked him. He felt the baby's tiny hands and stroked his soft head. Then he let his gaze wander around the room, and his thoughts returned to Danilo Peña.

A shiver suddenly went down his spine, as if someone were watching him from behind. He turned and looked out the window toward the dark yard. The glow from the closest streetlight stretched over the smooth lawn to the open area in front of their townhouse.

He couldn't put a finger on his sudden uneasiness, but something made an icy chill creep up his spine when he thought about Danilo Peña out there somewhere.

He looked at Vilgot again and saw that the baby was asleep. His heart was pounding as he laid him in the crib. Then he left the bedroom and went downstairs, going first to the entryway and checking that the front door was locked.

Not just once.

Twice.

The tomato soup was simmering in the kitchen.

Jana Berzelius left the pot on the induction cooktop and reduced the temperature. She still wasn't hungry, but she thought she should probably eat something anyway. She pulled the hollow-edged carving knife out of the knife block, cut a thick slice of leftover sourdough baguette and stuffed a piece of it into her mouth as she flipped through channels on the wall-mounted television in her kitchen to find the news station.

As she removed the simmering soup from the cooktop to the counter, she heard her cell phone ring from the bedroom. When she went and picked it up, she saw a familiar name.

Twice earlier that day she had ignored Per. This time, she knew she had to answer. She put the phone to her ear as she walked back to the kitchen.

"I think you're avoiding me," he said loudly to compensate for the noise in the background.

"What makes you think that?" she asked.

"Well, first of all, you didn't let me into your office today. Second, you haven't answered my voice mail."

"I've been busy. Something came up that…"

"I can hardly hear you," he interrupted.

"It was nothing," she said.

"I waited for you to come back, anyway."

Jana sighed, opened a cupboard and stretched on her tip-toes to reach a soup bowl.

"Why is that?" she asked.

"I was going to tell you something about a person in whom you might be interested…"

"A person?"

"Yes, a person who is now an escapee."

"And who is that?" she said.

"Danilo Peña."

The bowl slipped from her hands and broke on the tile floor. She tried to process the significance of Per's words, but it was hard to compose her thoughts as they raced around in her head. What? How had her nemesis, Danilo, escaped? It couldn't be true. Per must have said the wrong name, she thought.

"Could you say that again?" she said in an attempt to stay calm.

"You remember Danilo Peña, right?" he asked. "The Thai women, narcotics smuggling?"

"I remember," she said curtly.

"He escaped from the hospital today."

She leaned forward, supporting herself with her hand on the kitchen counter.

"And what are the police saying?" she asked.

"At the moment they have no knowledge of where he could be but believe that he's still in town. I'd love to tell you more over dinner."

"Dinner?" she asked.

"Yes—I left you a message about dinner. Asking if you'd like to come to my place for filet mignon tonight."

"Oh, well...I don't think that's such a good idea."

"But you have to..."

"...eat, I know."

Suddenly, she heard something knocking and stiffened. Slowly, she went out of the kitchen, looked down the dark hallway at the jackets and shoes and then into the bedroom.

"Hello?" Per said.

"Yes?" she replied.

"You don't even have to walk. I can come and get you, and later I'll drive you home."

"It's only a mile, Per."

"How can you say no to filet mignon?"

"I don't know..." she said, walking back to the kitchen. The light from the television colored the tile floor red, blue and white.

"I have a hard time understanding you sometimes," he said, and she realized she'd fallen silent again.

"We'll talk tomorrow," she said, hanging up.

She looked at the remains of the broken dish and picked them up, one after another, and tossed them in the garbage.

Then she stood at the kitchen counter to cut another piece of bread, but the knife wasn't there.

She looked around, thinking that maybe she had put the knife back in the block, but the slot was empty.

She muted the television. She listened carefully to the sounds of the apartment, but she heard only her own breathing.

Her hand steady, she took a second knife from the block,

gripped it securely and moved slowly toward the dark entrance to the living room.

The adrenaline pulsed through her body and heightened her senses, as she became more and more convinced that she wasn't alone in the apartment.

Her eyes scanned around the living room, seeing the contours of furniture, and then the wall. She hesitated for just a moment before reaching out and flipping the light on.

What she saw made her blood freeze.

She stood still, unable to move, not fully comprehending what she was looking at.

The man on the sofa smiled at her.

"So we meet again," he said.

Danilo.

CHAPTER
FOUR

HER BLACK NYLON SKIRT HAD INCHED UP TOO HIGH around her waist. She yanked it down, knowing it was far too short to be appropriate, but at Harry's, no one cared about appropriateness. They only cared about long, sexy legs.

Which Mia Bolander had known for a long time that she didn't have.

But she had a pretty smile!

Her teeth were chattering as she crossed the tram tracks. She hadn't bothered wearing a jacket. The fee for the coat check was too high—three dollars a night would add up to a significant monthly expenditure.

The chilly evening breeze played with her hair as she turned off Sandgatan. She looked at the construction cranes standing there and thought about how the naked blocks of concrete would soon become incredibly expensive condos. The ground floor was reserved for businesses and was sure to contain a pizzeria.

How fucking original.

Her fingers had become frozen stiff by the time she passed Strömparken. She tried imagining she was in some warm country like Spain, on the way to a club or bar without having to freeze her ass off.

Another five minutes and she had finally arrived.

There was a throng of people outside Harry's. She estimated maybe thirty people were waiting in line. Men and women with low shoes and high heels, tight shirts and plunging necklines, torn jeans and sparkly dresses.

A good night, in other words.

Mia pushed her way forward, and the bouncer waved her in. A few people whistled and muttered when she went past. She was a single woman moving slowly forward through a crowd, and in that moment, she was relishing the attention.

Men noticed her.

The music was deafening when she entered the bar. She worked her way in and studied a small group of about ten people, mostly men.

She kept her distance, watching them silently but with a wide smile on her face. She let her gaze rest on each of them for a few seconds, and prepared for the questions she could ask. It wasn't a problem if a guy had a ring on his finger or mentioned children—quite the opposite, really. It could lead to more questions, like: What are your kids' names? Are they twins? How old are they? Do they go to day care? What's your wife's name? How long have you been married?

And she knew that she would hear that the man in question was heavily dependent on his wife, who was a gifted graphic designer, or that he worshipped his twin sons, or that he had had two surgeries on his leg and liked model airplanes.

That was okay. Most just wanted to talk—about themselves. And those who did were the easiest prey.

The worst were the guys who showed off their muscles at every opportunity. She always avoided that type.

She also avoided talking about herself. But she did answer questions asked of her. It was important to be polite and pleasant.

And to smile.

It would be an exaggeration to claim that Mia Bolander was looking for steady companionship. She didn't want it to seem that way, at least. There was a certain level of turnover, and the men that she couldn't stand after the first night were sifted out. And those who got to go home with her more than once usually fell into the category of "ugly and horny."

Maybe tonight would be different?

She straightened her back, stuck her chest out and smiled even more broadly.

She was exhilarated and ready.

She prepared herself for the most important question of the night—and her answer.

Do you want to fuck?

Hell yes!

Her robe had opened so that her bra was showing. But Jana Berzelius didn't move. She didn't dare take her eyes off Danilo.

His beard had grown out, and his hair was an inch or so longer. It covered the letters carved into his neck, similar to her own. He was wearing scrubs and white sneakers. A bag sat on the floor in front of him.

"What are you doing here?" she asked.

He just stood up and walked toward her, his jaw clenched. She saw that he had the carving knife in his hand, and she gripped her own knife more firmly. She took a few steps backward, trying to maintain the distance between them, staying prepared.

"You deserted me at the boathouse," he said, referring to the last time they'd encountered each other in a manhunt.

She didn't answer. She didn't want to fan the hatred she knew he already felt for her. Before the police had arrived to the boathouse in Arkösund, she had gotten into a fight with him. She had sought him out at that cold place just to put him away for good. But when he'd told her he was working with her father, she had to restrain herself. And she had left him, wounded, yet alive in the snow.

The expression on Danilo's face changed. His eyes darkened.

"I just want to show you how I feel about that," he said, approaching her, the knife held threateningly in his hand.

The attack came quickly.

She raised her left arm to block. It burned as the sharp knife sliced her upper arm.

She dropped her knife but kept her eyes locked on him, saw him advancing again. Then all of her senses awoke at once. With a yell, she kicked the coffee table over and pushed it forward until Danilo was on the floor with the white tabletop over him, surrounded by overturned candles and a broken vase.

She attacked, hitting him in the face with brutal force.

He answered by forcing her and the tabletop off him, coming to his feet. She shook off her robe, grabbed her knife and jabbed toward his neck. But he had executed the exact same movement, and they froze with their arms parallel.

They stood eye to eye.

Her knife was against his neck. His was against hers.

"We have a problem," he said. "*You* want to see *me* dead. *I* want to see *you* dead. So what do we do?"

She was breathing heavily, yet noticed the beads of sweat that had formed at his temples.

They were standing far too close to each other, which made it difficult to anticipate his next movement.

"I don't know," she said. "I don't see any good reason *not* to kill you."

"I can give you one," he said.

She looked at him. She felt the urge to make her final attack, but something was stopping her.

The blood ran in rivulets from the wound on her arm, dripping from her elbow to the floor.

"The boxes," he said. "Your journals, your notes, your identity."

She looked at him. His facial expression changed, and he lowered his knife toward the floor and looked at her calmly.

She attempted to process the situation. She hadn't been prepared for him to retreat, so she waited a few seconds before taking two steps back and lowering her knife, as well.

"I don't know what you're talking about," she said.

"Yes, you do. And I know you want them back."

"You don't know anything," she said, picking her robe up from the floor without taking her eyes off him. The wound on her arm stung as she pulled the fabric over it.

"It just so happens that I do," he said.

She tied the belt as tightly as she could around her waist and gripped the knife again.

"What exactly do you want?"

"I thought we could exchange services."

"Exchange what?"

"Your boxes—the ones that hold your secrets—for you letting me stay here."

"What?"

"I'll give you your boxes back, safe and secure, and you'll let me stay here."

"Are you serious?"

"Yes."

"That's not possible."

"Why not?"

"You're a wanted man, Danilo. The police are searching all over for you."

"I'm aware of that, and that's why this is the best place to hide."

She felt her irritation growing and was having a hard time standing still.

"No," she said, shaking her head.

"I'll stay here until things have calmed down a little," he said. "You're a prosecutor. No one will suspect you."

"It won't work! Don't you understand? It's impossible!"

"You want your boxes back, right? They contain your letters, journals, evidence of things that could destroy you…"

"You're forgetting something. They contain information about you, too."

"But I'm the one who has them, and I don't care about my reputation. If you don't let me stay here, I'll make sure to send the contents to everyone who might be interested in getting to know the real you."

"You can't."

"Karl wouldn't like the truth coming out, either. Think about what he's done to you, to me, and all the other children who came here in those shipping containers. He has marked us as his own. Your adoptive father is evil personified. And you have been complicit in not turning him in to the police. Think about every one of his guilty cronies he has protected, all of the court cases he has manipulated, think about…"

"You're a part of all of that."

"And?"

"Is that all you have to say?"

"For me, there is no alternative," Danilo said. "Once I was victimized, I didn't have a wealthy family that adopted me, redeemed me, gave me an education, a job, a future. You've been handed everything on a silver platter, Ker."

"Don't call me that name."

"All you have to do, if you don't want anyone to find out about your complicit past, is let me stay here."

She took a step forward, trying to breathe more calmly, but the aggression held her in its iron grip.

"If they do catch me," Danilo said, "you can say goodbye to your job as prosecutor, goodbye to your luxury apartment, goodbye to your freedom…"

She examined his face, searching for any clues that he was bluffing, but he looked perfectly calm.

"You're lying," she said. "You don't have the boxes. You don't even know where they are!"

"I do."

"My father has them! He took them."

"Wrong, Jana. Your father and I took them together."

"Why should I believe you? Out at Arkösund, when I asked you, you said you didn't know anything."

"Oh, but I did."

Jana looked at him, breathing rapidly.

"Now I understand why my father saw you as a risk," she said, "why he wanted you gone."

"Maybe so, but now I'm the only one who knows where the boxes are and can get to them."

Jana's eyes narrowed.

"I still don't believe you," she said.

"You don't believe me?"

"Prove it to me."

The smile disappeared from his lips.

"Do you really think that I would bring them here, all wrapped up with a big bow on top? Think again."

"I want proof that you have them."

"You're just trying to buy time."

"That, too."

Danilo stood silently for a moment before walking toward her.

She stood completely still, unmoving, feeling her muscles tense as he approached. She let him come closer but was ready with the knife.

He leaned forward, hissing in her face.

"Is this proof enough for you?" he asked, pulling a torn piece of paper from his pocket.

She grabbed the paper and stared at it. It was a page of her journal that contained her own words, she saw, written by her child's hand many years ago.

"I'm staying here," he said, "and there's nothing you can do about it."

She gripped the knife tightly in her hand, wanting desperately to use it, but she knew that she had to release both the knife and the urge to destroy him.

Danilo was right. There wasn't anything she could do.

Not right now.

August 22

Dear Diary,
It started by first break today.

Martin and I hid in a corner of the schoolyard. Everyone else from class stared at me so strangely. They whispered and pointed and laughed.

I told Martin that we should go back into class. But when

we opened the door, the teacher said that we couldn't be inside during recess. So we went back out and huddled in the corner.

They kept it up during history lesson.

While Holger wrote the names of the Swedish kings on the whiteboard with marker, others started whispering. It began in the far back of the room, with Camilla and Markus, then traveled through the room. The longer Holger stood at the board, the more the gossip spread. Everyone listened and giggled before whispering to the next student.

When it was finally my turn to listen, Linus leaned toward me and said softly: "You are a disgusting freak."

I didn't say anything. I knew they wanted me to react, but I didn't. I just looked at Holger and tried to forget about everyone staring at me, about the mean words they said. But it was hard.

In the afternoon, I went to the hospital with my mother. It was time for yet another of her physical exams. I thought it smelled good in there, but I didn't tell anyone that.

I didn't say anything at all the whole time we were there. I just looked at the doctor, at his pale face. He tried to say he was sorry, that he understood that it could be confusing, that he knew that it wouldn't help, that it was highly unusual for an operation like the one my mother recently had to go wrong.

But how could I forgive him? He'd taken my whole world away from me.

The doctor had no answers; he sat with his head down. He couldn't say anything definite about the future. But he believed my mom would be okay.

Mom didn't think so. I could tell in her face, in her eyes. But she didn't admit that to me.

Don't worry, she said as we left the hospital. She said it again just a minute ago, too, before she went to sleep.

I'm also going to bed now, because tomorrow is a new day. A new shitty school day.

CHAPTER
FIVE

Thursday

AIDA NORBERG, HAVING RECENTLY GRADUATED from school, was on the morning bus heading home after working her overnight shift at McDonald's. Sitting beside her was her coworker Melvin Axelsson. Melvin was babbling on and on about how tired he was because he'd been running around for hours and hadn't even had the chance to drink anything his whole shift.

"Hello? We work in a total sauna. How the hell do you stand it?" he said to her.

She didn't respond. She let him continue complaining as she looked out the bus window. The glass was scratched and dirty, but she could make out the contours of people walking along the street.

At Eneby Center, she said goodbye to Melvin and stepped

off the bus. She could see her neighborhood more clearly now: children on scooters, businessmen in cars, students with backpacks.

She pulled out her cell phone and began walking down the street. She opened the newest version of Instagram and scrolled through the new filters, thinking how it wasn't very different from previous versions.

She selected another app.

Facebook, always Facebook.

Someone had added her to a group called Feminist Perspectives. She didn't want to be part of anything like that. She decided she would leave the group as soon as she had a chance. But for now, she was across the street from home, and it could wait.

A yellow-and-green tram went by, and garbage swirled around in its wake. She put her cell phone back into her pocket, crossed the tram tracks and went into the courtyard between two apartment buildings. She stopped outside the entrance to her building and looked up at the dark windows of her family's apartment. As usual, she felt anxious about coming home. Would it be yet another day of her mother's pitiful crying, followed by prolonged silence?

She didn't want her days to be like this.

Aida stood outside for a moment, trying to collect her thoughts. She had dreamed of getting her own place. Many of her friends already had their own apartments—studios, mostly, with kitchenettes. But it was one thing to leave home by yourself, and something completely different to leave behind your little sister.

She went upstairs and put her key in the door, and was just about to turn it when she realized that the door was already unlocked. Her forehead wrinkled in concern as she stepped into the apartment.

Her little sister Sara's backpack was still hanging in the hallway, as was her jacket. That meant Sara hadn't gone to preschool today. As Aida hung up her jacket in the hallway, she heard a weak whimpering sound. She glanced toward the room she and Sara shared. Something about the sound and the closed door made her nervous.

Was *he* here?

Aida's body tensed as she moved toward their bedroom. She noticed the key was in the outside lock. That was unusual. She had turned that key countless times—but always from inside the bedroom. This time, someone had locked it from the outside.

She swallowed, turned the key and opened the bedroom door.

The roller shade was pulled down and the smiling moon lamp above Sara's bed was turned off. Aida could barely see inside.

"Sara?" she whispered into the darkness.

There was no answer, but the whimpering sound became more intense, so she stepped in and turned on the ceiling light.

In the bed, almost fully concealed by a down comforter, lay her little sister. Her hair was tousled, and she was looking at Aida with a glassy gaze. Her eyes radiated confusion more than the fear they had when they were forced to listen to the abuse going on in the next room. But her little body was trembling.

Something unusual had happened in their apartment. What had he done this time, that fucking idiot?

"Come here," she said, reaching her arms out for her little sister. But Sara resisted.

"Calm down," she said, attempting to put her arms around her sister's small frame.

But Sara wrenched herself free from her older sister's attempted embrace, creeping even farther under the comforter. She was still whimpering.

Aida turned her gaze back toward the doorway, and at that moment began to understand. She stood up and listened intently as she quietly left the room. Various scenarios raced through her head, each one worse than the one before as she approached the living room, where she found an unbelievably gruesome scene.

She stood paralyzed with horror at the sight of her mother tied to a chair, covered in blood, her head hanging limply, her hands severed and lying on the floor.

Philip Engström was jerked hastily awake by the alarm in the ambulance station.

He swung his legs out of the narrow bed and immediately saw on his handset that the call was high priority. He had ninety seconds to get himself and the ambulance driver into the rig and on the road.

It had been a stressful night with nine calls and hardly any sleep. It was just eight o'clock now, and the second half of his twenty-four-hour shift was just beginning.

When he got to the ambulance, he saw Sandra standing there, waiting.

"What the hell are *you* doing here?" he said.

"Get in," she said, climbing in behind the wheel.

Philip raked his hands through his hair, hopped in the rig and pulled the seat belt across his chest. "Where is Katarina?"

Sandra drove quickly out of the garage, noting the address of the apartment in Eneby listed at the top of the navigation screen. She turned on the sirens and blue flashing lights while Philip began reading the information from dispatch.

"A woman has lost consciousness. Bleeding heavily from her wrists. Both hands severed. Police on the way."

"Her hands are severed?" Sandra asked.

"Yes," Philip said.

"Suicide attempt? Accident? Does it say anything more?"

He shook his head.

They drove past the hospital parking area and out onto Gamla Övägen toward downtown. Philip saw the industrial district, the fences and barbed wire that encircled the buildings.

"To answer your question, Katarina is apparently still sick," Sandra said.

"Strange. I talked to her just yesterday. She said that she would be back today."

"Yeah, but you know, the symptoms of exhaustion are nothing to play around with. I don't think she can handle the stress."

"No, not everyone can," he said.

Large clouds filled the sky, and a shadow lay over the road. The speedometer read 75 mph.

"My heart still pounds every time," she said, "as if I'm scared I won't be good enough, won't be able to help, that my efforts won't suffice."

"You sound like a professor when you use words like 'suffice,'" he said.

Sandra smiled. "Haven't you ever felt like that?"

"No." He raked his hand through his hair again.

"Not to change the subject," he said, "but you haven't seen a gold ring lying around anywhere at work, have you?"

"No. Why?"

"I've lost mine."

"You've lost your wedding ring? Nice move." She smiled.

"I already know it's not, but thanks for the reminder."

He rested his elbow on the door and looked out through

the windshield. He felt the vehicle swaying and closed his eyes for a second.

"You should stop taking those meds," she said.

"What the hell would I take meds for?" he mumbled.

"I don't know…"

"Do you think that I need meds?"

"No, but sometimes you slur your speech," Sandra said. "It's obvious you're on something."

"I'm just tired. Can't a person just be tired?"

She didn't answer. Or maybe she did; Philip didn't know. He was already in the borderland between dreams and reality.

She felt sick as she pulled her jacket over her shoulders. Jana Berzelius stood in her walk-in closet with her eyes on the mirror. The bedroom door was locked. She wasn't scared, that wasn't the issue. She wanted to be at peace with her thoughts. Her mother had just died. And now this. She had thought all night about the situation, about Danilo. About him staying in her apartment.

The police hadn't yet issued a description to the general public, which gave her some amount of relief. Just think what would happen if someone had seen him near her apartment and recognized him?

During the hours she'd been awake, she had heard him moving through the rooms, opening the refrigerator, flushing the toilet. Then finally everything had become silent. He had presumably fallen asleep, but she didn't want to know where, whether on the sofa, the floor or the chaise longue.

How had he gotten in? Through a window? Or had he been able to pick the front-door lock without her ever noticing?

Irritated, she fastened the top button on her jacket and adjusted her hair to cover her neck. She thought about how she should have been more aware, should have seen something, heard something. But she had been taken completely by surprise, and she hated it. Hated that he was unpredictable, that his movements were always so difficult to anticipate, that he could always get past whatever defense she put up. She hated his bold, competent, hostile, intense manner. Hated that he was the one who always made up the rules of the game. Hated their shared past.

Danilo was, in a way, uneducated—he had learned from experience, from practice. He had learned to navigate in *his* reality. He had no normal boundaries.

But then, she didn't, either.

Because of that, her reaction had already exposed her. That she hadn't killed him showed exactly how important it was for her to get the boxes back.

And he knew it.

She sighed, turned off the light and left her room.

"Philip!" Sandra said. "Wake up!"

"I am awake!" he shouted in the ambulance cab.

He met Sandra's serious gaze and knew that she had yelled at him more than once. They were already in Eneby.

"Bring the bag," she said, getting out of the cab.

Philip rubbed both hands over his mouth and eyes, grabbed the medical bag, and with the stretcher between them, they ascended the stairs to the second floor.

On the top step sat a teenager, her cell phone pressed to her ear. She was wearing a gray T-shirt and ripped jeans. Her hair was black, and she had a wing tattooed on her right lower arm. It began around her wrist and ended at her elbow.

When she saw Philip and Sandra, she pulled the phone from her ear and got up. Her shirt was bloody and her face pale; she was clearly upset.

"Hurry. My mom's in there," she said, pointing toward

the open door. "You have to help her. Her hands… They said that I should try and lay her down, but her arms are tied to the chair and I don't know how to free them. I tried, but I can't do it."

The girl's body was shaking.

"What's your mom's name?" Philip asked, examining the girl's face.

"Shirin."

"And yours?"

"Aida."

Philip and Sandra followed her into a room furnished with a leather sofa, round rug and long drapes. Tied to a chair in a sitting position was an attractive, middle-aged woman, wearing a black top and leopard-print pants. She seemed barely alive.

"What the hell…" said Philip, exchanging glances with Sandra. They heard Aida's voice behind her.

"She was like this when I came home," she said. "There's so much blood…oh god, I can't look…"

Both of the woman's hands had been cut off and lay a couple of feet from the chair she'd been tied to. Around each arm was a white zip tie, both pulled so tightly that they were cutting into her skin. The blood dripped slowly from her wrists. Judging from the amount of blood on the floor, Philip quickly surmised that the woman was in shock from extreme blood loss.

He rushed forward, lifted her head up and confirmed that her airway was free. He placed one hand on her forehead, two fingers under her chin, and gently tilted her head farther back. At the same time, he thought there was something familiar about her face. Had he met her before? When? Where?

"Shirin," he said. "Can you hear me?"

She didn't answer.

He leaned over so one ear was near the woman's mouth, looked at her rib cage and saw she was breathing.

"What happened? Who did this to you?" he said.

As he tried to find her pulse, he continued talking to her. He pressed his fingers to her neck and tried to establish the strength and frequency of her pulse, but he could hardly feel it.

"Shirin," he said, but she didn't answer. Only when he took her shoulders and carefully shook her did she react.

"We have to cut her loose," he said to Sandra, who was standing behind him. "Quickly."

"How should we do that?" she asked.

"I can't cut the zip ties without first stopping the flow of blood."

Philip opened the medical bag, pulled out the blood pressure cuff, placed it on the woman's upper arm. He closed the air valve and pumped it up as much as possible.

The blood flow stopped in that arm.

Now he had to stop the arterial flow in the other arm, but he didn't have another cuff with him.

"Shit, I need…" he began, but he faltered when he saw that Aida stood near the doorway with her back to them.

"God, god, god," she was whispering.

For the first time in ages, Philip felt his heart pounding.

The metallic scent of blood filled his nose as he thought about how he needed one more bandage to stem the blood flow. He stood up.

"Philip," Sandra said, but he had already left the room. He ran down the steps out to the ambulance. He found a tourniquet and ran back up the stairs with the strap in one hand. When he returned to the room, he saw that Aida had crawled into the fetal position in one corner of the sofa and was hugging a pillow so hard that her knuckles were white.

He placed the tourniquet around the woman's left arm and began to twist it to tie it more tightly. Just as he was about to tie it off, he heard a voice.

"Mommy..."

The voice didn't belong to the teenager. It was softer.

Philip lost his concentration when he glanced up and saw a little girl standing in the doorway, a scared look on her face. Her bangs were swept to the side, and her hair was messy. She was wearing a light blue nightgown with Princess Elsa from *Frozen* on the front.

"You were supposed to stay in our room," Aida said, getting up. "Go back in there, Sara!"

Aida pulled the girl's arm, but she resisted.

Philip and Sandra exchanged glances again before returning to the woman.

Philip was resolute as he released the zip tie.

"Help me now," he said, signaling to Sandra to get hold of Shirin's limp, heavy body.

They counted to three.

"One, two, three."

They placed her carefully on the stretcher, working silently, knowing what was at stake. Her condition was critical.

"The hands..." Sandra said, nodding toward the severed body parts still lying on the floor.

"We need to bag them and put them in an ice water bath," Philip said.

He opened the medical bag, pulled out two resealable bags. "Here, see if you can fill these in the kitchen."

He slipped on a pair of latex gloves, then reached for the hands. But because of all the blood, he lost his grip on one of them and it slipped to the floor.

"Shit, shit, shit," he said quietly and tried again as Sandra came back into the room with the bags filled with ice water.

His face was stony as he placed each hand into its icy bath and sealed the bag, then laid the bags next to Shirin's body. He and Sandra counted to three again and lifted the stretcher.

Then the younger girl peed. The puddle spread under her bare feet.

"Mommy!" she cried, beginning to stomp her feet in the puddle.

Aida picked her up and carried her out of the room.

"We have to go," Philip said to Aida. "The police are here now."

"Go, then," she said. "I'll stay here. With Sara."

Philip felt the bulk of the weight of the stretcher in his arms as he led them down step by step.

In the entryway, they met two uniformed officers who immediately continued up to the apartment.

As soon as they had gotten the patient into the ambulance, Sandra got behind the wheel as Philip connected the third wire of the EKG. He shook his head at the slow frequency. Usually he would have inserted an IV, but because of the severe blood loss, there was no chance he would find a large enough vessel.

He looked at the patient, studying her rib cage. It was hardly moving.

He considered using the intraosseous drill for access to the venous system through her bone marrow, but then folded the blanket back and looked at the tourniquet. He checked the strap multiple times and realized something wasn't right. It was loose.

It wasn't until then that he realized he hadn't tied it properly.

As he threw the blanket completely back, he saw the last sight he wanted to see. Blood flow to her arm hadn't stopped after all. It had continued to flow from her left wrist and collected under her body on the stretcher.

"For Christ's sake!" he exclaimed.

"What's going on? How is she?" Sandra shouted through the cab window.

"I can't stop the bleeding!"

She met his eyes in the rearview mirror, then swerved to avoid a truck that hadn't bothered to pull over for the flashing lights of the ambulance.

Philip pulled the tourniquet tighter, but the vehicle swayed and he lost his grip.

"Can you drive straight, please!" he screamed, reaching for the strap again. He pulled and pulled. He knew that every second counted now. Sweat beaded up on his forehead and his mouth was dry, but he was finally able to get the tourniquet in place. Just as he tied it off, he became aware of the sound from the EKG.

A single, solid tone.

And he knew. For the second day in a row it was the sound of a patient's death.

CHAPTER

SIX

THE PROTECTIVE PLASTIC FLUTTERED AS MIA BOLAN-
der entered the living room of the apartment in Eneby. She
surveyed the room. She estimated the ceiling height, length,
width. Three hundred square feet, she thought, which was
larger than her own living room.

But this room had blue wallpaper, knickknacks on the windowsill, and a leather sofa with a textured throw.

When she visited crime scenes in houses or apartments,
they often had broken glass or overturned furniture. But here,
everything seemed to be in its rightful place. That made it
even stranger to see the sea of blood on the floor. Chaos in
the middle of order.

What in the hell had happened?

She followed the red footprints with her gaze. It looked as
if someone had slipped around in the blood.

"Those are sock prints," Anneli Lindgren said, standing up.

"Someone walked around in socks, then took them off and walked around in bare feet. Looks like a women's size six."

"Could be her oldest daughter," Henrik said.

Mia looked at the floor again.

"The victim's name was Shirin, right?"

"Yes," Henrik said. "Shirin Norberg, forty-two years old. Born and raised in Iran. Two daughters, Aida, who's eighteen, and Sara, who's five. Was married to Magnus Norberg, who died in a car accident the same year Sara was born."

"There's a big gap between the children. Do they have the same dad?"

"Yes, Magnus was the father of both girls."

Anneli went to get her camera from the hallway.

"And the oldest daughter found her?" Mia asked.

"Yes."

"Jesus. Just think, finding your mom tied to a chair, her hands cut off."

"I can't even imagine," Henrik said.

Mia looked at Anneli, who had returned with her camera around her neck.

"Is Shirin in the system?" Mia asked, but Henrik shook his head no.

"You've checked the offender database?"

"Yes."

"And Social Services?"

"Yes, they don't have anything on her."

"The Women's Crisis Center?"

"Nothing there, either."

"Okay, so we have no known history. But she was born in Iran and has had both hands cut off. What should we call that, honor mutilation?"

Henrik looked at her without saying anything.

"I've read about thieves who've had their hands cut off as punishment," Anneli said from behind her camera.

Henrik nodded, still silent as if he were lost in thought.

"Well, should we go to Vrinnevi and take a look at the body?" Mia asked.

"It's already been transported to the Swedish National Forensic Center for the autopsy," Henrik said.

"That was fast," Mia said.

"Yes. The people at the morgue are always anxious to get rid of the bodies."

"Let's look at some of the photos, then," Mia said.

"Sure," Henrik replied. "But let's call in a prosecutor first."

The stairs down to the apartment garage seemed to take forever. Jana Berzelius took the last steps more quickly.

She had intended to work from home today but when her superior, Chief Public Prosecutor Torsten Granath, had personally called her, it was clear that she would have to get down to the station immediately. She had no choice but to leave Danilo alone in her apartment.

Her bag was heavy and was chafing her shoulder. She had packed it with things she didn't want him poking around in, like her computer and her most important personal papers and binders. It was bad enough that Danilo had taken up residence in her apartment, making it into some sort of idiotic hideout.

She had a difficult time shrugging off the unpleasant feeling of him being in her space and didn't really know how to handle it. Her whole adult life she had always lived alone, slept alone, eaten alone. She'd never had a visitor, never once let anyone come through the door.

When she'd left the apartment, Danilo had been standing in the hall, looking at her. His arms had been crossed and something resembling a sneer had been on his lips. But he hadn't said anything, and she hadn't, either. She had simply met his gaze and fantasized about putting her hands around his neck and squeezing until he was gasping for breath.

She would gladly break every bone in his body and would more than gladly erase him from the face of the earth. But killing him was not an option—not yet.

While driving to the police station she thought of her dead mother. She knew she had to make all the funeral arrangements. And she wanted to do them by herself, not involving her father.

She felt a few drops of rain on her face as she left the car and walked toward the station. She had decided she would not tell anyone at work about her mother's death…at least for now. The automatic door whirred open, and the hallway smelled strongly of disinfectant. Damp stripes trailed along where the polishing machine had traveled. Henrik Levin caught up with her; she heard his long strides before his greeting.

"So great that you could come right away," he said. "We're starting the meeting immediately in the conference room."

"Good," Jana said.

"That looks heavy. Can I carry your bag for you?"

"I'd rather you didn't."

Mia Bolander looked up and sighed when Jana Berzelius and Henrik Levin stepped into the conference room where she, Gunnar Öhrn and technician Ola Söderström were already sitting.

Jana Fucking Berzelius, Mia thought. Career whore. Beautiful and successful, interesting and gorgeous, on her way up in life.

Didn't they have any other choice to lead the preliminary investigation?

Mia had disliked Jana from the moment they'd met. But

why? Because she was upper-class, proud and stiff? Jana was the best resource of the Public Prosecution Office, a truly competent preliminary investigation leader, no one could deny that. But if she'd been just a bit less competent, she would've been kicked off the team long ago because of her snobbiness. Normally, Mia would have refused to work with someone like Jana, but nothing was normal anymore when it came to work.

Nor in her own life.

Mia looked down at her hands and scraped her chipped nail polish with her thumbnail. A feeling of emptiness had begun to form inside her. It wasn't exactly that she'd begun to doubt herself—she knew she was a good murder investigator. Her success rate was solid across the board, and she felt challenged by her work.

It wasn't police work that was the problem, and she had no intention of changing careers. It was that only two men had approached her last night. And they had only looked at her without saying anything, without taking any fucking initiative. They didn't even make a comment on her revealing blouse.

"Well, then," Jana said, tapping on the table with her pointer finger. "Let's get started, shall we?"

"Yes," Henrik said. "Shirin Norberg, female, forty-two years of age, was found near death in her apartment and later passed away in the ambulance en route to the hospital. She died from complications related to the brutal violence she was subjected to. There were large bruises on her body, and both hands had been severed. If you look here…"

He nodded toward Ola, who pressed a few buttons on his computer. A number of pictures were projected on the wall.

Mia looked at the photo of the dead woman, her pale face and dry lips, her arms, lying at her sides. The photo of the severed hands made her open her mouth.

"Jesus," she said, throwing her hand out in a gesture toward the photo, "this is so awful!"

"Yes," Henrik said, looking up.

"How the hell can someone mutilate another person like that?"

"That's a legitimate question," Henrik said. "I can think of possible motives—sadism, desire, power, revenge—"

He pointed his finger toward the naked body and looked at Jana.

"—do you see this?" he asked.

Jana nodded, following his finger. Mia let her gaze travel over the large bruises that were visible under her ribs, on her hips, her thighs, her shins.

"She was tied up," Mia said, "and it looks like someone beat her up really badly."

"Do we have a theory about how these injuries occurred?" Jana asked.

"Björn Ahlmann has the body, so he will be able to tell when he examines it. But this thing with the hands," Henrik said, sighing, "it's one of the worst mutilations I've seen, and…"

"What?" Jana asked.

"No, nothing," Henrik said.

"Yes, say it. What are you thinking about our course of action?" Jana said.

"What I'm thinking doesn't matter until we have all of the facts from Björn first," Henrik said.

"He couldn't give us anything more to go on?" Jana said.

"No, not just yet, but I hope that he'll get working on it soon. We're dealing with a very depraved perpetrator here, as you see," Henrik said, pointing to a new picture of the body.

"Those look like old burn marks on her chest," Jana said.

"Yes, and it's usually the case that violence like this is committed by someone close to the victim," Henrik said. "But her husband died five years ago."

"And now?" said Jana.

"No relationships we know of."

"What's next?" Jana said.

"We'll be questioning her children."

"Yes, do," Jana said. "Right away."

He sat unmoving on the couch and rested his legs on the table. She sat in one of the armchairs, wringing her hands. Philip Engström and Sandra Gustafsson avoided each other's eyes as they sat alone in the crew lounge.

"What did the boss say?" she wondered after a moment.

"I don't know. I haven't talked with Eva yet."

"Why not?"

He sighed.

"I have no reason to?"

"You know that we are required to self-report obvious cases of error…"

"For Christ's sake, Sandra, don't start with that again!"

"You promised to report yourself…"

"If I made a mistake, yes."

"And what do you consider malpractice?"

"Well, maybe we need to tease out the concept a bit. *Malpractice* could be inadequate routines, inadequate education, inadequate work relationships or inadequate equipment. And in this case, it was a tourniquet that didn't function properly."

"I assumed that…"

"You assumed what, that it was my mistake? Sorry to disappoint you, Sandra. It wasn't me, it was the tourniquet. And who the fuck cares about a fucking tourniquet when a patient's hands have been hacked off?"

The room was completely silent. He felt himself breathing more heavily; dizziness came and went. Just for a second or so, but he recognized it as the first sign that he needed a pill. He longed to feel its drowsiness wash over him, to feel his body relax.

"You'll never be able to admit to having made a mistake, will you, Philip?"

Sandra looked at him with a serious expression, and he thought about how her eyes were greenest when she was angry.

"I've never had to think about it," he said, "because I never make mistakes."

Jana Berzelius had absolutely no desire to visit the funeral home to make her mother's arrangements, but no one else was going to do it for her. And it had to be done.

Obviously, she'd lived her whole life knowing that her adoptive mother and father would pass away sometime, but she hadn't counted on her mother leaving the world so suddenly.

Because of that, she had no idea what her mother would have wanted for a coffin, for hymns, for a gravestone. And maybe it was just as well—it gave her the freedom to decide what the ceremony would look like.

She turned off the ignition, stepped out of the car and thought how the errand would have felt less unpleasant if it had been for Danilo's funeral.

The bell over the door jingled as she walked in.

A woman peered at Jana from behind the door to a break room. She had a light-colored, flowered dress on and permed hair.

"I'll be right there," she said with her mouth full. "Have a seat for just a moment."

Jana stepped in, surveying the place, feeling how it oozed sorrow and thinking the air was far too warm and humid. The funeral home was on the corner of Hospitalgatan and Gamla

Rådstugugatan. The windows facing the street were covered by vertical blinds, creating a gloomy atmosphere. A newspaper rack held several different brochures with titles such as "Arranging a Funeral," "Estate Inventory Proceedings" and "Your Will." Jana didn't even like the name of the funeral home— The Hourglass. It was as if they wanted to remind everyone that their days were numbered.

The door opened again.

"Hi, I'm Anna-Lena Hanberg," she said, reaching out her hand.

"Jana Berzelius."

They shook hands.

"How can I help you?" asked Anna-Lena, tilting her head to the side.

"I'd like to discuss some funeral arrangements. My mother has passed away."

"Do you have an appointment?"

Jana shook her head. "No."

"No problem. Follow me. Let's go into this room over here."

Anna-Lena opened the door to a smaller room and went in first. Jana looked at the blue chairs around the teak table, at the small stereo standing on a dresser and at the oil paintings on the walls.

Anna-Lena sat down and placed a folder entitled "The Eternal Rest" in front of Jana and opened a notebook in front of herself.

"I want to start by saying that it's important that you know you and your family aren't alone."

"I am alone."

"You don't have any siblings?"

"No. And my father is unable to come here."

"No relatives?"

"No. I'm solely responsible for the funeral arrangements."

"I understand, and I want you to know that we're here to support you. It's important to allow yourself to experience grief, to dare to really feel your emotions and not close them off. Sooner or later, you have to deal with them."

"I believe you," Jana said.

"You should also know that we are happy to help you with all of your practical questions."

"I really just have one question. How soon can the funeral be?"

"That depends. Most often, it takes place within two weeks of the death."

"I want it to be as soon as possible," Jana said.

"All right," Anna-Lena said and opened a calendar. "From what I can see the first available date is next week Friday."

"Good."

"But I must ask, has your mother left any documents stating her final wishes?"

"No."

"Have you had the chance to think about it?"

"No."

"Then I think it's a good idea for us to go through it step by step."

"I want the funeral to be private."

"Good, so that point is decided."

"There's more?"

Anna-Lena tucked her hair behind her ear and cleared her throat.

"There are a few more aspects to talk about," she said, "such as how the death announcement will look, what kind of flowers and what music you'd like. Will it take place in a church, crematorium chapel, fellowship room or outside? What type of casket? Size, color, material? Bedding, decorations, your own quilt, pillow, sheet?"

"I assume I'll be here awhile," Jana said.

Anna-Lena smiled vaguely at her.

"The first visit usually takes around two and a half hours," she said.

Jana looked at the clock. Anna-Lena noticed.

"I have a whole list of questions," she said apologetically. "It's unavoidable, really."

"And I can't take the list home?"

"No, unfortunately," she said. "So what do you think? Should we get started?"

"Are you sure she knew we were coming?" Mia Bolander asked after Henrik Levin had rung the doorbell for the second time.

He nodded.

"Yes, I talked to her on the phone. She stuttered a little, but she promised she'd be home."

Mia pushed her hands down into her pockets.

"How's the packing going, by the way?"

"Good, I think."

"When are you moving?"

"Next week Friday. You wouldn't want to help, would you?"

She shrugged her shoulders.

"Sure, but only if there's beer involved."

"It depends," he said.

"Depends on what?"

"On how expensive a housewarming gift you're getting us."

Mia raised her eyebrows.

"I'm just kidding," he said. "We don't want any presents. Your help is the best gift."

Henrik rang the bell again, and they stood quietly side by side until they finally heard sounds from inside: a coughing fit, then footsteps.

When the door opened, they were met by a peculiar odor, seemingly a mixture of smoke and wet fur.

Wearing a brown dress, Maria Ashour smiled in greeting. She had an enormous bosom, which she allowed to hang freely under the fabric.

"Hu-hurry in," she said, sticking her foot out to stop a cat trying to sneak out into the stairwell. She shook their hands before showing them into the kitchen.

"Aida is staying in the guest room. I—I'll get her."

Henrik and Mia sat down. There was an embroidered cloth on the table, and in the middle stood a bowl and a Russian nesting doll. The view over Norrköping would have been impressive if the drapes hadn't been pulled closed most of the way. Henrik instead turned his gaze to the floor and caught sight of a wine bottle and three plastic water bottles, all empty, in the corner. Large tufts of cat hair lay along the wall.

"Yes, yes, that...those probably should have been thrown away a lo-long time ago," said Maria, who had returned. She stood in the doorway with her arm around Aida.

"I—I didn't get Sara. She's playing in the bedroom. We—we haven't told her yet that her mother has passed away."

"Let her play," Henrik said.

"Come, sweetie," she said, nudging the older girl toward the table.

Aida sat down, looking first at Henrik, then at Mia, again at Henrik and then at Mia again.

Her hair was damp and hung down over her face. She was wearing a knit sweater, pleated skirt and a pair of black tights. She looked worn-out, yet composed.

"Hi, Aida," Henrik said.

"Hi," she mumbled, looking down at the table.

"Would—would you like something to drink before you start?"

"No, thanks," Henrik said. "We won't be staying long."

"Let—let me know if you change your mind."

Henrik turned toward Aida.

"We're here to ask a few questions about your mom."

"I know."

"We know you're very sad about what happened."

Aida nodded.

"Does it feel good to stay here, with your grandma?"

"Yes, it's good."

"Of—of course she would stay here, with her nana," Maria said, stroking Aida's hair. "Tha-that's what she calls me. I—I wouldn't let her stay anywhere else. Never. It—it would feel completely wrong."

"I understand," Henrik said, folding his hands on the table.

He studied Aida, thinking that it would be difficult for someone to guess her age solely based on her appearance.

"You work full-time, I understand?" he asked.

"Yes," Aida said. "I was lucky to get a job immediately after I graduated."

"Aida is smart, you know. Highest grades in everything. I—I'm so proud of her."

Henrik gave her a slight nod, showing he was impressed by the young, ambitious woman.

"We are going to need to talk to Aida alone," he said, turning toward Maria.

"I—I'll go," she said. "Come here, Kitty, let's leave them in peace."

She picked the cat up from the floor before leaving the kitchen.

"Can you tell us a little more about your mother, Aida?" Henrik said when the door had closed. "What did she do?"

"She was a surgery nurse," Aida said, "at Vrinnevi Hospital."

"So she worked shifts, right?"

"Yes, that's right." Aida nodded several times. "But never overnight," she added. "I just started to work nights so I could help her to take care of Sara during the day."

"What did your mother do when she wasn't at work?"

"What did she do?" Aida repeated. "She didn't do all that much. She mostly just stayed home. Took care of Sara and me. Cooked for us. Got Sara to school. She'd watch TV with us and stuff."

"I know your father died some years ago. What were your mother's friends like?" Henrik asked. "Did she have company to the house? Did she visit with anyone in particular? Did she have a lot of friends?"

Aida straightened her back and looked at him.

"No, she mostly just stayed home with us when she wasn't working. Sometimes we would visit Nana."

"Your mother wasn't in a relationship, as far as you know?"

"Relationship?" Aida said, taking a deep breath.

"A boyfriend?"

"No, she wasn't."

"Do you have any idea who might have hurt her?"

Aida looked up at the ceiling, as if she needed to think about it. Then she shook her head. "No, I don't," she said, looking worried.

Henrik looked at Mia, who had pulled the nesting doll toward herself and opened it. It contained five progressively smaller dolls.

"Aida…" he said, getting the girl's attention. "We'd like you to describe for us as best you can what happened when you came home and found your mother. What did you hear? What did you see?"

Aida began shifting in her seat.

"It's hard to talk about that," she said,

"We understand," Henrik said, "but it's important for us to hear it in your words."

"We know it was an awful situation," Mia said, picking up the nesting dolls again. "But can we try talking about it? You left your workplace after the night shift, you came home, and…?"

"The door was open when I came home."

"Open?" Henrik asked. "Do you mean that it was standing open or that it was unlocked?"

"Unlocked," she said, meeting Henrik's gaze for a brief moment. "So I opened it and went into the hallway."

"And what time was it then?"

"Just after eight o'clock in the morning."

"Okay. And then?"

"I hung up my jacket, took off my shoes, and then I noticed a key in the door to our bedroom. The door was locked from the hallway and I thought…well, I just thought it was strange."

"And when you say 'our room,' you mean…?"

"Sara's and mine. We share a room."

"Did you think it was Sara who had locked it?"

"No. I just assumed Sara was in the room and that it was locked from the outside. That's what was so strange. Mom would never lock us in…"

Aida swallowed. "And then I heard Sara whimpering in there, and so I unlocked the door. She should have been at preschool. I could tell from the way she looked that something bad had happened, and I tried to talk to her, hug her and stuff. Then I went into the living room, and that's where Mom… well, that's where I found her sitting in the chair."

"Besides Sara, was your mom alone in the apartment when you came home?" Mia asked.

"Yes."

Henrik rubbed his hand on his chin, thinking.

"Your mom was badly hurt," he said.

"Yes."

Aida's lower lip had begun trembling.

"I went up to her," she said. "But I didn't know what I should do. There was blood all over her, everywhere, and her hands...her hands were lying..."

Aida held her hand to her mouth to suppress a gag.

"Was she able to say anything to you?"

Aida was beginning to retch behind her hand and finally couldn't hold it any longer. She stood quickly and left her grandmother's kitchen.

"Sh-should I bring her back in?" Her grandmother Maria asked, appearing in the doorway.

"No, that's okay," Henrik said. "But we are going to need to talk with both you and Sara, too."

It was quiet for a moment, then Maria said: "No."

"No?" Henrik raised his eyebrows and was struck by how completely at a loss for words he was.

"You—you can talk to me, bu-but not to Sara," Maria said.

"But we need to talk to her," Mia said. "She was home at the time that her mother was tortured. You'll be sabotaging our investigation if you don't let us speak with her. Don't you want to know who murdered your daughter and see the monster brought to justice?"

"But—but Sara is so young."

"We have staff who are specifically trained to talk to children," Henrik said.

"I—I understand that, but, no..." Maria shook her head.

Henrik combed his hand through his hair.

"We respect your desire to protect Sara," he said, "but in this situation, it's incredibly important that we learn what she knows."

"I—I'll think about it."

"Please do," he said. "I want you to know that the only thing we want is to find out who did this horrible deed to your daughter, Shirin."

"M-me, too."

"Do you have any ideas about who could have been involved?"

"N-no, I don't, but whoever…"

Maria looked up at the ceiling, mumbling something to herself.

"I'm sorry, what did you say?"

"I—I said that whoever did this to my daughter will fry in the flames."

Jana Berzelius looked at the clock and saw that the meeting with the funeral director had taken far too long. There had been too many questions, and she still hadn't been able to decide what kind of ceremony to have and where to have it. Plus she needed more time to think of where she wanted her mother to be buried.

She had planned on heading to the Public Prosecution Office and working a few more hours, but decided instead to return home, even though she wasn't looking forward to seeing Danilo there.

She got into her car and drove to her parking garage at Knäppingsborg. She parked and grabbed her bag, but then changed her mind and put the bag in the trunk.

Less than two minutes later, she stood outside the door to her apartment. She turned the key, opened the door a little and listened.

Slowly, she pushed the door open all the way and stepped inside.

The mail was usually lying on the floor mat, but today it had been slung onto the kitchen table. Had he gone through it?

She tried not to lose her temper, tried to breathe calmly and quietly. But the thought that Danilo had gone through her personal mail gave her an almost tangible sense of claustrophobia.

He was on the floor in the living room, doing push-ups. He stopped in the middle of a repetition and looked at her. His face was red and tense, and he seemed distant.

He opened his mouth to say something, but when she walked straight past him, he remained silent. She continued into her bedroom, closed the door behind her and sat on the bed.

Ignoring him wasn't such a bad strategy after all, she thought, smiling to herself. Not bad at all.

Henrik Levin put his coffee cup down on the table and looked at Mia Bolander. She was staring at a point far beyond the bakery window toward the shops of Gamla Stan.

"I just don't get this murder," Henrik said.

"Me, neither," Mia said in subdued voice. "Obviously we're dealing with one sick sadist."

"You think so?" Henrik asked wearily.

Mia looked at him.

"Why, what do you think?" she said loudly before forcing herself to lower her voice again. "The victim's hands were cut off. Or did you miss that?"

"No," Henrik said.

After all of these years as colleagues, Henrik had come to see that Mia had both a positive side and a negative one. On the positive side, she was a tough woman with broad experience, especially with complicated investigations. On the negative, she was an egocentric with a loud and overly blunt demeanor that was sure to rub any decent person the wrong way.

Including Henrik.

Not always, but right now it did.

But fine, he was tired, and he knew that there wasn't any point in giving his opinion on her loud-mouthed behavior because doing so tended to make it even worse.

He took a bite of his open-faced liverwurst and cucumber sandwich, chewing slowly before swallowing. He used the time to decide that in spite of everything, Mia was right. The murder was bestial, and it wasn't often that their investigations included severed limbs.

"What are you thinking about?"

The wrinkle between her eyes had smoothed as she raised her eyebrows and looked at him.

"About the course of events," he said. "That someone went into Shirin's apartment and tortured her—cut off her hands in cold blood while she was still alive—with her youngest daughter right there in the apartment."

"Yes, pretty fucking sick," Mia said. "If the goal had been to kill her, the murderer could have just shot her in the head. Bang. Quick and easy. Instead, he tied her to a chair and hacked her hands off."

Henrik took another bite of his sandwich.

"Someone wanted her to suffer."

"Someone who was likely close to her," Mia said, "as most perpetrators are."

"Absolutely, but whom? Shirin didn't seem to have many friends or even a boyfriend. According to Aida, anyway."

"Parents don't always tell their children everything, though, right?"

Henrik picked at his sandwich with his thumb and index finger.

"But Aida seems so mature in a way," he said. "She would have known if things were amiss. She seems down-to-earth, practical, doesn't seem to have her head in the clouds like many teenagers."

"You think so?" Mia asked.

"You don't?"

She shrugged her shoulders.

"You don't seem to agree with me," he said, "but I thought she seemed very mature."

"What if Aida is not telling us everything about her home life?" Mia asked. "Maybe she resents having to take on responsibility for her little sister."

"Right. Or more. It was actually her little sister she first thought of when she entered the apartment, wasn't it?" Henrik said. "She was focused on her, as if she were worried something had happened to her."

"Where are you going with this?"

"I'm not sure. I'm just not completely convinced that Aida isn't holding something back. About their family situation, I mean. She seemed so composed, so resigned, despite having just lost her mother in such an horrendous way."

"How should she have seemed, then?" Mia asked. "People react in different ways."

"Yes, but it seems to me at her age she should have been more hysterical, more in shock. It feels as if the family is hiding something, and…" Henrik picked up his sandwich and raised it to his lips, but then put it back down again. "We really need to talk to the little sister. She's the one who was home when all of it happened, after all… She must have heard her mother's screams. She would know if someone else was in the apartment and if it was someone she recognized. I don't understand why the grandmother doesn't want us to talk to her. What's she scared of?"

"That something really fucking unpleasant is going to come out, probably?" Mia said.

"For example?"

"I don't know! Something!"

"Well, if you hadn't gone at it so hard, we maybe could have coaxed a little conversation out of her, in spite of everything," Henrik said.

Mia sat up in her chair. "What? So you're saying it's my fault?"

"I'm not saying anything, Mia. I just think it's damn unnecessary for them to prevent us from talking to the girl. Someone locked her in. It was presumably not the mom, so it's very possible that the girl saw the perpetrator. We really need to talk to her."

"Okay, the situation is really fucking frustrating," Mia said. "But don't fucking go saying it's my fault."

"For the second time, Mia, that wasn't what I said. We'll have to concentrate on finding new leads for now."

"Have we gotten anything from neighbors?"

"Not yet. We've only just gotten a hold of the neighbor in the next apartment over. We'll be questioning him later."

Henrik took another bite of his sandwich.

"And Shirin's coworkers at the hospital?" Mia asked.

"We haven't talked to all of them, but she clearly missed work a lot. But otherwise no interesting information yet."

"So what's our next step if we don't get to talk to Sara?"

"Don't forget that we have two other very important people to question."

"Who's that?"

"The two paramedics on the scene."

CHAPTER
SEVEN

PHILIP ENGSTRÖM PUSHED A SOBRIL OUT OF ITS BLIS-
ter pack, slipped it into his mouth, cupped his hands under
the running water and swallowed as he drank.

With his wet hands still against his face, he sat down on the
toilet and tried to collect his thoughts for a moment.

He recognized her. He had seen the victim before, somewhere.

Or was it just déjà vu?

He shivered and saw that someone was trying the door
handle. Far away he heard a voice calling for him, and he was
able to make out words like *police questioning*. How long had
he been sitting in the staff bathroom?

Shit, he really had to get himself together.

He held his hands up. The shaking had decreased.

Slowly, he got up and washed his face again.

Was it true that he hadn't tied off the tourniquet properly?

He was almost certain that he had, but he wasn't absolutely sure. His memory was cloudy. Again. Maybe the pills were beginning to have side effects… Maybe the tourniquet *had* failed, but he probably couldn't have saved her anyway, she probably would have died anyway.

While he dried his hands, he repeated to himself that few reports were filed among paramedics. Because people worked so closely with each other, it was a big deal to report a colleague. Any mistakes simply went unrecorded. And no one would self-report a mistake. Not among the old crew, at least.

But Sandra was new, and Philip was unsure how to act around her. She had said that she wouldn't hesitate to report him if he made another mistake. But he hadn't made a mistake. The tourniquet must have failed. He hadn't.

He raised his hands in front of his face.

Examined them.

They were completely steady.

Jana Berzelius turned off the warm water, stepped out of the shower, and wound the towel around her body. She opened the bathroom door and looked out into the hallway and noticed the late-afternoon sunbeams creating abstract patterns on the parquet floor. Then she snuck toward her bedroom.

"Why are you acting so nervous? I've seen you naked before."

Danilo stood there with his arms crossed over his chest.

She quickly walked past him into the bedroom and locked the door behind her. She reminded herself that she had to pretend he wasn't there.

She had to ignore him completely. That was the only way to bear this torment.

She took clean lingerie from a drawer. She pulled on her panties, dropped the towel and hooked her brassiere. She was just thinking that she should dress in black for tonight's dinner with Per when she saw a bit of dust float across the floor. She looked toward the door and saw a shadow through the crack at its bottom.

"What the hell are you doing?" she said.

"Looking at you," he said from the other side.

She grabbed the towel from the floor.

"Stop it."

"Or what?"

She heard his muffled, irritating tone through the door and felt infuriatingly frustrated. First, she had broken her promise to herself not to talk to him. Second, he clearly hadn't understood what she had said. But there were other ways of communicating.

Most people understood pain. Even Danilo.

She waited to get dressed until the shadow had disappeared. The hangers scraped against the pole as she pulled them back and forth in her closet looking for the black suit that she had purchased six months ago and worn only once. As she pulled the pants on, she felt how tense her arms were. She tried to relax before leaving the bedroom.

Danilo was sitting in the kitchen, and she felt his gaze as she silently walked past. It was as if he'd expected that she would go in to him.

Her high heels felt cold when she put them on her feet.

"Where are you going?" he called out.

But she didn't answer. She grabbed her coat and left the apartment.

Mia Bolander sat next to Henrik Levin in one of the interrogation rooms at the police station. She pulled her hands into the arms of her ribbed knit sweater and sank down a bit in the chair. She looked at Philip Engström, who was sitting directly across from her.

"We've just talked to your colleague, Sandra Gustafsson. We might as well start right away with what happened this morning," Henrik said. "From what we understand, you two were first on the scene?"

"Yes," Philip answered.

"We appreciate that you both gave us your fingerprints and DNA so quickly," Henrik said.

"We were just following protocol," he said.

Mia studied the man in front of her. He was in his thirties, and even though he had dark circles under his eyes, he appeared to be in excellent shape. He probably worked out regularly, only drank water, and avoided alcohol and junk food and candy, to stay in condition. But who the hell wanted to save lives if you can't have a life yourself?

"Tell us what it looked like when you arrived at the apartment," Henrik said.

"When we got there, the daughter was sitting on the stairs outside the apartment door. The older daughter, that is. She was waiting for us. Then, when we came into the apartment and walked to the living room in the back, we saw the patient tied to a chair and her hands...well, they were completely severed and lying on the ground."

"And by 'the patient,' you mean Shirin Norberg?"

"Her last name is Norberg?" Philip asked with raised eyebrows.

"Yes," Mia answered.

"Okay."

"Why are you wondering? Did you know her?"

"No, no," Philip said. "I must have confused her with someone else."

Mia looked at him and nodded slowly.

"Was there anyone else in the apartment when you were there?" Henrik asked.

"Yes. The little girl, the patient's daughter Sara," Philip said.

"And besides her?" Henrik asked.

"No one else, from what I know."

"Are you sure?"

"Yes," he said. "We were mostly focused on the patient, but there wasn't anyone else in the apartment."

"Okay," Henrik said. "And how would you describe the older daughter's frame of mind?"

"Her frame of mind?" he repeated, thinking. "Of course she was extremely upset."

"And how was she acting?" Henrik said. "Did she say anything?"

"She mostly stood with her hands covering her face. She understandably didn't want to look."

"Did she say anything?"

"No, not directly. She told us that she had tried to free her mom's arms, but it was too much for her. I understand it, too. I could hardly bear to look. How her hands were…it feels unreal in a way. I can't understand how someone could do that."

"We can't, either," Henrik said.

"But what I'm wondering about," Mia said, "is how it happened that you left Aida and Sara behind on their own? Even though their mom had clearly been subjected to deadly force, you left them alone in the apartment? Was that really good judgment?"

"That was our best judgment call," Philip said. "We knew that the police were on the way. We even met them in the stairwell on our way out. And however bad it sounds, we have to focus on saving the patient. It's our job to save lives."

"Yes, but this time you weren't able to," Mia said.

"No," Philip said, "we weren't."

★ ★ ★

The slices of rosemary-rubbed venison on the plate displayed a faint pink center.

"Oh, that looks good," Per Åström said, taking the plate from the server.

"In contrast to filet mignon," Jana said, swirling her wineglass two times.

Per was dressed in a dark suit and white shirt. It was evening, almost seven o'clock, and the restaurant Durkslaget was almost fully booked.

The table near the window was set with candles.

"Tell it like it is. You don't want to come to my place," he said.

"I want to save you the trouble of fixing dinner," she said.

"That's nice, but I had already bought all of the ingredients."

"Then you have dinner all set for tomorrow."

"Can I invite you? We can have ice cream for dessert."

"I don't like ice cream."

"Is there anything you do like?"

"Eating in peace."

"Just for that, I'm going to talk the entire time."

"Do you see how surprised I look?"

"Yes, truly."

"Cheers."

They raised their glasses, drank and began eating. The venison was accompanied by potato gratin, steamed beans and cream sauce.

"You did a nice job on the radio, by the way," Per said.

"You think so?"

"Of course. No doubt about it. You have, what should I say, a natural authority. You disarmed the program host completely. It's obvious you're an expert on the subject. You can

also formulate your thoughts in a way that listeners understand. Your voice is perfect for radio."

"How touching."

Per laughed and combed his hand through his blond hair.
"I agree with you that the primary duty of the criminal justice system should be to prevent crime. And I think that we
have to further increase our standards for the burden of proof."

"Really?"

"You heard about the innocent father who was released
after nine years in prison, right?"

Jana nodded. The case had received a great deal of attention
in the media. A sixty-six-year-old man had been sentenced
to fourteen years in prison for extensive, ongoing abuse of his
daughter. He allegedly raped her up to two hundred times
over the course of many years. The man was also said to have
tortured her with razor blades and lit cigarettes. But as he sat
in prison, it turned out that the daughter was making similar
accusations toward other people, one of whom was a trusted
police officer.

Per wiped his mouth with his napkin.

"And then a new affidavit showed that the injuries that the
daughter supposedly sustained from the father's alleged abuse
didn't match the accusations, either. He was awarded a new
trial and was freed. He asked for a record amount in repara-
tions."

Jana raised her eyebrows.

"Oh, really," she said.

"Guess how much."

"I don't know. A lot?"

"Good guess," Per said. "It's difficult to place a value on
suffering, of course, but he requested two million dollars and
received one and a half. It's the highest amount ever paid out
by the Office of the Chancellor of Justice."

"That type of case is problematic," Jana said.

"Yes, it's typically one person's word against another, but what I wanted to say was that what happened to this father could very well happen to another father. That's why we should increase our standards. More?"

Per held out the wine bottle.

"Yes, please."

"Now, tell me what you're thinking about," he said as he filled her glass. "And don't go saying you weren't thinking about anything, because you knew exactly how much he received. You just didn't want to say so."

Jana laid her silverware on her plate, took a sip of wine and looked at Per. His differently colored eyes met hers. One blue, the other marbled brown. She didn't want to tell him about her mother's death. It was personal and she wanted to keep it that way. Instead, she continued their conversation.

"I wonder how many of those in prison right now are innocent," she said.

"I don't know," he said. "All of them claim they are, right?"

"Just like Danilo Peña."

Jana lingered a little on the words, then reached for her wineglass and took another sip. She knew that she was taking a risk by saying his name, so she swallowed slowly as she waited for his reaction.

"Danilo Peña, right," he said, cutting the last bit of the venison. "Why bring him up? Do you think he's innocent?"

Jana shook her head and took yet another sip. Should she ask more? Or let it go?

"You said that he'd escaped. Do you know anything else about him?"

Per shrugged his shoulders. "The police have searched everywhere. He used to have an apartment in…"

"Söder…" Jana stopped herself. Per looked at her with his forehead wrinkled.

"…Södertälje, yes," he said, nodding. "But he isn't listed at that address anymore. And he has no family, no relatives, probably not many friends, and no home. He's like a ghost."

"So where is he, then?"

"Still in the city, the police think. I do, too. But don't worry. We'll catch him soon."

"I'm not worried."

"That's too bad."

"Why is that?"

"Because then I'd get to hug you and tell you everything will be okay."

"Per…"

"Jana?"

"Stop it with that."

"A person can dream, can't he?"

"Please don't."

"Okay. In that case, I'll take the check."

"No, let me."

"But I asked you out."

"You always ask me. Let me pay."

"If I know you, there's no sense in protesting."

"You're learning," she said, waving the server over.

Philip Engström loosened his belt and let his pants fall to the floor. His legs immediately felt cold. It was just past 8:00 p.m., and he was glad that, despite the conversation with the police, he'd been able to end his twenty-four-hour shift on time. Working in emergency services was like playing the lottery. Either you were lucky and got to leave the station on time, or you were unlucky and got a call just before your shift ended, which meant you were heading out again instead of heading home.

He pulled his work shirt off and thought how only losers had regular hours. And in this line of work, you had to be available to put the needs of others before your own.

When he opened his locker in the changing room, he thought about the staff in Stockholm Värnamo who, a few years ago, had defied their directive and changed shifts in the middle of a call. They had been called to a man in his sixties who was having chest pains. After examining him, it was decided that the man should be taken to the hospital in Jönköping. But the ambulance staff's shift was almost over, and so that they wouldn't have to work overtime, they changed both ambulance and paramedics in Värnamo. This meant that this life-or-death ambulance ride was delayed by at least fifteen minutes. Upon their arrival in Jönköping, the patient was unconscious; they couldn't save him in the end.

Philip put on his jeans and shirt. Then he looked at his cell phone and thought about Katarina Vinston. He had called her earlier in the day, but she hadn't called back. Where the hell was she?

He shoved the phone into his pocket, locked his locker and left the room. Just as he took the first step down the stairs, he heard a voice.

"Philip?"

He stopped, turned around and saw his boss, Eva Holmgren, holding her hand out toward him.

"Yes?" he said.

He saw a tense smile on her face. She walked toward him, laid her hand on his shoulder and wrapped her fingers around it.

"I need to talk to you," she said.

The temperature had dropped below fifty degrees when Jana and Per stepped out of Durkslaget.

"Should we walk?" Per asked, pushing his hands into his pockets.

They began strolling side by side. Jana pulled up the collar of her coat as they turned onto Kvarngatan. They continued into the industrial district, where many of the windows were dark. She thought how it was right here, among the city's characteristic textile factories, just three months ago in early December that she had caught sight of Danilo. She had at first followed him out of curiosity, and then had been attacked and threatened.

Stay away from me, he'd said.

Now he was the one who had gone looking for her.

"Thank you for tonight," Per said, interrupting her thoughts. "When can I invite you again? For filet mignon, with no ice cream?"

She gave him an exasperated look.

"Okay, I get it," he said. "But can I at least treat you to lunch at Fiskmagasinet tomorrow?"

"Maybe," she said.

They continued walking awhile longer. She thought about Danilo again. Even if she'd been aware that the police were going to search for him in the city, it was unpleasant to have it confirmed by Per. Not least because it meant that officers were on the lookout on the streets and in the neighborhood centers.

"You're quiet," Per said, interrupting her thoughts yet again.

"Yes," she said.

"And it feels like you're in a hurry to get somewhere…?"

"No," she said.

"Could we slow down a little, then?"

She slowed her steps, reluctantly. They walked toward Holmentorget and stood under a streetlight.

She met his gaze and saw that his eyes were smiling.

"Thank you for tonight..." he said, shifting his weight from one foot to the other.

"You've already said that," she said.

"But I wanted to say it again."

She saw that he had taken a step forward and suddenly she felt a strong desire to turn around and flee.

"Good night," she said curtly. Then she turned around and fled.

Philip Engström stretched his back where he sat in the visitor's chair and looked at his boss, Eva Holmgren. She sat behind her large desk, which was clean and tidy, with just a couple of binders and a few yellow Post-it notes.

"A lot has been happening lately," she said, looking down at the papers she had in front of her.

"Yes..." Philip said expectantly, studying her. Her arms were slim and her hands were freckled. She was wearing a simple T-shirt, and around one wrist she had a silver bracelet.

She looked up and gave him a questioning look.

"Should I be worried?" she asked.

"About what?" he said. "Are you thinking about what happened in Eneby today?"

"That, too, but above all, I'm thinking about how I got a report that you and Sandra took unusually long with a patient having heart trouble yesterday morning. According to the log, you received the call at 05:44:38."

"Yes?" he said. His breathing became heavier.

"And when did you arrive there?"

"It was the call to Lindö, right? It was probably about ten minutes before we were there."

"Ten minutes?" she asked.

"Do you want me to give you how many seconds, too?"

He wondered what she was getting at, and he had an uneasy feeling that she was heading toward something he didn't want to talk about.

"And what happened next?" she asked, picking up a pen.

"What do you mean, what happened next?" Philip said. "We loaded the patient in and left."

"You did?"

"Yes, we did."

He pulled his hand over his mouth.

"How is it that it took twice as long for you to get to the hospital?" she asked, beginning to tap the table with the pen. She tapped in an even tempo, which sounded like the second hand on a clock.

His body was becoming sticky with perspiration while he searched for a good explanation. He couldn't rush it now.

"Ten minutes there, load up, but then twenty minutes to get back," Eva stated. "I'm wondering why it took such a long time to drive back to the hospital."

"Okay," he said.

"I've also talked to Sandra, who also doesn't have any explanation. But I can see that you've taken on multiple twenty-four-hour shifts over the past month."

"But that doesn't have anything to do with this," he said.

"Not everyone can manage such long work shifts," she said.

"Yet you're willing to put them on the schedule and approve them," he said.

Eva looked at him, her eyes narrowing.

"When I go through the protocol from the yearly workplace meetings, not a single person breathes a word about it being too difficult to work twenty-four-hour shifts. I know that you all really want these long shifts because it gives you more consecutive days off. But when the situation begins to look like this, you also have to take responsibility for the shifts you're taking."

Philip looked down at the desk. He felt her eyes on him.

"I am going to say this very carefully," she said. "I know that twenty-four-hour shifts can cause an enormous stress. You know that already. But what I'm getting nervous about is that other factors are at play here. You can't, for example, drink alcohol and work this way, but I assume you know that."

"I don't drink," he said.

"Maybe not," she said. "But I still have to keep an eye on you."

"What do you mean, *keep an eye on me*? What do you want me to do?"

"I want you to do a good job," she said. "There are factors that indicate that you aren't dealing well with the stress of this type of work. I, as your employer, become responsible for these things if you neglect your work. Remember that."

CHAPTER
EIGHT

FOR FOUR MINUTES AND THIRTY-TWO SECONDS MIA
sat and listened to classical music coming from a stereo as large
as a microwave. She was probably going to have to listen for a
full hour or so that evening. *Shoot me*, she thought, scratching
her forehead. She and Henrik were about to question Göran
Karlgren, a neighbor of Shirin Norberg who lived in the apartment next to the family.

"Well, then," Göran said, setting a tray with coffee on the
table. "There you go."

"Thank you," Henrik said, accepting a coffee mug. "You
didn't need to."

"I know. Sugar?" Göran said.

"No, thank you," Mia said, taking a sip of her coffee right
away. "Aren't you having any?"

"No," Göran said. "I never drink coffee this late."

Henrik cleared his throat.

"We're glad you could see us," he said.

"As a retiree, I should have all the time in the world, but actually I've never had so little free time. Now, let's hear it. You had a lot of questions about the neighbor, I understand."

"Yes," Mia said, setting her mug on the table. "The music, can't we..."

"It gives me peace in my heart and provides a breeding ground for constructive thoughts," Göran said ceremoniously, smiling.

Mia smiled back, irritated.

"You said you had heard sounds from Shirin's apartment?"

"Yes, some screaming back and forth, but mostly verbal nonsense."

"What do you mean by nonsense?"

"I can't really explain," Göran said, "but now and then I heard them raise their voices."

"Were you home yesterday?" Mia asked.

"No, I can't say that I was. We had cleaning day for the housing association..."

"Did you hear any screaming last night?"

"No. As I said, I wasn't home until very late."

"And when you came home, did you see or hear anything?"

"No, nothing in particular...or, well, what do you mean?"

"I mean did you see something you don't usually see, like a car or a person or something."

"No, everything seemed normal."

Henrik took a sip of coffee.

"Have you met your neighbor Shirin?"

"Yes, a few times, in the stairwell."

"How did she seem to you?"

"Same as most folks. Stressed."

"Was she usually alone when you met her?"

"Yes."

"And the children. Have you had any contact with them?"

"Not exactly. The older gal, she comes and goes fairly regularly. But the little girl, I see much less often."

"Oh?"

"Yes, and she's more shy, almost in a way that makes me feel a little worried about her, really."

"Why worried?"

"She's usually alone when I see her.

"And last Christmas, I saw her with a black eye."

"A black eye?"

"Yes, it was fairly faded, so it was probably a few days old. She was holding her hand over it. But I saw it anyway."

"And how did you react? Did you say anything to her?"

"I was appalled, of course. But I didn't say anything. She ran past me so fast. I thought that maybe I should contact Social Services and make one of those reports."

"And did you?"

"No, I never did. I wasn't sure how to go about it. I saw the mother, Shirin, right afterward and stopped to talk to her. It seemed to me that she took my concerns about her daughter seriously."

"It sounds as if you thought the family needed help. Was there anything else that pointed to things not being quite right?"

Göran scratched his cheek before continuing: "I don't know… I really can't tell. You know, I forget how it was. My children are grown up now."

"The music…" Mia tried again, pointing toward the stereo.

"It's wonderful, isn't it?" Göran smiled again.

"Very," Mia said, sinking even deeper into the armchair, making the leather creak under her.

"And so you've heard arguments from the apartment, or 'verbal nonsense,' as you called it?" Henrik asked.

"Yes," Göran said, becoming still. "They'd been quiet for a while, but a few days ago, I heard it again. I heard Shirin shouting and screaming."

"Do you know what time it was?"

"It was probably around now, around eight or nine o'clock in the evening. But that wasn't too unusual. I've heard that before."

"How often?" Henrik said.

"A few times a week."

"A week?"

"Yes."

"But did you only hear Shirin?"

"No. I know the children's father is dead, that I knew, so I just thought that it was a boyfriend or some male with whom she has a relationship and she liked to argue with, but..."

"But you don't know who he is?" Henrik asked, stroking his hand over his chin.

"No, I haven't met him exactly, but I've seen him, you know, and..."

"So if we ask you to describe him, can you do that?"

"Somewhat, in any case."

"And when did you last see him?"

"That's what I wanted to get to. I saw him come up the staircase the other day, go up to the little girl, who was just standing there at the door, and hit her in the back of the head. She didn't look all that surprised, more just sad, or scared. Then Shirin came up the stairs, and she must have seen the blow. But she didn't seem to react. The three of them just went into the apartment, and then it was quiet."

"How did you see all of this?" Henrik asked.

"Through the peephole of my front door."

She heard a clinking sound from the kitchen when she stepped into the hall. Jana Berzelius stepped out of her heels and checked that the front door was locked before going into the kitchen.

Danilo sat at the kitchen table with a glass of water in front of him. He looked up at her, and she saw that his otherwise dark gaze was gone. Instead, his eyes had a different expression, one that she couldn't quite make out.

"Did you have a good time at dinner?" he asked.

She should have let it be, but maybe it was the wine she'd drunk.

"What do you mean?" she heard herself asking.

"You and that…Per Åström, did you have a good time?"

She glanced toward the kitchen counter and the knife block before stepping forward and sitting across from him.

"Why do you care?"

He shrugged his shoulders, picked up the water glass with his left hand and let the right one sink to his knees.

"Have you looked at my cell phone?" she said.

He sneered at her.

"I've always said that you should be more careful, Jana. Don't leave your phone in the bedroom next time you shower. And it might be time to change your PIN code."

She clenched her fists.

"Calm down now," he said.

"I am calm," she said.

"You don't look calm."

"What do you think I'm going to do, attack you?"

"I am worried that you're going to hurt me," he said in an affected tone and took a sip of water. "Over this thing with your phone."

"Is that why you have a knife pointed at me under the table?"

Danilo looked at her with a curious expression.

"How did you know?" he said.

"In the first place, you're right-handed," she said. "If you were just sitting and drinking water, you'd be holding the glass in your right hand. In the second place, one of the knives is missing from the knife block. Since there's no knife on the counter, I assume you have it in your hand."

"It's just a precautionary measure. Answer my question now. Did you have a nice dinner, you and Åström?"

"That's not something you need to know," she said, standing up.

"Maybe not," he said. "But you shouldn't see him anymore."

"What did you say?"

"You shouldn't see him anymore."

"We're colleagues, we…"

"That's why," he interrupted. "If I find out that you're going behind my back, Jana, I'll kill Per. I'll slit his throat all the way through to his vertebrae. I hope you understand me well enough."

January 18

Dear Diary,
Typical shitty day again. The teacher Mr. Thomas pointed to a table next to the window and asked me to sit there. Only Linus was at the table. When I started to pull the chair out, Linus moved away from me and said I "smelled like eggs."

I looked down so no one would see me cry. I didn't want to make them happy.

But at the break I couldn't hold it in any longer. I cried even before I could get to the bathroom. I didn't think anyone saw me, but my teacher came by and put his hand on my shoulder. When he asked why I was crying, I told him what Linus had said to me. But when he scolded Linus, Linus said I had lied. *He hadn't changed sides because I smelled badly. He only wanted to see the whiteboard better.*

Now everything will only be worse. I can feel it. Linus is going to tell everyone. He probably already has.

The teacher says I should focus on my schoolwork. But I can only think about being as invisible as possible. It's harder than you think. Especially during recess. I usually lock myself in the bathroom. I don't want to be in the corner of the school-yard anymore.

In art class, I finished my star. I painted it blue, wrote my name on it and tied a piece of string on it. Camilla said it was as ugly as I was. Then she stole it and hid it. I finally found it, in the garbage can in the hallway.

I took the star home. Mom thinks it is pretty. She wants me to hang it in the window. She says that it will always shine over us, that love is eternal. Our love.

I hope Mom means it, because it's hard to know. It's hard to know anything in this shit world. The only thing I know is that life hurts. Life means a wheelchair for my Mom. It means scratches on your face, calls for help, handfuls of pills.

I just want to close my eyes, put my hands over my ears and silence all the screaming, all the yelling, not have to hear all the stupid words.

I think about Dad sometimes. I almost miss him in spite of everything. And I'm actually more scared now, scared of being alone. I'm most scared at night. Last night I dreamed that Mom would see me, hug me, love me—forever.

That's the only thing I want.

CHAPTER
NINE

Friday

THE MORNING LIGHT TRICKLED IN THROUGH GRAY steel blinds. Jana Berzelius lay in her bed and tried not to think about Danilo lurking in the other room. Over the past days, she had spent twice as many hours in her bedroom when she was home as she normally would.

During the night, she had even dreamed about him, about how it had been between them. She was sitting in a dark cellar with a damp earthen floor, and she'd felt the cold in her legs, her bottom. She could still feel the chill, because she had sat like that in reality, too—huddled up, her heart pounding.

In the dream, she attempted to find a way to conquer the darkness, but in the end, she'd felt the panic come anyway. She had reached out her hand in a sweeping gesture to find something to hold on to when she discovered him. Touched him. Danilo. He had jerked when her hand made contact with him, and she'd felt how he was shaking just as much as she was. They hadn't had any idea how long they were going to sit in the cellar, but they knew that a girl had sat there previously, alone, and when the door was opened after multiple days, she had starved to death.

Weak, they'd called her.

Neither Jana nor Danilo had wanted to be called weak. That was why they'd held each other's hands there in that cold cellar. Held hands to show that they were not going to fold, not even in the darkness.

They'd been only seven years old when they experienced their first endurance exercise together. During that time, she learned more about him than she had wanted to know. She had tried to stay away from Danilo—or Hades, as he was called then…the name they had carved into his neck.

She had tried to forget about those dark years they had shared together as child soldiers. And now, after all this time, he had forced her to hide him in her own apartment.

Jana pulled the comforter away from her body with the thought that the memories of their common childhood had now also wormed their way into her dreams. She didn't want that, didn't want to think about Danilo at all. But no matter how much she tried to ignore him, she couldn't get rid of him. Not even in her dreams.

And now, on top of everything else, he was threatening to kill Per.

She got out of bed slowly. It wasn't that Danilo had threatened to hurt Per that bothered her. It was knowing he would actually do it, if he felt he had to.

He wouldn't even blink, she thought.

Philip stood naked in the kitchen and looked at the pills he was holding in his hand. They were his lifeline; they allowed him to function. He thought about his conversation with his boss, Eva. Had it really taken almost twenty minutes for them to transport the woman who had suffered a heart attack to the hospital? Twenty minutes was inexplicably long; he agreed with Eva on that point. But what was there to say?

Sure, he'd taken a pill during the night, but he shouldn't have fallen asleep because of that. Or had he made a mistake and mixed up the Sobril with the Imovane? Sobril was supposed to calm him. Imovane made him sleep.

If so, that would also explain why he didn't know where he had put his wedding ring. He'd looked at work, in the locker room, in the lounge, in all of the bunk rooms. He'd looked everywhere at home, too, but hadn't found it.

I should stop the pills now, he thought, putting a pill on his tongue. He drank some water before going back to the bedroom. Lina had rolled over and lay on her back with her legs straight up in the air. She was pressing her hands against the sides of her bottom as she followed him with her eyes.

"What were you doing out there?" she asked.

"Nothing," he said. "But what in the hell are *you* doing?"

"I've heard that you maximize your chances of getting pregnant if you lie in bed like this for a half hour afterward."

"Who said that?"

"I read it in a magazine. There's no scientific proof behind it, really. But it also said you could strike a compromise and lay like this just for a little bit, say, ten minutes or something. And definitely on your back, maybe with a pillow under your butt or sort of pedaling your legs with them up in the air like this..."

She began pedaling her legs.

"It isn't scientifically established, either," she continued, "but it sounds logical, so why not try?"

She kicked more energetically with her legs and expected

Philip to begin laughing. But he didn't. Instead, he sank down with his head on the pillow and listened to the patter of raindrops against the window.

"What are you doing?" she asked.

"Thinking."

"About what?"

"That it rained the first time we had sex."

"You remember that?" Lina giggled. She lay on her side, supporting her head with her hand. She became serious and looked at him for a long moment.

"What's going on?" she asked. "What has happened?"

"Nothing."

"Yes, something did. Tell me. I can see in your face that something has happened."

The bed rocked as she moved closer. She began caressing his chest.

"Wow, you're so sweaty," she said.

He took her hand in his, stopping her movements, and pressed it against his cheek.

"What's going on with you?" She giggled.

"Nothing."

"But it's got to be something."

"No, it's nothing."

"Yes, tell me. Tell me what it is, my love. Do I have to persuade you?"

She smiled at him, kissed him on the mouth, draped her leg over him, pressing her naked body against his. He tried to keep her hand in his, but she pulled it free and pinched his nipple.

"Stop it," he said, tossing back the comforter.

"Where are you going?" she asked, disappointed.

"I'm going to get something to eat," he said.

"I'm hungry, too. Would you toast some bread for me?"

"Of course."

He walked out of the bedroom and went back into the kitchen. The window was open, and raindrops were puddling on the windowsill, but he didn't bother to close it. Instead, he picked up the glass he'd left on the kitchen counter and let the water run from the tap as he drank.

He was just about to put the glass down when he began thinking of Katarina, his best friend and colleague.

How could she still be sick? She hadn't seemed sick when he'd talked to her the day before yesterday. And why hadn't she called him back yet?

"How's my toast?" Lina called from the bedroom.

"Good," Philip said, finding his cell phone.

He dialed Katarina's number.

Anneli got up from the mattress on the floor in her mother's house and was aware of the pain in her back. She opened the curtains and squinted out toward the rainy street. There had been a time when she would stand at a window and hear Gunnar approach her from behind, would feel his hands around her body and listen to him breathing. But that was another time, another window.

She considered going in to where her son, Adam, was sleeping and lying next to him and giving him a hug. But she stayed where she was, thinking that it was crazy that they were living with her mother now, his grandma. She had told Adam that it was just temporary, that she and his dad needed to be apart for a while, that they just needed a break. Grown-ups need breaks sometimes.

Adam had taken all of it in calmly. Maybe he was used to it; the number of times that she and Gunnar had separated was already far too high. But they had always found their way back to each other and would move back in together eventually. She had always known how he felt about her.

But now she had to admit that everything felt different. Tears sprang to her eyes at the thought of how she had lost control and let her feelings take over. How she had cheated on Gunnar.

Would he ever forgive her?

She longed to go home to him, to crawl next to him in their warm bed, feel his chest move as he breathed, hear his snoring.

Her palm became wet from her tears as she wiped her face. She picked up her cell phone and started to compose a text, but she deleted it and put the phone down.

There was no point. He wouldn't text back.

Jana Berzelius stood in the doorway to her bedroom. It was quiet in the apartment in the dark, except for the patter of rain against the window.

When she walked toward the bathroom, she caught sight of him, lying on the sofa with his eyes closed, seeming to be asleep. His clothes were on the floor, his running shoes unlaced and his gym bag closed.

She thought about the knives in the kitchen and wished she were holding one of them in her hand; wished she could thrust it through his body with all of her strength.

Or she could just use her hands.

She had killed a man like that once. She'd crushed his larynx by striking him with the side of her hand, just as she'd been taught. But that was a long time ago. She'd been young and afraid for her life. Now she wasn't terrified, just furious.

"What do you want, Jana?"

Danilo was almost whispering.

She raised her eyes and looked at him. He had opened his eyes and pushed one hand under his pillows.

"I don't think you want me to answer that," she said.

"You don't need to answer," he said. "I already know what

you want. Killing me would be a *small* problem for you. But afterward, you'd have a *big* problem. And when it comes down to it—" he pulled a pistol out from under the pillow and aimed it at her "—I believe you think it's more important to get back what's yours than to kill me. It would cost you much less to let me live."

She didn't move a muscle. She didn't even blink.

"If you kill me," he said, "your career and your life will be ruined in the same moment. So make sure to leave me alone."

"I hate you," she said.

"That's what you always say," he said, replacing the pistol under the pillow before closing his eyes again.

She went into the bathroom, closed the door quickly and locked it.

Her skin was covered in goose bumps as she got into the shower. She stood under the warm jets for a long time before sweeping a terry cloth towel around her body and a second one around her hair.

A white jar stood in the middle of the shelf. A faint scent of citrus spread through the room as she forcefully rubbed lotion on her face, arms and the deformed letters on her neck. She twisted the lid back on the cream, put it back on the shelf and reached for the electric toothbrush that always stood next to it.

But it wasn't there.

She looked around and found it farther down on the shelf.

The thought that he had used her toothbrush made her see red. She took it and threw it against the tiles. Then she cursed herself for not having ended his days at the boathouse three months ago when she'd actually had the chance. That way she would've avoided all of this.

The stairwell of the police station was empty. Henrik enjoyed the silence as he walked slowly up to the third floor.

Once upstairs, he saw Mia, who yawned exaggeratedly. She had just pulled on a gray knit sweater, and her fine blond hair was standing straight up with static electricity.

"Good morning!"

Gunnar Öhrn rushed past. A deep furrow was visible on his forehead.

"Already on the move?" Henrik asked.

"Yes," Gunnar said. "The media is here and writing about the new reorganization. It's not enough that we have crimes to solve—I have to go down and answer questions about *how* we are going to solve them, too. And how can I answer who does what, when we have new colleagues with titles I don't have the faintest idea of?"

"Like coordinator Britt Dyberg?" Henrik said.

"Yes, for example," Gunnar said.

"Who the hell is Britt Dyberg?" Mia asked, smoothing her hand over her hair in an attempt to get it to lie flat again.

"A *coordinator*," Gunnar said.

"Now that's a fucking title," Mia said. "Whatever happened to 'police officer'?"

Gunnar pulled his hand over his face, making his skin flush red.

"You look like you're ready to drop," Henrik said.

"Yes, because I see that we've created an organizational nightmare and a worse operation for the near future. The goal was to put more police resources closer to the public, but if we can't decrease the administrative work, there won't be any change. The police will just sit there and do paperwork instead of being on the ground preventing crime."

"I've heard a lot of people say that things on the ground are working," Mia said. "On the supervisory level, though, it's a fucking mess."

"But we got a new regional boss, anyway," Henrik said. "Carin Radler."

"Thanks for reminding me. That doesn't exactly make me feel less shitty," Gunnar said.

"Be careful so it doesn't rub off," Mia said.

"It doesn't matter," Gunnar said. "Everyone already feels shitty, and it's not so strange when we, who have supervisory positions, who are supposed to make quick decisions every day, aren't really settled in. In front of my title is the word 'Acting.' No one knows who has the authority to make decisions, no one knows what they're supposed to be doing, or with whom, and so nothing happens. And that's going on all over the country. There are supervisors who still haven't received their new job descriptions, so they're just sitting on the sidelines and watching."

"So they're just walking around not really doing anything?" Mia asked.

"That's about it," Gunnar said. "It's the worst for those who are older than fifty. They can't even be on patrol. They have to guard cells and answer telephones."

"Yes, I was one of the ones listening with great interest when the implementation committee was going around the country and saying that all of the decisions of the new organization would be understood as far down as possible in the ranks," Henrik said.

"What are you getting at?" Mia asked.

"That it was a nice thought."

"A nice thought, yes," Gunnar said. "But it hasn't been implemented. All of the decisions come from a central location in Stockholm, and from there it must be terribly difficult to get a feel for the regional conditions. It works just as poorly as I had thought, maybe even worse."

He fell silent as Anneli walked past in the hallway.

"I know you don't like to talk about it, but to change the subject," Henrik said, "may I ask, how are things between you two?"

"Between me and Anneli?"

"Yes."

"Our relationship is like the Police Authority after the re-organization. It exists in a vacuum."

Mia laughed.

"So what are you going to do to regain order?" she said.

"Everything rests on finding a new role, and in order to do that, a significant amount of desire is required," he said.

"I was talking about your relationship."

"So was I," he said.

Just then, Henrik's cell phone began ringing.

"Excuse me," he said, and left to go down the hallway.

Philip put the last bite of toast into his mouth and sank back on the sofa. Lina settled in next to him and the two of them watched the morning news on Channel 4, where a panel of entertainment reporters were discussing the participants of *Let's Dance*.

Lina reached for the cup of tea on the coffee table, but ended up in a coughing fit.

"Are you okay?" he said, feeling how nice it was to think about something other than work.

"I don't know," she said. "I'm just so terribly tired. Maybe I'm already pregnant."

"Pregnant?!"

"I'm just joking."

"That's nothing to joke about."

She giggled and kissed him, lifting his arm and laying her body along his.

"I really want this to happen," she said.

"Me, too," he said, stroking her hair.

"Just think if we can have a baby. We should have four kids, don't you think?"

"Four? Never!"

"At least three, then!"

"I'd just be happy if we had one," he said. "Why do you want to have so many kids?"

"Because I love you. I love the thought of having children with you. I love trying to make a baby with you. I would love being pregnant with you. Going through labor next to you…"

"Take it easy now," he said, pulling his arm from her shoulders. He sat up and felt her gaze on his back.

"Children are the whole purpose in life, aren't they?" she said, caressing up and down his spine with her fingers.

"Yeah," he said, getting up.

"Where are you going now?" she asked.

"I have to take care of something…at work," he said, the worry apparent in his voice.

"You're always working."

She sounded disappointed.

"Can't you stay home?" she continued. "So we can lie here on the couch all day long and snuggle?"

"I can't. I have to get going," he said, putting on a pair of pants and a shirt that lay on the floor.

He heard Lina sigh as he left the living room.

"No more sex, then?" she called.

"Not now. Tonight, maybe?"

"Sandra is coming over tonight."

"Why is that?" he asked, turning around.

"We're supposed to have dinner with her. Didn't you remember?"

"Yes, yes," he said doubtfully. "But you two are always here. Can't you go to her place for a change?"

"But we've already decided that she's coming here at six thirty. Maybe we'd have time for a quickie before that?"

"Sure," he said, grabbing his car keys.

Water dripped from the buildings and gutters.

Jana Berzelius walked with brisk steps toward the police station and focused on her breathing. She had only her briefcase in her hand; she'd left her computer and binders in the car. It didn't actually matter how much she tried to hide from Danilo, she realized. He had already been snooping around on her cell phone, scrolling through her messages and emails. She shuddered.

That Danilo had shown up in her dreams made her even more worried. He had appeared in them before, but never so intensively and clearly as he had the previous night.

She thought about how she had been nine years old when the nightmares had begun. The nights became torture. As soon as Margaretha and Karl said good-night and turned off the light, she had opened her eyes and wondered how she would be able to keep herself awake all night. She had never turned on the light; she'd let the room remain dark. The fear didn't come with the darkness. It came with the dreams.

She had never been afraid of the sort of things a person's imagination could come up with. She'd been afraid of what she'd experienced herself as a child.

She had tried to swallow her fear, pretend it didn't exist, forcing herself to stay awake at night. But in the end, she hadn't been able to fight it. She had fallen asleep. And she had dreamed.

Every time she awoke, the sweat lay like a film over her thin body. She had sat up, pulled her knees up to her chin and dried her tears with the sleeve of her nightgown.

Jana crossed in the crosswalk and thought how Father used

to bolt her door from the outside so that she wouldn't come into their room at night.

But that had never stopped her.

Silently and slowly she would climb out through the window, out of her room and into theirs.

Mother always slept on her side, breathing so quietly it was almost inaudible. Jana would sneak up to the bed, stretch out her hand and hold it in front of Margaretha's mouth, feeling how it tickled when she exhaled.

Carefully, she would pad around the bed to Father's side and stand close, holding both of her hands an inch from his face and feeling his breaths come in deep bursts from his mouth.

Then she would huddle up, lie on the floor and wait.

Wait for the fear to come.

They never had any idea that I was there, she thought, pushing the door to the police station open. *They never had any idea what I was actually dreaming about.* And now her mother was gone.

But everything was collected in her journals, and right now that was what meant most to her. She would do anything and everything to get them back.

Henrik Levin had just closed the door to his office when he again heard his cell phone ring.

"This is Henrik," he said, sitting down in his chair.

"Do you have a minute?" pathologist Björn Ahlmann said. "For the Shirin Norberg case?"

"You're done with the autopsy report?"

"I will be soon."

"Tell me what you've found," Henrik said, pressing the phone to his ear even harder as he observed the tangled pattern of roads, tram lines and bus routes below him.

"This has nothing to do with rape or attempted rape. But she has been subjected to extremely aggressive violence directed at her arms, legs and kidneys. Her hands, as you know, were severed."

"With what?"

"Probably a Gigli saw."

"Which is?"

"A surgical tool used to saw through bone. It's a long, saw-edged wire that's fastened to handles."

Henrik let his gaze wander up the dismal facades on the other side of the street.

"Had she been drugged?" he asked.

"I haven't received the results back for all of the tests yet," Björn answered.

"DNA?"

"I can't give you any more than that right now. But I want to make you aware of the time line. The bruising on the body occurred much earlier and separate from the severing of the hands."

"How much earlier?"

"I would guess upwards of four days, at least."

With both hands on the steering wheel, Philip turned his Audi A5 onto the E4 highway and continued toward the Klinga interchange. Just before the exit, his gas light came on, and he swung into the gas station. The credit card reader beeped loudly as he entered his PIN code.

He put the pump handle back after five gallons and got back in his car. He continued past the Go-Cart arena, turned left on Linköpingsvägen and then left again, onto a narrow gravel road to a neighborhood called Borg Boklund.

Katarina Vinston's house stood on a small hill on the left. On the right, barely visible, were two other single-family homes.

Philip parked on the side of the road, opened his car door

and got out. He stood with one leg still in the car for a moment.

The house was red with white trim. All the windows were dark, and he couldn't help but think that the house looked almost abandoned.

When he left the car, the gravel crunched under his feet. He opened the gate to the yard, walked onto the lawn and up to the house. A broom had been leaned against the front door.

He rang the doorbell, waited a moment and then rang again. He tried the door handle twice, but it was locked.

He listened at the door, but all he heard was the whispering of the trees. Everything was quiet—unnervingly quiet.

Philip peered carefully in through the narrow window next to the front door, trying to see any evidence that Katarina might be inside. But all he could see were a jacket and scarf hanging up on the wall at the entrance, and, farther down the hallway, the kitchen with its long, narrow wooden table, Windsor-style chairs and braided rug.

He rang the bell one more time, waited and then backed away from the porch. He looked around, thinking maybe there would be someone to ask, someone who might know her whereabouts, but the only thing he saw was a deer at the edge of the woods, standing completely still, its head high. There were the two houses farther off, but he would feel odd going there and making such a big deal out of it.

He hesitated at first, but then he stepped around into the flower bed and stood on tiptoe in the black soil to look in the side window, but was met only by darkness.

He stepped back and walked around the back of the house. At the rear was a glassed-in sunroom, the door to which was also locked.

He went back around to the front and stood in the street

and looked at the upstairs windows for two full minutes. Then he tried her on his cell, but her voice mail picked up.

Finally he pulled the pills from his pocket, pushed one out of the blister pack and swallowed it before getting back in his car.

He couldn't shake off the feeling that the house appeared abandoned, as if no one lived there anymore. The entire way back to Norrköping he asked himself the same question: Where had Katarina disappeared to?

CHAPTER
TEN

"SO WHAT BJÖRN AHLMANN IS CLAIMING, THEN,"
Gunnar Öhrn said, resting his elbows on the table in the conference room, "is that many of the bruises on Shirin Norberg's body happened a few days before her hands were severed?"

The meeting had been going on for five minutes, but it was already warm in the room at the police station. Henrik Levin was drinking from his coffee cup, Mia Bolander was twirling a lock of hair around her finger, Ola Söderström was rocking his chair, and Jana Berzelius and Anneli Lindgren both sat still with their eyes on Henrik.

"Is that right?" Gunnar asked.

"Yes, that's right," Henrik said, putting his coffee down. "The bruises on her body did not appear to occur at the same time as her hands were severed. And according to Björn, there is no doubt that someone had abused her. There are also signs that indicate that she was subjected to systematic violence for a long time. The question is whether the person who abused her over time is the same one who mutilated her in the end."

It became quiet in the room. Gunnar swept his gaze over the faces around the table. He met Anneli's eyes for a moment, but he didn't linger there.

"And her hands?" he continued.

"Yes," Henrik said. "Her hands were probably amputated using a surgical instrument like a Gigli saw, but…"

"I'm sorry to interrupt," Jana said, spinning her pen with both hands, "but this possible boyfriend that the neighbor described, do we have any trace of him? Have you checked the victim's computer, what she downloaded, what sites she visited, if she chatted…"

"Yes, of course we did," Henrik said.

"And her cell phone?"

"I've gone through it," Ola said. "She or someone else appears to have erased all of the texts."

"Why would she do that?"

"If you look here," Ola said, putting a bunch of papers on the table, "you'll understand why."

The list of calls was four pages long.

Jana cast a quick glance at them.

"Numerous times every day, Shirin received ominous text messages," she said.

"Ominous?" Mia snorted, pulling the papers toward her. "These clearly are murder threats, plain and simple." She read aloud: "'You are worth nothing. People like you need people like me. See you tonight, whore.'"

Mia flipped through the pages and continued, "'You will let me in. Otherwise I'll wake you up at night, force you to say your last words and then I'll kill you and your daughters and no one will even care.' And 'Don't you even dare to answer now? *Ha ha*, you're so disgustingly pathetic. Answer, for Christ's sake. Answer!'"

Mia put the papers back down. "Seems to me these were sent by a real knight in shining armor."

"But who *did* send them?" Gunnar asked.

"Unfortunately," Ola said, "all of the texts came from a prepaid phone."

"No other phone numbers that we can track from the list?" Mia said.

"No," Ola said. "There are a few calls to and from the oldest daughter, Aida, but nothing else."

"Maybe Aida knows who sent the threats?" Gunnar asked.

"She seemed ignorant about most of it when we talked to her, right, Henrik?" Mia said. "Either she is still in shock, or it simply hasn't sunken in yet that her mother is dead."

"Yes, she did act a little strange, you could say," Henrik said thoughtfully.

The room fell silent.

Gunnar clasped his hands on the table.

"Or did she feel afraid and threatened into silence?"

"I could buy that," Mia said. "But then her grandmother Maria Ashour must also have been threatened, because I still think it's damn strange that she didn't know that her daughter was being abused in this way. It seems completely bogus that she's not letting us talk to the youngest daughter, even when we gave her assurances that the interrogation would be handled sensitively. Maria didn't say anything useful at all during our questioning."

"It could be taken that both Aida and Maria are trying to hide something," Henrik said. "But I don't quite know what they would have to gain from that."

"Yes, I have a very difficult time seeing how Maria would

have been able to turn a blind eye to this recurring abuse of her daughter," Mia said. "It's not likely at all."

Gunnar nodded.

"Okay," he said. "But the hands? What do we think about that aspect? Why cut them off?"

Everyone fell silent.

"He's a fucking sadist, if you ask me," Mia said after a moment.

"Punishment for something," Anneli said.

"Yes, she suffered enough, that's for sure," Henrik said.

Jana laid her pen on the table.

"But the neighbor attested that Shirin had someone in the apartment at least from time to time. He had even seen the man, if I understood you correctly, Henrik."

"Yes," Henrik said, "the neighbor had seen a man with both Shirin and the youngest daughter, Sara. A man with broad shoulders and black hair. Not a very good description, maybe, but he only saw him through the peephole."

"In which case, we can't lose sight of the fact that Sara has seen things she shouldn't have seen," Gunnar said. "That makes her our most important witness."

"Exactly," Mia said.

"And if we can't question her, we can at least talk to Aida right now," Gunnar said. "I think we should call her in for at least one more questioning. We'll start there."

She tried to look relaxed but was afraid that she wasn't very successful. Aida Norberg glanced at the policeman sitting across the table from her. It was the same friendly detective as last time, Henrik Levin. They sat alone in the little interrogation room in the police station.

Aida placed both of her hands between her thighs and rubbed them slowly against each other. The chair was hard, and the Dictaphone lying on the table before her was small. She looked up at it a few times, but quickly looked back down again.

"I have to ask you a few follow-up questions," the detective said.

"Okay," she said, swallowing.

"And we might as well get right down to it," he continued. "We know that your mother was being threatened by someone. We've found texts that she erased from her cell phone. The neighbor has also seen a man visit your mother."

She blinked a couple of times, continuing to rub her hands against each other.

"I want you to be completely honest with me now, Aida. Who is that man? Who threatened her?"

"I don't know," she said, shaking her head.

"Try to think. This is important."

"I can't."

"Why can't you?"

"I just can't."

She felt the tension in her shoulders.

"Is it someone who also threatened you?"

"No."

"Are you sure?"

"Yes."

"Is it someone who has done something bad to you?"

"No."

"You have to tell us."

"I know," she said, her heart pounding. "But there's nothing to tell."

"She's clamming up," Henrik Levin said in a low voice. "It's obvious she's keeping something from us."

He was standing in the hallway with Jana, who had followed the interrogation with Aida from the observation room.

"I agree," Jana said. "There's a scared look in her eyes."

"You saw that?"

"Yes."

"And how did she seem to you?"

"Well, as you've already said, she's very composed," Jana said.

The fluorescent lighting fully exposed her face. Her skin was pale, her throat long and slim.

"It's remarkable," he said.

"But not everyone is sentimental," she said.

"Maybe not," he said. "But still…"

He crossed his arms over his chest, looking up at the ceiling for a moment. Then he leaned toward Jana and said: "Aida is never going to give us the perpetrator. Even if she knows, she's not going to say anything."

"You don't think so?"

"No. If she were going to, she would have already."

He looked at her.

"Would you have told even if someone threatened your family?" he asked.

"I don't have a family," she said, meeting his gaze.

"But if you did?"

"There's something called the duty to report misconduct."

"Yes, there is. But would you take the risk?"

"It would depend on the circumstances."

"Of course it does," Henrik said, releasing his arms. He lowered his gaze to the floor and looked at his shoes, thinking for a moment.

"I really want to question the little sister," he said then.

"I think we should," Jana said. "Call Special Victims Investigator Mikaela Lundin."

"Even though the grandmother Maria doesn't want us to?"

"Yes, I think so. Considering the seriousness of this crime and the principle of proportionality, we have leeway for the decision to bring the youngest daughter in for interrogation. She can help us find the perpetrator. According to my judgment, witness statements are very valuable, and when you set that in relation to other evidence, the interrogation is absolutely necessary. I'd like you to tell Maria that."

Philip walked straight through the gym to the row of treadmills. He stepped up on one and began maniacally punching in his weight and distance on the panel. The machine thudded loudly as he began to jog.

On the TV screen mounted on the wall in front of him, he saw a woman holding a children's book about Native Americans. It made him think about all of the stories his father had told him when he was young. Stories about tents in desolate forests, paths through the wilderness, trampling herds of buffalo and loud birdcalls. Stories that were realistic and detailed.

He thought it was ironic that the memories of the stories his father had told him were stronger than most of his memories of the man himself. His father had worked and mostly kept to himself. *He worked and mostly kept to himself.* It struck Philip that this sentence could just as well be a description of his own existence.

What sort of spouse was he that he'd allowed himself to become so absorbed in his professional priorities? How had pills become his best friends?

Just as he felt his pulse increasing, a man walked into the gym. Philip didn't know him but recognized him as a regular.

"My grandma runs faster than you do, dude," the man with a wide back, muscular arms and skinny legs said, grabbing a barbell.

"What did you say?" Philip said, staring at him as he ran.

"I said, my grandma runs faster than you. And she has a prosthetic leg."

"What the fuck do you mean by that?"

"Calm down, for Christ's sake," he said. "It was just a joke."

"At least I do legs," Philip said.

"When I do legs, it's by spreading my girlfriend's," he said, grinning.

Irritated, Philip began pressing the button to increase the speed. He should have laughed at the joke, but instead he felt pissed off.

He pressed the button hard, but the speed didn't change. He pressed multiple buttons, but in the end didn't know what buttons he was even pressing. He couldn't think straight anymore, and it scared him and made him feel like a failure.

Over the years, he had amassed a whole archive of failures. As a son, he had failed his father by not following in his footsteps. As a spouse, he had failed Lina by not getting her pregnant. Now he had failed a patient. Or two patients, if he also counted the woman with the heart attack.

It wasn't the first time he had failed in his work. The greatest mistake he'd made had been ten years ago, but his brain had its limits, and after grappling with his past torments for a minute, it shut itself off. His thoughts were just getting in the way. He pushed the stop button and stepped off the treadmill.

Special Victims Unit investigator Mikaela Lundin sat in a blue armchair in the small, eight-by-ten interrogation room. She was wearing a pair of light-colored pants and a thin blouse. She had blond hair and light eyebrows. Sara Norberg sat diagonally across from her, also in a blue armchair, and her legs dangled slowly back and forth.

Sara had been shown the camera that was mounted in one

corner of the room near the ceiling, but she'd already forgotten that it was there. She had a stuffed animal, a pony, on her lap and was wearing blue-and-white-striped pants and a pink long-sleeved shirt. Her hair was messy, and her bangs hung to the right.

In the adjoining observation room, Henrik Levin and Jana Berzelius sat on office chairs, following the interview.

Everything was recorded and archived on a computer.

"What a nice pony," Mikaela said. "Do you like playing with ponies?"

"Ye-es," Sara said, smoothing her hands over the black mane.

"Have you ever ridden one?"

"No."

Mikaela waited for a moment, letting the girl stroke the mane a number of times before continuing.

"How old are you, Sara?"

Sara held up her hand and stretched out all five fingers.

"So you're five years old?"

The girl nodded.

"Who do you live with?" Mikaela asked.

"Mommy."

"What does Mommy look like?"

"I don't know."

Mikaela moved a little closer to Sara, trying to establish eye contact with her, but the girl kept her eyes on the pony.

"Sara, can you tell me a little about where you live, about your sister..."

The girl pressed the pony's muzzle against her nose.

"Can you tell me a little about your sister...or your grandma?" Mikaela said.

"Aida has a tattoo, right here," Sara said, pointing to her arm. "She said it hurt."

Mikaela studied Sara as she again pressed the pony's muzzle to her nose, longer this time.

"What does it look like where you live?" she asked.

"I live with Grandma now."

Sara laid the pony in her lap.

"Because Mommy is sleeping," she said.

"Is Mommy sleeping?"

Sara nodded again.

"Yes, she's sleeping."

"What do you usually do at Grandma's?" Mikaela asked.

"Aida and I play hide-and-seek."

"Where do you like to hide?"

"Under the bed."

"Is that your best hiding place?"

"Yes. Mommy also likes to hide."

"Why does Mommy hide?"

"I don't know."

Sara shrugged her shoulders without looking up.

"Can you tell me where Mommy hides?" Mikaela asked.

"She hides when she's bloody."

"Bloody? Why is Mommy bloody?"

"Mommy's sweetheart."

"Is Mommy your sweetheart?"

"Mommy isn't my sweetheart."

"No?"

"No."

Sara stroked her hand over the pony, first with the hair, then against it.

"Sara?"

"Yes?"

"Do you see that the door to this room is closed?"

"Yes."

"Is the door to your room usually closed?"

"Yes."

"Do you lock it?"

"No. Aida locks it."

"Is there anyone other than Aida who locks it?"

Sara shook her head and stroked the pony again, quicker this time.

"What's your pony's name?" Mikaela asked.

"His name is Pony," she said, looking up at Mikaela for the first time. "I'm thirsty."

"There's water if you want some."

Mikaela filled a glass for Sara.

"I want juice."

"Do you like juice?"

"Yes."

"What kind of juice do you like?"

"Red juice."

"Fruit punch?"

"Yes."

Sara smiled and deep dimples appeared in her cheeks.

"Do you usually have juice at your house?"

"Yes."

Her smile disappeared.

"But Mommy doesn't like juice," she said. "She likes coffee. I don't like coffee."

"Children don't usually like coffee," Mikaela said.

"Coffee hurts."

Mikaela swallowed.

"Why does coffee hurt?"

"It hurts here," Sara said, pointing to her chest.

"Did you get coffee there?"

Sara nodded.

"Was it on purpose that you got coffee there?"

Mikaela tried to meet her gaze, but it was impossible. The girl didn't want to talk any more about it.

"Is there anything else that happened at home that you want to talk about?" she asked.

"Yes…" Sara said.

"Can you tell me what happened?"

"Mommy's bloody."

"Why is Mommy bloody?"

"Mommy's sweetheart."

"Who is Mommy's sweetheart?"

"Ted."

CHAPTER
ELEVEN

"UGH, WHAT A HORRIBLE CASE THIS IS, AND THE GIRL is so young!" Anneli Lindgren said when Henrik had held a quick briefing about the interviews they'd conducted with both of Shirin Norberg's daughters.

The whole team was gathered around the conference table.

"And for us, it's even worse, because we only have the name Ted," Henrik said. "She didn't say anything else."

"If she was even telling the truth," Gunnar said. "Maybe she just made up the name?"

"Ted is probably his real name," Henrik said, "and I don't think she made up the thing with the coffee, either, even though it doesn't have to mean anything...and she has unquestionably seen blood. I absolutely think that Ted is an important clue."

"Okay," Mia said. "So now we need to know who this Ted

is, where he is, and if and why he killed Shirin. But you can do that easy as pie, right, Ola? Poke around a little online."

"I'm working on it," Ola said, "and thanks for the tip, I'll *poke around a little online.*"

"Good," Gunnar said, slapping his hand on the table. "Find everyone with the first name of Ted in Norrköping, and do it quick."

Ola nodded and got up from the table.

"Anneli, check with the National Forensic Center and see if they've gotten any matches on the fingerprints from the crime scene. Understood?"

She had heard his voice, knew that he looked at her, but she couldn't bear to meet his gaze. Normally, she wouldn't have reacted at all to his command, but now she sat there, cheeks blushing, like she had just been scolded. What had happened to her self-esteem?

"Understood?" he said again, a little harder this time, and she nodded slowly.

"Good, then let's get going," he said. "Time to get our butts in gear."

The chairs scraped the floor as everyone stood up. They left the room one after another, and she was going to do the same when she looked up and saw that only Gunnar remained.

She followed his movements as he pushed the papers together on the table and saw that he was being unusually precise about it.

Maybe he wanted to draw the moment out, simply enjoy being together just for that moment?

She couldn't ruin it by getting up.

So she remained in her chair.

"What do you think about her story? Is Sara telling the truth? Or is she just a child in shock who's fantasizing?" Hen-

rik Levin asked as he walked down the hallway with Jana Berzelius after the meeting.

"She doesn't need to fantasize. She's experienced enough
trauma firsthand," Jana said. "Now we should instead gather
all conceivable information about this Ted person as quickly
as possible."

"You think he's the one who cut off Shirin's hands? But we
still don't know if Shirin and this so-called Ted had a closer
relationship."

"How else do you interpret her saying that Ted was
'Mommy's sweetheart'?"

"Yes, that's true," Henrik said thoughtfully. "But we don't
know anything about Ted. She named him when she said that
Mommy was bloody...*that* makes Ted suspicious in my eyes,
not just that he is her sweetheart."

"Because you believe that the murder is about something
other than their relationship?" Jana said.

"Yes, the MO is too extreme. It suggests that it's something
other than relationship trouble. Tying someone to a chair and
chopping off her hands is perverse violence, I would say."

Henrik stopped outside his office. Jana looked at him with
a serious gaze. "I don't think we need to be so creative about
this investigation," she said. "It's better if we stick to the facts
and focus on finding Ted."

She looked at her watch.

"Another meeting coming up?" he asked.

"Just paperwork," she said. "Let me know as soon as you
get anything."

Henrik nodded and watched as she disappeared down the
hallway.

Per Åström straightened his tie again. He was impeccably
dressed in a gray tailored suit and white shirt and had just been
shown to a table at Fiskmagasinet.

He was waiting for Jana. It wasn't one of their usual spots, but the decor was decent. The chairs were large, comfortable and high-backed. Large windows faced the inner courtyard.

The restaurant was filled with the right sort of people. There were men in jackets and women with perfect hairstyles. The ideal place for networking. Per sat at the table and listened to cheerful calls of greeting from the entryway, saw people's wide smiles and listened to their small talk about a soccer match, a new TV series, the weather. More people streamed in, introduced themselves, exchanged pleasantries and tried to be entertaining.

"Is this chair free?"

Per looked up to see a woman in front of him. She had her hand on the chair on the other side of the table and was preparing to pull it away.

He studied her. She looked around forty years old but was dressed like a teenager. She seemed to enjoy wearing red lipstick and a plunging neckline, and she had long, sparkling earrings. On her left hand was a simple gold ring.

"Sorry," he said. "It's taken."

"Okay."

She smiled at him. He smiled back but quickly looked away. There was nothing wrong with her, but another woman occupied his thoughts. He cast a glance at his Breitling watch. Eight minutes until she was to arrive. She usually came exactly on time. At the precise minute, even the second. He preferred a wider margin. He'd been brought up to come at least ten minutes early to dentist appointments, meetings with clients, tennis matches or whatever else might be on his schedule.

He felt like someone was watching him, turned his head and saw that the woman with the gold band had fixed her gaze on him. Like him, she sat alone at a table, and he saw that she still hadn't found a chair for whomever she was waiting for.

She smiled at him and he smiled back, a little self-consciously, and wondered what she was thinking about him.

He looked at his watch again. Five minutes left before she would come.

He straightened his tie one last time and continued listening to the cheerful, pleasant small talk going on around him.

Anneli Lindgren fiddled with her earring and saw Gunnar Öhrn reach for the last paper on the conference table. He looked quickly toward the door, and she knew that he was getting close to leaving the room.

She had to move.

She walked slowly toward him. She tried to suggest with her pace that she wanted to be seen. As she walked so incredibly slowly, she was swept back in time to the day when they had stepped forward together, side by side, toward an altar and a priest. They had promised each other eternal love, had sung about belief and hope, and had whispered about the forgiveness of sins.

She had sinned, but he had still not forgiven her. She could understand him, of course, understand that he couldn't deal with her betrayal, but at the same time she didn't really. Their love couldn't just disappear, not like that. It had to be there still.

That was how she felt about their situation, and she so badly wanted him to say the same. She wanted to forget about walking slowly; it was making her crazy. She wanted to rush forward, embrace him, say that now, now, now it was time to move on with their life together. Again.

"Hi," she said, trying to catch his eyes.

Suddenly, she felt the nervousness fluttering in her stomach. The feeling surprised her. She hadn't expected to be standing before the man she had lived with for over twenty years with her eyes darting about and her mouth dry from anxiety.

Then he turned his face up and looked at her. A smile began to spread from one corner of his mouth to the other.

He was just about to open his mouth to say something when she heard someone clear their throat behind her. She spun around and saw Britt Dyberg in a knee-length skirt and light gray cardigan.

"Am I interrupting?" she asked.

"Not at all," Gunnar said. "Come in."

He waved her in with his arm, and Britt walked toward them with steady steps.

"Hi, Anneli," she said.

"Hi," Anneli said, looking away, feeling a strong desire to be elsewhere.

"I tried calling," Britt said. "But you didn't answer your cell phone."

"We were just in a meeting..." Gunnar said, scratching his head.

"I figured as much. But because it was urgent, I thought it best to come here in person. It's about the man we're looking for."

Britt held out a piece of paper.

"Here," she said. "We've gotten new information about where Danilo Peña is."

"Reliable information?" Gunnar asked.

"Very reliable," she said.

He gave Anneli a look, then took the paper, skimmed it and said, "This will have to wait." But then he fell silent.

"Or, well, wait a minute. Henrik!" he yelled.

Jana Berzelius stepped into the elevator. She greeted two uniformed police officers and was just waiting for the doors to close when she heard Gunnar yell for Henrik. She stuck her foot out and stopped the doors. She saw how Gunnar's facial muscles jerked as he rushed toward Henrik, who was just coming out of his office.

"Are you coming or not?" one of the officers asked.

She took a step back, but just then heard Gunnar say: "Officers on the lookout think they've seen Danilo Peña in an apartment in town."

The doors thundered shut and the elevator began traveling downward.

Jana stood still and hoped that the officers couldn't tell how hard her heart was pounding.

What had Danilo done? Had he been spotted through the windows? Or had he, despite everything, gone out and been recognized? Were the police already there? Had they stormed her apartment and captured him?

In the elevator, the officers were talking about some course in mountain climbing, about ropes, carabiners and chocks.

Her palms were sweating and her mind was racing. What should she do? Was there anything she *could* do? How was she going to be able to explain that she had an escaped murderer in her apartment? She would hardly be able to deny knowing who he was, or what he was doing in her apartment. He would just give her away anyway.

Maybe she should have wished the elevator would move more quickly, but in that moment, she wished she could stop time so she could think clearly.

Just then, her phone rang. She quickly pulled it out of her pocket and saw Per's number on the display.

"Yes?" she answered.

"Are you on your way?"

Lunch!

Her body became ice-cold. She had completely forgotten. What should she do? Should she, despite everything, eat lunch and pretend like nothing was going on? Or should she go home to her apartment and try to salvage the situation?

The elevator doors opened.

"Per, I'm sorry, but I've been delayed," she said.

"But…" she heard him say.

"I can't talk now. We'll have to talk later," she said, ending the call.

Then she dropped her phone back into her pocket and hurried out of the elevator.

"Hello? Jana?" Per Åström said, but she had hung up.

He put his phone back in his pocket. Alone at his table, he felt like people were staring at him. When his gaze fell on people he recognized, they just looked stressed and depressed, turned their faces away and pretended they didn't see him. The murmur of voices was muffled. Even the smell of the place was strange now. It didn't smell like food anymore; it smelled like resignation.

He looked at the empty chair across from him. It wasn't the first time she had canceled lunch. He wasn't bothered by it. Honestly. What bothered him was her manner. She was so distant, and he thought it had gotten even worse recently. Regardless what they talked about, he felt like he was talking to a wall. Even if she were sitting right across from him, she wasn't really there. It was as if her mind were always somewhere else. Because of that, the empty chair across from him wasn't much different than her company.

He grinned at his pathetic thoughts and looked up at the woman with the gold band. He met her eyes again and wondered what she was thinking about him now. Maybe she saw a naive idiot who thought that where there was someone who loved, there was love.

He got up from the table, picked up the chair and went to her.

"You can use this one," he said.

"You don't need it?" she said with a smile.

"Not anymore," he said.

There was a loud crash as Jana Berzelius drove over a manhole cover. The beams of sunlight hit the wet asphalt, and the sharp light made her squint. She was forced to brake when a short, muscular woman in black jeans and a black leather jacket biked quickly across the road without looking for cars.

Jana followed her with her eyes before stepping on the gas again. With a sharp left turn, she was home. She parked her black BMW X6 outside a fashion boutique, under a sign warning that parking was only allowed for fifteen minutes.

Her high heels drummed against the asphalt as she approached the apartment. She attempted to take in her surroundings and stopped on a street corner, pretending she was removing a pebble from her shoe and taking the opportunity to look around. For a brief moment, she wondered if she had ever looked at Knäppingsborg in this way before. She could perceive every sound in the neighborhood, and it was almost as if she could see each brick in the facade of the building she was standing in front of.

Her heart beat even harder as she continued onward. But nothing seemed different or strange. Had the police already been in her apartment? Were they watching her that very minute? Waiting to capture her? They surely knew by now who owned the apartment.

She walked quickly along the street, looking straight ahead yet quickly registering the people who looked at her, who noticed her but who then presumably didn't give her another thought.

Jana arrived at the street entrance, opened it and listened. She prepared to meet someone or hear voices.

But the stairwell was deserted.

She tried to walk quickly, but her shoes still clicked under her weight. Finally, she was on the top floor of the building. With both feet on the last step, she stood still and listened. There was the noise of water rushing through a pipe, but otherwise, her breathing was the only sound.

She continued cautiously toward the door. She stopped and stood still with her hand on the doorknob. She inserted her key and stepped in.

She began to walk toward the kitchen, but she stopped short with the thought that she usually heard him. Footsteps in one of the rooms. A door closing. Panting from the living room as he did push-ups.

But now—no sound. Not one.

Had they already taken him?

Or had he been able to get away?

The thought made her heart pound faster.

She went into the living room and looked around—and then saw him lying there. He was stretched out and his hair was messy, and it was obvious he'd been working out. The shirt from the hospital, which he was still wearing, was damp with sweat.

"What do you want?" he asked without looking at her.

"The police know you're still in town. Have you been outside the apartment today?" she asked.

"Of course," he said. "I went to the grocery store, met a few neighbors, introduced myself and all that."

"You're funny," she said. "Great."

"And you seem to have a fucking vivid imagination," he said, standing up.

"I just happen to know that the police are looking for you, and someone saw you. They could be anywhere."

"How the fuck could someone have seen me?"

"I don't know. But there's a hatch in the attic that you can use."

He looked at her.

"Aren't you overdoing it a little now?"

She shook her head.

"Through the attic storage area, you can get out onto the roof. Two chimneys down there's a hatch that takes you down into the next building, and from there you…"

"Are you worried about me?" he asked, smiling.

"I don't give a damn about you. I'm trying to save my own skin," she said, turning on her heel.

CHAPTER
TWELVE

MIA BOLANDER STOOD IN THE WINDOW OF THE CON-
ference room, waiting for Henrik and Gunnar. She looked
out over the world below. Stroking her hand over her lank,
blond hair, she wondered how long it had been since she'd
had her hair cut.

An old man walked along the sidewalk below, holding a
yellow plastic bag from the discount grocery store. Wearing
a faded black parka over his rounded shoulders, he glanced
around shiftily before stumbling on in the search for empty
PET bottles, or whatever it was he was hunting for.

She sighed at the man, at her hair and at the feeling that she
couldn't shake—that damn feeling of futility.

Just then, the door opened. She looked quickly at Henrik
and Gunnar as they entered. As Henrik walked to the table,
she thought he looked bored. He walked slowly, moved his

hands slowly, and when he opened his mouth, he even talked damn slowly, too.

"Four men in the apartment," he said, releasing the report onto the table. "But no Danilo."

He looked quickly at her before pulling out a chair, sitting down and clasping his hands behind his neck.

"It's a setback," Gunnar said as he also sat down.

"He's probably skipped town altogether," she said.

"So what do we do?" Henrik said. "Please, Mia, come and sit."

"Sure," she said, walking to the table.

"I need more resources, more manpower, so that we can intensify our hunt for him," Gunnar said.

"And if they don't agree?" Mia said, sitting down.

"If I'm going to keep my reputation and my value to this place, I have to have the resources I need."

"Officers are already looking for him around the clock," Henrik said.

"That's not enough," Gunnar said. "We have to have more people on it, leave no stone unturned. Danilo Peña has appeared to have found a place where he believes he can hide until the worst blows over, and we are damn well going to find where that is."

Three minutes later, Henrik walked down the hallway. What a defeat this was. Their only job was to find Danilo Peña—or understand why they couldn't. But aside from the failure of the apartment tip, no information at all had come in. After Danilo escaped from the hospital, all traces of him had disappeared.

Despite the comfortable indoor temperature, he felt sweat running down between his shoulder blades under his thin

Oxford shirt. He tugged on it as he pushed open the door to his office. The chair squeaked as he sank down in it.

"I've got a hit."

He spun around and saw Ola Söderström, who had come into the room without Henrik noticing.

"Hit on what?"

"The name Ted."

Henrik tugged on his shirt again.

"So we have a Ted in the system?" he said.

"Yes, several, and some in the area with criminal records. A Ted Henriksson, a Ted Kjellson and a Ted Strandberg… Should we pass their photos to Aida and Sara? Or wait until Anneli has gotten the results of the fingerprints found at the crime scene?"

"Fingerprints can take time," Henrik said. "Let's go with the photos in the meantime. But I think we should just show them to Aida."

"Not Sara?"

"No, I think that first we should let Aida take a look at them. Maybe we can get her to open up a little more."

"Should I print them out?"

"Immediately."

Jana Berzelius gave the clerk a long, almost empathetic look when he pressed the wrong button on the register for the second time. His hair was red and combed back, and the name tag on his chest said "New Employee." His nervous manner didn't make her any calmer. It was humiliating that Danilo thought she cared about him. The reason she had gone home to the apartment was to protect herself. Nothing else. He shouldn't get any ideas about it.

The clerk stuffed the receipt in the bag, as if to show how conscientious he was at his job.

Jana took the bag and took a roundabout way home to Knäppingsborg to avoid any police seeing her. When she entered her apartment, she went straight into the bedroom and put the bag on the bed.

"You're home again?" Danilo said.

She spun around and saw him coming out of her walk-in closet.

"Get out of here," she said. "I don't want you in here."

"I understood that when you locked the door. What do you have in the bag? A present?"

"It's a new toothbrush. I don't have the slightest desire to share one with you."

He grinned lopsidedly at her.

"Knock it off," she said. "And leave my room right now."

He walked slowly to the door, stopped in the doorway and turned toward her.

"That's a beautiful safe you have in your closet. What do you keep in it?"

She met his gaze but said nothing.

"You should have a smarter place to hide your stuff, Jana."

"Who says I don't?" she said, stepping toward him.

He smiled more broadly now.

"Good," he said. "Just so you don't need to waste time gathering your things if everything goes to hell. I keep a few things hidden, too."

"Where?" she said, gripping the door handle.

"The closest one is under the floorboards in an abandoned building here in town. Things I need are there."

"A pistol?"

"Yes, and money, a few picklocks, a passport...the usual stuff."

"But no clothes, I take it," she said, examining him.

"No clothes," he said. "Or toothbrushes. So, it was really thoughtful of you to buy one for me."

"I bought it for myself," she said, closing the door.

The first minute passed in silence. No one said a word. Mia Bolander sat still in Maria's kitchen and felt the chances of having the right man singled out quickly fade. She looked at Aida, who sat with her arms wrapped around herself, her eyes wandering. Mia heard the hum of the stove fan, saw a few unwashed plates and a baking dish with the dried remains of fish on the counter. The fish was cold and half-eaten.

She really fucking wanted to leave that kitchen, no question about it. The atmosphere was as dismal as the dried-up food. It was as if she, Henrik and Aida were sitting at a wake.

"Aida?" Henrik tried again cautiously, but she didn't lift her gaze. "Is it okay if I show you the pictures now?"

She shook her head.

"It's important to us that you look at them."

"I don't want to."

"Why not?" Mia asked, a little too irritated, and immediately received a look from Henrik.

Aida didn't answer. She just hugged herself even harder.

"And the name Ted," Henrik said, "Are you sure that name doesn't mean anything to you?"

She shook her head again, but this time her nostrils flared.

"You have nothing to lose by talking to us."

"Yes, I do."

"No, you don't," Mia said.

"Yes… Sara."

The room fell silent. A tear squeezed out from the corner of Aida's eye and rolled slowly down her cheek, but she didn't wipe it away. It was as if she were pretending it wasn't there.

"What do you mean by that?" Henrik asked.

A new tear on her cheek.

"She'll die, I know it."

"Why do you think that?"

"He said that he would kill her if I told."

She buried her face in her hands.

"Who said that?" Mia said, who now felt like she'd fully woken up. "Who in the hell said that to you?"

She didn't answer.

"Aida," Henrik said, "who said that to you?"

"I can't say."

"Was it Ted who said that?"

"I don't want to say his name."

"Should I go get your grandmother?" Henrik asked. "Do you want me to?"

"I don't want to have her here, she doesn't know anything. I just want Sara... If anyone..."

"Why don't you want her here?" Mia asked.

Aida dried the tear, and her face took on an introspective look.

"Tell us, Aida," Henrik said calmly. "We're here to help you. You are completely in safe hands. No one but us knows where you and Sara are living right now."

He gave Mia a look as if to say she should hold back. She knew the look well. He didn't want her to interfere right now.

"I just want to...think a little..." Aida said.

"You can think as much as you want," Henrik said.

She took a deep breath and then turned her face toward the window.

"I..." she began but trailed off, as if she didn't know how to continue. She opened her mouth again, looked up at the ceiling and started over.

"It's strange," she said. "But I remember the first time the

Mercedes parked outside our building. Sara was just a baby. He…"

She took another deep breath.

"He introduced himself, shook Mom's hand and asked her out. Alone. Sara and I never got to go with them. So I always took care of Sara. I think I tried five times before I made the formula correctly. But I had to learn, that's just how it was."

Aida's shoulders sank.

"Sara learned to walk when she was about nine months old. Mom was scared that something would happen to her, and so I knew it was my responsibility to take care of her when Mom wasn't home."

Mia sat quietly, listening to every word the teenager said.

"We didn't have much money. After Dad died, we moved to that little apartment, so Sara and I shared a room. It was always me who put her to bed, got up in the night to find a clean diaper, that sort of thing. Until I got my overnight job."

Aida pulled her legs up onto the chair and hugged them as if she were freezing.

"Mom often stayed in bed when she was not at work. *Mommy needs to rest*, she would say, things like that. *Can you get Sara from preschool?*"

Aida fell silent for a moment.

"Mom cried a lot, too. You could tell. Then the phone calls started. I didn't mean to eavesdrop, but I couldn't help hearing through the walls. She was always saying 'sorry,' and I hated her for that."

Aida stopped again.

"Go on," Henrik said. "You're doing great."

She nodded, speaking quietly.

"He kept asking her to go out. He would come to our door to pick her up. It would be early in the evening, and she would be back home before I left for work. I remember Midsummer holiday last year. She didn't want to go with him that evening. She said *No* a bunch of times, but in the end she got into his car after all. He was taking her to a place in the archipelago, he said."

"When was this?"

"Sara was four years old then. I didn't work yet."

Her eyes filled with new tears.

"A few days later, when Mom came back...I still remember how she looked...but I don't want to talk about it now..."

"You don't have to," Henrik said calmly.

"She was hurt...and you couldn't see her eye, it was swollen all around and it looked like it wasn't there..."

Aida's voice trembled.

"Mom didn't want to see him after that...but he wouldn't listen to her. He ignored what she said to him and kept coming to our apartment and forcing his way in, forcing himself on her. Mom wanted to keep us safe so she told us always to stay in our room. But Sara didn't want to be locked in. She would always start crying and screaming. And I would let her cry, let her scream. I didn't want to make her be quiet."

"Why not?" Henrik asked.

"Because *I* didn't want to hear Mom's screams."

The room fell silent. Aida's eyes were fixated on the table as if she'd said something stupid. Henrik laid his hand on her shoulder. "It is very important for us to find the man you're talking about," he said. "Is it okay if I show you the pictures now?"

She nodded slowly.

Henrik slowly laid out the pictures of the men. Only when all three pictures were lying there did she look up. Her eyes suddenly widened.

"That's him," she said, pointing to the picture in the middle.

She couldn't hold back the tears any longer.

★ ★ ★

Jana Berzelius didn't answer on the first ring as she usually would when Henrik called. She was sitting on her bed with her computer on her lap, preparing her presentation for an aggravated extortion case scheduled for the following Tuesday. In one hand she held a cup of yogurt she had brought from the kitchen to avoid eating in Danilo's presence. She couldn't stand being around him. It was far too risky and distracting to have him here. But she *had* to get her journals and notebooks back, by whatever means necessary, and then it was goodbye, Danilo.

She looked at her cell phone as it rang, and finally decided to answer.

"This is Jana," she said.

"Hi, it's Henrik."

"Anything new on the Norberg case?"

"I thought you'd be interested in the information we've gathered about Ted. His last name is Henriksson."

"You thought correctly." She heard him flip through papers, then listened as he told her it had been easy to find Ted Henriksson. The authorities had been involved in his life since his birth in 1978. First Social Services, then the police, then the penal system.

"At five years old, he was pickpocketing," Henrik said. "Petty crimes all through his school years, spent time in a juvenile detention center, then he moved on to drugs. He's been previously convicted of felony domestic violence. In the verdict, eight separate offenses are described. He allegedly threatened his live-in partner, hit her in the face, pulled her hair, pressed a pillow to her face, threw boiling water on her, grabbed her by the throat, spit on her and called her whore, cunt, useless, worthless..."

"Thanks," Jana said. "I get the picture."

"Eight months in prison," Henrik said.

"So he's a repeat offender."

"Which also means that he should be in the DNA database."

"Have you brought him in for questioning?"

"Not yet. We're on our way right now. He lives at Ban-dygränd 4."

"Good," Jana said. "Take him to an interrogation room, but make sure he doesn't call anyone. I'll be there shortly. We have to buy ourselves a little time. When his lawyer comes, we probably won't be able to hold him long."

"The children can identify him."

"There's still no evidence tying him to the murder yet, is there?"

"We'll have to hope there's something in the samples from the autopsy."

"And that we get a confession."

When Henrik Levin and Mia Bolander stepped out of the car, the evening air was raw and chilly. They nodded toward the uniformed officers who met them there and began walking across the parking lot. Two men in jackets from the X-Force Factory Fitness gym stood at the other end, watching them.

Both were in their twenties with shaved heads. It looked as if they were weight lifters or kickboxers. They might have been high and carrying knives.

He knew that it was wrong to think like that. He should push away those stereotypes, but lately, violence in the city had escalated. Over the course of six weeks, no fewer than eleven serious knife attacks had occurred, and none of the perpetrators had been over twenty-five years old. The attacks all had some connection to drugs, and the editorials and stories had dubbed Norrköping, "Narco-ping."

"Fuckin' white boy," one said, standing taller as they passed.

Henrik pretended he didn't hear him, and they continued toward the entrance to Bandygränd 4. He felt the men's eyes on him but didn't try to make eye contact, because if he did, the situation would only become threatening.

It was completely backward that he, an officer of the law, chose to look down at the ground and not say anything. But what should he say? It was better to ignore them and focus on what they'd come here to do.

Besides, he had Mia next to him, and he didn't want her getting upset. She could really go off on guys like this. Not a good thing.

The door slid open and, together with the other officers, they went up the stairs to the door with the name "Henriksson" on it and rang the doorbell.

They waited a moment, knocked, then waited again.

"Maybe he's not home?" Mia said.

Henrik pushed the mail slot open with his hand and called in: "Henriksson? My name is Henrik Levin, and I'm with the police."

A sound came from inside as if someone were moving across the floor.

"I haven't done anything," said a man in a tired voice from inside the apartment.

"That's fine, but we still need to talk to you."

"Go away."

"I want you to open the door and talk to us."

"Leave me alone, you bastard."

The voice came closer.

"Open the door," Henrik said.

"Why should I?"

"We just want to talk to you."

"About what?"

"About Shirin Norberg."

It was silent for a moment.

"I haven't got anything to do with that whore. I don't want to get involved, do you hear me?"

"So you know who she is?"

It sounded as if the man slammed his hand against something in the apartment.

"Did you not get that I don't want to talk to you?" he said.

"I understand that, but I want you to open the door, look at me and tell me why you don't want to talk to me."

"What the hell!"

Footsteps came close. Mia did the same as her colleague— she released her service pistol, stood with her legs apart and got in a ready position.

There was a clattering sound as the door opened. Henrik had time to see white teeth in a confused face and a pair of broad shoulders before the door quickly began to close again. But Mia was ready with her foot; she stuck it in the doorway and stopped the man from closing it. At the same time, Henrik got a hold of the door and pushed it forward.

"Let go of the door," Mia said, pointing the mouth of the gun toward the man. "Let it go!"

He looked at her, looked at the gun, swore loudly again and let go.

The traffic on Södra Promenaden moved slowly due to road construction. Anneli Lindgren sat in the driver's seat with one hand on the steering wheel.

Next to her sat her son, Adam, with his huge headphones and his blue-and-white tracksuit. He yawned loudly, having allowed himself to be lulled to sleep by the car's forward movements.

"Are you excited for the game?"

He didn't answer, and Anneli poked him in the side.

"What do you want?" he said, irritated, pulling his head-phones back.

"Are you excited for the game?"

"No."

"I'm sure it'll go well," she said.

She slowed down and looked to the right, toward the avenue and public library.

"Grandma is going to pick you up."

"Why Grandma?"

"I have some work I have to do."

"What about Dad?"

"I don't know."

Adam sighed and leaned his head against the window.

"How long are we going to live with Grandma, really?" he asked.

"I don't know. Not too long."

"But why don't you live with Dad anymore?"

"Have you been thinking about that?"

"I've been thinking about a lot of things," he said loudly, too loudly.

"You don't have to yell."

"Forget I said anything."

Anneli looked at him with heavy eyes and wished that they had talked soccer, German or English leagues, instead.

She had avoided talking to him about the separation; instead she'd managed the day-to-day, tried to find a normal routine, but maybe she hadn't realized the impact, the huge change this had meant for him. She had had the impression that his nonchalance came from his acceptance of the situation. Now, her heart pounded in her chest when it started to become clear to her that Adam had been hiding behind a facade.

"Dad and I are just taking a little break," she said.

"You've said that."

"But I truly believe we'll find our way back to each other."

"Oh, really."

"Why do you say that? Has Dad said something…"

"No, he hasn't."

She reached her hand out to touch his cheek, but he turned his head away.

"Is there anything else you've been thinking about?" she asked.

"No."

"Are you sure?"

"Seriously, Mom, can't I just listen to my music now?"

"Of course…"

The car behind her honked, and she began rolling forward. She couldn't let her life go on like this. It was obvious that Adam was affected by the separation, that he was truly sad because of it.

But what else was he thinking?

What was he feeling? How did he experience it?

She tried to get his attention again, but he had turned his gaze out of the window. Her throat was so tense it hurt, and tears welled up in her eyes. She didn't want it to be like this.

She had to talk to Gunnar and make him understand that she really wanted to become a family again, that she'd do anything for that to happen.

Anything, in all honesty.

"It will all be fine," she said, quietly.

A fluorescent bulb flickered above her. Jana Berzelius was approaching the interrogation rooms at the police station when she saw Mia Bolander leaning against a wall, chewing gum.

"So you have him now?" Jana said, mostly just to have something to say.

"As if you didn't know," Mia said.

Jana smiled stiffly at her. "That was quick," she said.

"We usually work quickly."

"But not when it's Danilo Peña."

She surprised herself that she had allowed her irritation with Mia Bolander to sweep over her.

"Why do you care about him?" Mia said. "That's not your case, is it?"

"No."

"Well then."

"Well then, what?"

"Then you needn't worry about it."

"You're right," Jana said. "It was silly to show an interest in what happens here. A person can risk being seen as competent."

Mia stopped chewing, instead letting an irritated smile spread across her face.

Jana nodded curtly at her and went into the room.

It was a standard four-by-six photograph. Color. Glossy paper. Henrik Levin held it between his thumb and forefinger as he displayed the large bruises visible on the dead woman's body to Ted Henriksson.

Jana Berzelius sat next to him, ready as usual with a legal pad and pen.

"Can you explain how Shirin got these bruises?" Henrik said.

Henriksson's eyes darted toward the camera that was pointed at him from the corner of the ceiling. He was ordinary-looking, with black curly hair. But there was something unpleasant about him. His voice was low and gruff.

"How would I know?" he said, breathing heavily.

"You've admitted to knowing her," Henrik said.

"I only said I knew who she was."

"So have you met her?"

"Once. Maybe twice. Maybe three times. Who knows?"

"What is it, then?"

"Okay, we've been seeing each other for a while...actually a few years."

"So you had a relationship?"

Henriksson sneered.

"Yes, we had a relationship, Commissioner."

"For how many years?"

"Three, four, five."

"And when did you last see her?"

He smiled and tilted his head to the right, then to the left.

"Last weekend."

"Where did you get together?"

"At T3."

"Where?"

He smiled again.

"The bar at Trädgårdsgatan 3."

"How long were you there?"

"One hour, maybe two."

"And what did you do next?"

Henriksson looked at Henrik, then at Jana.

"How much detail do you want?"

He held his gaze fixed on Henrik, laid both hands on the table and let them rest there. Henrik reached for a few papers and said: "Can you read what's written here?"

Henriksson looked down at the papers that Henrik held out to him and then shook his head.

"Why would I do that? Don't you think I can read?"

"Yes, I think you can," Henrik said. "But I want to hear you read this aloud."

"Forget it," Henriksson said.

Henrik pulled the papers toward himself and read: "'People

like you have nothing to give. People like you need people like me. See you tonight, you whore.' Did you write this?"

"You don't know, do you?"

"No, that's why I'm asking. Did you write this?"

Henriksson looked up.

"You took my cell phone. Haven't you checked it?"

"Do you have more than one cell phone?"

"No."

Henrik pushed the papers away from him and scratched his nose before continuing.

"What were you doing yesterday morning?" he asked.

"I was at Vitamex."

"You work there?"

"Yes, I do. My colleagues and I produce food supplements and such."

"What time do you start in the morning?"

"I don't start in the morning. I work overnight."

Henriksson raised his chin.

"Have you ever been to Shirin Norberg's home?" Henrik continued.

"No."

"Never?"

"No."

"That's funny," Henrik said. "We have witnesses who say that you've been seen at her place."

It was silent around the table. Henrik looked at Ted, who looked like he was about to react, but something made him stop.

"I'll ask you again, have you spent time at…"

"I haven't *spent time* at…"

"But we have witnesses who…"

"They're lying!"

Henriksson's voice thundered through the room. The outburst came without warning.

Henrik looked at Jana, who gave him a calm look.

"Who's lying?" she said.

Henriksson stared down at the table, looking different now as his lower lip hung slack. He had clenched his fists and mumbled almost inaudibly: "They're just lying, they're just lying, they're just lying…"

"Who is it that's just lying?" Jana repeated.

Henriksson looked up and examined Jana up and down.

"Say it again," he said.

"Excuse me?" she asked.

"Say it again."

"Why?"

"I like hearing your voice."

She held him riveted with her gaze.

"Because it reminds you of Shirin's?" she asked.

"No," he said. "She had a much softer voice."

"You say 'had.'"

"Yes? She had a softer voice."

Henriksson wrinkled his forehead. "So that's why I'm here?" he said. "You think that I did something to her. But I would never do something so stupid. I admit that I may have become bored with Shirin. But I am not a killer. I'm a nice person. People like me. I'm sure that you would, too—just let me come to your place and show you how nice I am. I can come to your place and…"

"Don't do that," Jana interrupted him.

"I know how to make you feel really special…"

"That's enough," Henrik said sharply.

"I'm not dangerous. I won't hurt you, I promise."

"Just answer the questions, nothing else," Jana said.

A bubble of saliva had formed in the corner of his mouth.

"I'm absolutely not dangerous," Henriksson said.

"I can guarantee you, you are going nowhere," Henrik said, his voice raised in anger.

"Maybe not today, but," he said, looking at Jana, "I'll take care of you later. Caress you. Would you like that?"

Henrik was having a hard time sitting still, he was so embarrassed by the words that had just come out of the suspect's mouth.

"Or maybe you wouldn't want me to be nice to you. Maybe you like rougher treatment."

"Did Shirin?" Jana asked.

"Yes…" he said. "She liked it. Begged for it."

"Have you ever been violent toward her?" Henrik said.

"Once. Maybe twice. Maybe three times. Who knows?"

A small lamp shone behind the drapes in the window. Philip Engström stood in the dim room and looked at his reflection next to the beam of light.

He held his phone in his hand. He'd called Katarina four times, but she still hadn't answered.

From the kitchen he could hear Lina and Sandra laughing, and he knew that he should go back to the dining room table and the pasta with chanterelles and pork chops. He should take part in the conversation they were having, should discuss TV series, gossip about celebrities and laugh at jokes like he used to.

But he had no desire to talk with either of them right now. He felt tired of his wife tonight, tired of his colleague Sandra. There wasn't a single person he really wanted to talk to, that he wanted to be with right now—except Katarina.

In the middle of his thoughts, he heard footsteps approaching.

"Oh, is this where you are?" Sandra said as she pushed open

the door. "What are you doing in here? It's so dark in here," she continued, turning on the ceiling light.

The brightness made Philip squint.

"I just wanted to say goodbye," she said.

"Are you going already?" he said, hearing that his voice sounded a little too pleased, almost happy, but he didn't have the energy to care, couldn't be bothered to be fake, ingratiating. He didn't have the energy for anyone but himself right now.

"Thanks for tonight," she said. "See you at work."

Philip didn't answer. He turned his gaze out the window again. Sandra didn't say anything, either; she just turned off the light and left him alone in the room.

He stood for a moment in the darkness and listened to the sound of the front door closing. From a distance he could make out sirens of an emergency vehicle. Not a police car or his EMT colleagues—it was a fire truck. The sirens came closer; now they were behind him, on the road leading downtown, and he wondered where the fire was.

Then the light in the room turned on again. He turned around and saw Lina playing with her necklace.

"We missed you at the table," she said.

"Oh," he said.

"What's wrong?"

"Nothing really. I just wanted to be alone."

She let go of her necklace and went to him. "I thought you liked Sandra."

"We work together," he said, seeing that her eyes were bloodshot. "But that doesn't mean I like her."

"That's my friend you're talking about," she said.

"Exactly, so it's better if you sit and gab with her than if I do."

"Okay," she said. "I know Sandra can be a little naggy sometimes."

"A little?" he said.

"But at least she's honest."

"What do you mean by that?"

Lina avoided his eyes.

"You said you were at work today," she said.

"And?"

"So how was it?"

"It was fine," he said, shrugging his shoulders. "Why are you asking?"

"Because Sandra said you *weren't* at work today."

It took more than ten seconds for Philip to respond. It felt like a long time to stand in front of your wife trying to come up with a good explanation while you can't hear anything but the sound of her breath.

"I…" he began, but fell silent again.

"You're seeing someone else."

When she met his eyes, he suddenly understood why her eyes were red. She'd been crying.

"No!" he said. "Why would you think that?"

"You aren't even wearing your wedding band anymore. Where is it?" she asked.

"I lost it at work."

"Oh, sure."

"Don't you believe me?"

"What should I believe when you lie to me?"

"But…" he said.

She interrupted him.

"Where were you, then? If you weren't at work, where were you?"

"I was at the gym."

"All day? Really?"

He felt himself beginning to get irritated.

"I went to Katarina's, too."

"Katarina Vinston? I knew it."

"Knew what? I just wanted to talk to her!"

"And by 'talk' you mean…?"

Philip didn't answer.

"Fuck you," she said, leaving the room.

Philip stood there with his cell phone in his hand. He had wanted to call Katarina again, but this time he let it go.

"Wait!" Henrik called.

Jana Berzelius was on her way to the elevator when he caught up with her.

"I've talked to Anneli," he said. "She has gotten results from almost all of the tests from Shirin Norberg's apartment."

"And?"

"We now know that there are fingerprints that match Henriksson's, so it's obvious that he *has* been in her apartment."

Jana slowly shook her head and resumed walking. Henrik followed her.

"But you know as well as I do that that's not enough to convict him," she said. "Clearly he knew Shirin. I have no idea why he's trying to hide having been at her apartment, but it would be best for him to just admit that he'd been there, and then the fingerprints are worthless."

"Yes," Henrik said, "but the fingerprints together with a confession?"

"A confession that he's hit her, yes," Jana said. "But not that he intentionally killed her. Or even mutilated her. We need more on him."

"Yeah, you're right," Henrik said, rubbing his eyes. "And can he even use a Gigli saw?"

"We'll have to press him harder in the next interrogation if we're going to get anything of use out of him," Jana said.

They arrived at the elevator but chose to take the stairs instead to the first floor. Outside the window to the stairwell, the lights of the city glittered. Jana looked at the red bands of car lights when she heard Henrik yawn again.

"I'm sorry," he said. "It's been a long day. First Peña, then this Henriksson."

"Peña…you mean the perp who escaped from the hospital?" Jana said cautiously, feeling again that she was on thin ice.

"Yes. The hospital…yes. He's impossible to find. We'd gotten a tip on an apartment today, but it was a dead end. We just have to keep looking."

"For how long?"

"Until someone tells us to stop."

"And now they've asked us to do just that," came Gunnar Öhrn's rumbling voice from behind them. He had come down the stairs, too, and was about to put on his jacket.

"What do you mean?" Henrik asked, turning around. "Are we going to give up the search?"

"Yes, you might think so," Gunnar said.

Jana felt her pulse quicken as her hopes rose.

"I tried to tell the brass that this is a high profile, high priority case," Gunnar said as he approached them. "I also said that I wanted to allocate more resources there, but the only thing I got as an answer was: Not possible. *Not possible*, can you believe that?"

Jana knew she shouldn't ask, shouldn't show too much interest, but it was as if the words slipped out of her.

"What does that mean?" she said.

"It can mean a damn lot of things," Gunnar said. "But to my ears, it means that we have to get help from another direction."

"So you'll continue looking?" she asked, immediately feeling less hopeful.

"Yes," Gunnar said. "And I've decided that we should turn to the public for help. Danilo Peña is crazy. And dangerous. We must not forget that he is suspected of being responsible for the murder of several young Thai girls. We can't have him running around right under our noses."

"Have you thought that through?" Henrik said. "Issuing a description can lead to—"

"—better chances of finding him. Yes, I've considered the decision carefully, and I want to send out his name and picture first thing tomorrow morning."

October 3

Dear Diary,
In geography today, we were split up into groups. I hate working in groups. Usually the kids I'm supposed to work with disappear, going off together and hiding so that I can't find them.

When I finally saw Linus, who was in our group, I asked him what I should do. He said, why not kill yourself. I was just in the way.

How am I supposed to work with kids who hate me?

After class, our teacher and I had a talk. She asked me if I had any friends.

I lied and said, "Martin." I think it made her feel better. She knew I was lying. But I think it's easier for her to accept lies instead of dealing with tough problems.

So now I'm grouped with the weirdos Markus, Theodor and William. We have nothing in common. Never will, either. I find myself mostly in my own world and detest this fucking loneliness.

On the way home from school, they stood outside the schoolyard and waited for me. I thought about turning around, but knew they'd follow me anyway if I did. So I continued toward them. Tried to pretend I didn't care. But they surrounded me and said: "Are you scared now? Are you scared now, you fucking monster?"

And I was scared, really. But I didn't say that. Those guys are so much bigger and taller than I am.

Then one of them grabbed me from behind, grabbed my shirt, and I knew that I didn't stand a chance. There was no corner to hide in, no bathroom to run into, no teacher who was going to see what was going on.

They pushed me up against the wall, and they yelled and cheered. A fist punched me, landed in my stomach. In my face. I thought it was Linus hitting me, but it wasn't. It was the tallest of the boys. He smiled the whole time, as if it were fun.

I tried to get away, but every punch pushed my body into a wall. It didn't really matter that I was being hit. It didn't hurt all that much.

But yet I cried. Because it was Martin who was hitting me.

Mom didn't see my bloody nose when I came home. I tried to hold her hands. I tried to catch her eye. But I only saw her blank, distant gaze. I want her to look at me like she did before her operation. But we've become strangers.

CHAPTER
THIRTEEN

Saturday

ON THE WAY OUT OF THE APARTMENT, MIA BOLAN-der attempted to zip up her jacket, but the zipper got stuck. She carefully tried to ease out the fabric that had caught in it, but after a few seconds her patience was gone. She pulled and tugged on the zipper until she heard the fabric rip, but she didn't care. She swore loudly when the zipper pull broke off and disappeared down the staircase.

Most of all, she wanted to run up the stairs again and crawl back into bed. Preferably not alone. Unfortunately she didn't have anyone else in her life right now, so instead she just continued down the rest of the stairs to the lobby.

Her wine-red Fiat Punto was parked outside on the street. She put the key into the ignition, but the car wouldn't start.

She tried again and again, but the car was as dead as a door-nail. Just then, her damn cell phone rang.

"Yeah?" she answered. "What now, Henrik?"

"There's been another murder," he said. "Where are you?"

"At home. My fucking car won't start."

"I'll pick you up in five minutes, okay."

"Where are we going?"

"To Borg, near the golf course. It's going to be an unpleasant sight."

Jana Berzelius stood in the kitchen with her eyes fixed on the TV. The evening news was just about to start.

"The police have announced today that they are looking for one of the main suspects behind the narcotics ring that was revealed in Östergötland in December, the so-called Police-gate scandal in which National Police Commissioner Anders Wester is involved. On Wednesday, Danilo Peña escaped from Vrinnevi Hospital, where he was being treated for the injuries he sustained in connection with his capture. The thirty-one-year-old man is considered dangerous and is believed to still be in the Norrköping area. The police are interested in all information that could lead to the man's capture."

Jana felt the noose being tightened around her neck. It was no longer *if* he would be found, but *when*. She gave in to an urge and threw the remote control, blood pulsing in her temples.

"Did you know about that?" Danilo said, standing in the doorway. If he was surprised, he hid it well.

"Yes," she said, turning her gaze to the floor.

"So today's the day they'll come here to get me?" he said with irritation.

"You were lucky yesterday," she said.

"You were, too," he said. "More problematic than anything was that you didn't know what was going on. Sloppy."

"I played it safe. I can't afford to take chances, and neither can you."

He went to the table and sat down. "Just think, the police are so desperate to find me that they've turned to the general public…"

"You're a person of interest for them," she said. "They need you as a witness against Wester, if nothing else."

"Interest," he said, snorting. "Do you think the media will also think I'm interesting?"

"We just saw proof of that, didn't we?" she said. "Every detail of your escape seems to be a media magnet. You should probably prepare for being on the run for a few more days."

Danilo's eyes gleamed when she said that. He leaned so far forward that his chest pressed against the edge of the table. But suddenly, when the first enthusiasm had passed, he regained control of himself and leaned back.

"But this BOLO could be very significant," he said.

She lifted her gaze and looked at him.

"What do you mean?"

"The police really want to find me," he said.

"Yes," she said.

"So maybe we should let them."

"What do you mean?"

"The only way for me to leave Norrköping safely is to let the police believe that I'm somewhere else."

"How? By calling in a false tip?" she said.

"That's not enough," he said. "We have to give them physical evidence."

"Who's 'we'?" she said.

"Sorry," he said aggressively. "I mean *you*. *You* have to be the one to throw them off the trail."

"How is that?"

"Think of a scheme."

They sat silently across from each other while Jana thought about what he could possibly expect of her.

"Exactly what type of scheme were you thinking?" she said.

"This," he said, tugging on the dirty shirt he'd been wearing since he escaped from the hospital. "It's crawling with traces of me. You could plant it somewhere."

"And possibly my DNA, too," she said. "So that won't work."

"Don't be so damn nervous. But if we're going to use this shirt, you'll have to buy me a new one. And pants. Basically a set of new clothes."

"New clothes?" she said.

"Yes," he said. "I can't leave the apartment naked."

He was serious. She saw it clearly in how his jaw muscles tensed and how he was breathing. It was a strange feeling to sit across from him, so close and for so long a period of time, she thought.

"This is how it's going to play out," he said. "You'll buy me some new clothes and plant this shirt as a false lead in another city, not too close or too far away, and it absolutely shouldn't be Södertälje."

"Why not?"

"Because I have a meeting there."

"I don't know if I want to know any more."

"Now listen up and listen carefully," he said. "When you've planted it, call in a false tip. We have no time to lose. I have to be in Södertälje on Tuesday at exactly 8:00 p.m. I'll go disappear from there."

"Who are you meeting?"

"The less you know, the better."

Jana's eyes narrowed.

"I don't want to be seen with you. Nothing can connect me with you."

"Listen. I'd always rather be safe than sorry."

"So how have you been communicating about this Södertälje meeting?"

"Cell phone."

"Cell phones are dangerous," she said. "The police can trace you. They have a whole room filled with investigators whose sole purpose is to find you."

"That's why I used yours."

"You can't have used it again. I've had it on me the whole time since..."

"The shower, I know, but that's when I took care of all of my business."

"So..."

"Shut up now, Jana. The only thing you should be worried about is that I don't miss that meeting on Tuesday."

She looked at him, at his dirty shirt, and in just that moment the thought popped into her head: that although she'd made such a concerted effort to tolerate him these past few days, this involvement wouldn't ever end. It would just get worse and worse. He would be able to continue setting whatever demands he wanted, as long as he had control of the boxes that contained her journals.

"It's not actually so difficult, is it?" he said.

"What?"

"What you're thinking about."

"It might be difficult," she said.

"Possibly," he said. "But it's easy to see that you're going to go along with it."

Philip Engström shoved a slice of cheese into his mouth and set the orange juice, butter and a tube of caviar spread on the table.

Lina didn't look at him when she came into the kitchen. She pulled the comforter along with her and sat cross-legged on the chair, letting the thick down of the duvet warm her shoulders. Her light brown hair was gathered in a high, tight ponytail.

Philip reached his hand out, but she didn't take it.

"I don't want to…" She fell silent.

"What don't you want?" he said.

She lifted her gaze and looked him in the eye with a gravity that made him scared. "I don't want to have children anymore."

"Why do you say that?"

"I don't want to have children at all."

"Okay," he said, pulling his hand back.

"Okay?" she said. "Is that all you have to say?"

"What *should* I say? If you don't want to have children, there's not much I can do about that, right?"

"No, I've already decided," she said, blinking quickly a few times as if trying to hold back tears.

"Good," he said. "So now that that's decided…so I guess we're done, too."

He leaned back in the chair and turned his gaze to his coffee mug. He knew he should go to her, comfort her, say a few well-chosen words. But he couldn't move.

"But I don't want that," she said quietly, drying the tears from her cheeks. "I don't want us to be done."

Philip sighed.

"What do you want, then?"

She stared at him, now with a disappointed look.

"I want to hear you say it," she said.

"Say what?" he said, looking down at the table.

"That you love me. But only if you mean it."

"I love you," he said, tired. "And I mean it. Do you want me to say sorry, too?"

"No, that's not what I mean," she said, reaching her hand toward him. "But sometimes it feels as if I don't know you."

"You know me better than anyone else."

"Why did you lie about being at work?"

Philip met her gaze, leaned forward and squeezed her warm hand.

"I don't know," he said. "I really don't know. It's all just so damn exhausting."

"What else have you lied about?"

Henrik Levin laid his hand on the cold door handle and let it rest there for a moment.

The house in Borg was red with white trim at the corners. All the windows were dark, and the drive was covered in gravel. There was a mailbox in a hole in the fence. It was filled with mail and advertisements.

"Someone has been here recently," he said, pointing to the shoe prints visible in the flower bed under one of the windows.

"Who called it in?" Mia asked, looking at the tracks.

"A neighbor. She came here with a cat she saw rubbing around her house, which she knew belonged to the woman living here. That's when she…well, discovered the victim."

"So, these could be the neighbor's footprints?"

"They look a bit too large to be a woman's," he said, pushing the door handle down. "But we'll have to see what Anneli says."

The door swung open, and they stepped in.

They heard voices in the house. Anneli Lindgren stood against a door, camera around her neck, talking with a colleague. Several thick winter coats hung in the hallway.

They walked into the kitchen, noting the flowers on the

wallpaper, the long, narrow wooden table, the Windsor-style chairs and the braided rug.

The bedroom was surprisingly large. A double bed with a purple spread was on the left, and several closets with mirrored doors lined the wall on the right. The different flooring stood witness to two rooms that had been merged into one. One wall featured three windows in a row, all with the blinds closed, yet the room was as bright as a stage. Anneli had placed several floodlights on the floor and directed them toward the woman sitting on the chair.

"You were right," Mia said to Henrik. "This is some fucking sight."

"Yes…"

It looked like the blood had come from the woman's face and head, then had run down over her shirt, over her pants and onto the floor. But it was difficult to make out what exactly had happened. Her head was bowed down to her chest, and her long, dark hair covered her face and large parts of the bloody gray shirt. Her arms and legs were tied to the chair with zip ties.

"It's the same MO, the same perpetrator…" Henrik said.

"Henriksson?" Mia asked. "But isn't he in jail?"

Henrik shook his head.

"It may not be Henriksson. Depends on how long she's been sitting here."

He pulled on his plastic gloves, feeling his pulse increase as he slowly approached the woman. He reached out his hand, put one finger to her forehead and carefully pushed her head up until her face was visible.

The victim hadn't yet been identified, but he assumed it was the woman on record as owning the house—Katarina Vinston.

Her gaping mouth was just a dark hole. He turned his eyes away for a brief moment.

"What is it?" Mia asked.

"Her tongue has been cut out."

"What the fuck did you say? Really?"

"Yes."

Henrik looked around the scene as if expecting it to be chaotic, but he verified that everything seemed to be in its place. The perpetrator must have been in control and done the deed very methodically, he thought. But what had made him cut this woman's tongue out?

"They say that those who lie get their tongue cut out," he said aloud. "And those who have their hands cut off are thieves."

"You're thinking of Shirin?" Mia asked.

"Yes."

"But what do Shirin and this woman have in common?"

"That's just it…" he said. "I don't know. But this is the same perpetrator, without a doubt. The MO, how the victim is placed, the chair, the zip ties…"

"Yes?"

"Someone is sending a message, trying to tell us something."

It was warm in her office after the sunny morning. Jana pressed the send button on her new cell phone, letting all of her contacts know that she had a new number. She then pulled the SIM card out of her old phone and broke the phone in half. She would throw the battery and the rest of the phone into different garbage cans. The idea that Danilo used it to set up a meeting made her furious. How dumb can a person be? Or he didn't care.

That he was now also forcing her to plant false evidence had given her a serious headache.

She sat at her desk in front of her computer and rubbed her temple with her fingertips to get the pain to subside.

It did sometimes happen that a perpetrator would place personal belongings, like a glove, receipt or wristwatch, in different locations to divert attention and buy time.

She needed to find a place where no one would raise an eyebrow at a dirty, strange man who didn't identify himself. A homeless shelter, of course.

She googled shelters in Östergötland. She looked south in areas like Borensberg, Mjölby and Skänninge, but in the end decided on Motala.

It was completely possible that a person on the run would be able to hide at a shelter, and Motala had multiple shelters and transitional housing for the homeless and for migrants from within the EU.

The first shelter she clicked on had strict requirements that guests lock their doors and remain in their rooms between eleven o'clock at night and six in the morning. It didn't sound like a place for a man on the run.

The second shelter was located in a school. But just a few weeks ago, the building had been ravaged by fire and the reconstruction was just starting.

The third alternative seemed just right. It was a shelter located in an old industrial area about a mile from downtown. A community college, museum and cultural center were nearby.

Jana scrolled through the pictures of the building, looking at the hallways, stairwell landings and doors as she considered the challenge she was just about to take on. And the freedom she hoped to gain afterward, when she had gotten rid of Danilo and gotten her possessions back.

This might work, she thought.

This has to work.

CHAPTER
FOURTEEN

MIA BOLANDER STEPPED INTO THE CONFERENCE room and closed the door behind her. Everyone except Anneli Lindgren was there: Gunnar Öhrn, Henrik Levin, Ola Söderström... Jana Berzelius was in charge.

Mia sank down onto a chair and avoided Jana's gaze by examining the map of Norrköping hanging on one of the long walls of the rectangular room. Next to the map hung photos from the crime scene investigation in Eneby. In one of the photos, Shirin's body was visible.

On the other long wall, there were photos of her daughters, Aida and Sara. And a photo of Ted Henriksson.

"It has just been confirmed that the woman in Borg is Katarina Vinston," Henrik said, turning first to Jana. Then he turned to Ola.

"Can you..."

Ola pulled his computer toward him and enlarged the photo of the woman tied to the chair.

"Katarina Vinston, forty-four years old, born and raised in Eskilstuna," Henrik said. "She was trained as a paramedic in Stockholm and worked for many years on an emergency medical helicopter before transferring to ambulance work in Norrköping. No intimate relationships as far as we know. Her parents still live in Eskilstuna. One sibling, a younger brother who lives in Lund."

Everyone examined the photo.

"And as you see," Henrik continued, "Katarina's body is positioned in the same manner as Shirin. They were both tied to a chair using the same type of tie."

"Yes," Gunnar said, scratching his scalp hard several times. "Here the tongue was severed and with Shirin, the hands…"

"But aside from that gruesome detail," Jana said, "what else do they have in common?"

The room fell silent while the photos of the two women were displayed.

"They're both in their forties," Mia said.

"They work in health care," Ola volunteered.

"And Ted Henriksson?" Jana said. "Could he be the common denominator?"

Everyone turned their eyes to the wall where the picture of Henriksson's face looked back at them. The glossy, black hair, the white teeth. And the look that made him seem pleasant.

"You and Jana both questioned him, Henrik," Gunnar said. "What do you think?"

"Now everything has taken on a different order of magnitude," Henrik said. "But I was already skeptical of the idea that he was the one who had cut Shirin's hands off. He doesn't quite fit…"

"Wait a minute, now," Mia said, putting her hand in the

air. "He *does* have a history of violence and is in the system. He's said that he had a relationship with Shirin. And he has as much as *admitted* that he'd been rough with her."

"Definitely," Henrik said. "But still. Chopping off hands and cutting out tongues. That kind of mutilation is in a whole other league."

Gunnar said, "Still, Mia has a point. Henriksson is our main lead at this point…"

"We could check dating sites," Ola said. "Maybe that's how he's meeting these women…"

"Fuck," Mia said. "Think there are any more single women out there that he's done this to? That we don't even know about yet?"

"Henriksson is at least still being held," Jana said. "So if it *is* him, at least for the time being there won't be any more victims."

"But do we have any time line here?" Gunnar asked.

"This latest victim died approximately twenty-four hours before we found her," Jana said.

"Yesterday morning. Since Henriksson wasn't brought in until last evening, he could very well have been at her house," Gunnar said.

"What size shoe does he wear, by the way?" Mia said. "We found clear footprints in the flower bed outside the house."

"We'll check on that," Jana said.

"We also found a man's wedding ring beside Katarina's bed," Mia said, "so she must have had *some* sort of relation-ship."

"What did the ring look like?"

"It was a typical gold band, completely smooth. It's inscribed with 'An extraordinary Tuesday in the Archipelago 2012.'"

"Good," Jana said. "And while we're waiting for responses, let's go through Henriksson's background. What connection, if any, does he have to this victim? Have they met, dated, chat-ted online…you know."

"We know," Mia said.

"Apparently they both worked in the health-care industry…" Henrik said, looking at the papers he had in front of him. "I see that they both worked at Vrinnevi. Katarina Vinston as a paramedic and Shirin Norberg as a surgery nurse. That may factor in…"

"Possibly," Gunnar said. "Maybe he has a weakness for women in health care. Check that, too."

His eyelids were heavy, but he forced himself to stay awake. The pattern on the wallpaper appeared to move, the small white stripes pulled together and drew apart.

Philip Engström sat on the sofa in his living room as Sandra Gustafsson's voice droned on and on from his cell phone. He had stopped listening long ago, couldn't understand anything more after he heard her say that Katarina was found dead, tied to a chair, in her home.

He didn't believe what she was telling him. Why should he, really? Sandra, who let him sleep in the ambulance. Who then threatened to report him to his superiors. Who nagged, nagged, nagged. Why should he believe her?

What sort of fucking joke was this? Katarina wasn't dead. She was alive, of course she was alive; she had to be alive. He needed her in his life. She couldn't be dead. It couldn't be. It simply couldn't be.

With trembling hands, he pushed two pills out onto the table.

"Are you there, Philip?" Sandra asked.

"Yes," he finally said.

"Tell me what you're thinking."

"That I've felt better."

"Yes, it's terrible," she said. "Is there anything I can do?"

"No."

Philip poked the round tablets on the table with his finger.

"I've talked with the boss. You and Katarina worked together for many years. We understand if you need to stay home tonight. Someone else can take your night shift."

"No," Philip said. "I'm coming in to work."

"You're not listening to what I'm saying."

"Of course I am."

"You're in no condition to work."

"I think I'm the one to decide that, not you. You're not my boss."

"But Eva asked me to call."

"So you've talked to her about me?"

He could hear her irritation growing.

"Both she and I only want the best for you," she said. "We understand that you feel bad about this, everyone understands that you feel bad about this."

"I said that I've felt better, not that I *feel bad*."

He heard her swallow. He raised his gaze and saw a pale light streaming in through the window that faced the street.

"I'm really getting angry now," she said.

"Don't get angry."

"But what should I say to Eva?"

Philip tried to speak calmly but was having a hard time controlling himself.

"Tell it like it is," he said. "That I'm coming to work."

"I'm just concerned about you," she said.

"You know you're treating me like a child."

"But you're so...so..."

She swallowed hard before continuing.

"...so bullheaded."

"Thank you," he said.

"I'll let Eva know, then," she said quietly.

"Good," he said, ending the call. The display went dark. The black screen reflected his face. He was completely white.

Was Katarina really dead?

The thought was impossible to grasp. He couldn't comprehend the world, couldn't comprehend anything right now.

Philip put down his phone and then, in a rage, swept the pills from the table, put his hands over his ears, pressed as hard as he could and screamed loudly.

She found a vacant space at the top of the parking ramp. Jana Berzelius parked and got out of the car. The stench of exhaust and dried urine hit her immediately.

She took the stairs down to the street level and looked at all of the silent people moving around in the bustling commerce of Drottninggatan. The chain boutiques attracted customers with sales, and the cafés tempted shoppers with coffee, sandwiches and baked goods. As she crossed the street, she heard a man playing guitar and a child crying.

A garbage can rattled as she tossed the last parts of her old cell phone into it.

She went into the Linden shopping mall, rode the escalator to the second floor and went into a clothing store. Throughout her short walk, she had felt a certain calm, but now as she entered the men's department, she felt the tension return. Jana knew exactly how to sever a person's jugular, but she had never bought clothing for a man.

"May I help you?"

She turned her head and saw a man with slicked-back hair and a high forehead.

"Yes," she said. "I need to buy an outfit for a man who is about six feet tall. Shirt and pants."

"Okay...?" he said in surprise. "Any particular color you were thinking of?"

"No."

"Should it be business or casual wear?"

"Casual."

"Can I trouble you for the size?"

"What size are you?" she said.

"Small."

"Medium, then."

The salesman began looking through clothes on the shelves; Jana wished he would hurry up. Maybe she should have told him that she was in a rush, that she had to get to a meeting or had only a few minutes left on her parking meter.

"There we go," he said, finally. "What do you think? Will these items work for your husband?"

Jana cast a quick glance at the dark blue long-sleeved sweater, and beige chinos.

"Yes, that'll be fine," she said, reaching into her pocket for cash.

"Jana?" came a familiar voice from behind her.

When she wheeled around, she was met by Per Åström's smile.

No, she thought. *Not Per, not now, not here.*

"Doing some Saturday shopping?"

She bit her lip.

"For my father," she said quickly, meeting the annoying gaze of the salesman. "He needs new clothes. He spills easily, as you might guess, and it's hard to get the spots out, so..."

Per nodded slowly.

"You don't need to explain," he said. "I believe you..."

"That will be two hundred sixty-two even," said the salesman.

Jana counted the bills and held them out.

"And what are you doing here?" she asked.

"Johan Klingsberg and I had lunch after tennis, and I thought I'd buy a new suit."

She took her change and glanced quickly at her wristwatch.

"You seem stressed," Per said.

"I have a meeting and have to go now," she said.

"Do you want these clothes gift-wrapped?" the salesman asked.

"No," she said. "Put everything in one bag."

"A pullover sweater??" Per asked. "I thought he only wore button-downs."

"Who?"

"Karl."

"Yes," she said, taking the bag, "but...not since he got sick. I'm sorry, Per, I really have to go now."

She moved quickly toward the exit, feeling Per's searching gaze on her back and hearing him call: "Say hi to your father for me."

Henrik Levin tried to ignore the sweet smell coming from the woman opposite him at the interrogation table.

"Rita," he said, and Rita Olin, clearly completely lost in thought, looked up quickly, as if he had just come into the room and surprised her.

Her outfit was simple, and she seemed mature in her manner. Definitely not the type to overdramatize, exaggerate or crave attention for the sake of it.

"Importing scented candles," she said, pushing her glasses farther up the bridge of her nose.

"Scented candles," Henrik repeated.

"Yes. I've always dreamed of owning my own business," she said. "So I quit my job in pharmaceutical sales, and my husband and I began importing children's clothing. Then we got into home decorating products of various sorts, and that went fairly well. But we noticed that what always sold well were our candles, so we decided to focus solely on those. Our business is called LLJ, for Light, Love and Joy."

"So you both work with that now?"

"Yes, we do."

"You have an accent," Henrik said.

She laughed.

"Yes, I've traveled a lot over the past few years. That might be why."

"Where do you travel to?"

"Mostly to China, actually, where the factory is. My husband and I are going there in a week."

"So you're married?"

"For twenty-six years."

"Do you have children?"

"Adult children; four boys and all of them have moved out, thankfully."

Henrik felt a headache starting behind his eyes. He hadn't eaten since breakfast and knew it would be a while before he would be able to get something in his stomach. Two more people to question after this. And then a conversation with Katarina Vinston's boss, Eva Holmgren. He didn't have time to continue the small talk.

"Let's take it from the beginning," he said, asking her to tell him what had happened from the time she got to Katarina Vinston's house until the police arrived.

"I can do that," she said.

Henrik listened carefully as Rita described how she found the cat outside her house, recognized it, and around eight o'clock in the morning had gone to Katarina Vinston's house. She had rung the doorbell and waited a few minutes for Katarina to open the door, and when she didn't, she had unlocked the door and gone in.

"I have one of her spare keys, and she has one of ours."

"It says here that you didn't see anyone else in the house while you were there."

"That's right," she said. "But I never went farther in than the hallway, from where you can see into the bedroom, and that was where she…well, sat. I turned around immediately. I couldn't stay, not even for a second. It was completely horrible."

"I understand. And when you left, was there anything else you noticed?"

"No," she said.

"Okay," Henrik said, feeling how his shoulders sank.

"But it depends on what you mean by 'anything else.' The mailman was driving past."

"Yes, we've talked about the mailman."

"And then there was the Audi."

"The Audi?"

"Yes, it was around yesterday morning. But your typical Audi maybe isn't so suspicious?"

Jana maintained a steady grip on the bag of clothes. She wanted to get rid of it as soon as possible and walked with determined steps toward her apartment.

As she turned down Skolgatan, she noticed a car with two men in it. They were drinking coffee. She felt the hair on the back of her neck stand up when they noticed her. They seemed to follow her with their eyes. There could have been a number of reasons why they were looking at her, of course, but the only thing she could think of was that they were on a stakeout.

With her gaze straight ahead, she continued to walk, all

the while listening for the sound of a car door being opened or closed.

She stepped into the hustle and bustle of Knäppingsborg, but instead of going straight home, she rounded the building, stopped and looked around from behind the corner.

She'd been right.

The men were no longer in the car, but she didn't see them anywhere. A tall, blonde woman with coarse features walked past. She hunched her shoulders to appear shorter and not stick out. A bike messenger pedaled by in a red shirt and wearing a helmet and sunglasses. Farther down were two younger men in ball caps. Behind them, she suddenly caught sight of the two men from the car again. They had their hands in their pockets and their eyes on the ground. They were walking away from her.

She gave a sigh of relief, rounded the corner and continued home. The whole time, she wondered what was going to happen to her. Why did she think that the police would have put officers on her? If they suspected she was hiding Danilo, they would have kicked in the door to her apartment—not sat in a car and drank coffee.

She went up the stairs, thinking how Danilo had now been able to hide in her apartment for a number of days. The neighbors didn't know a thing. A whole winter could pass without you even seeing your neighbors.

She cast a glance backward before unlocking her door.

Danilo sat on the floor with his arms around his knees. Beads of sweat glistened on his forehead.

"Enjoy," she said, tossing the bag onto the floor.

He pulled it toward himself and pulled out the pants.

"What the fuck are theses? Chinos?"

"That's what they had," Jana said.

"You couldn't have bought a pair of normal jeans?"

"Aren't chinos normal?"

"And a pullover," he said, pulling the top from the bag, yanking off the price tag.

She looked away when he pulled off the filthy shirt. She wasn't quite fast enough and noticed how developed his chest muscles had become from exercise; a web of veins stood out along his arms. His features were symmetrical and sharp, but didn't attract attention. She also saw the scar that shone white against his skin, just under his ribs on the left side.

She was the cause of that wound. She, three months earlier, had left him to die near a boathouse in Arkösund. It was her fault that he'd ended up in the hospital.

"What do you think?" he asked. "Does it fit?"

She glanced at him, at the tight-fitting shirt.

"It fits," she said, leaving the room.

Mia Bolander looked quickly at the sunlight streaming from the clear blue sky. For over a half hour, she had been trying to get a hold of some friend or acquaintance who could help with her car again. After a number of unsuccessful attempts, she impatiently regarded her cell phone, wondering if there was anyone else she could bother.

Ola or Henrik?

She chose the latter and went to his office, but the room was empty. She had better luck with Ola, who sat with his nose to the screen, as always. She could hear him humming some tune as he tapped on the keyboard.

"My car is dead once again," she said. "Do you know anything about cars?"

"What kind?"

"Fiat?"

"Wait a minute," he said without looking away from the screen. "Let me just finish this first."

Mia stood there, looking around his office, looking at all of the gadgets he surrounded himself with: the custom keyboard, the black headphones, the new cell phone lying on his desk.

What did she wish for that she didn't already have? Everything, she thought. She also wanted to be able to afford a new cell phone, and to travel south in the dead of winter. A larger apartment, downtown. An even larger apartment in Spain. No, not that. She'd never enjoy that, surrounded by strange people who spoke a language she would never care enough to learn. She didn't even like paella.

"There we go," Ola said. "It took a while, but I've been able to find exactly the model of the Audi the neighbor saw near Katarina Vinston's house. An Audi A5. Blue metallic."

"How did you do that?" Mia asked. "Are you sure it's the right model?"

"Completely sure."

"How so?"

"I called her and asked her to describe the car in more detail. It was simple."

"You know cars, then?"

"Only their appearance. What's wrong with yours?"

"It won't start."

"Did you buy it from a dealer or privately?"

"A dealer, place called Biva."

"Make it easy on yourself, call them and ask them to look at it. They're open until six. The address is Fjärilsgatan 2. They're open until four on Saturdays, too, I see."

"Thanks," Mia said. "I don't understand how you know so much."

"I used Google."

The website of the local newspaper showed a picture of Katarina Vinston. In the photo, her face was alive and almost shamefully pretty. Henrik Levin brought the phone closer to his face and skimmed through the article entitled "Forty-four-year-old woman found dead."

He looked at the photo and thought that someone, maybe her mother or father, was also now looking at the photo and he felt his stomach tighten. Her parents and brother had been notified, and they'd be called in for a longer questioning as soon as possible. Notifying next of kin was the hardest part of the job. Being confronted with the sorrow, hearing the screams and seeing the pain of the victim's loved ones. Looking on as they realize there was nothing they could do, only the unrelenting emptiness that tears apart their existence. And then the questions, which in this early stage, seldom had answers.

Across the region, people were seeing the same picture. And everyone was wondering collectively: Who did this, and why?

Henrik had just thought how it was up to him to deliver answers when he heard steps in the hallway outside his office. He looked up and saw Mia approaching.

"Ready?" she asked.

"Yes," he said, getting up from his chair.

In his heart of hearts, he was a bit nervous to have Mia in the interrogation with Ted. She wasn't usually good at ignoring provocations. Another mark against her.

They walked slowly to the interrogation room.

"I've talked with Katarina Vinston's boss at the hospital," he said.

"Could she give us anything to go on?"

"Unfortunately not," he said. "The only thing I found out, really, was that Katarina had been sick this past week. But I requested the call list from her cell phone, and the forensic techs are going through her computer."

"So we still haven't found a clear connection between her and Ted Henriksson?"

"No," he said. "Not yet."

★ ★ ★

Jana Berzelius slowed her steps when she heard her new cell phone ringing. She'd run six miles at top speed, and her heart was pounding. She took two deep breaths before answering. She'd expected the slow, thick voice of her father, but it was Elin, his caretaker, she heard on the other end.

"Am I bothering you?" she asked.

"No," Jana said. "What's this about?"

"I don't know. Karl asked me to dial the number. He wants to talk to you."

"Okay," Jana said.

She heard the nurse's soft voice call for her father. She heard him mumble something and then heard his shuffling steps as he pulled himself forward in his wheelchair.

"Nn... Jana," he said.

She lifted her eyes, looking at Louis de Geer Concert Hall lit up by artificial lights, thinking how her mother and father had visited the concert hall regularly over the years, sometimes to experience the symphony orchestra, sometimes to listen to some of the world's best opera singers. Mother had loved classical music. Jana thought she had, at least. Or maybe it was one more way for her mother to suit her father's interests.

"Abut funrl...funerl," he said.

"It's on Friday, in a week," she said.

"Whr?"

"Where will it be?"

She didn't know what to tell him. She still had no idea where the ceremony should be held, nor had she decided where Mother should be buried. She had avoided even thinking about it.

"What do you think?" she said, with her gaze still on the concert hall.

He breathed heavily into the phone.

"Matts chrch."

She tried to imagine the ceremony in a church, tried to see the flowers, casket, a choir singing psalms, but it didn't feel right.

She closed her eyes and saw her mother in front of her, standing on a cliff and looking out over the sea. An image of Swedish summer: an older woman in a dark blue vest, white knit sweater, carefully pressed pants and clean tennis shoes. The woman walked slowly across the stones, her short hair ruffled by the wind. Her face was relaxed, happy. She turned around and waved with her whole hand. The sunlight filtered down through the branches of the trees.

When Jana saw the image of her standing there waving, she understood. She knew where Mother should find her final resting place.

"No," she said. "The funeral won't be held in any church. I've decided that her ashes will be spread at the summerhouse in Arkösund."

"Need prmissn."

"I know that requires permission from the county board. But you can see to that through your contacts."

"I cnt takk."

"Send an email, then," she said, irritated. "You have a week."

He was breathing even more heavily now. Whether it was because she'd gone against his suggestion of a religious ceremony or if it was because he had a hard time forming the words, she didn't know.

"I wnt to see hr," he said.

"Sorry?" Jana said. "I didn't hear…"

"If shs gong to becm ashs I wnt to see hr!"

"She's at the morgue. Ask Elin to set up a time for you."

"Yu do t."

"Me?"

"Magrtas deth concrns yu an me onl. Nt Eln."

"But…"

"No!"

She fell silent, understanding it was pointless to argue with him now.

"Whatever you want. I'll set up a time," she said, hanging up.

Mia Bolander looked down at her papers while Henrik Levin tapped his upper lip. The silent tension in the tight little interrogation room was palpable.

Ted Henriksson had refused the offer to have a lawyer present. In the beginning, it was an advantage because it gave them more room for questioning. At the same time, it was a signal that Henriksson didn't think he had much to hide.

He thought that the interrogation was going to be about his relationship with Shirin Norberg.

Mia turned her gaze to him and tried to interpret his facial expression. What was it she was seeing? Distrust? Or self-righteousness? Yes, she thought. Henriksson was self-righteous and was not thrown off by long silences. After he had commented that Henrik had a "new little dame" at his side, he hadn't said a word.

Mia and Henrik waited a long time before beginning their inquiry. Usually, the silence and the wait made the suspect more nervous, more open. But Henriksson looked calm.

"Tell us about your relationship with Shirin Norberg," Henrik began, a simple question to get the conversation started.

"What do you want to know?" Henriksson asked, looking at him.

"Were you engaged to her? Or somebody else?"

Henriksson sneered.

"No," he said.

"So this isn't your ring?" Henrik asked, showing the picture of the gold ring they'd found at Katarina Vinston's house.

Henriksson shook his head.

"A ring on the finger isn't really my style," he said. "Why limit yourself to one, when you can have a good time with many?"

"So you have other women friends that you see besides Shirin Norberg?"

"I haven't been seeing anyone *besides* Shirin. But I'm not exactly a stranger to seeing someone *with* Shirin. What do you say? Do you like to share, Commissioner?"

Henriksson looked suddenly at Mia, who didn't move a muscle. That seemed to provoke him.

"Do you know who this is?" Henrik asked, placing a picture of Katarina Vinston on the table. Henriksson cast a quick glance at it, pulling air in slowly through his nose, delaying his answer.

"No," he said finally as he exhaled. "But I wouldn't have anything against getting to know her."

Henrik placed his fingertips against each other.

"Your girlfriend has just been murdered, and you don't seem particularly bothered by it..."

"Yes, I am. I just show it in my own way."

"Your own way?"

Henriksson sank back in the chair.

"Yes, my own way."

"I think you really need to start talking now, Henriksson. Otherwise this could end up with you in jail for murder," Henrik said.

"Exactly," Mia said. "We know you had a relationship with Shirin Norberg. We also know that you systematically abused her. But why did you kill her?"

"I didn't kill her."

Mia examined him. Had she underestimated him, in spite of it all? He was hard to read. The method of suggesting they already knew everything wasn't working on him.

"We just want to understand you, Ted," Henrik said. "What drives you?"

"Pretty girls," he said, looking at his palms. "Pretty girls drive me."

"You like girls? Not women?" Mia sighed. She felt like they weren't getting anywhere.

She would have preferred that she and Henrik just walk out of the room. It didn't feel worth their while to continue talking to this clown.

"I didn't know you were so up on things," Henriksson said. "The combination isn't bad, is it?"

He spit in one palm, observing the gob as he continued: "One experienced and one…less experienced. It makes the game much more interesting."

"What game?" Mia asked.

"What game!" he said and began laughing. "Let's say this, my friends. I prefer two to one."

"It'd be best if you speak in more obvious terms," Henrik said.

"Can I be any more obvious? I thought that you'd at least be familiar with these things, but does the word 'threesome' mean anything to you?"

"No, can you tell us?" Henrik said wearily.

"Seriously?"

"You like to tie people up, cut them a little, whip them?" Mia said. "Is that what you like, Ted?"

She was quiet for a moment and looked thoughtfully at him.

"That was why you tied Shirin Norberg up, but what was

it that happened next? Did you get scared and run away when you were done, is that what happened?"

"What?"

"It's okay," Mia said. "We're listening, you can tell us."

"There's nothing to tell! I haven't done anything."

The room fell silent.

"You say that," Mia said, "but I don't believe you."

"It doesn't matter if you don't believe me. That's not reason enough to keep me here, is it?"

CHAPTER
FIFTEEN

"JUST GIVE ME THE MOST IMPORTANT POINTS," GUN-
nar Öhrn said, stressed.

He had asked for a quick briefing in his office and, in addition to Henrik, had also called in Mia.

The air was thick. The windows and the blinds were closed,
so that it was almost dark in the room.

"Ted Henriksson seems to have been at work when both
Shirin and Katarina were murdered. We're still investigating,
of course, to be sure that it checks out," Henrik said.

"Good," Gunnar said.

"I also have people checking out that Audi that was seen
in Borg."

"Unfortunately, Ted doesn't own an Audi," Mia said. "No,
damn it, it couldn't be that easy."

"He could have borrowed, rented or stolen one, of course,
so we'll go down that route, too," Henrik said. "When it

comes to the footprint in the yard, Anneli isn't done with the analysis yet, but she knows that it's a footprint from a pair of gym shoes, size nine and a half, so in all likelihood too small for Ted."

"And what do our friends at the National Forensic Lab say?" Gunnar asked.

"They promised to prioritize the body, but I can't say if that means they'll have the time to look at it today."

"That was a shit briefing," Gunnar said.

"That's where we are right now, unfortunately," Henrik said. "So there's not much that connects Ted to either of the crime scenes."

"And then we have the ring," Mia said. "The one we found at Katarina's, but Ted didn't seem to recognize it...we'll have to see what the forensics say."

"Two spectacular murders and no suspects besides Ted Henriksson. We're in a really weak position, in other words," Gunnar said, looking instantly tired.

He pulled his hand over his face, then told them what they'd gotten about Danilo Peña so far.

"Fourteen tips, of which four are from the regular informers who always call in whether they've seen something or not."

"But there are some people who've seen him?" Henrik said.

"Yes," Gunnar said, "or who think they've seen him. A pizzeria owner claimed that Peña had come into his pizzeria on Kungsgatan, ordered a house special, drank a Coke, went into the bathroom and then climbed out the window. The only problem was that there wasn't a window in the bathroom."

"Why lie about such a thing?" Mia asked.

"I don't know," Gunnar said. "To get noticed, maybe. If the newspapers think it's a good story and write about it, the pizzeria gets a lot of publicity."

"You mean this is about free advertising?"

"Something like that."

"But is there anyone out there who's actually seen him?" Henrik said.

"No, I don't think so. Some kids saw him running along the train tracks toward the bridge, you know, where Ingelstagatan goes over the tracks, and then he disappeared. Tips like that *could* be true."

"So in other words, the BOLO hasn't given us anything?" Mia asked.

"It's still early," Henrik said.

Gunnar nodded, but his facial expression gave anything but positive signals. They knew that the earliest responses were the most important. The news would soon be lost in the flood. People forget so easily.

The stairwell smelled of oregano, basil and garlic. When Jana Berzelius opened the door, she heard clinking glass and music coming from the television.

She pulled off her running shoes and went into the kitchen. There she froze and just stared.

Danilo stood at the kitchen counter. In one hand, he was holding a knife and in the other, a hunk of bread.

"What happened to your hair?" she managed.

"Scissors," he said. "Scissors happened."

He was wearing the new pants and sweater. His hair was cut, yet it resembled a hairstyle. A dark lock hung down onto his forehead. His chin was freshly shaven.

"You obviously found a razor blade, too," she said.

He grinned at her.

"I've just made soup," he said.

"Don't let me stop you. I'm going to shower."

"Here, help me instead."

He threw the bread at her, hard. She reacted instantaneously, raising her hand to catch it without taking her eyes off him.

"I don't—"

"—cook," he said. "I figured as much. Here."

The knife blade sliced through the air. She caught it with her other hand, gripping it securely, which Danilo noticed.

"We should act normal, don't you think?"

She didn't say anything as she walked slowly to the cutting board. She cut the bread in thin slices, keeping an eye on Danilo the whole time as he made small talk.

His manner irritated her. The situation wasn't normal. Didn't he understand that her actions over the coming days would be decisive for both of their lives? If she wasn't able to plant the shirt in the shelter, he wouldn't be able to escape, and she'd never be rid of him.

But he didn't seem to care about that at all; rather, he seemed more worried about the simmering soup. He took the saucepan off the burner and took out two bowls. He removed the lid from the pan and stirred the soup with a ladle. He filled the bowls halfway and set them on the table, which was already set with two wineglasses and an open bottle of wine.

"Sit down," he said, muting the television.

"What's the point of all of this?" she said, feeling how the sweat on her back had turned cold.

"I want to eat. Sit down!"

She hesitated at first, but then sat down across from him.

"What the hell is it now?" he said. "You aren't going to eat?"

"Do I dare?"

"Considering you had four packages of this soup in the refrigerator, I assume that you like it."

She picked up the spoon and lowered it slowly down into the soup.

"I haven't poisoned the food, if you're thinking I did."

"I never know with you."

"We can switch bowls if you want."

"No, thanks," she said, tasting the soup.

Just then, the doorbell rang. Danilo froze in the middle of a movement and looked at her.

"Are you expecting someone?" he asked tensely.

"No," she said, feeling her heart begin to pound.

Anneli Lindgren opened a folder and inspected the photographs from the crime scenes, closely examining those of the victims—Shirin Norberg's severed hands and Katarina Vinston's pale face. She shuddered with disgust but continued scrolling through the photos. She didn't like being unsure. She wanted to have control, wanted to understand. That was why she liked her work, and that was why she could sit for hours examining textile fibers, DNA analyses and other technical traces.

In one of the photographs, the footprint from the flower bed in Borg was visible. She had examined it previously, but she zoomed in close to the print now. She twisted and turned her head, squinted, and zoomed in again.

She saw the pattern from the sole. It matched what she thought, a cross-trainer or running shoe, size nine and a half.

Suddenly, her cell phone rang. It was Gunnar.

She smiled as she answered. "Anneli speaking."

"Why didn't you call me about the footprint?"

Her smile evaporated. "I told Henrik, and he said he was going to tell you."

"I know you did. But next time, call me first. Is that understood?"

"But, Gunnar...what does it matter? What did Henrik tell you about the footprint?"

He was a completely different person from three months ago. From a year ago. From ten years ago. Gone was the easy-going soul, the warm and thoughtful man, replaced by a strict and serious person speaking to her on the other end of the line. Over the years they had had their disagreements, separations even. But this hardening against her felt permanent.

She squirmed in her seat, upset by the sound of authority in his tone of voice. In what he said, there was a subtext: you are sloppy and aren't doing your job.

Clearly, he couldn't forgive her cheating on him. But it had only happened once, she thought. Once in twenty years! It had been uncomfortable at times to have her live-in partner as her boss, but it was damn unpleasant to have her boss as her ex. Her *ex*! She sighed that she had to call him that.

"Henrik told me it was a cross-trainer or running shoe, size nine. Did you tell him something more?"

"Yes," she said, "I told him that I figured out the brand."

"What brand is it?"

"I can see the swoosh."

"What?"

"The Nike logo."

"Yes, I know what it is. Are you sure?"

"Yes," she said.

"Good," he said and hung up.

She put her phone down, feeling sad. Studies showed that emotions could be measured, analyzed and compared. But it was harder to understand them. And when it came to the love between her and Gunnar, it was impossible to understand.

Jana Berzelius cast a quick glance behind her to ensure that Danilo was staying out of sight before she opened the front door.

On the other side of it stood Per, smiling at her. The green athletic jacket was zipped up to his chin, and the color accentuated his differently colored eyes.

When he took a step forward, she gestured for him to stay where he was.

"What is it?" he asked, stroking his hand under his chin.

"What are you doing here?"

He laughed. "We didn't get to have lunch at Fiskmagasinet, so I thought..."

"But you can't be here. Not now."

"What do you mean?"

"You have to go!"

He laughed again, but more nervously this time.

The laugh echoed in the stairwell before dying out and being replaced by a dull silence.

Calmly, she stepped outside and let the door close behind her. Most of all she wanted to disappear into the apartment again and avoid dealing with the unavoidable.

"I really want you to go," she said, giving him a quick look.

"You aren't exactly one to encourage friendship, are you?" he said.

"No, and I want ours to end," she said tersely.

"Did I do something wrong?"

"No, I just want to be on my own and left alone."

He looked at her, now with an expression of both disappointment and confusion. His chest heaved under his jacket.

"I've understood that you want to be left alone," he said, "that you don't want anyone to be involved in your personal life, and I've really tried not to."

"Why did you come here, then?"

"Well, I regret that now."

She looked at him, searching for his eyes.

"Don't be mad," she said.

"I'm not," he said with irritation. "I'm disappointed in myself because I put so much time into nothing."

At the same time, Danilo moved inside the apartment. She

heard it. Per should also have heard it. And then again. The wood floor creaked, and she pressed herself against the door.

"I thought you were alone," he said.

"I'm always alone," she said curtly.

"But…"

"Go," she said. "Now."

"I just don't understand…"

"What is it you don't understand? Go!"

"Jana…"

"You and I have nothing more to say to each other, Per. Our so-called friendship is over. End of story."

Their eyes met.

"Our so-called friendship…" he repeated quietly.

Then he didn't say anything else.

No more words were necessary; there was only one path for each of them to go.

She saw him nod in disappointment, take a few steps back and turn around.

Suddenly she was struck with the desire to put out her hand and pull him back.

But she didn't.

She went inside and closed the door behind her.

The highway rushed by outside the window. Philip Engström sat in the idling ambulance with his gaze fixed on an indefinable point beyond a field. It was Saturday evening, and they were busy.

Certain weekends almost every call was for a young person who'd been seriously injured in a pointless traffic accident. Like two weeks ago—a kid drove off highway 210 south of the city and broke through a deer fence near Söderköping's golf club. His car ended up deep in the forest, and he was stuck inside. It took twenty hours for him to free himself and reach the highway, where he was able to flag down a car.

Eighteen years old. A high school student.

"You missed a button," Sandra said.

Philip looked down at his soft, worn work shirt and was silent. He was thinking about Katarina again.

How long had she been there in the house, tied up? The bedroom was surprisingly large. A double bed with a purple spread was on the left, and a number of closets with mirrored doors lined the wall on the right. The different flooring stood witness to two rooms that had been merged into one. One wall featured three windows in a row, all with the blinds closed...

Had she called for help? Had she been conscious when he was looking for her, had she heard him knocking at the door?

The thought made him dizzy; no matter how much he thought about her, how much he longed to see her, she would never come back.

"What are you thinking about?" Sandra asked.

"Rainbows and kittens."

"You're thinking about Katarina, aren't you?"

He didn't answer.

"It's like pulling teeth to get you to talk."

"I'm just wondering how she died," he said.

"I told you that," she said.

"Told me what?" he said, looking at her.

"On the phone," she said, meeting his gaze for a brief moment.

"What?" he asked.

"That her tongue was cut out. She drowned, in her own blood."

"What?!"

"I'm not lying."

He heard the engine become quiet, almost strangely muffled. At first, Philip thought that his ears had plugged up, but it was his thoughts taking over. With a shudder he repeated the words in his head: Tongue. Cut out. Whether or not she'd heard him knocking didn't matter. She wouldn't have been able to yell.

"How do you know that?" he said.

"Richard Nilsson. It's lucky he was the one to go on that call, that it was someone experienced."

Philip turned his head, looking at the field along the road.

"Can I ask…" Sandra said. "Did you and Katarina have something going on?"

He looked at her, confused.

"She was a friend," he said, sounding offended.

"Not the sort of friend you sleep with?"

"What the hell? Why does everyone think that?"

Sandra passed a Winnebago.

"So that wasn't how it was, then?" she said.

"No," he said. "It wasn't. Katarina was a friend. The sort who listens."

"I'm happy to listen if you…"

"Thanks, but there's nothing I want to talk about right now."

"It's not good to keep everything inside," she said, swerving back into the right lane.

"Then you talk," he said, "if you think it's so damn important."

"I *do* think it's important. There are actually people who feel alone who need…"

"But I'm not one of them. Nor are you. So I really don't understand why you go on and on about it all the time," he said, turning his gaze out toward the field again. "No one here is alone," he mumbled.

Jana Berzelius stood still for a moment, holding her hand on the handle of the front door as if she didn't want to let it go.

She listened to the sounds of her apartment and walked through the hallway, passing the kitchen and into the living room. She looked out through the window at the world outside, which was dark and quiet, cold and sleepy, and wondered what Per was thinking.

She lowered her gaze, looking down at her tightly clenched fists.

There is no other way out, she said to herself, than the one she had just chosen.

"Who was that?"

Danilo was suddenly standing behind her.

She stopped but didn't turn around. She didn't want to see him, didn't want to have anything to do with him.

She wanted to return to being alone in herself.

To the silence and stillness.

"You know who it was," she said curtly.

"What did you say to him?"

"What I had to, to make him go away."

She walked forward again, into her bedroom, closing the door with a quiet sigh and sinking to the floor. She leaned her head against the wall and felt the pain from her clenched hands. She didn't care. She clenched them even harder.

She remained there a long time.

April 16

Dear Diary,
When I came into the locker room after gym class today, I couldn't find my pants at first. Someone had thrown them in the toilet because "they smelled like alcohol."

It's Martin's fault, I know it is. I should never have said anything to him about you, Daddy. I told him in confidence, and anyway, it was a long time ago when he and I were still friends.

Now he's told everyone else in class about you. Now every-

one knows that I used to hide your liquor bottles in my closet. Do you understand how embarrassed I am, Daddy? Do you know? I hope you do, because it's your fault, your damn fault that everything is how it is. It was you who made sure I was alone when I was just little.

Do you know what my first memory is, Daddy? It's from the kitchen. I remember you lying there, under the kitchen table, your eyes closed and something sticky on your skin. All I wanted was for you to snuggle with me.

If I could have, I would have gotten out of my high chair and lain down beside you.

I remember that I was crying, Daddy. Come, I yelled. Come here. Please get up, hold me. Don't lie there. Hold me.

But you didn't.

I think about you more and more, Daddy. I think that even if you never did anything for my loneliness, at least you brought my new mom into my life.

Daddy, I wish you were still with us. But you let us down.

So I was happy when you finally disappeared from my life.

But I didn't know life would be like this. The doctor said everything was going to be fine. Why? It's not fine. It's never going to be fine, even in the end. I know that.

The worst thing is that I feel overwhelmed inside me. I can't handle it anymore, knowing that I'm soon going to be completely alone.

Completely fucking alone.

But what is loneliness, really? Why does it exist? And what does it do to us?

Can anyone answer that?

Can you answer that?

Daddy?

CHAPTER
SIXTEEN

Sunday

HE WAS THE FIRST ONE UP, EVEN THOUGH HIS YOUN-
gest son had kept him awake almost all night. The kitchen was
bathed in a captivating light from a blue sky. Henrik Levin
stood by the window and looked out, noticing the beginning
of light green colors and a multitude of buds in the yard.

"You're up early."

He turned around and saw Emma come in dressed in her
gray pajama pants and top, her hair in a ponytail.

"Yes," he said.

"What a beautiful day," she said, looking at him, yet past
him, out through the window and toward the blue sky. Then
she went to him, put both arms around his waist and leaned
in close.

They stood like that for a long time.

"I'm going to miss this yard," she said.

"It's small," he said.

"That's why," she said, hugging him harder.

"You haven't started to regret moving, have you?" he said.

"No," she said. "It just feels strange to move back to the house I grew up in. Everything looks like it did when I moved out, down to the striped wallpaper in my old room."

"But if I know you well enough, the whole house will be painted white even before we've arrived with the moving boxes. You can choose whatever shade of white you want, I promise."

She laughed and kissed him.

It was just after eight o'clock when Henrik walked out the front door. He was about to get in the car when his cell phone rang. On the other end of the line, Björn Ahlmann cleared his throat. "The report is done," he said.

"What?"

"That's what you wanted. For it to go quickly. The autopsy of Katarina Vinston is complete. I've been up half the night finishing it."

"Thanks, Björn."

"No problem."

Henrik rested his elbow on the car door. "What do we know, then?" he said.

"Nothing more than what we already know, probably."

"But we hardly know anything."

"You know the victim's tongue had been cut out."

"With what sort of tool, though?"

"A single-use disposable scalpel."

"How do you know it was disposable?"

"Because the blade was still there inside her."

Henrik fell silent; he was having a hard time seeing in front of him. The scalpel was still inside her? A wave of nausea hit him. He swallowed, then swallowed again to try and get rid of the terrible taste in his mouth.

"Växjö?" Björn said.

"What?"

"Växjö, do you remember what happened in Växjö?"

"I don't remember."

Björn related, in his characteristically factual way, the story of a woman with self-harming behavior who had swallowed two scalpels. The psych ward was familiar with the woman; she'd been seen earlier at an Urgent Care facility. She had previously brought attention to herself by swallowing sharp objects such as razor blades and knives.

"When the second scalpel was being pulled out, her esophagus and the blood vessels in her neck were injured so seriously that she died on the operation table at Central Hospital in Gothenburg," he said. "I seem to remember that it resulted in a Lex Maria report to Social Services, because the hospital's actions may have contributed to the patient's death. Katarina had only the blade in her stomach. I believe it may have come loose when her tongue was being cut."

"And she swallowed it?" Henrik said.

"You understand what that means?" Björn said.

"No, but I assume you're going to tell me."

"It means that Katarina was conscious when her tongue was cut out."

Henrik grimaced.

"Does it require a lot of strength to...?" Henrik asked.

"Not really."

"And what kind of scalpel is it?"

"I can't say anything about the brand, but it says that it was made in Tuttlingen, Germany."

"Okay, I'll get someone to trace it."

"That might be difficult. Countless disposable scalpels are sold all over the world."

"Send me a picture anyway, please."

"I will."

"Did she have any other visible marks on her body? Wounds, bruises?"

"No."

"Is there anything else you can tell me?"

"Yes," he said. "From the analysis, we've seen that both Shirin and Katarina were both injected with a fast-acting anesthetic, a narcotic."

"Which is called...?"

"Ketalar."

Jana Berzelius clasped her watch around her wrist. She was still thinking about Per and his sad, disappointed look. His only crime was that he was her...colleague? Acquaintance? Friend? She didn't really know; no matter what word she used, their relationship was very likely over now. He would probably never want anything to do with her again.

It made her furious.

And it was Danilo's fault.

She moved slowly through the bedroom, turned off the lamp by the bed and opened the door.

He was on the floor in the living room, doing his push-ups slowly and methodically. Every day, the same exercises.

"Give me the old shirt."

He looked up quickly, stood up and went over to her chin-up bar, wrapped his palms around it and lifted his body multiple times.

"You look angry again now," he said. "And you are, aren't you, Jana?"

She took a deep breath, trying to calm herself. "You think you're smart?"

He let go of the bar and shook his arms.

"I'm not angry," she said, "but I will be if you don't give me the shirt."

"It's on the sofa."

"So I'm supposed to get it myself?"

"Yes, who else is going to? Per?"

She raised her eyes and saw him smile, saw him open his mouth to say something else. But she didn't intend to let him.

It was as if all of her hatred for him exploded inside her. She advanced without hesitation, twirling around in a single graceful movement and swinging her arm hard horizontally, striking his arm where the shoulder meets the upper arm.

He was surprised by her sudden attack and grimaced from the sudden pain. But she continued, taking two steps to the left and striking his other arm with a hard backhand.

Then one kick and another. She rotated her hips, braced with the back foot and connected with his waist. She ended by kicking him away from her.

She didn't want to stop, but she checked herself, lowered her arms, stood still and breathed. She saw him lying on the floor underneath her, saw him bleeding. She saw that he was going to say something again, and this time she let him.

"Okay, I get it, I get it," he said. "Sensitive subject."

"If you want me to help you escape, you had better go get your shirt. Now."

It was nine thirty in the morning and Mia sat rocking in her chair in the conference room while Henrik briefed the group about his conversation with the National Forensic Lab.

"Björn didn't find anything of value, unfortunately. No

sperm, no blood or anything else on Katarina Vinston's body," he said.

"Nothing from Ted, then," Mia said. "Well, shit!"

"I've said this before," Henrik said. "I don't think Ted Henriksson is our guy."

The room fell silent. Mia looked around and met cheerless, bleary-eyed looks from Gunnar and Ola.

"Besides, the morning someone was torturing Shirin, Henriksson was at work," Henrik said. "It's been confirmed."

"But couldn't he have snuck out for an hour or two without anyone noticing?" Ola said.

Henrik shook his head.

"He works with the production of supplements at Vitamex here in Norrköping."

"Sounds a little advanced for an idiot like him, if you ask me," Mia said.

"Even men like him have to earn a living," Henrik said. "The point is that he works on a production line, and if he hadn't been at his station, his coworkers would have known and reacted, I guarantee it."

"And when it comes to Katarina?" Gunnar asked. "Where was he then?"

"At work then, too. Henriksson certainly has a lot on his conscience. But we have to look a little wider..."

Gunnar drew both hands over his head, back and forth multiple times.

"You're right, Henrik," he said. "We no longer have a suspect for the murders of Shirin and Katarina."

Mia sank into her chair. "Damn it," she said. "I really thought it was him."

"You said that Björn reported no sperm on the victims? Interesting," Gunnar said.

"What's interesting about that?" Mia said.

"It seems odd that the perpetrator didn't sexually assault them in any case. And in turn, it means we can eliminate a lot of perpetrators in our own database. These crimes are about something else."

The room fell silent again. Gunnar clasped his hands together and leaned over the table. "We have a crazy person who tortures his victims in their own homes. Nothing points to a fight, or a break-in, so it's likely that both Shirin and Katarina knew their torturer."

"Yes," Henrik said, "but from where?"

"Well, this is what I'm thinking," Mia said. "The perp is probably smart and lives a seemingly normal life with a job and a family. But something sick and twisted inside him makes him need to tie up his female victims and dismember them. And so far he's managed to do this while keeping a somewhat normal profile."

"Sounds like a true psychopath," Ola said. "Probably a state employee. I can imagine that from his desk at his day job at some government agency, he follows his crimes in the media and is proud of them, as if he were involved in some sort of large-scale art project."

"The fucker must be getting quite a charge now," Mia said, "since the newspapers are having a field day with these murders."

"Let's not get too far ahead of ourselves here," Gunnar said. "We have no idea if we're dealing with a psychopath or not."

"But when it comes to serial killers, anyway, the victims often have something in common," Ola said, "like career, ethnicity, hair color or sex. Both Shirin and Katarina worked in health care."

"I think we're dealing with a fucking serial killer, too," Mia said.

"As I said, let's not get ahead of ourselves here. There has to be three murders for it to be a serial killer," Gunnar said.

"Who said he's done?" Mia said.

Gunnar scratched his earlobe.

"Okay," he said. "Both Shirin and Katarina worked in health care, but there has to be something in addition to that."

"The ritual of tying up the victims and severing limbs is identical, which might point to some form of serial intention, anyway," Henrik said. "What says he will ever stop?"

Henrik looked out over the team.

"Nothing," Mia said. "Not if he gets off on reading and hearing about his crimes in the news. That's why it is our job to stop him."

"We can hardly stop the media from writing about the murders," Gunnar said.

"True, and by the way," Henrik said, pointing to a paper he had before him, "there was one more important thing Björn said. Both Shirin and Katarina had been injected with the anesthetic Ketalar."

"So the perpetrator has access to drugs," Gunnar said.

"Yes, and he seems to be able to use a bone saw and a scalpel, too," Mia said.

"The common denominator between the victims and the perpetrator can, despite everything, be their work," Henrik mumbled. "Maybe the killer is a doctor?"

CHAPTER
SEVENTEEN

JANA BERZELIUS SLOWED DOWN, STOPPED AND scanned the industrial district in Motala. So this was what the district looked like for real, she thought.

Just a hundred yards away, a rabbit bounded off over asphalt and gravel. Two hundred yards past that, she caught sight of the shelter building, and right next to it was a white building called Konsum Ringen. The building apparently had previously featured a grocery store. Now it housed a cultural center, and a poster advertised an exhibition featuring a young talent from Linköping.

Jana drove on behind the Konsum Ringen building and parked the car so it was well hidden among a string of garages with rusty doors.

Was it really such a good idea to step right into a shelter and plant a trace for a man who was suspected of murder?

She heard something outside the car, something that

sounded like footsteps. She listened, but the sound disappeared. Maybe it was her imagination.

She rubbed her hand over the initials carved into her neck and sank back into the driver's seat, trying to breathe calmly. She persuaded herself that it was a simple plan. Without anyone seeing her, she would place the shirt in an obvious place in the shelter. Nothing too complicated. Just plant the shirt where someone would notice it and then get out of there.

What did she have to lose?

Not much, she thought, and got out of the car.

Lucas Bratic looked at himself in the mirror and thought how everything had gone to hell: yesterday's earnings, the miserable weather and the fact that someone had just knocked on the door.

"Open up," he heard a harsh voice say.

There was no mistaking whose voice it was. Dragan Sandin, a forty-five-year-old man with an exaggerated accent, was making his usual collection rounds in the shelter.

"Or we'll break down the door, cockhead."

The fact that Dragan had said *we'll* break down the door instead of *I'll* break down the door made Lucas nervous. In other words, multiple people stood on the other side of the door. Just the thin piece of wood separated him from their hard fists.

Lucas saw the door handle move up and down. He'd been sitting in the shared bathroom for a half hour, pretending he had a stomachache. In actuality, he needed the time to figure out a plan.

Yesterday, he'd only been able to beg $10.53 out of people. The money was in his right pocket, and that was what Dragan was after. He wanted all of it—the money in Lucas's other pocket, too. A wad of ten-dollar bills. It was money Lucas had been able to hide and that he needed.

Carefully, he removed the lid of the toilet tank. He rolled up the bills and tried to fasten them to the float as he heard Dragan's voice again.

"If you don't open up, we'll do it for you."

Bang.

Then there was the first kick. The whole door rattled.

Bang. The second kick.

Lucas broke out in a sweat. He tried to attach the money to the tank in some way, but he had nothing to fasten it with.

Bang. Now the bathroom door was beginning to splinter.

Lucas struggled, finally getting the lid back on. He sank down to the floor, closed his eyes and prayed to higher powers as they broke through the door.

She took a cautious step to the side, then held her breath and listened. Jana heard the front door close behind her and then voices behind a corner, farther down the hallway. She saw a pale light trickle in through a window in a door marked "Staff." She tried the door handle, but it was locked. She began walking down the hallway, keeping close to the wall. She found another door and tried it. It opened into a storage closet with vinyl flooring that had peeled up in places probably because of dampness. The shelter emanated a smell, a mixture of dust, sweat and garbage.

She held the bag containing the shirt and continued down the hallway. It looked as if there were ten rooms ahead, five on each side of the corridor. She would leave the shirt in whichever one was the most likely it would be found.

Quick in, quick out was her plan.

She nudged another one of the doors open and saw that the room was empty.

No dresser, no closet. Just two bunk beds.

Two bunk beds. She looked at the lower bunk with its thin mattress, and quickly stepped inside.

In a police cruiser in Motala, Officer Joel Marklund had just taken a call about an in-progress disturbance at the shelter in the industrial district. The call had come from staff who had locked themselves in the staff office.

"Aren't there any officers closer?" he said. "We're a ways outside of the city."

"There's no one else," said the voice from the central command.

"Then we'll take it," Joel said, confirming before an "over and out" that they were on their way.

He started the car, signaled left and told his partner, Kim Heist, that it had been unusually unruly at the shelter lately.

"Toby and Danny were there twice yesterday, and on Friday I think Vlad and Anna had to spend the whole damn day there. There's a new guy who seems to be using the shelter as a base to shake people down. We think he's organizing begging in some way, and not always by very pleasant means."

"Then let's go and clean things up a bit," Kim said.

The fist came immediately and the pain was like an explosion. Lucas stumbled backward but steadied himself on the sink. Dragan sneered. Behind him stood two of his men, one with a shaved head and the other with wide, dark pupils. They took hold of him, one on each arm, and Dragan head-butted him so hard that he crumpled to the floor. When he looked up again, he was looking straight at the gleaming tip of a knife.

"Give me the cash. Now."

"In my pocket," Lucas said.

The blood from his nose was running into his mouth.

Dragan counted the money and began laughing.

"You foolin' me, man," he said. "Now show me the *real* cash."

"That's all I got, I…"

"Shhhh…"

Dragan laid a hand over Lucas's mouth.

"I know you have more. And do you know how I know? That guy there told me," Dragan said, pointing to the man with the shaved head. "He said he saw you counting. What to do? You no money, others no money, me problem. You understand? Problem!"

Lucas stared at the tip of the knife as it neared his face. He tried to breathe through his bleeding nose.

"And now I teach you a lesson. I teach you, no fuck with me."

Lucas began screaming with Dragan's hand over his mouth, but he felt the pressure increase.

"Calm," Dragan said. "I only take *one* eye."

Lucas should have struggled, should have thought of something, but now he couldn't think at all. Stiff from fear and with his eyes wide open, he couldn't avoid the movement of the knife.

"Dragan?" said the man with the shaved head.

"Shut up."

"But it's important. Look. The door over there is open."

He pointed down the hallway.

Dragan rolled his eyes, took his hand from Lucas's mouth, looked at the blood that had run over his palm and wiped it back and forth on Lucas's shirt to clean it.

"Check it out."

"I will," Dragan said. "I'm just going to solve this problem first."

Lucas took short, quick breaths, gasping for air. One part of his brain told him he should try to get away. Another part said he should attack the men in front of him and at least make an attempt to defend himself.

But fear has a peculiar effect on people. Even when standing before certain death, there are people who, despite a complete lack of alternatives, simply can't fight back. It was as if Lucas was paralyzed. He simply couldn't move. So he sat there, with his hands on the floor. He saw when Dragan raised his fist and felt how it split the skin on his forehead. He was deafened by the blow and knew that if it had been any harder, he would have passed out. Then he wouldn't have had to see when the next blow came.

But he did.

Jana lifted the thin mattress, shook the dirty shirt out of the bag and shoved it almost completely underneath, backed up a few steps and checked that it wasn't visible at first glance.

When she turned around, three men were standing there.

"What the fuck," one of them said, revealing his gold teeth. "What we have here? Smells like cash. Or is there something else you gonna give me? Huh?"

He walked toward her, around her. She could smell him: grease and sweat, alcohol and cigarettes.

He opened his mouth and waggled his tongue. He stood in front of her and tried to touch her hair, but she slapped his hand away as quick as a blink.

He laughed. "Well, well! Did someone wake up on the wrong side of bed?"

He tried again, and again she slapped his hand away. This time, he didn't laugh. Jana saw the transformation in his face. She knew what was about to happen and began counting backward.

She estimated it would take a full twenty seconds before

he attacked her. Twenty seconds, she thought, before the first attack.

It was risky to stay there. She should get out, but she knew that she couldn't turn her back on this type of opponent. It was better to look him in the eye.

"I don't want to fight," she said.

"We don't have to fight," he said, sneering. "If you do what I say."

"And what exactly are you saying?"

The man sneered and pulled one sleeve up to his elbow. The hand on his watch was glowing a strange shade of blue. He tried to appear calm and relaxed, but she saw that he was nervous. All three of them were.

Fifteen seconds.

But Jana felt the usual sense of calm filling her as she lifted her head and appraised the situation. She remembered the green exit signs at the end of the hallway that led to two es- cape routes. Three, if she counted the window behind her.

Ten seconds.

She examined the other two men carefully, one with a shaved head and the other with large pupils. In compari- son, the man with the gold teeth seemed old. He was small, round-shouldered, wrinkled. He probably wasn't older than around fifty, and clearly he enjoyed demanding things from other people. He looked determined and held a steady grip on the knife in his hand.

"What are you gonna give me? Huh?"

He took a step toward her, and she could almost hear the ticking of his watch. The other men stood to either side of her, breathing heavily.

She also took deep breaths, not because she was nervous, but to fill her blood with oxygen so that she would be ready to act when the moment came.

Five seconds.

The man with the dilated pupils clenched his fists. Only then did she realize how muscular he was. Any blow from him would knock her out without a problem.

Then the man with the gold teeth gave the signal.

Go time.

Jana held her breath.

Officers Joel Marklund and Kim Heist double-parked their cruiser outside the shelter. They didn't say a word to each other.

Joel examined the surrounding buildings nearby, scanning for movement. The shelter was relatively new, and not just a temporary place to sleep. When morning came, the guests were allowed to stay. They didn't have to wander around Motala with a suitcase or plastic bag containing their possessions, didn't have to wait for evening to be allowed back into the warm shelter again.

But there was a limited number of beds; only forty-odd people could stay here. No one knew how long the municipality's pilot project would last, if the shelter would still be there in a year or two.

"It looks calm," he said, biting his thumbnail.

"I think the instructions were to go inside," Kim said.

"Really?" Joel said.

"Come on now, for Christ's sake."

The man with the gold teeth advanced. But Jana Berzelius was ready. She shifted her weight and pressed her elbow against his temple. In her next movement, she jerked the knife from his hand. He faltered, staring uncomprehendingly at his empty hand.

"Give me the knife," he said.

"I don't want to hurt you," she said. "But I will if I have to."

He laughed, more unsure of himself this time.

"She has the knife. Get the knife!" he said.

As the man with the dilated pupils approached, she dodged him, spun around and thrust the knife toward the man with the shaved head. She scratched his throat with it, then slammed him hard with her left hand. It felt like punching a brick wall. He didn't move an inch. Instead, he hit her so hard that made her double over. If he had made contact a few inches higher, he would have broken at least one rib, maybe two. She didn't even try to block. She attacked him with everything she had, getting in an uppercut and feeling his jaw break. He swore, spitting out blood and teeth. She followed with a fist directly over his nose, which made the blood spatter and the color drain from his face.

He cupped his hand over his nose as he staggered and sank to the floor. He looked ready to pass out.

The man with the gold teeth nodded at her and smiled a chilling smile. He seemed reluctantly impressed and waved his hand at the man with the dilated pupils, who pulled out a pistol.

Jana stared into its muzzle.

She knew better than to run.

You couldn't run from a Glock, not without getting a bullet in the head. And the man's empty, easily confused expression meant that he wouldn't hesitate to pull the trigger.

She glanced at the man with the gold teeth. His sneer was wider now, more superior.

"I'm sorry about this," he said.

"So am I," Jana said, flinging the knife.

It sunk straight into his shoulder, going through cartilage and tissue. Before he understood what had happened, she kicked the pistol out of the other man's hand, stepped forward and gripped his right arm, twisting his wrist until it tightened the nerves of his forearm. He moaned.

In her next movement, she grabbed the pistol from the floor.

The man with the gold teeth looked at her. Blood was pulsating from his shoulder, staining his shirt a deep red. His arms hung at his sides. He tried to say something, but Jana didn't have time to listen.

She pointed the weapon at his head and pulled the trigger.

Joel Marklund twirled around. Three birds took flight and disappeared behind the rooftops, cawing. He met Kim Heist's gaze. Kim had assumed a wide stance, hand on her holster. They were standing right outside the shelter.

"That was a gunshot," Joel said.

"Yes," Kim nodded.

They heard one more shot, and then another.

Joel ran back to the car with his head down and, in a shaky voice, requested reinforcements.

Lucas Bratic had come to, but he quickly realized he was still in the shared bathroom in the hallway at the shelter.

Blood dripped from his broken nose, over his chin and down onto his sweatshirt.

He had heard the shots, and now he heard footsteps approaching.

He thought his last moment had come. Dragan would probably shoot the top of his skull off, too. Spray his brains all over the bathroom.

But Lucas didn't want to die in a bathroom, not for the sake of a few bucks. He didn't want to be shot, either, for that matter.

When he heard the steps disappear, he thanked the higher powers again. This time, he did so with clasped hands.

Joel Marklund and Kim Heist stood unmoving on either side of the open front door. They listened to the sounds coming from inside the shelter.

Joel gripped his weapon, saying nothing to Kim because he wanted to be able to register any potential whimpering or moaning from any of the rooms. But he didn't hear anything. Experience told him that the silence didn't bode well.

It was important to act quickly. So they wouldn't risk that the perpetrator or perpetrators would be able to leave the building, they decided to go in without waiting for reinforcements.

They opened the front door.

Joel knew he had to do more than just that.

"Police!" he yelled into the building.

Jana Berzelius pressed her body against the facade of the shelter. She saw the police cruiser parked in front of the entrance and felt some hesitation about which way she should go. Her car was a hundred yards away. If she chose the quickest route, she would be completely visible from the shelter entrance.

She heard sirens far off; they were slowly becoming louder, coming closer.

She turned her head in the opposite direction and looked at the window standing wide open in the neighboring cultural center. If she took that route, through that building, she'd be able to stay out of sight.

Then she heard the officers' yells and assumed they had entered the shelter and caught sight of the dead men.

She never even considered letting the men live. Showing

mercy would have been a mistake that would have haunted her. As long as they were alive, they would have presented a threat to her.

She climbed inside the building through the window and saw cabinet drawers and empty frames. Farther off were a number of paintings. She presumed she was in a storage room.

She moved nimbly toward a wooden door.

She put her ear against it and heard a quiet voice and a muffled laugh. The laugh subsided. When she listened again, there was silence on the other side of the door. She pushed it open, peered out cautiously and looked straight into a bright, well-lit space. Large paintings adorned the walls and sculptures of various sizes stood on white tables.

It was a gallery.

She straightened her coat, smoothed her hair and stepped into the room, walking with quick steps toward the exit. Just then, she heard the laugh again, followed by approaching footsteps.

Quickly, she stood with her nose pointed at one of the paintings and pretended to observe it with squinted eyes.

"Yikes! Oh, you scared me!" said the woman, who entered from an adjoining room. She held her cell phone in her hand. She had a wide smile and twinkling eyes, and was wearing a knee-length skirt and long-sleeved blouse, bracelets in various shades of red around her wrist and matching red earrings that bounced as she spoke.

"I didn't hear you come in," she said.

"No?" Jana said.

"The door usually jingles."

"Maybe it's broken."

Jana turned her gaze to the painting again.

"Do you like Julius Nord?" the woman asked.

"Who?"

"The artist? The exhibition is comprised of his paintings, which…"

"I'm just looking around."

"Okay, but just tell me if you need help with anything. We have a newly opened exhibit on the second floor. Acoustic installations."

"Thank you, but I see from the time that I have to hurry off," Jana said, beginning to walk toward the exit.

"Come back soon. Both exhibitions are open until May," she said. "Wait, let me hold the door open for you."

The glass door jingled loudly when she opened it.

"The bells seem to be working again," Jana said as she left the gallery.

She saw her car parked just a dozen yards away. She walked slowly toward it, thinking how she wasn't in much of a hurry anymore. If anyone, contrary to her expectations, happened to ask, she had both a reasonable explanation for why she was in the area and a believable alibi.

She opened the car door and sat behind the steering wheel. Farther up the street, she saw the flashing blue lights. She sighed in relief and put the car in Drive.

Officers Joel Marklund and Kim Heist remained on either side of the shelter's entrance. Reinforcements had arrived. The lead officer shouted orders at the units to surround the building. Two men immediately disappeared to place themselves at the back exit, if the shooter attempted to escape. All other doors to the shelter were secured.

Joel heard the sound of weapons being loaded in the cool afternoon, then the sound of a door being kicked in.

His colleagues rushed past him and shortly he heard calls from inside the building, first announcing three dead bodies. Then he heard the capture: "Hold your hands where I can see them!"

He went in.

"Hands up, I said!" he heard.

Joel followed the voice and found a colleague with his weapon pointed into a bathroom. And there, sitting on the floor, he saw a man, his head hanging and hands up in the air.

The man's breathing came in large, sudden gasps, as if he were about to have a panic attack.

Joel listened for a moment while the man hyperventilated, and he wondered if the man was dying. His sleeves were stained red; he'd probably dried the blood from his nose on them.

"Are you armed?" Joel asked.

"No," the man whispered.

"Are you injured? Shot?"

"Just my nose."

"What's your name?"

"Lucas."

"Okay, Lucas, can you tell us what happened here?"

CHAPTER
EIGHTEEN

IT WAS LATE AFTERNOON WHEN HENRIK LEVIN squeezed into his townhouse in Smedby. Emma had stacked boxes four high in the hallway.

He took off his shoes, hung up his jacket and listened to the children's merry voices upstairs. He stopped and stood in the living room. More boxes, filled with things he hadn't even known existed. Things that might never be unpacked again, that would be stashed away in an attic or storage closet and forgotten. Again.

He began to think of Danilo Peña. He thought how the escapee might be sitting hidden in an attic or closet. But he was probably in a more secure location. He'd probably already had a whole plan for where he would go when he left the hospital. Peña didn't seem like a man who left that sort of thing to chance. They should also question former National Police Commissioner Anders Wester, since he and Peña were involved in the Policegate scandal. But, he thought, it was unlikely that he would give them any information they could use.

Outside the window, Henrik saw the light fog rising between the treetops. He went closer to the window and stood thinking how all too infrequently he had taken the time to appreciate the views from this townhouse.

How many years had they been there, actually?

As he counted in his head, he thought back to the day they had first stepped into the house. The sun had just begun to warm the earth, and Emma had taken off her cardigan, rested her hands on her big belly and stood beside him. While gazing through this window, they'd decided that this was where they would live for many, many years.

That had been eight years ago, he thought. Eight years since Felix was born.

He hadn't known then that this was the life he was going to be living when he was forty years old. Now as he stood and looked out over the fog-covered yard, he was on the way to a new house, with a wife who had just given birth to his third child.

Henrik went up the stairs, and when he reached the top step, he met Emma with Vilgot in her arms.

"Hi," she said hurriedly. "Great that you're home. Can you make sure that Felix and Vilma pick up the Legos? I have to feed Vilgot."

"Of course," he said, going into Felix's room.

The floor was chilly underfoot, and Lego pieces were everywhere. Both Felix and Vilma sat on the bed with the iPad in front of them and were watching a movie with two yellow characters dancing and singing.

"Time to clean up now," Henrik said.

"Noooo!"

"Yes."

"But, Daddy, can't we finish watching first? Please."

"No. Turn off the movie right now."

"There's only three minutes left. Please, Daddy, please!"

"Okay."

"Yay!"

"But then you need to turn it off."

Both of them nodded and turned their gazes back to the dancing yellow characters. Henrik sat down and picked through the Lego pieces as he began thinking about work again, about the possible suspects in the investigations surrounding Shirin and Katarina. There weren't many, unfortunately.

There weren't any, to tell the truth.

Ted Henriksson had already been cut from the list.

Still there was that car, the Audi. What had it been doing in that isolated residential area at the time of Katarina's murder? And who'd been driving it?

Was it a doctor? Who wore a nine-and-a-half-size shoe?

Henrik lined up a row of Lego figures. He thought about the Gigli saw, the scalpel and the narcotic.

Three more clues, he thought. *But where can they lead us?*

Jana breathed deeply. Yes, her pulse had slowed now, but the strange feeling remained. The whole way from Motala, she experienced a mixture of anger and nervousness. She had been forced to kill three men in the shelter, play for high stakes, risk altogether too much, just to plant Danilo's shirt somewhere far away from her apartment. But at least she was able to accomplish that and, she hoped, thus throw investigators off Danilo's track.

When she stepped into her apartment, all of the lights were off. Only a weak light from the windows found its way into the hallway.

She pulled off her shoes by the door and lifted her gaze. His shadow appeared on the floor. He stood there, looking at her.

"I assume it went well," Danilo said.

She didn't answer. Didn't feel like talking.

"But you understand that there are more conditions, don't you?" he said.

The rage returned. She looked at him and couldn't help but admire him—in the way you admire a cockroach you've stepped on that keeps on crawling. On and on. And on.

"The shirt's been planted," she said.

"That's not enough. You have to call."

"Unnecessary," she said. "The police are already there and have probably found the bodies of the men in the same room as I planted the shirt. You'll have three new murders on your conscience…"

"What the hell did you do?" he said with a furrowed brow.

"I had unwanted visitors at the shelter."

He grinned doubtfully. "Okay, but I don't trust the pigs. They don't always come to the correct conclusions."

"I'm not going to call," Jana said. "I think that's overdoing it."

"And I think you aren't a stranger to overdoing it. Three murders just to plant evidence that I was there?"

"I really had no choice."

"You don't now, either. You're going to call and say that you saw that dangerous man, Danilo Peña, near the shelter, and that you saw him there today."

"And you don't think they will trace the call?"

"Not if you are quick enough."

"And my motivation is still to get rid of you?"

"And get your boxes of journals back."

She knew that it was pointless to continue the conversation, so she turned her back on him and began walking to her bedroom.

"I know," he said behind her, "that you've gone through the alternatives. And that you don't really have any. I'm leaving the apartment in two days. It's too bad, really. I've begun to like it here."

She went into her bedroom and locked the door. She didn't want to call, she wouldn't! But she realized that she had to. It wasn't a sure thing that the police would come to the right conclusion. If she called, the possibility of getting rid of him increased considerably. He knew it, and she knew it. As long as she wasn't found out.

She slammed her hand against the wall.

Bang!

Bang!

Bang!

Then she walked slowly into her walk-in closet. She opened the safe and looked in at the wrinkled journal page Danilo had given her. Then she let her gaze sweep over the bundle containing cash, knives, passport, cell phones and SIM cards.

She took out one of the cell phones and inserted a SIM card into it. She turned it on and saw that there was enough battery left, so she sat on her bed and silently rehearsed what she was going to say. She intended to sound calm and factual, but then she changed her mind. It would be better to release what she was feeling, let both the anger and irritation she felt for him speak. It would sound more real then, more believable.

She dialed the number to the police tip line. She did it slowly and braced herself as she heard the phone ringing.

A woman answered, her voice clear and calm.

"Hi," Jana said. "First, I want to stay anonymous. Second, I have something important to report..."

My Journal, November 1

Dear Diary,
We worked in groups again today. This time we were supposed to paint a skyline. Our art teacher tore off a large sheet of paper and placed it on the table in front of me. There were five people in my group. I said that I could paint a boat sailing along the horizon. But they gave me a brush and said I could paint the water. In one corner. I was almost done painting when Linus dipped his brush into black paint and drew a dark line through the blue.

"They're waves," he said. "Fucking tall ones."
I didn't say anything. I just stared at the table.
When it was time for break, I waited until everyone had left, as usual.
Just as I was about to leave the room, I heard their voices, Linus, Martin and the others. And I heard them loud and clear because the door was open.
When I walked out, I saw that Martin was standing with his fingers wrapped around the doorframe.
I didn't hesitate. It was easy as pie. I grabbed the door handle and slammed the door. It didn't bounce or anything, just made a crashing sound and then Martin howled.
It's awful to say it, but I still smile when I think about his crushed fingers. So darn wonderful! So wonderful to get revenge. Fucking idiots!
And no one saw that it had been me, either, because I took the back way through the group room. Viveka said that the door must have slammed shut because of the crosscurrent, because a window had been open in the room.
I'm going to ignore anything Martin says tomorrow, if he even comes to school. He won't be able to do anything bad to me. I took the power from him, the power to do bad things to me.

Do you understand, Diary? Martin is the monster now—I've taken away his ability to hit! It's probably the greatest thing of all. Oh Mom, who always says that revenge doesn't get you anywhere. Nowhere good, anyway. But it does. You can have an effect if you really want to. You can, truly.

I wish I could tell her. But it's the middle of the night now. I should sleep, but my mind is racing. Thinking about a future that doesn't exist. It sounds awful, I know, but there is no future. Not the future the doctor promised, anyway. Time is running out. And there's nothing I can do about it. Nothing at all.

CHAPTER
NINETEEN

Monday

PHILIP ENGSTRÖM LEFT THE CREW LOUNGE AND walked toward the ambulance. It was fifteen minutes into his shift, and they had received a request for medical transport for a fifty-eight-year-old man who was having problems with his urinary catheter. Philip felt alternately cold, sweaty, jerky and thirsty, and the physical unpleasantness became even more painful when combined with his awful thoughts about Katarina.

He caught sight of Sandra walking toward him. They exchanged a quick glance before sitting silently next to each other in the vehicle. She took the wheel and turned out of the roundabout and continued at legal speed toward the E4 highway. The clouds had dispersed, and the sun's sharp beams made the waters of Lake Bråviken glitter.

Suddenly, a voice from dispatch broke the silence.

"Dispatch to Ambulance 9110, come in."

"Ambulance 9110, over."

"We've got a call about a man with a serious leg fracture. Don't know any more than that because we lost contact with the caller. But switch calls and go Code Three to Stavsjö, Tintomaras väg 37."

"Copy, affirmative, over."

"Dispatch over and out."

"Stavsjö?" Philip asked.

"It's near Nyköping," Sandra said. "About ten minutes away."

Ten minutes, Philip thought.

These minutes were long, crucial, when it was a serious case, and his heart pounded just a little as Sandra increased her speed.

"Code Three, lights and sirens, for a leg fracture?" Philip said. "What the hell happened?"

Sandra didn't answer. She kept her eyes on the road.

Just before Stavsjö Pub and Café, on the boundary between the counties of Östergötland and Södermanland, they turned off the highway and continued into the little community.

The hill after the lake was steep, and Sandra was forced to slow down as she turned left.

The house was located on a cul-de-sac. They parked by a tall hedge and saw a neighbor who had hurried out of her house and followed them with a curious expression. Philip grabbed the medical bag and noticed the garden implements in the yard. A lawn mower, a rake and a wheelbarrow.

Wooden stairs led to the front door, and they rang the doorbell. They waited, but nothing happened.

Sandra tried the door handle, and the door swung open.

They looked into a small foyer with black-and-white-patterned wallpaper.

"Hello?" she called. "Paramedics here."

They stepped in and saw a woman with light, chin-length hair, sitting on the kitchen floor, cell phone in hand. Her upper body was rocking back and forth. She was visibly shocked. Sandra sank to her knees and talked calmly to her.

"Here," Sandra said, handing the oxygen bag to Philip.

Philip continued down the half flight of stairs and came to a living room and dining room. A half flight farther brought him to bedrooms, an office and a laundry room.

It was a large split-level house, and it wasn't until he was down in the basement that he found the man sitting in a pool of blood on a chair with his hands tied and his head hanging down to his chest.

Philip would never forget the sight.

The man's legs were missing. They had been cut off above the knees, and a shining sea of blood had formed around him.

His chest was heaving. He was hyperventilating.

Without saying a word, Philip went to him. He dropped both the oxygen bag and the medical kit on the floor, placed his hands on the man's head and leaned it back carefully. The man was ice-cold; his skin was deathly, almost bluish green. A moaning sound escaped from his mouth. "Ph…Philip?"

The man looked at him with hazy eyes, and it was only then that Philip recognized him. The narrow mouth, liver spot on his cheek. A former colleague. Johan Rehn.

"What the hell happened?" Philip said, feeling for his pulse.

"My legs…my legs… I…" Johan closed his eyes and tried to control his breathing. "I can't breathe…it…"

Philip opened the oxygen bag and brought the oxygen mask toward his mouth, but Johan shook his head.

"No," he said.

"Johan," Philip said. "Stay still."

"No."

"Breathe!"

"It won't help...it..."

"Now stop with this craziness," Philip said sternly, knowing it was his stress talking. He quickly took out tourniquets and placed them in the man's groin area to stop the arterial flow to the legs. But he knew that it was an impossible task.

Johan had closed his eyes.

"Shit, shit shit!" he screamed. "Sandra, come here and help me, now!"

Blood was everywhere.

It would take twenty minutes to get to the hospital, and the only thing to do at that very moment was to load the dismembered Johan up and get moving. Sandra appeared in the doorway, and with her help, he released Johan from the chair. Then they placed him on the stretcher. Neighbors had gathered by the time they carried Johan out of the house. Philip immediately began working in the ambulance, connecting the pulse oximeter and beginning to insert catheters into his arm so he could administer fluids.

Johan opened his eyes and met his gaze. One hand was looking for something to hold on to. Then he closed his eyes again.

His hand became still.

He had lost consciousness.

Philip felt the vehicle sway as he tried to read the man's pulse.

But Johan's heart wasn't beating anymore. He was in traumatic cardiac arrest.

Philip began CPR. He pushed furiously with both hands against Johan's chest. He counted to thirty and blew air into

Johan's lungs until his rib cage rose. He finished two breaths and then continued pushing on his chest.

"Don't give up now, Johan. For Christ's sake, don't give up," he said, even though deep inside, he knew Johan already had.

Mia Bolander stood in her office with her cell phone pressed against her ear. She tried to figure out what had just happened in her conversation with the salesman at the car dealership. He had talked with the mechanics who had gone through the car and found that the cylinder head gasket had blown. It wouldn't be hard to replace, but it would take time. Then there might be other problems, that the cylinder head edge was uneven or that the cylinders had been damaged, and it was right about then that Mia had bit her lip. She'd bit it even harder when the salesman told her that the mechanics had also found other small, irritating problems such as a loose door handle and a broken fan.

"So you can probably count on the whole thing being about two thousand, if not more."

"Well, shit!" she said.

"What happened?"

"I bit my lip. It's bleeding, too…shit."

She dried the blood with the arm of her sweater.

"Are you there?"

"Yes."

"I'm sorry to say, but it will take at least a couple of weeks to fix your car because we're not sure the shop has the spare parts in stock. Well, it's very possible they don't. The car isn't exactly new, if I may say so."

"A couple of weeks?"

Her phone beeped, and Mia saw that it was Henrik Levin.

"I'm getting another call, and I have to take it. Sorry," she said.

"But I have a solution for you, Mia. We've just gotten in a shiny, new Fiat Lounge with a sunroof and leather seats that would be perfect for you."

It beeped again. Henrik didn't give up; it was presumably something urgent.

"I have to take this," she said.

"And do you know what the best part is?" the salesman said. "This car is available immediately. So my suggestion for you, Mia, is that you trade in your old car and come here and pick up this beauty. And do you know what's even better, Mia? That you'll only have to pay two hundred and fifty dollars a month, and that includes basic service. And with a new car, you'll never have to worry about your car not starting. What do you say?"

"I really have to take this," she said.

"You can't miss a chance like this, Mia. What do you say, do we have a deal?"

"Hold on a minute," she said and switched over to the other line.

"Mia?" Henrik said. "Why didn't you answer?"

"I was on the other line. What's up?"

"You were right," he said.

"About what?"

"That we're dealing with a serial killer."

"Why do you say that?"

"Because there's been another murder."

There was blood on his collar, chest and arms. Philip Engström had pulled off his work shirt before going up the stairs to the locker room. The on-call doctor was taking care of Johan Rehn. His death needed to be confirmed with the date and time. The ambulance had to be cleaned, the medical kit needed to be filled with new medicine and the oxygen tank had to be changed.

Philip went into the silent locker room. He leaned his head against his locker and tried to comprehend what was going on around him.

Johan Rehn was dead.

Katarina Vinston was dead.

And Shirin Norberg was dead.

He knew Johan and Katarina, and he was certain that he'd also seen Shirin somewhere; she looked so familiar to him.

He felt an unpleasant lump in his throat. It couldn't be coincidence that he knew, or knew of, all three.

When he looked at his watch, his hands were shaking so hard that it was difficult to see the time. With his forefinger and thumb, he found the pill he kept in his pants pocket. He always had a single Sobril there for when he needed to calm himself because it was easier to hide one than a whole pack of pills.

He brushed away the lint that was stuck to the coating, opened his mouth, stuck the pill as far back on his tongue as possible and swallowed.

But his body wouldn't obey.

The pill didn't want to go down.

He gagged.

He went to the sink, turned on the faucet and slurped the ice-cold water as it filled his cupped hands.

After retching once more, the tablet slid down.

He looked at his reflection, saw the drops of blood on his cheek and tried to rub them off with his hand. Then he noticed the blood on his neck and ear and rubbed even harder, as if it were a poisonous substance he had to get off.

It hurt, but he kept going.

Rubbing, rubbing until it was completely gone.

★ ★ ★

"So who is he?" Mia asked.

"Johan Rehn, fifty-eight years old," Henrik said. "I've asked Ola to gather any and all information on him for the meeting."

Mia looked at Anneli, who was kneeling to get fingerprints from a dresser. Henrik stood next to her, his shoulders drooping and his face weary.

The chair the man had been sitting on was covered in blood. There was blood on the floor, blood everywhere. An adult has about six liters of blood, and Mia wondered how much of that this man had lost. Far too much, clearly, since he hadn't made it.

"Was he home alone?" she said.

"Yes, at least when it happened," Henrik said.

"So who called it in?"

"His wife. She came home from a trip this morning and was seriously shocked when she found him without legs."

"I'd fucking think so," Mia said.

"The same perpetrator," Anneli said, still kneeling by the dresser.

Henrik nodded, troubled.

"But this time he killed a man instead of a woman," Mia said. "Why?"

"Good question," Henrik said.

The room fell silent.

Mia observed the scene of the crime. The similarities with the brutal scenes at Shirin Norberg's apartment and Katarina Vinston's house were remarkable. But what did a widowed mother of two, a single working woman and a late-middle-aged man have in common? Why had these three fallen victim to the perpetrator's violence?

"Whose footprints are these?" she said when she looked down at the prints from shoes next to the chair.

Anneli turned around and looked toward the great sea of blood.

"They're from the paramedics," she said. "Unfortunately, they didn't have any protective gear and left a whole lot of traces behind them, and also potentially destroyed some. But we just have to live with that."

"Do we know who was here?" Mia said.

"Yes," Anneli said. "Philip Engström and Sandra Gustafsson."

Mia nodded thoughtfully.

"Have you found any traces of anyone else but his wife?" she said.

"Not yet," Anneli said. "But I'm not by any means even close to finishing."

Mia looked around again, taking in the room and all of the details. She heard footsteps from the floor above and thought it must be the forensic techs doing a thorough search of the house.

"There's one thing I'm wondering about," Henrik said. "How did the perpetrator get in? Anyone can use a crowbar or break a window, but getting into a residence without leaving a trace is an art."

"The victim must have known the perp," Mia said. "There is no other explanation."

"But how could he know that the victim would be home alone when he was going to attack? I mean, he needed a bit of time to saw off the legs, right?"

"Shirin wasn't alone," Mia said.

"Okay, but he locked her daughter in her room. Katarina and this man were completely alone. I'm thinking he must have had a very good sense of their schedules."

"Like I said…he knew them," Mia said again.

"Or he'd made a detailed investigation of their lives. We

have to talk to all of the neighbors right away. Ask if anyone saw someone hanging around the area, or maybe saw an Audi A5."

Jana hurried across the crosswalk. Her coat flapped against her legs, and the sound of her footsteps was drowned by the noise of the traffic, of the crowd, of a bustling Norrköping.

Because of the most recent murder, she had been called to a meeting at the police station, and she had promised Henrik Levin she'd be there by ten o'clock at the latest.

She was just about to ascend the steps to the entrance when she saw a bicycle chained to the bicycle rack.

She recognized it as Per Åström's. For a brief moment, she froze, as if she was hesitating over whether to continue or not. The indecision irritated her. What was stopping her?

She hadn't had time to answer her own question when she heard the sound of jingling keys. She looked up. Even though she had seen his bicycle, she was surprised to see him in person. Per was dressed in his usual athletic jacket over a dark suit. His bag hung on a shoulder strap.

They stood quietly and looked at each other, Jana with her briefcase in hand, he with his key ring.

All that existed was the hustle and bustle of the city.

And the two of them.

He looked tired.

"It's just me," he said, and walked toward his bicycle.

"Yes," she said. "It's just you."

Then she walked past him and dashed up the steps. She didn't look behind her, but she heard him unlock his bike and pedal away. In her mind's eye, she saw him moving along Kungsgatan, biking quickly, braking now and then to look around, maybe to continue along a cross street or in among all of the people that filled the street farther down.

She ran faster now, listening to her steps and noticing that she didn't hear the roar of the city anymore.

Three people gruesomely killed, Philip thought. Johan, Katarina—and Shirin. Shirin had worked as a surgery nurse, that much he knew. He'd read it in the newspapers, and now he began to realize where he'd met her. It was strange he hadn't come up with how he knew her right away.

Johan was a surgeon.

And was he...

This is crazy, Philip thought again. *This can't be about that.* He walked back and forth across the floor in one of the bunk rooms at work.

No, it couldn't be about that. Katarina hadn't been part of it originally. Not then, when the unthinkable happened. Or had she?

He slapped his palm to his forehead, multiple times. Wake up, brain! Think!

He sat down on the bed while he tried to understand how Katarina fit into all of this. But he couldn't piece it together.

He turned his gaze out the window, tried to focus, tried to gain control and return to reality.

But he couldn't.

When Jana Berzelius arrived on the third floor, Henrik and Mia were standing and talking to Gunnar outside the conference room. Mia was wearing jeans and a sweater. Henrik was also in jeans, with a blue-checked flannel shirt and a silver watch around his wrist. Gunnar's hair was uncombed; his face gray and jowly.

Jana greeted them all with a nod and thought multiple times as she approached that she wasn't going to stop, that she would instead continue into the conference room. But just as she passed, she heard Henrik say, "According to our colleagues in Motala, there were three dead and one injured."

"Any motive?" Gunnar asked.

"The witness whom they found injured in the bathroom said it was some sort of dispute."

"That must have been one hell of a dispute," Mia said.

Jana stopped. As she stood there, the same thoughts churned around in her head. Could this actually work? Would the shirt and her phone call really produce the result she was hoping for?

"What are the shelter staff saying?" Gunnar asked.

"They've been having problems there for a while. Some criminal gang has been active at the shelter and has subjected both guests and staff to threats and abuse. Various reports have been filed."

"And what measures have been taken? What have the police done?" Mia said.

"Well, who should they blame?" Gunnar said.

"They probably blame the reorganization," Mia said.

"They can blame whomever they want," Gunnar said, looking at Jana as he rubbed his hand along his stubble. "The media will dig around in everything. Security at the shelter will be under the microscope, and what's more, the whole immigrant question will flare up again. It'll be worst for the shelter staff. They're going to be up to their ears in it. Poor devils."

"It'd be just as well to shut down the shithole even if it is new," Mia said.

"That would be a great quotation for the newspapers," Henrik said.

"But seriously," Mia said. "The municipality uses taxpayer money to provide places for homeless people to sleep, and what do we get as thanks? Oh, right, we have to pay even higher taxes to deal with threats and violence and a little bit of murder, too. What's wrong with people?"

"What's wrong with you?" Henrik said.

"I'm just saying what I think," Mia said. "Maybe you should try it sometime."

They fell silent.

Jana looked at Mia, who had placed her hand on her waist, thinking how Mia always gesticulated as if she needed to reinforce what she was saying. Jana opted to stand still, and now when the irritating silence had fallen over them, she thought she should say something. She really wanted to know if her call had had any impact, if Danilo Peña had been connected with the events, but she couldn't ask about that, of course. Instead she said: "And do we know anything about the murder weapon?"

"I only know that a pistol was involved," Gunnar said. "Who shot whom will be revealed by the investigation. The preliminary investigation has been initiated, but Motala has to take care of all of that. We have other things to deal with."

Henrik looked at his watch.

"Oh, we're supposed to be starting the meeting."

"Well, we'd better go in, then," Gunnar said.

The corners of his mouth twitched slightly from exhaustion. Philip didn't usually feel like his shifts were so interminably long. But now he was standing in the empty locker room, completely wiped out.

And he couldn't escape his thoughts.

Shirin.

Katarina.

And now Johan.

He stood in the stark light from the fluorescent bulbs. The hot metal clicked. He locked his gaze on a speck of dust that danced aimlessly in the air and thought, that's me. A fucking piece of nothing, all alone, fumbling around in a giant emptiness.

Even in his relationship with Lina, his own wife, he felt alone. He hadn't let her in, couldn't let her in, and he wondered how many times during their marriage he had given excuses to avoid revealing things about himself.

Avoid talking in general.

This need to hide his past, his mistake had been doomed to fail. He knew it. It would catch up with him. Everything would catch up with him. Everything always catches up.

And now the only person he wanted to talk with was dead. The only one he *could* talk with because Katarina had been there originally.

He didn't want to burden Lina, and she wouldn't want to listen anyway.

That left only Sandra.

Slowly, he began to walk toward the bunk rooms that lay at the other end of the hallway. He looked at the closed door for a moment and then knocked lightly on it.

"Sandra?"

"What is it, Philip?" she said.

Her voice was sleepy.

"Can we talk?"

"Is it urgent, or can I wake up a little?"

"It's fairly urgent," he said, clearing his throat.

"Come in, then," she said.

He stepped in, making sure the door closed fully behind him, and then stood next to the bed where Sandra was sitting up, supported by her elbow.

"I don't know who else to talk to…" he said. "I'm not paranoid…but you know the murders, the severed limbs…"

"Yes?" she said.

"I knew all three victims."

The last statement he almost whispered.

"What do you mean?"

"I know that it sounds crazy, but it's true."

His eyes darted around, and beads of sweat on his forehead collected into rivulets.

"What do you mean, *knew*?" she said, her voice more awake now.

"We all worked together at one point," he said. "Shirin, Katarina, Johan and I."

"I don't understand," she said, rubbing one eye.

"Katarina and I..." he began, but she interrupted him.

"...had worked in the ambulance together, and I know you know her. But Shirin and this..." Sandra said.

"See...this is crazy, this is crazy," Philip said loudly and began pacing back and forth.

"Calm down now," Sandra said, "and tell me what..."

He stopped, standing still with one hand on his forehead.

"I think I might be the next victim."

"What? Hey, wait a minute, now..."

"It's true," he interrupted. "I might be the next victim. What should I do?"

"What would make you say that? Have you contacted the police?"

"What could I say? They probably won't believe me."

"Why won't they believe you?"

"It's completely fucked-up," he said, turning toward the door.

"Philip, you have to..."

"No, it won't work," he said. "Forget what I said."

He ended the conversation and opened the door, already regretted having said anything at all. Regretted letting Sandra in. It was a bad feeling, and he wanted to get rid of it immediately.

★ ★ ★

On the whiteboard were written three names.

Shirin Norberg, Katarina Vinston and Johan Rehn.

Henrik Levin let his gaze wander from colleague to colleague as he summarized everything they knew up to this point. He looked at Mia, who was thoughtful; at Anneli, who was polishing her glasses; and at Gunnar, who had his arms crossed over his chest.

He turned his head in the other direction. Jana Berzelius. Attentive, as always.

Ola Söderström. New cap today, purple this time.

He continued by describing the murders and knew that he should push aside the images of the mutilated bodies and not show too many emotions. Just keep his gaze forward, be analytical and bite the bullet.

"These murders don't give me any peace," Anneli said when he was done.

"They don't give any of us any peace," Henrik added.

"You've checked on Johan?" Gunnar said.

"Yes. He was married and is the father of two adult children who both live in Stockholm. But the most interesting thing about him is that he was a doctor. Worked as a surgeon."

"At Vrinnevi?"

"At Vrinnevi."

"So all three victims worked there," Gunnar nodded.

"Yes," Henrik said, and saw Jana write something on her legal pad. "And that's where we stand now. We have three victims: a surgery nurse, a paramedic and a surgeon. We have Vrinnevi Hospital, the narcotic Ketalar, a Gigli saw and a scalpel. Everything points to the hospital. But how these are connected and why are still a mystery," he said, throwing his arms up.

"So the hospital is the common denominator?" Gunnar said. "Could the murderer also work there?"

"In which case the next victim is almost guaranteed to be from there," Mia said.

"There won't be a next victim, Mia," Gunnar said severely. The room fell silent.

"I've been digging around in Katarina's history," Ola began. "She was unmarried and lived alone in the house in Borg. Aside from an old boyfriend, a relationship from three years ago, she's been fairly careful about relationships…"

"Careful?" Mia said. "What do you mean by careful?"

Ola sighed.

"Well, how should I say it, then? She hasn't had many relationships, it seems…and I've checked her cell phone conversations, and it's the same thing there. She doesn't seem to have many friends. The only thing that sticks out is that she talked to a Philip Engström fairly frequently, and he's the last person she talked to before she was murdered. He also works as a paramedic."

"Well, Christ!" Mia said.

"What?" Henrik said.

"I was just thinking…" she said, but fell silent as if she wondered if it were too early to complete the thought.

The others sat quietly, looking at her as if they knew she had understood something that they all should have understood right away.

"What is it, Mia?" Gunnar said.

"I just think it's damn remarkable that Philip was called to two of these crime scenes. I don't think he's been completely honest with us."

She paused before continuing: "Specifically, I think he knew Shirin. I got that sense when we interrogated him. I saw him raise his eyebrows when I mentioned her name. It would be interesting to know what size shoe he wears. And if he knows how to use a scalpel."

Gunnar stood up, looking first at Mia and then at Henrik.

"We aren't going to make any assumptions," he said. "But we probably need to have a chat with this Philip Engström. Hear what he has to say about his relationship with Katarina."

"And his relationship with Shirin Norberg," Mia said.

CHAPTER
TWENTY

HENRIK LEVIN LEANED BACK IN THE CHAIR IN HIS OF-fice, took out his cell phone and dialed the number one more time. He had already made three attempts, but hadn't gotten a hold of Philip Engström. When the voice mail picked up, he put down the phone, put his thumbs in the corners of his eyes and closed them tightly. His thoughts were racing, and he wasn't sure what he was looking for. But he knew that he was beyond eager to get in touch with Engström.

He took his phone, dialed the number again and listened to it ringing.

When he looked up, he saw Mia suddenly appear in the doorway. She pushed her hair behind her ears.

"Are you talking to Engström?"

He shook his head.

"You already talked to him, then?"

"Christ, Mia. I'm on the phone."

"I can see that. I'm not blind. But you don't seem to be talking to anyone. So what did Engström say? What did you set up?"

"What?" Henrik said, putting the phone down.

"You and Engström? What did you agree on?"

"He didn't answer."

"Is that why you look so strange?"

"No," he said, meeting her gaze.

"I take it back," she said, "because now you look fucking serious."

They fell silent. He leaned his head back and sighed. Then he glanced up at her and tried to decide if he should continue calling or not. But Mia had already decided for him.

"That isn't going anywhere," she said. "We're going to his house. Where does he live?"

"In the Skarphagen area."

"Good," she said, hitting the doorframe lightly. "Come on, there's nothing to sit around here for."

"I'm coming," he said. "But all of the company cars are taken, so we'll have to take my car."

"Or mine," she said.

"Did you get it fixed?"

"Something like that."

Jana Berzelius put her coffee mug on the table. She sat in the break room at the police station and felt like she wasn't comfortable being anywhere. She didn't want to go back to the Public Prosecution Office because then she risked seeing Per again. And she didn't want to go home, because Danilo was there. And she had absolutely no desire to go to the morgue and be forced to see her mother's pale body again. She didn't want to face the sorrow...had already pushed it out of her mind…had decided that there was no reason to be overly sentimental.

Most of all, she wanted to be left alone in peace.

Slowly, she leaned back in the chair and thought about what a long day it was going to be. Besides the unavoidable visit to the morgue with her father and his nurse, she was going to have to participate in meetings and run-throughs, listening to preliminary reports, prioritizations, witness statements, blood analyses, clues, murder weapons, *et cetera*, *et cetera*. She usually found her work challenging and satisfying, but now all of her thoughts centered on Danilo and on confirming that the shirt she planted had been found so that she could drive him to Södertälje with a somewhat lower risk.

She still didn't know if the police had downgraded their search for him in Norrköping. The police in Motala had begun to investigate what they called "a dispute." But the false witness statement she had called in yesterday evening hadn't seemed to get through. Not all the way to Norrköping, at least. It seemed unusually quiet.

What was their *modus operandi* in Motala? Hadn't they found the hospital shirt? Wouldn't that have provided fresh tracks from the escaped murderer Danilo Peña in the same room that three men had been executed in? But no one seemed to be putting one together with the other.

She pushed her coffee mug away and got up from the table.

She tried to think about something else, but she ended up in the same train of thought. What if this didn't work? What if she never got rid of him?

Anneli Lindgren greeted the administrative assistant Britt Dyberg, who stood in the hallway with a bundle of papers in her arms. She noticed Britt's pink cardigan didn't fit her well at all. It hung over her shoulders and looked many sizes too large.

Anneli, on the other hand, was wearing a light blue sweater and a pair of slim-fitting jeans. Her hair swayed in her ponytail as she continued toward her office.

When she saw the light on in Gunnar's office, she peeked in. She greeted him, and he waved to her without removing his eyes from the computer screen. She continued past, but then she stopped, backed up and went back in.

"Don't have time," Gunnar said when she opened the door completely.

"Yes, you do," she said calmly.

"I'm in the middle of something important," he said.

"Like reading the newspaper?" she said.

"The media is already all over the third murder," he said, looking up at her.

She had hoped to be met by a smile, but that didn't happen. Instead she was met by a tired expression and the question "So what is it you want?"

"I need…to talk to you."

"Not now," he said.

"I just want…to talk."

"Talk, then," he said.

"God, you're in a bad mood," she said.

"One minute," he said. "Our private matters have already taken a minute of our workday, and that time could instead have been used to check fingerprints, footprints or whatever the hell else. We have a lunatic running around loose out there who likes to cut body parts off people, and I want us to find this lunatic damn fast. I don't want any more headlines in the newspapers."

"Of course," she said, hearing how disappointed she sounded.

"And close the door after you."

"Of course," she said again, closing it. Hard.

★ ★ ★

"Here it is," Mia Bolander said. "My new ride."

It took Henrik five seconds to close his mouth, which gaped in astonishment. Mia had been counting.

"You bought a new car? When did you do that?"

"An hour ago, on my lunch break. It was going to cost so much to fix the old one," she said, "that I decided on a new one."

"That sounds reasonable," he said cautiously.

And it *was* fucking reasonable, she thought as she unlocked the car. Every day she'd feel the usual irritation when she saw someone driving a Lexus, BMW or Tesla. Every day, she would see them in roundabouts and at intersections, seeing them as impossible dreams, as missed chances, bad choices and limitations. Almost as if they were a mockery of her and her life.

But that was over now.

Because now she had a red Fiat Lounge.

And it had suddenly made that meaningless feeling disappear. Okay, the men at the pub hadn't paid her enough notice, so she needed to notice herself. Simply speaking, she was worth this far-too-expensive car. She was worth it a hundred times over.

She and Henrik sat next to each other in the soft seats, surrounded by the wonderful new-car smell. She started the engine, pulled slowly out of the parking lot and left the police station behind them. Ten minutes later, they turned in at Engström's house in Skarphagen.

Henrik was three steps ahead of Mia and had already knocked on the door when she caught up.

Engström's wife, Lina, opened the door. Her face showed no trace of makeup. She had freckles and smooth skin and wore her hair in a braid. She was wearing a red sweater and pants that were a bit too large.

She let Henrik introduce himself first.

"And I'm Mia Bolander," Mia said, reaching her hand out. "We're looking for your husband, Philip."

"He's not home."

"No?"

"No, not yet. Did something happen?" Lina asked, staring at them with a worried expression.

"We've been trying to reach him on his cell phone," Henrik said, showing his badge. "We need to talk to him. Do you know where he is?"

"He's probably still at work," Lina said, beginning to breathe more rapidly. "He often can't answer his phone. He's a paramedic."

Mia surveyed the hallway, the hat rack with a cap and a scarf, the hangers with a jean jacket and a leather coat. And a shoe rack.

She nodded toward it, and Henrik also noticed what was sitting there.

A pair of Nikes.

"Whose shoes are those?" he said, pointing.

Lina turned around.

"Philip's," she said.

"What size are they?"

"Nine and a half, ten, something like that," she said, picking up one of the shoes.

Henrik exchanged a quick glance with Mia.

"We're going to need to take those with us," he said then.

"Why is that?"

"A print from that type of shoe was found at a crime scene."

"A crime scene? But what would Philip have to do with that?"

Mia thought that was a reasonable question to ask, but she didn't intend to answer it.

"Can we bother you for a bag?" she said instead.

"Yes…" Lina said, confused, and disappeared into the kitchen. She returned with a white plastic bag.

"But what did he do?" she said as Henrik put the shoes in the bag.

Mia looked at Henrik.

"We're just anxious to get a hold of him," he said. "Would it be okay if we looked around the house for a moment?"

"Of course," she said.

Henrik and Mia went into the living room, looked at the sofa and blanket, at the flickering television, at the books lying in stacks, the laptop computer on a table.

They also saw leftover take-out food cartons and candy wrappers.

"I'm sorry," Lina said. "It's a bit messy. I'm studying for an exam, that's why it looks like this."

"What type of exam?" Mia asked.

"I'm going to become a teacher."

Mia looked at Lina as she stood under the dim light fixture. In some way, the light and shadows brought out her wrinkles, Mia thought. Even the ones that were almost invisible stuck out.

"Poor thing," Mia mumbled, thinking about both her choice of career and her wrinkles. Then she turned her face away, looked into the bedroom at the unmade bed and the rectangular picture that depicted a white-sand beach and clear blue sea.

In the window in front of the closed Venetian blinds stood a plastic fern.

"What sort of car do you have?" she asked.

"An Audi. Why?"

Mia turned around quickly, as if the words came out of Lina's mouth like a whip.

"What model?" she asked.

"Hmm, what is it…"

Lina whispered to herself as Mia and Henrik held their breath.

"I think we have an Audi A5."

Mia examined Lina, looked watchfully at her and saw that she was a bit heavy in her movements, hesitant in front of them in some way.

"Where is the car?" Mia said.

"Philip took it to work," she said, gesturing with her hand and making the wedding ring on her finger glitter in the light from the ceiling lamp. "He always does."

"How long have you been married?" Mia said.

"In July, it'll be exactly three years."

"Three years?"

"Yes."

"Where did you get married?"

"In Saint Anna's Archipelago."

Mia gave Henrik a knowing glance.

"Has Philip seemed strange recently?" Henrik asked as he opened the door to the bathroom, looked in, noted the empty toilet paper rolls on the floor, and continued to the kitchen.

"No."

"He hasn't shown any signs of stress or trouble sleeping?"

"No."

She stared at him nervously.

"So you don't think he's been affected by his colleague Katarina Vinston's death?" Mia tested.

"Katarina Vinston?" Lina said, gasping.

"Yes?" Mia said.

"That…oh my god…is she dead?"

"Philip hasn't told you?"

"No, but wasn't he with her the other day?"

Mia raised her eyes, looked at Henrik and back at Lina.

"What did you say?"

"He was at her house, he was there. Dear lord…dead?"

"Did you know her?"

"No, I didn't know her. I knew who she was. I've met her a few times, in town and such, but we just said hi to each other. But she and Philip were fairly good friends, I think."

"You think?"

"I don't know…they worked together."

"Are you okay? You look pale."

Lina supported herself with her hand on the white refrigerator door. "The thought that she and Philip…"

"You think they had something together?" Mia asked.

"No, absolutely not," Lina said, shaking her head indignantly. "They couldn't. They just couldn't. It just couldn't be."

"Why not?"

"Because I'm pregnant."

CHAPTER
TWENTY-ONE

SHE STARED INTO THE COLD-STORAGE ROOM OF THE Vrinnevi Hospital morgue at the stainless steel drawers and wondered how many bodies lay behind them waiting to be delivered to their graves. Then Jana walked slowly down the hall toward the visitation room.

She could hear someone approaching her from behind. When she turned around, she saw a young man with long blond hair walking toward her. He was wearing a white coat and white pants. He shook her hand and looked at her almost shyly.

"I'm Sören Erixson," he said. "Welcome."

"Thank you," Jana said.

"There will be two of you?"

"My father is on his way with his caregiver, I'm sure."

"You're welcome to go into the visitation room now," he said, "if you feel ready."

"I don't know if..."

She fell silent, looked toward the door to the room and hesitated about going in. A few seconds passed as she attempted to compose herself, then she cleared her throat and opened the door. She stood still with her hand still on the door handle as she let her gaze wander over the heavy drapes, sofa and the burning candles in the black, three-armed candelabra. She looked at the chairs and the painting hanging on the wall. Finally, her gaze rested on the gurney covered in linens that stood in the middle of the room.

She stepped in, leaving the door open, and stood a few yards away from her mother, who lay there with her eyes closed and her hands folded peacefully over her chest. Her hair was combed and her lips looked moist, probably from lip gloss or Vaseline.

Jana walked toward her, reaching out her hand and holding it over her mother's mouth, as if she were waiting to feel the tickling of her mother's breath that she used to look for when she was younger.

She heard steps in the hallway through the open door, so she quickly pulled her hand away. It was then that she again noticed the slight bruise marks on her mother's nostrils.

She took a careful step closer and leaned in to examine her mother's face more clearly. Her gaze shifted from her mother's nose to her mouth, and then she gently lifted her mother's upper lip and looked even more closely. Could the bruise marks really come from the normal course of CPR? She wasn't really sure now.

Quickly, Jana pulled out her cell phone and snapped a few pictures before putting her phone back in her jacket pocket and then lifted her mother's sweater to check her stomach. She searched for more marks, but didn't find any.

Before the others reached the door, she looked at her mother's right arm, letting her eyes sweep from the upper part past her elbow to her hand and nails.

One of her nails appeared broken off.

She took her mother's hand into her own and felt its chill and lifelessness. Under all of her nails she could see a thin layer of dirt. Or was it dried blood?

She broke off a piece of a nail that was cracked, took a tissue from her pocket and placed the nail in it and put it away. Then stepped backward from the gurney and stood still as Sören Erixson came into the room with Elin Ronander pushing her father in his wheelchair.

Jana met Elin's gaze and could read the sorrow in her face. She listened to Sören's words of condolences, saying that it was fully normal to stay in the room for a long time to say goodbye, as she observed her father's calm, attentive face.

"Now I'll leave you in peace," Sören said, leaving the room.

Elin pushed the wheelchair to the opposite side of the bed until Father held up a hand to show that he didn't want to move any closer. She rested a hand gently on his shoulder and whispered, "I'll wait outside." Then she closed the door behind her. The flames from the candles flickered, but after that, the room was completely still. An almost unpleasant silence filled the room.

Jana didn't move. She stood silently, her gaze on her father. His face was suddenly strangely pale. Slowly, he lifted his gaze to her, and there was something different in his eyes. They were bottomless.

"We...we met n," he said, "to a wondrful... Now I dnt rember what they playd, Beethovn, I thnk..."

She could barely understand what he said. She looked at him, saw his serious gaze, how he concentrated to control every twitching nerve, every tremble, as he talked.

"I don know f you can unnerstan dit," he said. "But I've ben proud tht she nvr wanted fr anything."

He carefully touched Mother's thin arm as he whimpered, a moaning sound. It came from deep within, as if he only at that moment understood that she was truly dead.

"Margaretha…"

He fought to bring his hands to his face and cried quietly.

Jana moved back and felt an urge to leave the room immediately.

"We're done here, aren't we," she said.

"No," he said, irritated, and rubbed his trembling hands over his face in an attempt to wipe the tears from his eyes.

"It wasn't a question," Jana said. "I have a meeting to get to."

"Go, then," he said.

"I'll see you at the funeral," she said, walking quickly across the room. She turned around in the doorway.

"I almost forgot. I want you to order the flowers for the funeral."

"Flwrs?" he said.

"You know what kind she liked, right?"

He was silent.

The realization of how little he actually knew about Mother made her sick. She swallowed multiple times, repressing her anger toward him.

"Peonies," she said sharply and left the room.

Philip wanted to be left alone with his thoughts, felt pursued by them. He was sweaty, trembling and tired.

I'm not crazy, he thought as he stepped into the empty crew lounge. *It's just a part of me that has given way, burst at the seams.*

He sank onto the sofa and thought about Sandra Gustafsson. He regretted having dragged her into his problems. She would only see it as an invitation and continue with her nagging questions—questions he couldn't stand. Why had he confided in her?

As he rested his feet on the table, his cell phone rang again. It had been ringing all fucking day, and he had just decided to let it ring when he realized that at least this time it was a number he recognized. He answered.

"You lied again," she said. "I don't get how you can stand..."

"Wait a minute, Lina," he said, looking over his shoulder. "I'm just going to..."

"Just what?"

"Get out of here. I'm not in a good place for talking."

He left the lounge and went into the locker room, checked that he was the only one there and sat down on the bench in front of the lockers.

"What did I lie about now?" he said.

"As if you don't know?" she said. "Katarina is dead and you knew it, didn't you?"

Philip closed his eyes. It took a moment before he answered.

"Yes."

"You knew it," she said, "but you didn't say anything to me?"

"I forgot."

"How could you forget that?"

"I don't know."

"Where are you now?"

"At work?"

"Are you sure?"

Philip opened his eyes and leaned back, feeling the cold locker door through the fabric of his shirt.

"Why would I lie about that?" he said.

"You lie about absolutely everything else," she said.

"No, I don't."

"You lied that you'd been at work," she said. "But in reality you were at Katarina's."

"That's true," he said.

"You're an idiot."

"That's also true."

Lina was quiet. After a moment, he heard her take a deep breath.

"Were you having an affair?" she said.

"What sort of question is that?" he said. "I've told you no. Don't you believe me?"

"I do, but the police don't. They're probably on their way to you now."

"Here?"

"Yes. You didn't answer your cell phone. They asked a bunch of questions about Katarina, but I said it would be better if they talked to you. They took your shoes, too, and they asked what sort of car we have. What did you do, Philip? Did you kill Katarina?"

"Fuck!"

He stood up and raked his hand through his short hair. He felt the sweat break out in his armpits.

"Philip!" he heard Lina say, but he didn't answer. He put down his phone, already lost in thought.

It was an absurd idea, but he still couldn't let go of it: he wasn't only the murderer's next victim; he was also suspected of murder.

What the hell was going on?

The room was spinning, he felt something closing in on him, and he heard a voice. It nagged him.

They think it's you.

Shirin, Katarina and Johan.

He was having a hard time breathing. He tried to focus his gaze, searched for the exit.

They're coming to take me in, he thought before putting his phone in his pocket and hurrying out of the locker room.

"Can I help you?"

A mustached man in his thirties looked questioningly at Detective Chief Inspector Henrik Levin and Detective Inspector Mia Bolander, who had just walked into the ambulance station in Norrköping.

"We're looking for Philip Engström," Mia said.

"I just saw him in the locker room. You can check there."

"And that is…?"

"One floor up, to the right."

"Thanks."

Henrik and Mia walked between two ambulances, past a room intended for outerwear and shoes, and continued up the steps to the second floor.

Three men and two women were sitting around a table discussing vacations, but they fell silent when Henrik and Mia stepped in.

"We're here to talk to Philip Engström," Henrik said after introducing himself and Mia.

"Sandra, do you know where Philip is?" one of the girls asked, nodding expectantly toward a woman wearing work clothes who was standing in the kitchen. She had green eyes, and Mia remembered her from the questioning.

"Sandra Gustafsson, right?"

"Yes," she said.

"Do you know where your colleague is?"

"He got sick suddenly and just left for home. Said it was something with his stomach. He looked really pale."

"That's too bad," Mia said, "but before we go, do you know if your boss, Eva Holmgren, is here?"

"She was just in her office," Sandra said. "Her office is down the hallway to the right. I can show you."

"Thanks."

Henrik and Mia followed her.

"Would it be possible to have a few words with you after we've talked to your boss?" Henrik said when they stopped outside Eva's room.

"If I'm still here," she said. "It might be that we're out on a call. But you can definitely call me if there's anything."

Philip walked quickly out of the ambulance station. His cell phone rang and rang, but he didn't feel like answering. He continued walking forward and only stopped when he'd gone a good distance.

What was he going to do? Where was he going?

He was having difficulty collecting his thoughts, and his heart was pounding in his chest.

At the entrance to a footpath, he turned off and started to run straight through an apartment complex. He jumped over a low fence, walked through a sandbox and continued to run diagonally across a soccer field.

I shouldn't be running, he thought. *People will notice me and begin to wonder.*

But he couldn't stop. His legs were moving as if of their own accord.

When he got to Vilbergen Center a few kilometers away, he was having a hard time breathing and slowed down. He went as slowly as he could, keeping to the side of the square and trying to appear as normal as possible. Yet he felt all eyes were on him. And only then did he realize he was still in his work clothes.

Everyone is looking at me, he thought.

The panic welled up inside him, and he began running again.

★ ★ ★

"I assume you'd like to speak privately," Eva Holmgren said, closing the door to her office. "Please sit."

The office was small, light and Spartan. No flowerpot in the window, but there were nicely framed pictures of children, probably grandchildren, Mia Bolander guessed.

"You have some further questions about one of our staff members?" Eva said, clasping her hands and laying them in her lap.

"Philip Engström," Henrik said.

"Philip…" she said, pushing a lock of hair behind her ear. "He has worked with us for many years."

"Can you tell us about him?"

Eva took a deep breath, as if she wanted to have time to think before answering.

"Philip is an ambitious person who likes working hard," she said. "He is punctual, professional and engaged in his work."

"Sounds like a perfect employee," Mia mumbled.

"No one is perfect. Even Philip has his faults."

"Such as?"

Eva took yet another breath, more like a sigh this time.

"Philip has been having a fairly rough time as of late. Our staff must be ready for anything when they go out on a call. It might be a car accident, fire, murder, suicide, suicide attempt, rape, illness, drowning and so on. The list goes on and on. And in these situations, you must assume that the person who comes to the rescue will be able to work under circumstances the patient can't handle themselves, not only medically, but also the situation itself and everything related to it."

"I understand," Henrik said.

"These work conditions are tough. Our staff experience

things daily that many others don't experience during a whole lifetime, such as severed limbs, dead bodies, decay... It also doesn't have to be the horrible sight with a lot of blood and serious injuries. It might be a loved one standing and screaming in their ear, 'Do something! Do something!'"

Eva leaned forward and picked up a pen, which she twirled around her fingers.

"I'm saying this so you understand that this is about extreme pressure. At the same time as we must provide physical care, we also must comfort grieving loved ones. You can't even imagine how difficult it is to guess exactly how a person is going to react to all of this. Some dare to show what they're feeling, others don't seem to be bothered at all. It can also vary from call to call. And when we've finished a call, we're supposed to just deal with our own feelings. It's impossible to get used to the seriously ill, dying and dead."

"We know," Mia said.

"I know that you know, but I just want to...I don't know... clarify it, maybe. And now we've been hit by a terrible death ourselves...it wears on the staff, it really does..."

"But what do you do to manage these feelings?" Henrik asked.

"We talk to each other," Eva said, putting the pen down. "We have something called 'peer support' here. Peer support requires that people feel they can trust each other, which I think the vast majority of our staff does. They spend many hours at the station in between calls. They eat, work out and sleep together, and because of that, a particular togetherness is formed in the group. A good partner is ninety-nine percent of the job. I know that Philip and Katarina worked really well together. They were a tight-knit team."

"So Philip and Katarina worked together," Henrik said.

"I don't remember you saying that when we talked on the phone."

"I hardly remember what I said. This thing with Katarina, it's so…terrible. It's incomprehensible. But yes, they worked together a lot."

"So how did Philip react to Katarina's death?" Henrik said.

"I don't think it has really sunk in yet for him…"

"What do you mean?"

"As you know, even before the event with Katarina, he had been witness to a very unpleasant call. He was first on the scene at the murder of the surgery nurse who has been featured in the newspapers. Additionally, he was first on the scene at the murder of the surgeon… Considering everything that has happened, he has, if I can be honest, hardly shown any emotion at all."

"And what do you think about that?" Henrik said.

"I've offered him a few days leave, but he refused. So actually, I'm not thinking about it much right now. Many times I've seen staff who consciously distance themselves from what they're thinking and feeling. It's a strategy that largely comes from experience and number of years in this career."

"You mean that you get desensitized?" Mia said.

"Don't you?"

They fell silent. Mia opened her mouth, but it was Henrik who answered.

"As in all lines of work, we gather experiences that we always carry with us," he said. "But certain images you never forget…"

"Yes, true," Eva said. "Even if the staff talk about it and work through the situations they've experienced, these images always remain. We carry them with us, unfortunately, like a little backpack. The older you are and the more you've worked, the larger the backpack you have to carry."

"But sometimes it must get to be too much," Mia said.

"Absolutely," Eva said. "It does. We've obviously had staff who haven't worked for more than a couple of years, who couldn't handle the physical and psychological stress of this job. We've seen personality changes and dealt with all sorts of drug abuse. We are constantly watching our staff and help them in any way we can."

Henrik raked his hand through his hair. "We're hoping to have a chat with Philip," he said, "but he seems to be sick?"

"Yes," Eva said with a troubled expression. "He is...he's seldom sick, but I can imagine it's a reaction to recent events."

"So you don't think it's odd that he is sick today of all days?"

"No, why would I think that? It must be almost healthy to react to the loss of a colleague in some way? Not to mention he is entitled to be sick." Eva nodded.

"You spoke earlier of the fact that Philip doesn't usually show any emotions," Henrik said, turning his gaze to Eva. "Has he ever overdone it?"

"What do you mean?"

"Well, to the point that he couldn't take it, that it became too much?"

"No, not from what I know. Philip is a very good employee. But he's human."

"What do you mean by that?"

"I don't know what I am trying to say by that, really. It's maybe just my way of excusing Philip."

"For what?" Mia said.

"It's obvious that those of us in health care also make an occasional mistake," Eva said.

"What did he do?"

"I don't know if I can say anything. I'm bound by professional secrecy."

"Well, then I'll inform you," Henrik said, "that our query is regarding an ongoing investigation."

"That's what I assumed...but I don't want to muddle up the investigation in any way with outdated information."

"We don't think you will."

Eva was quiet for a moment.

"As I said before, we all have our own tools for coping with stressful events in our lives. Many turn to alcohol."

"And Philip? Does he turn to something?"

"I stumbled upon his pill use once."

"At work?"

"Yes. But it was five years ago, when he'd just started. He had left a pack of pills in one of the bathrooms. We had a conversation about it, and ever since then, I haven't had any reason to suspect him. But now, with you sitting here in front of me, of course I'm beginning to wonder. How nervous should I be for him?"

She sat at a table at a restaurant called Fresh Market and waited for the rice noodle salad she had ordered. Jana looked forward to being alone, in peace and quiet.

She took out her cell phone and looked closely at the pictures of her mother that she'd taken at the morgue. She lingered a long time on what might be bruises on her mother's nose, then flipped to the photos of her mother's upper lip before dialing the number to the crime lab.

"Björn Ahlmann speaking."

"Hi, Björn, this is Jana," she said. "I'd like to talk to you."

"Not about Johan Rehn, I hope. I haven't had the chance to perform the autopsy on Johan Rehn's body yet..."

"No, it's something else."

"Tell me."

She fell silent, listening to the murmuring of others around her, the clinking of silverware on china, then suddenly she heard herself saying: "What conclusion would you draw if you saw bruises on the nose of a dead body?"

"Child or adult?"

"Adult," Jana said. "An older woman."

She swallowed and looked around to confirm that no one was eavesdropping.

A man came in through the door and walked clumsily over the floor toward a girl who was slim and short—she didn't even reach his chest. The girl gave him a quick hug, and he smiled at her, kissing her on the head.

"As you know, bruises and other signs of violence can show up many hours after the time of death," Ahlmann said.

"I know," she said, feeling a chill spread through her body.

"But it's difficult to draw a conclusion off the cuff like this, without knowing what we're talking about," he said. "You have to give me something more to go on. Are the bruising marks symmetrical? Do they run together? Do they cover the whole nose, or just parts of it?"

"The woman has bruising on the wings of her nose and hemorrhaging on the inside of her upper lip."

She heard Ahlmann breathing, followed by a long silence. The silence made her heart begin pounding.

"The way you describe it…" he began.

"Yes?"

"It could be from an attempt at resuscitation. But it sounds as if they are the type of injuries that might have arisen if someone wanted to obstruct the breathing passages, in other words, as if the person had been smothered."

Two people remained in the crew lounge after Henrik Levin and Mia Bolander left their meeting with Eva Holmgren. To their disappointment, neither of them was Sandra Gustafsson. They arrived at Mia's car and got in. Henrik pulled out his cell phone.

"I'm going to try Philip again," he said, dialing the number and listening to it ring.

"Fucking suspicious that he's not answering," Mia said when Henrik shook his head.

He dialed the number to Philip's wife instead.

"This is Lina."

Her voice was soft, almost a whisper.

"Hello, this is Detective Chief Inspector Henrik Levin again. I'm wondering if Philip has come home."

"No, he's still at work, like I said."

"They said that he's on his way home."

"Why would that be?"

"He was feeling sick, they said."

"What?"

"So you don't know?"

"No, I haven't talked to him."

"Can you ask him to call us when he comes home? We're very anxious to get a hold of him."

"Of course…"

"Thanks."

Henrik ended the conversation and looked straight ahead. They had looked for Philip Engström at home, at work, and called him multiple times. They had talked with his wife and his boss and now knew a little more about him, but Henrik still couldn't say that anything had actually become clearer. Quite the opposite, in fact.

He was just about to ask Mia to start the car when he caught sight of it.

"The Audi A5," Henrik said, opening the passenger door.

"Where are you going?" Mia called after him.

But he had already started over the parking lot.

★ ★ ★

She had ended the conversation with Björn without saying goodbye. Jana Berzelius was in shock and was now trying to grasp the thoughts whirling around in her head.

Smothered? Could that be possible?

"Here you go, one rice noodle salad," the waitress said. She barely noticed the woman placing the plate on the table in front of her.

Jana considered asking for a take-out container. But instead, she sat there, trying to collect herself, her gaze unfocused on the food for a long time.

Smothered!

Chief physician Eliasson, an acquaintance of her father's, had told her that her mother had died a natural death from a heart attack. If a clinical autopsy were required for cases of natural death, the bruising would probably have been found earlier, and the cause of death would have been different. Now, she was the only one who knew.

As Margaretha's daughter, she could request an autopsy. But what would that lead to? *Only problems*, she thought. The police would start an investigation, begin looking at her and her father in detail, asking questions and digging in the past.

She didn't want to involve the police. But she wanted to know what had exactly happened and why.

She picked up her fork and slowly twirled the noodles as she formulated her thoughts. Mother had been home alone when she'd had the heart attack. Father had been at the rehabilitation center in Örebro with Elin, and even if he'd been home, it wouldn't have been physically possible for him to smother her. Not in his current condition, at least. But could someone have smothered her in order to get to Father? Did all this have to do with his role in the Policegate scandal?

Mother had called the ambulance herself in the middle of

the night, and it had come quickly. She didn't want to disturb Karl. Despite this, they couldn't save her. Had she already been dead when the ambulance arrived?

No, she thought. If Mother had been dead, the ambulance personnel wouldn't have taken her body; they would've contacted the police.

So what had actually happened between the time they picked her up in Lindö and when they arrived at Vrinnevi Hospital? Only the ambulance paramedics could answer that. But who were they?

Henrik Levin was confused. He stood facing four cars parked in a row and thought how there were even more questions surrounding Philip Engström now. He had quickly pulled out his phone and dialed Gunnar's number before Mia even caught up with him.

"Yes, Henrik?" Gunnar Öhrn sounded stressed on the other end of the line.

Henrik spoke as quietly as he could even though no one besides Mia was nearby. Mia kept her eye on him, her arms crossed over her chest.

"Things are taking shape," Henrik said. "We found a pair of shoes at Philip's house, Nikes, size nine and a half."

"So, it could have been Philip who was walking around in Katarina's yard?"

"Yes, with great probability...because we've now also discovered that it was Philip's wedding band that we found in her bedroom."

"Has he said why?"

"That's just it. We can't get a hold of him. He isn't answering his cell phone, and he's not at home or at work."

"But where could he be, then?" Gunnar said.

"Per his coworkers, he got sick and was heading home."

"Okay."

"There's just one problem," Henrik began, looking at the sign that said the parking spaces were only for staff. On the asphalt under the sign lay an ice-cream wrapper and a receipt.

"Tell me," Gunnar said impatiently.

"His car is still in the parking lot outside the ambulance station."

"Are you sure?"

"I'm standing in front of it right now. An Audi A5. Blue metallic paint."

"An Audi A5," Gunnar repeated. "So he could just as well still be there?"

"Yes, or he left work some other way. What should we do?"

"And no one knows where he is?"

"No," Henrik said, watching a gust of wind that moved across the asphalt and made the wrapper whirl up into the air. "Maybe Philip chose to leave the car because he didn't feel well. Maybe he took the bus. Or did he suspect something?"

"Do we have a reason to think that he is purposely avoiding us?" Gunnar said.

"In which case, he becomes more and more interesting to the investigation," Henrik said.

"You mean more and more suspicious?" Gunnar said.

"In short, yes," Henrik said. "We need to get a hold of him."

"So then," Gunnar said. "I suggest that we find him as quickly as possible. Have the uniformed patrols been informed? And the on-duty officers?"

"Not yet. We wanted to know what you thought first."

"What I thought? I just told you what I thought. Let's get out there and find him."

He sat completely still with his gaze fixed on a single birch tree. It was a straggly, wild little birch tree that had fought its way up beside the other trees in the small grove. The tree was twisted from its struggle for light and air, first in one direction, then in the other. A few feet above the ground someone had carved something into its bark. Two letters, maybe?

With shaking hands, Philip Engström pulled out his cell phone and saw that he had missed multiple calls from the same unfamiliar number again. Lina had called, too.

He returned her call, and heard her pick up after three rings.

"You just hung up before," she said. "What are you doing?"

"I've done something stupid," he said.

"What did you do?"

He could almost see her in his mind's eye, standing there with her hand in front of her mouth.

"I'm hiding. The police are looking for me, and I think I'm being hunted by a murderer..."

She gasped.

"What are you talking about?" she said.

"I don't know."

"What do you mean, you don't know? I'm in a state of total panic over this. Where are you now?"

"Where am I?" he said. And what the hell should he say? That he was hiding behind a tree, in a grove, near a soccer field? It sounded too dumb.

"I ran because I didn't know what I should say," he began. "It's too much, Lina... I don't know what I should do anymore. I've made a mistake, I know it. I was stupid and I lied, and you're right, you don't know everything about me, and I should have told you the truth from the beginning, but I just couldn't, I just couldn't, and now it's too late, and... goddamn it!"

"What did you do? Tell me, please, Philip!"

"There's nothing to say," he said.

"There's lots to say if you just start talking, but you never want to talk!"

"It's not so easy…"

"Do you know that I go around all the time wondering whom I'm married to? I have no idea who you are anymore, Philip. You never tell me anything. And now this…"

"I understand that you're angry, but…"

"Don't say you're sorry," she said.

"Sorry," he said. "I make so many mistakes all the time."

"But I'm the one who made the biggest mistake by getting pregnant with you."

Philip blinked hard, as if he was having a hard time understanding what she had just said.

"You're pregnant?" he said.

"Yes."

"Really?"

"Yes."

"And you haven't said anything?"

"I took the test this morning after you'd gone to work."

She heard only silence.

"You're not going to say anything?" she said, irritated now.

"What should I say?"

"I don't know, but how about that it's fantastic, magnificent, wonderful news?"

"But it *is* completely fantastic," he said, drawing a deep breath.

"It doesn't sound like you think so."

"I *do* think so. But the timing is all wrong. You don't understand…and I need to tell you…"

He fell silent again. He heard her breathing and leaned his head back, looked at the birch tree in front of him for a long time. He looked at the carving, the two letters, and only now did he realize what they were.

Two halves of a heart. A heart broken in two.

"Lina?" he said.

"Yes?"

"Don't hang up. Stay with me."

CHAPTER
TWENTY-TWO

HENRIK LEVIN WAS BACK IN HIS OFFICE AT THE PO-
lice station. He hung up his jacket and wondered where the day
had gone. It was already late afternoon. Gunnar had called a
meeting that was to begin in five minutes, and Henrik wanted
to talk to the paramedic Sandra Gustafsson before then.

She answered on the second ring.

"This is Detective Chief Inspector Henrik Levin. Can you
talk?"

"Yes," she said. "I may have to hang up if there's a call. But
how can I help you?"

"I need to talk to you again," he said, "about your colleague, Philip Engström."

"Have you gotten a hold of him?"

"No, he wasn't home. Do you know where he might be?"

"He said that he was going to go home, but if he's not there,
I don't know where he could be."

"This is how it is," Henrik said, looking at the clock, which showed there were three minutes left before his meeting, "we're investigating the murder of another one of your colleagues, Katarina Vinston. We've gone through her cell phone and saw that she and Philip have had quite a bit of contact between shifts. Do you know what sort of relationship he had with Katarina?"

"They almost always worked together," Sandra said. "And I know that they're friends."

"Could they have had a…romantic relationship?"

"That's possible, of course. But I doubt it."

"Why is that?"

"Well, first, he is married. And besides, I would say that Katarina is a fairly sensitive person, and Philip simply isn't…"

Sandra fell silent.

"I'm not following," Henrik said.

"Well, it's a little difficult to get close to him. I think most would say that he's a…well, a little bit aloof, a bit cocky."

"And is he?"

"He likes to be in charge, to be right all the time and stuff like that. Even when he's wrong."

She laughed a little.

"I remember once when we were playing cards with another coworker, I think it was poker, and we'd bet something silly, like three dollars each. Philip lost the pot, got really upset and accused our coworker of cheating. Then he threw his cards on the floor, left the room, and went and lay down in one of the bunk rooms. I don't think I ever saw him play poker again."

"Has he always been like that?"

"I think so…"

"How long have you worked with him?"

"Almost a year," she said. "But we hang out outside of work, too. Or rather, I hang out with his wife."

"You know her, too?"

"Yes. We met at a staff party."

Henrik looked at the clock again.

"Both you and Philip were called to *two* crime scenes this past week."

"Yes, unfortunately. You never know what's going to be waiting for you when you go out on a call, but I don't think I've ever seen or will see anything like this week. That thing with the hands, and, well…ugh. You have to shut yourself off, just do your work, not think about the person who's been injured. But I think that was easier for me than it was for Philip."

"Why is that?"

"He knew all of them, of course."

"Wait a minute, now," Henrik said. "All of them? Who do you mean?"

"Well…"

Sandra took a deep breath as if to summon all of her strength before she continued.

"…he knew all of the victims. I guess he'd worked with all of them."

The line went silent.

Henrik wrinkled his brow.

"And by 'all,' you mean Shirin, Katarina and Johan?" he said.

"Yes," she said.

"How do you know that?"

"He told me himself. Before he went home today, actually."

Henrik focused his gaze on a notebook that lay on the desk. He felt his heart pounding faster. It was amazing, he thought, how things began to create a pattern.

"How had he met them, do you know?"

"At work, as I said...but he was upset this morning when he told me and..."

She stopped.

"...he isn't usually, but lately..."

"Yes?"

"I don't know if this is right. But he has actually been...a little different."

"What do you mean?"

"He's stressed out. Angry, things like that. Has a hard time focusing and is always tired."

"Do you know why?"

"I don't think I should be answering all these questions, actually," Sandra said. "Even if I wanted to. It'd be better if you talked with Philip yourself."

"I think it's best if you say what you're thinking," Henrik said. "It's important."

"Okay," Sandra said. "I've seen that he, or rather, I think that he's taking pills."

Henrik didn't say anything, instead letting her continue.

"It's gone so far that he has a hard time focusing on his work," she said. "He even fell asleep on a call last week. I think it was Wednesday. We were going to get a patient in Lindö who'd had a heart attack, and it was impossible to wake Philip up in the ambulance. I tried multiple times and finally..."

"And the patient?" Henrik said.

"She didn't make it."

"Who was it?"

"I don't remember, it was an older woman..."

His thoughts were racing.

"I'm glad you told me all of this," he said.

"Of course," Sandra said.

"Thank you very much. We may be in touch with you again," Henrik said, standing up.

The meeting was just about to begin.

★ ★ ★

She listened to the chairs scraping against the floor. While Henrik, Mia, Ola and Anneli took their places around the table, Jana looked out the window toward the horizon at the blue sky.

"Everyone here?" Gunnar said, getting multiple nods in response. He closed the door and sat in his chair.

"Well, then," he said. "Henrik, go ahead."

"Recently," Henrik said, "we've found out that Katarina Vinston and Philip Engström were in contact via cell phone before she was murdered. They were coworkers but, as it seems, also friends outside of work. We've been trying to contact Philip all day, but he's missing. No one knows where he is, neither his wife nor his colleagues. We've contacted patrol, and they're keeping their eye out for him right now."

"But why would he be hiding?" Ola said. "Any theories?"

"It's damn mystifying, I agree," Mia said. "His boss seems overly pleased with him. She called him professional and engaged, but she also said that he used drugs…"

"He takes pills," Henrik filled in.

"So he's addicted to some sort of medication?" Gunnar said.

"It seems that way," Mia said. "His boss happened upon him taking them a long time ago, anyway."

"Yes," Henrik said, "and Philip's paramedic colleague Sandra Gustafsson says he's still using some sort of drug."

Mia gave him a wondering look. "When did you talk to her?"

"I'll get back to that," Henrik said.

"But why are we focusing on this particular paramedic?" Jana said.

"Mainly because he's avoiding us," Henrik said. "He's also the last person who talked to Katarina, as far as we know. We found footprints outside Katarina's house, prints from a pair of Nikes in size nine and a half. Then we found the same type of shoes at Philip's house. We're having them analyzed now and hope that can go quickly. Also Katarina's neighbor saw an Audi A5, blue metallic paint, outside Katarina's house the same day she was murdered. Philip owns that exact same make, model and color of car."

Jana leaned back, thinking.

"But if Katarina and Philip had a romantic relationship, is it so strange that his footprints or his car would be seen at her house?" she said.

"That's true," Henrik said. "But then why would the footprint be in the flower bed right under a window? And what was he doing at her house the same day as she was murdered?"

"And what about the wedding ring?" Mia said. "Did he take it off when he was going to murder her or when they were going to roll around between the sheets?"

"If we believe their coworkers, they were nothing more than friends," Henrik clarified.

"But friends can also fuck," Mia said. "And friends can also fight. Maybe Katarina wanted him to get divorced, and so that Lina wouldn't find out he'd been unfaithful, he murdered Katarina?"

"By cutting her tongue out?" Henrik said skeptically.

"I'm just trying to find a fucking motive," Mia said.

"That's right," Gunnar said. "We're asking questions in the wrong order. We've been talking about who and how, but not *why.*"

"Okay, okay," Henrik said, "but just before this meeting, I talked with Sandra, and what really confirms my suspicions about Philip is that he actually knew all three victims, including Shirin and Johan Rehn."

"I knew it!" Mia exclaimed.

"According to Sandra, all four of them worked together, but I'm still not sure where that was."

Mia suddenly looked a little confused.

"But how does she know that? Isn't it a little suspicious that he'd tell her he knew all three victims? If he's guilty, wouldn't it be smarter to stay quiet about something like that?"

"And to follow up on what Gunnar just said, what would his motive be?" Jana said.

"I'm wondering about that, too," Henrik said. "And is it probable in general that Philip went to the victims' homes, murdered them, and then arrived in an ambulance and tried to save their lives?"

"Maybe that's a part of the plan," Mia said.

"If we could just get a hold of him, so much would become clearer," Henrik said. "But Sandra also said that Philip has been acting strange lately, that he's been stressed out, angry, has had a hard time focusing. She said he even fell asleep during a call and possibly contributed to the death of a woman having a heart attack a little less than a week ago."

"What?"

Jana looked up.

"Philip Engström fell asleep during a call to Lindö, which caused a delay in the ambulance getting to an older woman in time who apparently had had a heart attack death..."

"To Lindö?" Jana said. "When exactly did this happen? On Wednesday?"

Henrik looked down at his papers.

"Hmm," he said. "Yes, it was Wednesday."

Jana felt her body tremble.

"How do you know that he fell asleep?" she said.

"The colleague Sandra told me, as I said."

"So it was just the two of them in the ambulance?"

"Yes."

Jana looked out through the window again. The cloud had disappeared; only the blue sky remained.

"Do you have Sandra's number?" she asked quietly. "I'd like to have a word with her."

"I can call her again if there's anything you have questions about."

"I'd rather call myself."

Henrik clicked through to the number on his cell phone and wrote it down on a piece of paper.

"Here," he said.

"Thanks," Jana said.

"Okay," she heard Gunnar say, "so Philip Engström seems to be unstable. But it still doesn't clarify why he would have murdered and mutilated three people."

"And clearly caused a fourth person's death," Mia said. "I'll be damned if this thing isn't just exploding…"

"Undeniably," Gunnar said. "I'm so eager to bring this guy in and hear what he has to say. Who is he, really? Do we have any info on him?"

Silence fell around the table.

"He works as a paramedic…" Mia began.

"I know that already," Gunnar said. "But for how long? What did he do before that? What do we know about him besides where he works?"

"Let's see here," Henrik said, flipping through some papers. "He's worked in ambulance services for five years."

"And what did he do before that?"

Silence fell again. Jana let her gaze wander from the window to the people around the table.

"So we know nothing about him," Gunnar said. "How can we then assume that he has anything to do with the murders?"

"Have you been sitting there asleep? How can we *not* suspect him?" Mia said.

"I'm not saying that you're wrong," Gunnar said, "but we can't have such tunnel vision. Can you imagine that Philip might be innocent?"

"It is possible that he's innocent," Henrik said, nodding. "But if we think about the murder weapons that have been used—scalpel and Gigli saw—these are tools that appear in the health-care sector, tools that Philip would have access to, from what I understand."

Ola held his finger in the air.

"And sorry to be saying this," he interjected, "but tools like these can also be ordered online. One click and you've got a multipack of scalpels in your mailbox."

"I just mean that for Philip, these aren't unfamiliar tools," Henrik said.

"But his motive, then?" Gunnar said.

Henrik shrugged his shoulders.

"We have to find him," Gunnar said, standing up. "Then we'll be able to stop all this damn speculation. I want to know who Philip is and what, if this is truly the case, could have made him murder three people. There must be an explanation. So it's best that we get back to work."

He turned toward the map.

"So how do we find him?"

"Maybe we could track his cell phone?" Henrik asked.

All eyes turned to Ola.

"That shouldn't be much of a problem," he said. "If he has a contract and not a prepaid phone, that is."

"Good," Gunnar said. "You have one hour."

"Hi, my name is Jana Berzelius and I'm a prosecutor. I'd like to ask you some questions."

Jana had left the police station, taking out her cell phone, and called Sandra Gustafsson. She looked around, making sure nobody listened to her talking.

"But I've already talked to the police," Sandra said.

"That's great," Jana said. "Then I only have a few follow-up questions."

"Okay, but it has to be quick because I'm at work."

"On Wednesday of last week, you and your colleague Philip Engström traveled to a house in Lindö. You'd received a call that a woman was having a heart attack."

"That might well be. I don't remember all of our calls."

"You don't know?"

"Well, when I think about it, I think I know what you're talking about."

"Good. Then could you tell me what you usually do for a heart attack?"

"I don't understand what you mean."

"What is the protocol for a heart attack? What are your instructions?"

Sandra cleared her throat.

"Well, after you've established that it's a heart attack, it's important to open the clogged artery to get the blood and oxygen supply going again. The part of the heart that doesn't receive oxygen becomes more and more seriously impacted the longer it takes for the clot to dissolve. The faster we can restore blood flow to the troubled heart muscle, the less injury there will be from the heart attack."

"So it's very important to get to the hospital as quickly as possible?"

"Yes," Sandra said. "It's important. But it's not only the time that's crucial; there are also other factors that play a role…"

"Like what, the condition of the medical staff?"

Sandra was silent for a brief moment.

"Now I really don't understand. We do everything we can to save lives."

"But this woman died?"

"Yes, but I don't understand what you're getting at. Every year, around thirty-one thousand people in Sweden have heart attacks, and nine thousand of them die."

"Why was this woman one of the nine thousand?"

"I can't answer that," Sandra said.

"You were in the ambulance."

"I was driving the ambulance. Philip Engström was the paramedic in charge of taking care of the patient."

"But don't both of you have responsibility?"

"Yes, and I assure you that we always, always put the patient's needs first. I just don't understand what this has to do with the murders. Is Philip suspected of something?"

"Should he be?"

"I'm asking you."

Jana took a deep breath.

"At a meeting at the police station today, it was revealed that Philip Engström fell asleep during this call..."

"Yes, and I talked to Henrik Levin about that."

"And you also said that it was because of him falling asleep that the woman died."

Sandra cleared her throat again.

"It is true that there was an unfortunate delay on that call, and we were late getting back to the ER. But these things happen. It doesn't necessarily mean that it affected the patient's outcome."

"These things happen? That you fall asleep on a call?"

"If you have any more questions, you're welcome to call my boss, Eva Holmgren. She can surely help you find out if anything went wrong, and in that case, what."

"Thank you," Jana said, hanging up.

She needed time to think. Rethink. It felt like Sandra didn't want to or couldn't answer what actually happened in the ambulance. Did Engström have the answer Jana needed?

Jana put her phone in her pocket and began to walk. The afternoon sun was strong. But instead of turning her face toward its warmth, she turned her gaze away and wondered how she was going to get a hold of him.

CHAPTER
TWENTY-THREE

IT WAS QUIET IN THE DEPARTMENT. HENRIK LEVIN SAT on his chair and drummed his fingers against the keyboard while he waited for his computer to wake up.

In the light of the flickering screen, he tried to make sense of the facts and his conflicting thoughts about paramedic Philip Engström. It had been relatively easy to map his merits. There were hardly any of them.

Born on April 1, 1978, the only child of physician Charles Engström and teacher Rita Engström. Grew up in Vadstena and completed a three-year specialized high school program in biology. After graduating, he lived in Poland for a few years, but it wasn't until a number of years later, in the city of Uppsala, that he passed his exams in the specialist nursing program with a focus on ambulance services. He then moved to Norrköping and began working as a paramedic. Married

Lina Engström three years ago. Both registered as owning the single-story home in Skarphagen.

Two telephone numbers were listed for Philip's parents. Henrik chose the first, but when he got voice mail, he immediately dialed the second. He heard a man's voice after the second ring.

"Engström."

"My name is Henrik Levin, and I'm an inspector with the police."

Silence.

"I'd like to talk to you about your son, Philip."

It was still silent on the other end. It sounded like a gasp for breath and a phlegmatic cough resulting from innumerable cigarettes.

"Who did you say you were?"

"Henrik Levin. I'm an inspector with the police…"

He paused, waiting through another coughing fit.

"…and I need to ask a few questions about Philip."

"Over the phone?"

"I can come to you if you'd like."

"Here? No, there've already been so many police officers around here looking for him. If we're going to meet in person it had damn well better be worth the trouble. What do you want?"

"Talking about your son isn't worth the trouble, if I understand you correctly?"

"I've already talked about my son to these officers, and I think you should tell me what this conversation is really about before I lose my voice completely."

"Have you seen Philip lately?"

"No, we don't see him these days."

He heard the man clearing his throat.

"Is there a reason for that?"

"Of course there is," said the man on the other end.

"And that reason is?" Henrik asked.

"That reason is…that Philip made a choice some years ago."

"Okay."

"Yes, he changed then."

Henrik looked down at his lap, scratching his chin.

"Did something in particular happen?" he asked.

"He just changed, simply speaking."

"In what way?"

"In every way. He developed mental problems, went through a change in personality. And we lost him; we lost our son."

"Has he been treated for it?"

"He's taken most of the medications out there, in any case. I just don't know if they've helped."

"Helped for what? Do you mean he is sick?"

Henrik switched his cell phone to his other hand.

"Sick?" the man said and coughed again. His voice was hardly audible now. "A person must be sick to abandon a promising career."

"Did he abandon a promising career? In what way?"

"A career as a surgeon. Only an idiot throws away that sort of education, that's what I think. But I shouldn't have told him that. I have regretted it so many times. I even asked him to forgive me, but he hasn't said a word to me since then."

"So Philip was a doctor?"

"Yes, he was a doctor. Educated in Poland. He didn't have the grades that were required to study in Sweden."

"But why didn't he continue as a doctor?"

"That, my dear friend, is a question that I've asked myself many times. And I think I will never get the answer to it. At least not from Philip. Now I have to end this long-winded drivel. My voice is going."

Henrik thanked him for the help, laid his cell phone on

the desk and looked at the computer screen, which had gone to sleep.

This new information just seemed to complicate everything. What had made Philip Engström quit being a doctor? Something important, something decisive must have happened that made him change his direction in life.

But what?

"Are you still there?" he said, pressing the phone harder to his ear. He changed position, sitting with his back up against the birch. Philip Engström's legs were freezing so badly that they were almost numb. How could that be? It wasn't particularly cold out.

He wanted to run farther and find a new hiding place— he could now see the flashing blue lights between the trees.

"Yes," he heard Lina say. "I'm here."

He tried to stand, but his legs wouldn't obey him. A part of his brain said that he should stay, sit there and continue talking, but another part of him told him to escape. But it was a hopeless struggle against time, because every breath he took brought him relentlessly closer to the end. By continuing to flee he only delayed the inevitable; in the end, he would still be forced to turn himself in.

"Should I come and get you?" she said. "Tell me where you are and I'll come pick you up."

"No," he said. "That's a bad idea."

"What makes you say that? You're scaring me, Philip."

"I have to take care of this myself. Call Sandra and ask her to keep you company."

"But why, Philip?" she sniffed.

"Because then you won't be alone if I don't come home tonight."

"And why wouldn't you come home, Philip? What are you going to do?"

He hung up and let his cell phone sink down into his lap. He felt almost detached from the feeling of fear.

His heart pounded in his chest as he reached his hand out toward the ground and began digging with his fingers. The damp earth felt cold against his skin, and he let his fingers slip around in the cold dirt. He found a stone and gripped it. He didn't resist the idea that he felt a little less alone that way, with his hand around a stone.

"So Philip was a doctor?" Mia Bolander said. She sat on a chair in Henrik Levin's office with her legs outstretched.

"Yes," Henrik said, "and he wanted to specialize in surgery."

"How long ago?"

"He began his education right after high school, but instead of studying in Sweden, he chose Poland because it's easier to get into med schools there," Henrik said.

"But did he ever work as a doctor?"

"I'm not sure."

"But if we assume that he did, and we also assume that he worked at Vrinnevi, then it's possible that he met Shirin and Johan there," Mia said. "And if they worked in the same department, we should also check who else worked there at the time. The next victim might be on that list. Philip might be looking to erase other colleagues?"

"Hold your horses, Mia," Henrik said.

"But something must have happened, right?"

Henrik paused for a moment before turning to the door where Anneli Lindgren had just stepped in. She didn't say hello. Instead, she walked straight up to his desk. Henrik saw that she looked both tired and upset.

"I've gotten the results about the shoes you found at Philip Engström's," she said. "There's no doubt that his shoes made the impression in the flower bed."

"Just as we thought," Henrik said.

"I've also looked into this narcotic, Ketalar, which Ahlmann found in both Shirin's and Katarina's bodies. It's in the medical bag that paramedics use."

She examined Henrik and Mia.

"Now, I'm no tactical investigator, but doesn't it seem that all of the clues point in the same direction?"

"It can hardly be a coincidence," Mia said.

"And I'm thinking that Philip has had every opportunity to move freely about the crime scenes," Anneli said. "No one would question that he left traces there. No one suspects the one who comes to help."

I'm truly an idiot, he thought. *What the hell am I solving by sitting here? Nothing. I'm just making everything worse.*

Philip Engström had been gripping the stone for so long that his hand had begun to hurt. There was no point in running.

He was going to become a father, and that was his most important duty right now. And he realized that there was only one alternative left in which he could anticipate even an ounce of sympathy and possibly find a solution.

He saw the police cars and listened to the car doors opening. When he heard the yells, he felt a huge relief. He would give up; let them take him in.

He let go of his cell phone and felt the calm rising, straight through his body.

Then he stood, turned his back to the police and put his hands on his head.

She was almost to Knäppingsborg. Jana looked at the people moving around her, most of them with headphones plugged into their cell phones. Some were also carrying grocery store bags.

She walked past a newsstand and saw that the free newspaper had dedicated multiple pages to the police search for Danilo Peña. Jana grabbed a paper and flipped to the articles that described in detail how Danilo had escaped from the hospital and how he had then disappeared without a trace. On the cover was a blurry photo of him as he lay on a stretcher. The photo had been taken in connection with his capture at the boathouse in December. The same picture was probably being circulated around the social networks. Maybe it was even trending right now on Facebook.

That's not good, not good at all, she thought, tossing the newspaper in the nearest trash can.

Just then, her cell phone vibrated in her pocket. She continued walking as she answered.

"Jana speaking," she said.

"We have Philip Engström," said Henrik on the other end of the line.

She stopped.

"Are you sure?"

"Yes."

"Where did you find him?"

"In a grove next to a field. He gave himself up without any resistance."

Jana raised her gaze.

"And when will you begin the interrogation?"

"As soon as possible."

"Good," she said, turning around and heading back to the police station. "I'll be there."

"You don't need to," Henrik said.

"But I want to."

CHAPTER
TWENTY-FOUR

HENRIK LEVIN SAT AS COMFORTABLY AS HE COULD on the chair in the interrogation room. He carefully studied Philip Engström, who sat directly across from him, examining his face and noticing a certain anxiousness. The man's lips were pressed together in a thin line, his shoulders were drawn up, and his gaze fixed on the table in front of him.

Next to Henrik sat Jana, and behind the one-way glass stood Mia and Gunnar.

For a moment it was completely silent in the room, and Henrik used that silence to plan the course of the impending line of questioning.

He felt calm, relaxed, prepared. He thought about the questions he was going to ask and in what order he should ask them, without wasting energy on meaningless speculations or assumptions.

He observed the man who was still dressed in the ambulance uniform he had been wearing when he disappeared from his workplace that afternoon. He wondered what was going through this man's head at that moment.

Jana crossed one leg over the other. She simply sat there, back straight and pen ready with her legal pad. Henrik cast a glance at her and was met by her steady gaze. He noted her clothes, the jacket in dark blue fabric and the pure white blouse underneath. She nodded to him as if to say that it was time to begin, and he nodded back as if to confirm her encouragement. He began the interrogation by saying the date, time and the names of those present in the room. Then he leaned back, put his forefinger under his nose and asked: "Do you know why you're sitting here?"

Philip Engström nodded.

"We would appreciate it if you answer 'yes' or 'no' to the questions."

Philip nodded again, without saying anything.

"Would you begin by stating where you have been the last few hours?"

Philip took a deep breath, and on the exhale, his shoulders sank low enough that he didn't look as anxious anymore.

"I don't have a good answer," he said. "I think I panicked."

"Over what?"

"Over everything that's happened."

"So you hid in a grove of trees?"

"It was dumb, but, yes. I didn't know what else I should do. I really had no idea that I would end up there. Before I did, I mean."

"But you're aware that it could be seen as suspicious behavior to run away like that, above all when you know investigators are looking for you?"

"Yes, I understand that."

Henrik raised his eyes a bit. "So what's happened here," he began, "is that there have been three murders."

"Yes, I know," Philip said.

"And for some reason, your name has come up during our investigation."

Philip sighed. "Yes. I know."

"And we think that is *very* strange."

"I understand that," he said again.

Henrik thought for a moment before asking: "You're married, correct?"

"Yes."

"But you're not wearing a wedding ring."

"No, I lost it."

Henrik flipped through his papers and held out a photo.

"Is this your ring?"

Philip examined the picture.

"Yes, that's it," he said. "Where did you find it?"

Henrik didn't answer.

"But where did you find it?" Philip repeated.

"We'll get to that," Henrik said.

Jana took a piece of paper out of her briefcase just then and passed it over to Henrik, who placed it on the table in front of Philip.

"Can you explain what this is?" he said.

Philip leaned cautiously forward and read what it said.

"It's a document from the National Board of Health and Welfare."

"Exactly," Henrik said. "These are excerpts from the Registry of Authorized Health and Welfare Personnel, which covers people who sought and received authorization for careers within the health and welfare field. And can you tell me whose name is on this paper?"

"My name."

"So you've worked as a doctor," Henrik said, giving the paper back to Jana.

Philip sighed again.

"Yes," he said finally.

"But not anymore?"

The room fell silent.

"No," Philip said.

"Why not?"

"It's a long story."

"One which we really want to hear."

"I don't know if I can tell it," he said.

Henrik paused for a long time.

"Okay," he then said, "then maybe you can tell us about Shirin Norberg instead. How did you know her?"

"I...I don't know."

"But you know who she is?"

"No, see..." Philip shook his head stubbornly.

"Listen," Henrik said. "Right now, you can only lose by lying. The only thing you should be doing is telling us everything you know. So don't sit there looking at me as if I were an idiot."

Philip looked down at the table.

"But...but the ring..." he said. "Where did you find it?"

"Forget about the ring for now. We'll get to that. I want to hear about your relationship to Shirin Norberg first."

Philip sat quietly.

"Are you having a hard time talking?" Henrik said.

Jana stepped in. "Can I ask you something?" she said. "There's something I've wondered about a lot in recent days. How does it feel when a patient dies? I mean, when it's your duty to save someone who is hanging in life's balance, how does it feel to fail? Can you possibly...convey that feeling for us here?"

She looked at him as if she expected some reaction, whatever reaction, but it didn't come. He sat as if he were made of stone.

"I always do my best," he mumbled.

"Even in your sleep?" she said.

Philip looked at Henrik with a confused expression.

"You recently fell asleep on a call, is that right?" Jana said.

"Yes," Philip said dejectedly.

"I don't know if…" Henrik said, but Jana held her hand up to signal that she wasn't done.

"What happened with the patient?" she said.

"With the patient?"

"Yes."

"I don't know. I don't exactly remember."

"Do you usually fall asleep when you're out on a call?"

"No."

"But how did it happen that you did this time?"

"I'd been working a lot, sleeping too little…so that's how it was."

"So what happened with this patient…while you were sleeping?"

"Well, she…died."

"And what does that make you feel? Nothing? Do you have any reflections on it at all? Do you feel sorrow? Regret? Or maybe relief?"

Philip raised his gaze, shifted in the chair, and Henrik saw a faint flush appear on his cheeks.

"I accidentally fell asleep monitoring the patient in the ambulance," he said. "Ten minutes at most. And when I woke up, the patient was dead. But Sandra could damn well have woken me up."

"You mean Sandra Gustafsson?" Jana said.

"Yes, Sandra Gustafsson. We drove the rig together. She could have woken me up."

"But she didn't?"

"No, well, yes, she may have tried, but not hard enough, because I'm not such a sound sleeper that it should take ten whole minutes to wake me up."

Henrik looked at Jana, saw that she was pressing her lips together and thought she probably shouldn't ask any more questions just then—especially questions Henrik didn't understand the reasoning behind. If Philip had fallen asleep on a call or not wasn't exactly where Henrik's own focus lay.

"To return to what we were talking about before—and I want you to be honest now," Henrik said to Philip. "Who was Shirin?"

Philip's gaze wandered across the table.

"She was a surgery nurse," he said.

"We know that," Henrik said. "But what we want to know is how your paths crossed."

"We actually only met once."

"When was that?"

"Many years ago. She worked in surgery at Vrinnevi."

"And you?"

"I did, too. And Johan. That was where we met. All three of us."

"And Katarina Vinston?"

"She was already a paramedic at the time."

Henrik leaned forward, set his elbows on the table, and said, "I am not following you. I don't see how all this hangs together."

"I can understand that," Philip said.

"So you and Katarina worked together?"

"Later, yes. When I stopped practicing medicine and became a paramedic nurse instead. Before that, Katarina had flown a rescue helicopter. But she said that she realized she preferred to be on the ground rather than in the air. So she started working with the ground ambulance instead."

"I still don't get it," Henrik said. "You worked as a doctor but decided to quit and begin working in EMS instead."

"Yes."

"But why did you quit as a doctor?"

"A series of unfortunate circumstances."

"That have to do with Shirin Norberg, Johan Rehn and Katarina Vinston?"

"Yes. But mostly with me."

Jana tilted her head to the side.

"Shirin, Johan, Katarina and you worked in the same hospital," she said, meeting Philip's gaze. "Is that right?"

"Yes."

"So what is all this about?" Henrik said. "Three people have had body parts brutally severed…"

Philip looked down at his hands.

"A former patient," he said. "And now someone wants to hurt us," he said, "and I think I'm the next victim."

"You think or you know?"

"I'm sure of it."

"Completely sure?"

"Yes," Philip nodded.

"Okay, now," Henrik said, placing both palms on the table. "This is new information for us. What would make you think that *you* would be the next victim? And who is this former patient you're talking about? Is it someone you know?"

Philip turned his eyes away.

"Erika," he said. "Her name is Erika Silver."

Jana's pen stopped working. She laid it alongside her legal pad and reached into her briefcase for a new pen. She had heard

Philip Engström's own confirmation that he'd fallen asleep in the ambulance that her mother was being transported in.

The question was if it were the case because he was overworked, or if he had fallen asleep for some other reason, such as drugs.

Or was he simply lying?

She really wanted to meet with Sandra Gustafsson. Gustafsson was the only one who could say for certain what had happened in the ambulance and why someone had smothered her mother to death.

Jana stretched her hand in the other pocket, and when she felt the folded napkin, she realized how she would do it. Instead of pressing Philip and Sandra, she decided to find out the truth for herself. And she knew exactly who was going to help her.

It was chilly in the interrogation room.

Philip Engström pushed his hands between his thighs. He looked straight down at the table, listening to the investigator and the prosecutor breathe as they sat across from him.

"I'd almost forgotten all this," he said, closing his eyes. "It was so long ago."

But that wasn't true. What had happened with Erika Silver wasn't the sort of thing you forgot. Just the opposite; it had affected him more than any other specific event in his entire life.

His body was relaxed, at least outwardly. Inside, he felt an enormous amount of anxiety about digging up the past, what had been buried and forgotten long ago. Now all that was going to whirl up again like an autumn windstorm.

In his mind's eye, he saw a clear picture of a woman lying in bed. Her lips were taut, and drops of foam came from her mouth. She was screaming at him: he was the one who took her life from her. Strings of four-letter words.

He knew that he had made a mistake when he had taken her on as a patient. He'd known that from the very beginning.

Over the brief years he was in medicine, he had seen so many terribly tragic fates. People with neck injuries, back injuries, people who were aggressive, who cried or screamed, who had been beaten, abused, who had lost their children, who had been subjected to incest or rape or who had attempted suicide. Yet it was the memory of Erika Silver that affected him most. It was many years ago now, and it had been a mistake, a terrible, life-changing mistake. Not just for her, but for him, as well.

When she lay there in the hospital bed, she'd looked at him with contempt. She had repeated that she hated him, repeated it over and over. These powerful words had become sobs and finally just silence.

He had tried to say he was sorry, but the words meant nothing. He had fallen silent, too. Just before he left the room, she had said something to him, a few barely audible words.

Now an icy chill ran up his spine and down his arms. The hair on the back of his neck stood on end, and suddenly he heard a chair creak. He opened his eyes and looked at the man and woman who interrogated him. They were still sitting quietly there across the table from him. Their faces looked grainy. He swallowed hard and looked up at the camera in the corner of the ceiling. He wondered how many other people were looking at him right now, watching him, studying his body language and facial expressions. The situation was completely unreal. But he had chosen this for himself, and he had to follow through on what he'd decided to do.

He was going to tell them everything.

"A lot of things went wrong," he said, feeling his heart pound in his chest.

He took a deep breath, gathering courage.

"It was a Thursday in March. I was doing my residency and was going to help perform a gastric bypass surgery. On the operating table lay Erika Silver. I was told that she'd been looking forward to the surgery for a number of years."

He swallowed, trying to stay calm despite the thundering pulse in his head.

"The operation was to be performed with the aid of what we call 'peephole surgery.' There were six of us in the operating room. A surgery nurse, Shirin Norberg, and an OR nurse, Anders Svensson; a nurse anesthetist, Annikke Straum; and two surgeons, Joe Nordin and Johan Rehn, and myself. Johan was going to be the main surgeon, and I would be the observer. But at the last moment he delegated the actual surgery to me. I shouldn't have said yes, but I did, and I've come to regret it so many times."

Philip fell quiet and heard the whisper of the HVAC system.

"When I inserted the first trocar, her aorta burst..."

He fell silent again, couldn't bear to continue. He just wanted to leave the room, return home, take a pill and sleep.

"Please continue," said the investigator in front of him, and he knew that he had to tell the whole story. He couldn't go home, not now, not yet. He closed his eyes for a moment and then opened his mouth again.

"Puncturing the aorta is a dreaded, but highly unusual complication," he said. He remembered the panic that set in when he realized his mistake. "All surgeons know where the vessel is, but when the patient is lying down, the distance between the skin and the vessel is very small, and exactly where the abdominal wall lies can be difficult to judge. It's not an excuse, I just...wanted to explain it more fully."

He wrung his hands nervously. "I didn't know what I should do. Johan called for help, but there wasn't a vascular surgeon immediately available, so he had to act. Erika had already lost a lot of blood. I knew that it was terribly urgent to get the aorta sewn up, but I couldn't do anything. I was only the resident, the student, I just had to sit there and look on. Erika was placed under observation in the ICU. But when she woke up in the afternoon, she was complaining of severe pain in her legs. She couldn't move one leg. It turned out that Johan had made the sutures too tight so that the blood flow to her legs had been cut off. It was clear that she needed to be under the care of a specialist in Linköping, but the MedFlight helicopter was broken…"

He was talking to a point on the white wall, a few feet above the policeman's head.

"This must sound like I'm making it up, but it's true. All of it." He laughed oddly.

"There was some kind of engine problem, so it never came, but the ICU didn't know that until much later."

"And this is where Katarina comes into the picture?" the policeman said.

"Yes, she was the one who should have reported the situation with the helicopter. But she didn't. That's why it was eleven o'clock before Erika was transported to the university hospital in Linköping via standard ambulance transport. The legs can withstand six hours without oxygenated blood. But it had been eleven hours by the time Erika arrived in Linköping, and her legs had to be amputated."

Philip looked down at his hands.

"I destroyed her life. That was ten years ago now. And in a way…"

He shrugged his shoulders.

"…I maybe destroyed my own, too. I never wanted to have that level of responsibility for a patient again. Instead, I wanted to make sure the patient ended up in the right hands, in the right amount of time."

"Have you heard from her over the years?"

"No," he said, shaking his head.

"But you're sure that she's the one behind the murders?"

"Yes," he said.

"How can you be so sure?"

"She said so, she said it clearly, at her follow-up exam. I knew she was confused. I don't think I took it seriously then."

He felt his lips beginning to tremble.

"What exactly did she say, Philip?"

He sank lower in the chair and buried his face in his hands. And behind his closed eyelids, he saw the woman lying in the bed, heard her say that he was the one who'd taken everything from her, everything.

And as he was about to leave the room, she had said a few barely audible words: *I will get my revenge.*

CHAPTER
TWENTY-FIVE

JANA BERZELIUS FELT THE FLOOR VIBRATE. SHE WAS on her way up in the elevator of the police station along with Henrik and Mia after the interrogation was over.

None of them said a word to the others during the short elevator ride. Neither Henrik nor Mia looked at her or each other. They were presumably deep in thought about what Philip Engström had revealed.

It had begun to get dark when Gunnar and Ola met them in the conference room. Jana placed her briefcase on the floor before sitting down.

"Tell me right away what you're thinking after your talk with Philip," Gunnar said even before everyone had taken a seat.

"Yes, what do we think?" Mia said.

"If I can start," Ola said, pulling his light blue cap back so that his whole forehead was exposed. "I've looked, but there's no Erika Silver that's the right age in any database. Not with the IRS or the DMV or anywhere else, either."

"Nowhere?" Henrik said, looking inquisitively at Ola.

"No," Ola said. "There's no Erika Silver, and there may never have been one, either."

"Have we looked up this Joe, and Annikke?"

"Yes," Ola said. "Joe retired before he died of a cerebral hemorrhage a number of years ago. Annikke moved to Norway but died last summer. Breast cancer. I also looked up this OR nurse, Anders Svensson, and found that he'd also moved away from Sweden. He lives in Washington State, in the USA."

"Did he just make up someone to lay the blame on?" Mia said.

"You think Philip is lying?" Henrik said.

Mia laughed. "Yes! How else would you interpret what Ola is saying," she said. "It's not enough that he's a serial killer; he's a pathological liar, too. What a fucking combo."

"Or maybe he simply got the name wrong," Henrik said. "It was ten years ago that this happened, after all."

"He's lying," Mia said. "I know it. He's like a fucking puppet master who's playing with us. He came in through a blind spot, wormed his way into the investigation, and now wants to lead us down the wrong path. He has a fucking great disguise, too—a paramedic. Sorry, but I think we're sitting here like a group of lost idiots, making a fuss about motives and MO, and now we're also supposed to take a suspected murderer's statement seriously? Engström's doing it to fucking confuse us."

"But still," Henrik said. "We can't exclude any possibility. It's our damn responsibility to twist and turn every little detail."

"But Mia's right, we can't put all of our focus on a person

who probably doesn't exist," Gunnar said. "I can't put more resources on it just for Philip's sake."

"You can't? We just released staff from the Peña case," Henrik said, earning a look from Jana.

"What do you mean?" she said.

"Danilo Peña was seen in Motala and seems to have been involved in the dispute at the shelter there," Henrik said. "As a result, we've reprioritized our resources, and we could really use them now."

"But that doesn't mean that we can use them to exonerate Philip," Gunnar said. "There is no Erika Silver. End of story."

"Then I want to talk to Engström again," Henrik said, "because there's a motive here. To my ears, it sounds like Erika Silver, imagined or not, would have a very clear motive to kill. Revenge for what she was subjected to. A personal, emotional, aggressive reaction to a serious mistake."

"You mean that Erika would brutally kill three people in revenge for an operation gone wrong?" Gunnar said.

"Yes, that's exactly what I mean."

"But do we even know that such an operation occurred?"

"We haven't gotten confirmation yet."

"So we're just guessing?" Mia said. "Drop it, Henrik. Engström is the murderer. And furthermore, you're forgetting something: Erika Silver, *imagined or not*, is assumedly in a wheelchair."

Henrik took a deep breath, collecting himself.

"You might be right, Mia, but if she does exist, *in a wheelchair or not*, she has a clear motive. And perhaps she enlisted someone else to carry out the murders on her behalf. It's more than you have in your theory that Philip is the murderer."

Silence fell around the table.

Gunnar clasped his hands behind his neck and rocked slightly in his chair.

"There've been three brutal murders," he said, "and I want us to work ourselves to the max to solve them."

"So why won't you let us put some resources into searching for this Erika?" Henrik said calmly.

"Because I'm worried we'll be on the wrong track, that we'll waste time unnecessarily. We don't have that sort of time right now!"

Outside the room there were echoes of footsteps and a rolling cart.

"I know," Henrik said when the sound died away. "But I think we're going even farther down the wrong track by not listening to Engström. Everyone wants a solution, and I know you also want that."

"So we're supposed to take what he is saying seriously?" Gunnar said.

"He has an alibi for at least one of the murders," Henrik said.

"But is it tight?"

"His coworkers have confirmed that he was working nights when Shirin was butchered. He was the attendant on the scene when she succumbed to her wounds."

"What about Katarina Vinston?"

"He was supposedly at home with his wife. The same for the murder of Johan Rehn."

"And has his wife confirmed that one? Engström apparently was on the scene for that one, too."

"We haven't had the chance to check."

"You haven't had the chance to check…" Gunnar said.

Henrik crossed his arms over his chest.

"We *will* check," he said, "but in the meantime, isn't it silly to just sit here and wait?"

"Okay, okay, okay." Gunnar sighed again. "Ola, see to it that you find this woman."

Gunnar took his hands from his neck, pulling them over his head and making his hair stand on end.

"How the fuck are we going to find a person who doesn't exist?" Mia said dejectedly.

"Same thought here," Ola said. "Where am I supposed to look? There *is* no Erika Silver."

Jana met Henrik's gaze and saw a spark in his eyes. A thought popped into her head, and she leaned forward. "All surgeries are recorded," she said, and saw the whole team turn their faces toward her.

"Yes," Henrik said.

She straightened her back and continued: "And this surgery went wrong, right?"

"Correct," Henrik said.

"Then a report must have been filed somewhere in Sweden. All health-care workers are to report situations that have contributed or could have contributed to a serious injury to the Health and Social Care Inspectorate. If Philip is telling the truth, this botched operation should be documented. On every report, the patient's name will, in all likelihood, appear, and also the patient's social security number. If we find the report, we'll find Erika Silver."

Philip Engström sat on the floor of the interrogation room, his legs outstretched. He was exhausted, and his body was completely limp after the interrogation. His mouth was dry, and his head hurt.

Erika Silver, he thought. Finally, he had been able to tell someone about the botched surgery. He hoped every police officer was searching for her now. And when they found her, he would bury his memory of her and his involvement in her surgery forever.

He whispered to himself, letting his gaze leave the window and looking at the door. He wondered when he would be able to go home. He thought about Lina, about what she might be doing in that moment.

He saw her before him. He saw her face, the corners of her mouth turned down, sad and anxious. But she wouldn't need to be anxious much longer. He would soon be home with her again, would make everything right again, tell her everything, everything he had just told the police.

"You can speak undisturbed in here," her father's caretaker, Elin, said to Jana when she opened the door to the library at the house in Lindö. The bookshelves stretched from floor to ceiling and held masses of literature, most of it of a legal nature. Heavy curtains hung over the window, and a patterned rug lay on the floor. A brown leather armchair and round table were in the middle of the room. Elin pushed Jana's father's wheelchair in and stopped it tightly next to the armchair.

"Karl often likes to sit here when he wants to be left in peace," she said, smiling at Jana. "Would either of you like something to drink?"

But before Jana had been able to answer, Father had raised his hand. "Leave us," he said thickly.

Elin nodded, turning on a floor lamp with a bronze stand, and closed the door behind her. Jana heard her steps disappear.

The armchair was the only other seat besides his wheelchair.

She sat down and felt far too close to him. The sudden intimacy made her uneasy. She looked at her hands as she searched for the words.

"This is a little sensitive. And maybe not even a correct hypothesis. But I want to ask…for a favor," she said.

"What ist?" he asked in his thick, labored speech.

She cast a quick glance at him and saw that he was waiting for her to continue.

"I need a DNA analysis, but not an official one. So I'm wondering…what I mean is…you have to help me."

She interpreted his silence to mean he didn't understand what she had said, so she clarified.

"I don't want to file a report. Or more accurately, I can't, because then the police will begin a preliminary investigation, and neither you nor I want to be at the center of that."

She fell silent and looked urgently at him as if she were waiting for a confirmation that he had understood this time.

"I haf to know wht this is about."

"It's about Mother."

He met her gaze.

"Margaretha?"

"Yes," she said. "But I can't say any more than that."

"You hf to!"

"I can't," she said.

It was silent for a number of seconds. He raised his head somewhat. The circles under his eyes were dark. Maybe it was because of the dim light in the room, or perhaps the gravity of the conversation.

"Wht are you lking for?" he said.

"I want answers," Jana said.

She stuck her hand in her pocket and took out the napkin, laid it on the round table and unfolded it so that he could see the bit of fingernail. He opened his mouth, fighting with the words.

"You thik somthing hapnd to her…?"

His throat clenched, and his voice cracked when he said the words. He had probably tried to push out a rational question, but the emotional confusion and pain took over.

"I suspect that something happened to her, yes," she said.

"Wht? I want to know!"

"I can't say yet. The only thing I want to know is if my suspicions are right. I just want answers. And I want what is on this nail to be checked against a Philip Engström and a Sandra Gustafsson. Their DNA profiles are already in the system."

She looked at him and waited for him to say something.

"Ansrs take time," he said.

"I know," she said. "But I'm sure you can rush the process."

His tired eyes had taken on a sharp look. She pushed the napkin even closer to him and waited again.

"If not for my sake, you can at least do this for Mother's," she said.

He said nothing.

But then, completely unexpectedly, he reached his hand out. It trembled as he picked up the napkin and folded it. He made two attempts to put it in his own pocket before finally succeeding.

"I'll do wht I can," he said.

His mumbled promise was barely audible, and Jana realized that the conversation was over.

Anneli Lindgren stared at the computer screen and thought about Gunnar. She had attempted to make eye contact with him after the meeting, but he had just walked sullenly into his office and closed the door behind him.

She was tired of him now, she thought, tired of him and his dissociation. Recently, he had become closed off in his own world. Distant. He'd give her orders, point and patronize, but he didn't see her. She knew that it didn't have to be like this; she knew there was another Gunnar, a softer Gunnar.

All she wanted was for them to start talking again. For them to start figuring out what had happened. For him to hold her and say that he forgave her stupid misstep, and that they would never, ever again let anyone or anything come between them. That from now on, it would just be her and him and Adam—forever.

She looked up and checked the clock on the wall, which indicated it had turned into evening.

No, it couldn't be like this. They had to at least be able to talk to each other. They were grown adults.

She quickly got up from her desk, left her computer and went with determined strides toward Gunnar's office. She counted to five and took three deep breaths before gripping the door handle and stepping in.

But she didn't get any farther than just inside the door before the smile on her lips vanished. She saw Gunnar standing with both hands on Britt Dyberg's shoulders. He leaned right over her and kissed her. It took a second, maybe two or even five, before Anneli understood what she had just witnessed.

She stepped backward and closed the door behind her, letting it shut silently and returning to her office, her desk, her computer.

Like a fog lifting, it all began to become clear to her. She hadn't wanted to see it earlier; she hadn't understood why Gunnar had been so negative. But he had already moved on from their relationship. He had never planned on their being together again. Now he stood there touching another woman, caressing her shoulders, her hair, her arm, kissing her.

He wanted Britt Dyberg, and the realization was painful.

So, so painful.

Jana walked past the Italian restaurant Matbaren and looked in at the people sitting at their tables. A couple sat in the corner, and the light from the lamp above them fell on their wineglasses and interlaced hands.

The sky was full of stars, and the moon shone brightly above the rooftops. Jana was on her way home. She rounded a corner, walked under a wide archway and began thinking about the meeting with her father. Halfway through the arch, she put her hand into her pocket, feeling its emptiness.

The fingernail was in his possession now, and the question was how long it would be there. She hoped he would try to pull his strings already tonight. Exactly how he would go about keeping it a secret she didn't know, but she knew that if anyone was capable of keeping it quiet, it was her father.

She stepped into the lobby and heard steps in the stairwell, a door opening and closing, then silence. With her hand on the railing, she ascended the stairs.

The apartment was silent and dark. She took off her coat and shoes. She looked ahead of her and stopped breathing for a moment. Not because she needed to conserve oxygen but because he was standing there. If it hadn't been for the moonlight, she wouldn't have seen him. He stood against the wall, as if he were one with it. She didn't like his cold gaze, tense body or clenched teeth.

"Long day?" he said.

"It was a good day," she said, "because I've found out that the police have reprioritized their resources."

"So they aren't looking for me anymore?"

"They're looking, and they will always be looking for you."

He stared at her but didn't say anything. They both stood still in the dark hallway.

"So we'll soon be done with each other," he said.

"I hope so," she said.

"When you've dropped me off in Södertälje, you'll never have to see me again."

"I've understood that."

"Don't look so worried, then."

"I have other things on my mind."

"Don't think so much. Focus now, Jana. What route are we taking to Södertälje?"

"You should have figured it out," she said sourly.

"But you're the one who has the inside info from the police."

She looked at the ceiling, observing the darkness and moonlight that continued creating unpredictable patterns.

"There are a number of ways to get to Södertälje," she said in a long exhale. "The first is to take the main highway."

"That's probably not a good idea," he said.

"The second is to drive along the county road that runs parallel to the highway."

"But there we'd also risk being stopped by the police for some fucking traffic check. Not a good idea, either."

"The third is to try to make our way north through the maze of small, private roads."

"Sounds better," he said.

"The fourth way is to take the train."

"Fuck," he said. "I wouldn't risk someone recognizing me in the crowd even if I looked completely different. We'll take the private roads."

They looked at each other.

"I have to be in Södertälje at eight o'clock on the dot," he said. "Not one second later. Get it?"

"Believe me, I don't want to be late, either," she said.

My Journal, June 13

Dear Diary,
It started out as the best day ever. I was finally free. While the others were being met in the schoolyard by their families, I rushed home with my graduation cap in hand. I was happy it was finally over.

But the house was completely silent. I searched the whole house. Finally I found Mom on the floor in the bathroom. Her eyes were staring at me—white, but not yet dead.

I was scared, of course. I wanted to scream. But instead I started to stroke her hair. It was soft and smooth between my fingers. I leaned forward and took her hand. She wanted to say something...she tried, but she couldn't get the words out.

Instead, it was the voice in my head that I heard. And what it said seemed both smart and crazy at the same time.

It was there, on the floor, that she slipped away from me; she simply let go of my hand.

And I don't want anyone to know, so I've hidden her. I don't know if anyone cares, really. No one cared about her all these years since her botched surgery. No one helped us. It's always just been me.

And I'm not scared anymore.

Because I have you still, Mom. I feel it. You are with me. And you will always be with me. It's you and me, Mom. You and me.

CHAPTER
TWENTY-SIX

Tuesday

LINA LAY IN HER BED WITH HER CELL PHONE IN HER hand and a blanket around her body.

He hadn't come home last night. What had happened? Why hadn't he called? Can't he, won't he? What was stopping him?

Lina Engström's lips trembled, and she tried to hold back the tears.

There were moments when she had truly doubted their relationship. Many moments. His lack of communication. A sense of being walled off. Yet she had stayed, given him more love, more tenderness, more concern. But what had she gotten in return?

Lies, lies and more lies.

Why should they build a family if he was just going to lie all the time? If he never told her anything voluntarily?

She felt too warm and kicked off the blanket. She laid her hand on her stomach and looked at the ceiling. Was it all going to end now that she was finally pregnant?

She thought about Philip's words. This was something he would fix. Then she thought about his coworker Katarina Vinston—who was dead. *What had Philip to do with her death?* She shuddered at the thought. Could they have had a romantic relationship? But why would he have killed her?

No, he hadn't killed her. And he had no secret relationship with her.

Philip and I are married, she thought. *And he loves me. He has said it countless times*. And furthermore, he had said it first.

He had asked her out, first to a movie and then for dinner. She had forgotten the name of the movie now, but it was an action flick with Arnold Schwarzenegger. He'd already seen it once and said that he really wanted to see it again. With her. He had reserved seats in his name in the last row of the theater.

In hindsight, his intentions were obvious. She didn't even like action films. But she liked Philip. They'd made out through the whole film, and when they woke up in the morning in his bed, he had summarized the plot for her. That was when she had felt the anxious happiness. She buried her nose in his short hair as he said *I love you*.

She said, "I love you, too."

She couldn't hold back the tears any longer. How could everything have turned out like this?

Henrik Levin sat in the chair in his office. With a furrow in his brow, he opened the folder and began glancing through the reports from the preliminary investigations of the three murders. He looked at the photos and skimmed the autopsies.

Suddenly, Ola appeared in the doorway.

"We're finding ourselves in the same place as last night," he said.

"What you're saying is that you haven't found anything from Social Services?" Henrik said, slapping the folder closed.

"Right. They haven't found anything yet, but the bureaucratic machinery is at least in motion."

"Good," Henrik said. "It's obvious that Philip was a part of something, but I wonder if what he told us was really true."

"Should we use a lie detector on him?" Ola said.

Henrik grinned.

"I don't think so," he said.

"Torture, then?" Ola said. "We can pull his fingernails out."

"Tempting," Henrik said, getting up from his chair.

"What should we do, then?"

"I think it's best that we do what we usually do. Let's talk to him again."

Jana stood in the kitchen with a coffee mug in her hand, looking at the water move down the river. She looked at the black, straggly crowns of the trees against the blue sky and felt heavy inside.

Her cell phone lay in her pocket. She pulled it out and tried calling her father. When she heard the voice mail answer, she hung up.

She heard steps behind her and could feel his presence, but she didn't turn around. She just stood still with her gaze out the window and her thoughts on Father.

She saw a movement out of the corner of her eye and looked up.

Danilo had come closer. He stood in the middle of the floor just a short distance from the window with his gaze fixed on a faraway point.

"Do you have something against me being in peace?" she said.

"Yes," he said. "Who were you calling?"

"Someone I would really like to talk to," she said.

"Who?"

"The less you know, the better," she said, replacing her cell phone in her pocket. She was about to leave the kitchen when he took hold of her arm.

"Don't mess with me, Jana. If I find out you've snitched, you'll have dug your own grave."

The hold on her arm became harder. She met his icy gaze.

"I got revenge on a snitch once," he said. "I started by sticking a screwdriver in his brother's neck. Then I poked in his wife's eyes. She screamed, my god, how she screamed. Finally, I killed the snitch. He crawled after me on the floor with the blood running from his mouth before he finally gave up."

"What you do bores me to death," she said.

"Bores you?" he said. "I'm threatening to kill you and you think it's boring?"

"Yes."

His jaw muscles flexed.

"I never trust anyone I'm not absolutely forced to trust," he said. "And even now, I don't completely trust you."

"The feeling is mutual. How do I know you won't shoot me in the head the very second I've dropped you off?"

He smiled at her as if they'd just become friends.

"We have a few hours," she said. "But I still don't know how you're going to get down to the garage without being seen, and I won't have the chance to figure it out as long as you're standing here holding my arm. So if you'll excuse me, I also have work to do."

He raised his head, then let go of her arm.

★ ★ ★

"You've talked about a woman named Erika Silver," Henrik Levin said, observing Philip Engström. "But the problem is that there doesn't seem to be anyone named Erika Silver."

"Yes, but…"

"There's no Erika Silver that matches what you've described, in any case. You didn't make all of this up, did you?"

"No, I didn't."

"Well, I suggest that you tell the truth instead," Henrik said. "We have people in this department who would really like to throw you in jail forever."

"But her name was Erika," Philip said, looking immediately a little confused.

"Erika Silver?" Henrik repeated, placing his elbows on the table. "I really want to believe you, but I'm having a hard time doing that when what you're saying doesn't fit any records."

Philip's eyes darted around.

"But I don't remember her name being anything other than Erika Silver…"

"You might as well let it go now," Henrik said, irritated. "There's no one by that name."

"But what was her name, then? Simonsson, Sandell, Sander… I don't know…?"

"You can't come up with it?"

Philip shook his head.

"I don't fucking remember…in that case."

"You know that you have the right to have a lawyer?" Henrik said.

"Yes, I know that, but I haven't done anything. I'm sure it's Erika who wants to hurt us."

"You still claim that's the case?"

"Yes, it's obvious."

"And she is supposed to have murdered three people because they, along with you, had accidentally caused her harm during a surgery ten years ago?"

"Yes!"

"Do you know what I think?" Henrik said. "If you are going to get away with this, you're going to have to come up with a much better lie. You mean in all seriousness that I should believe that a legless woman named Erika Silver tied three people up individually and savagely severed parts of each of their bodies?"

"It has to be that," he said, unsure now. "I can't come up with any other explanation."

"But how is it, then, that we can't find a single trace that proves this woman exists?"

Philip looked up at Henrik, furrowing his brow as if this were a new thought for him.

"The only 'proof' we've gotten came from you," Henrik said. "Therefore, right now I can't come to any other explanation than that it's you who went to the homes of Shirin Norberg, Katarina Vinston and Johan Rehn. How did you get in, though? Through a window?"

"What? No…"

"Or did they let you in? Did Katarina open the door and let you in?"

"I wasn't at Katarina's!"

"But you're lying, Philip…"

"No, I'm not. Why do you always think I'm lying?"

"You say you weren't at Katarina's on that day, but we have proof that you were."

"What kind of proof? I've never been inside her house."

"How is it that we found your wedding ring there?"

"What? You found it there?"

"Yes."

"But that's impossible, it…" Philip fell silent again.

"If I were you," Henrik said, "I'd ask for a lawyer."

★ ★ ★

Lina picked up a shoe that lay in front of the front door and placed it on the shoe rack before opening the door.

"I saw through the peephole that it was you," Lina Engström said, reaching her arms out toward Sandra, who was wearing jeans and a black polo shirt.

"I'm sorry I couldn't come yesterday," Sandra said, hugging her, "but we're short-staffed now that Philip is also gone. But you don't know how glad I am that you called."

Sandra had a backpack over one shoulder and white gym shoes on her feet. She tilted her head to the side and smiled.

Lina couldn't hold back the tears anymore.

"Is it that bad?" Sandra said.

Lina nodded.

"The police are looking for Philip, and I don't know why," she said. "Do you?"

"No," Sandra said. "I thought you did."

Lina wiped the tears from her cheeks. "Come in," she said.

Sandra stepped in.

"Did you close the door all the way?" Lina asked.

"Yes."

"Lock it, too."

"I locked it."

"Are you sure?"

Lina stepped forward and tried the door handle.

"I think you should try to calm down a little now," Sandra said.

"Yes," Lina said, breathing heavily. "I will. But Philip has been so strange. He thinks a murderer is hunting him. And he's been gone all night."

Sandra looked at her with a worried expression.

"I don't want to sound mean, but you look a little tired."

"I am tired," she said and smiled. "But do you really not know where he could be? I'm so nervous."

"Yes," Sandra said slowly. "Maybe I have a feeling."

"Tell me!"

"Only if you get me a cup of tea first," she said, dropping her backpack to the floor.

Mia placed a mug in the coffee machine and received a message that it was conducting an automatic cleaning cycle. She tried to remain calm and stood at the kitchen counter to wait.

It felt like she was waiting for everything right now. Philip Engström's wife wasn't answering the phone; Henrik hadn't come back from the interrogation; Ola still hadn't gotten any hits on anyone named Erika Silver. And now the fucking coffee machine was making her stand there and wait.

She looked at the clock. The machine had promised service in one minute, but two had already passed.

Standing there was beginning to feel annoyingly uncomfortable when Henrik came into the room.

"Philip Engström is being evasive," he said bitterly.

"What a surprise," Mia said, sitting in a chair.

"He's standing by his story, though, that there *is* an Erika Silver, and he seems to be going with the idea that her last name was something different," said Henrik. "But I don't know what I should believe anymore."

"You're doubting his story?"

"No, I'm not doubting it. He does actually have an alibi for the murder of Shirin Norberg. I have a hard time seeing his colleague being mistaken about such a thing."

"But he has no alibi for the murders of Katarina Vinston and Johan Rehn."

"He doesn't?"

"Not yet."

"Didn't you get a hold of his wife?"

Mia shook her head no. "But I'll try again."

Just then, the machine beeped. It was ready for use.

Mia stood up and filled her mug to the brim. She blew on the coffee just as Ola was coming in to join them. His excitement was visible.

"Good news!" he said triumphantly. "We have her name. It's Erika Sandell. Had surgery in March of 2005 at Vrinnevi. No husband, no children. She's lived in Fiskeby, west of town, for twenty years."

"Where in Fiskeby?" Mia said, signaling to Henrik to get moving.

"Drive over the bridge, get off at Sörbyvägen, take a left on Leonardsbergsvägen. The house should be at the end of the road."

CHAPTER
TWENTY-SEVEN

JANA BERZELIUS CHECKED HER CELL PHONE BEFORE stepping into the courtroom. Father hadn't called back—yet. She knew that the analysis itself would take time and she shouldn't have called, but she just wanted to make sure that he had done what she had asked him to.

She had never before turned to him for help, and the nagging uncertainty of whether she had done the right thing made her tense. It was likely he was the only one who knew how the contacts in his intricate network functioned.

She heard subdued voices when she stepped into Courtroom 2 for the hearing about an aggravated extortion case. She shook hands with the plaintiff, a young, twenty-two-year-old man, before sitting down beside him. He was nervous and chewed on the inside of his cheek constantly.

She looked at the presiding judge and the lay judges, and at the defendant and his scurrilous defense attorney, Peter

Ramstedt. Peter's wide grin was impossible to misinterpret, nor was his clicking pen. He was confident he would win.

She took a number of papers from her briefcase, among which was her summons application, which she would soon request to have read. She only had time to skim through it quickly before the presiding judge greeted everyone and thereby began the proceedings.

She looked at her cell phone one last time before turning it off. Then she prepared to begin.

The house was the farthest one on the street, as Ola had said, and almost out of sight, but the white facade and the dirty clay roof tiles were still visible.

There was nothing suspicious about the house itself. It looked like any other single-family home, on any other road, in any other midsize city.

There was a satellite dish on the roof, a straggly apple tree in the yard and an overturned ceramic pot on the stone pathway.

The gate squeaked when Henrik Levin opened it. He heard Mia Bolander's steps behind him and looked at the windows, noticing that some of the blinds were down and thinking it was far too quiet and calm for anyone to be home.

He pressed the doorbell, but he didn't hear any sound on the other side of the weather-beaten door. With his hand in a fist, he knocked hard three times, took a step back and waited. They waited for three minutes, then one more, and then two more to be on the safe side. Experience had taught him that if no one answers within six minutes, no one is going to. Ever.

They went around the back of the house, but nothing indicated the house was anything other than empty.

"There," Mia said when they had come full circle, pointing to a small window next to the front door. "I can get in there if you let me stand on your shoulders. That way we'll avoid a little paperwork and gain a few hours."

Within a few minutes, they were both standing inside the house.

It smelled closed-up and almost a little sweet. Cobwebs covered the corners of the ceilings and the light fixtures.

"Hello?" Henrik called despite the house seeming completely abandoned.

The kitchen was small and square and was located next to a living room that was twice its size. Pots and pans and boxes covered the countertop. There was a thick layer of grime covering the sink, and crumbs on the floor.

Henrik looked around, thinking that the silence felt ominous.

They turned around and left the kitchen. They walked past boxes and tin cans and continued into what seemed to be a path through the garbage.

The door to the bathroom was open and Henrik went in. There was filth everywhere he looked.

He went out again and looked at a wooden star hanging in one of the windows in the living room. Its blue paint had faded. Someone made that many years ago, he thought.

He moved his gaze to something in the hallway, right behind Mia.

"What are you looking at?" she said, turning around.

"A door," Henrik said.

He stepped over the garbage, carefully moving the cans of food that stood in front of the door before placing his hand on the door handle. He pulled on it, but it only opened an inch.

"Help me," he said to Mia.

"Damn, it's stubborn," she said, bracing with her foot against the wall.

The door opened and Henrik staggered back, stopping himself with a hand against the wall. Then he went to the doorway and saw stairs leading straight down into pitch-black nothingness. A musty smell wafted up from the darkness. Mia made a face and covered her mouth with her hand to try and stop herself from gagging.

"After you," she said.

"My whole body hurts when I think about Philip," Lina Engström said. She pulled on the arms of her sweater, avoiding looking at Sandra. Even though they had talked so many times before, she still didn't feel completely comfortable talking about her husband with her. Maybe it was because Sandra and Philip worked together.

Lina and Sandra sat on opposite sides of the sofa in the living room. The teacups sat on the table, and they'd been empty for a long time.

"It's awful," Lina said, "and I really wish I could not think about him at all. You know how it is…you think you know someone, that what you read in their eyes is true. That what they say is what they actually mean. And then you find out that's not the case at all."

Sandra nodded but didn't say anything.

"And now you're saying he made a mistake at work," she continued. "But why would the police be hunting him down for that? What sort of a mistake?"

"There were many mistakes," Sandra said. "I can't say any more about that because of…"

"…professional secrecy, I know. But where is he, then? And why would a murderer be hunting him down?" Lina tugged on her sweater again.

"Yes, it sounds crazy, I agree…but I don't know if you know that Philip…"

"What?" said Lina. She stared suddenly at Sandra.

"I don't know how much you talk to each other…" Sandra said.

"We don't talk to each other at all," Lina said sharply. "What is it?"

"Did you know that Philip takes pills?" Sandra said.

"No. I did suspect it, but I never…"

"Okay," Sandra said, taking a deep breath, "I think that his strange behavior lately is because he's addicted to these pills…"

Just then Lina's cell phone rang. Her heart began pounding as she picked it up from the table.

"Who is it?" Sandra said.

"I don't know," Lina said, stressed. "I don't recognize the number…"

"But maybe it's Philip. Why don't you just answer?"

"I don't dare."

"What are you scared of?"

"Everything, I think. But mostly that someone is going to call and say that something happened to him."

"Now you're blowing everything out of proportion again."

"Yes, maybe I am," she said.

"You should call back and see who it was," Sandra said when the ringing had stopped. "It's better to know than not, right?"

"Yes…" Lina said hesitatingly.

She looked at Sandra again.

"But how do you know he's taking pills?"

"Lina, he and I are work friends; we're together around the clock sometimes and we talk. Besides, a few things have happened at work that…"

"But…what sort of pills are they?"

"Sedatives…sleeping pills…" Sandra said.

"Sleeping pills? But that can't be true. He has a terrible time sleeping."

"That's exactly it."

★ ★ ★

Mia was still holding her nose and staring straight into the darkness. She stood behind Henrik, who fumbled around in his jacket pocket, pulled out his pocket flashlight and turned it on.

He took a step down the steep stairs, and she heard the wood creak under him. She followed his steps, thinking of all the horror films she'd seen.

As a little girl, she had hardly dared to be alone in the bathroom, even to wash her face. The sink was right across from the bathroom door, and she always had the crazy notion that if she looked into the mirror, she'd see someone in the doorway behind her. A classic fucking horror film cliché.

She still didn't like mirrors, which explained why she was so startled to see the dusty mirror standing near the stairs on the rough cement floor.

The low ceiling meant Henrik had to walk hunched over, and he swept the beam of light over the walls and some drapes, looking for a light switch. But there weren't any.

It smelled like mold and old basement—and something else.

Henrik suddenly gasped.

Mia looked at him and then at what was illuminated by his flashlight. In the light she first saw a wheel, then a wheelchair, and then she saw that in the wheelchair sat a woman. Or what was left of a woman, at least.

"Is that Erika Sandell?" Mia said, exhaling.

"I assume so," Henrik said.

CHAPTER
TWENTY-EIGHT

"SHE'S BEEN DEAD A LONG TIME," ANNELI LINDGREN said, pulling on a blue glove that snapped against her wrist. She had just arrived with two other forensic techs who would now work through the house room by room.

Henrik Levin and Mia Bolander stood to her left, both with their eyes on the woman in the wheelchair, her hanging head and her amputated legs.

"How long?" Henrik asked.

"Hard to say at first glance. But considering how far the decay has gone, she's probably been here a few years."

"A few years?" Henrik said.

"Yes, or even longer. It's hard to know exactly."

Henrik sighed and looked around in the now brightly illuminated basement, letting his gaze sweep over the walls and the curtain hanging behind the dead woman in the wheelchair.

"And poof, there goes Philip's story," Mia said.

"Yes," Henrik said, "but Erika existed, anyway. Even if her condition was worse than we'd expected."

"Yes," Anneli said, "and if you'll excuse me, I'd like to have her to myself now."

"We'll take a look around upstairs, then," Henrik said.

"I'd rather you didn't," Anneli said.

"You know we're careful," Henrik said, looking at Anneli with a knowing gaze.

"You can never be too careful," she said, turning her back to him.

Henrik and Mia left the basement and went up the stairs to the first floor.

"What are we to think about Philip after this?" Henrik said. "Innocent or not?"

"It's obvious he's not innocent. Either he's completely off his rocker from all of the pills, or he's just trying to confuse us."

"We have to try to get a hold of his wife," Henrik said. "See if she can confirm his alibi, if nothing else."

He stepped onto the first floor and shivered as the cold, damp air from the open front door permeated his jacket. He looked around and thought about the sequence of events. Shirin Norberg, whose hands had been severed, Katarina Vinston, whose tongue had been cut out, and Johan Rehn, who had lost both legs.

And he thought about Erika Sandell, sitting in her wheelchair in the basement, dead.

"And for all of these years, no one missed her," he said aloud but to himself.

He went back into the square kitchen. The words echoed in his head as he looked around. He looked at the pans and the boxes, at the food scraps.

"But someone must have helped her get down into the

basement," he said. "And someone must have been paying the bills all these years."

He walked to the sink and looked more closely at the scraps, then opened the kitchen cupboards and looked.

"Not all of the porcelain is dusty," he said.

"Okay…?" Mia said.

"Look here," he said, pointing to two cups standing side by side. "One has a layer of grime on it, and the other one looks almost freshly washed."

Mia turned to him.

"But only Erika is on the books as living here?" Mia said.

"Yes," Henrik said.

"Husband and children?"

"No," he said. "She didn't have any family."

"So who the hell has been living here these past few years?" she said.

"It feels like I'm the only one who wants anything out of our relationship. Philip just always clams up," Lina said, meeting Sandra's gaze. "And now that all of this has happened—the police, the pill addiction, the murders—I feel like I don't know anything anymore."

"I understand," Sandra said.

"Ugh, it feels like I'm the only one talking."

"You need to vent, and I'm a good listener."

"Maybe that's why it's so easy to talk to you," Lina said, smiling. Then she turned her gaze to the blanket that lay beside her and starting fiddling with it.

"Now you look worried again," Sandra said. "It'll work out. You'll see."

"But," Lina began, "I have this picture in my mind of a family, and I don't know why I've been holding on to it so hard. It isn't real."

"What does it look like?"

"You're going to laugh."

"No, I won't. Tell me."

"It's the traditional picture with a mom, a dad and children, a house with a white picket fence, Volvo station wagon, a dog…"

"Sounds like a beautiful picture to me."

"Yeah." Lina nodded, turning her gaze to the window. "But when you find out that the man you're married to and love is a pathological liar who's addicted to pills…do you know how that feels? How tricked I feel?"

"No, but I can imagine."

"I'm so angry, I could almost kill him."

Sandra gave a short chuckle.

"Now *that* I can understand!" she said.

Lina smiled, but her smile evaporated as her cell phone rang again.

"You should probably answer this time," Sandra said.

"I probably should," Lina said, feeling her hand tremble as she picked up the phone.

"Hello?" she said.

Jana Berzelius left the courtroom without speaking to anyone, which seemed to bother attorney Peter Ramstedt. It seemed like the drawn-out hearing had gone in her favor, but the judgment wouldn't be handed down until the following day.

She went out through the lobby, down the stairs, then walked quickly through downtown toward her apartment.

As she walked, she thought through everything one more time. There weren't many escape routes. The way she had chosen was the simplest, but she wanted to be sure that she hadn't overlooked any obvious difficulties that would prevent

Danilo from getting from the apartment to the car in the garage. She hadn't.

She was more worried about how they would manage any unexpected problems that could crop up.

As she entered the apartment and took off her coat, she saw him out of the corner of her eye. Danilo held his head high, as if he were already certain everything would go according to plan. In reality, his entire disappearance had had to do with confidence. It didn't matter if you had a fake passport or driver's license, convincing wigs or disguises, if you couldn't talk, move and act with confidence. People saw what you told them to see.

Danilo was probably a good actor, but the only role he was playing right now was himself. He had clean clothes, a new haircut and a freshly shaven face, for sure. At first glance, he bore no resemblance to the man who had broken into her home wearing scrubs almost a week ago. But a practiced eye would recognize him, she was sure of it.

"Have you decided?" he asked.

"We'll go through the basement," she said. "I'll go first, then you."

Then he turned toward her, his muscles tense under his sweatshirt. Their eyes met for a brief moment, and Jana felt a rush of emotional relief pass through her. Danilo would finally be leaving her apartment, finally be disappearing from her life.

"Good," he said. "I'm ready. Are you?"

Henrik Levin took a deep breath when he stepped out into the fresh air. It was a relief to leave Erika Sandell's house.

He heard children laughing as they crossed the street and, a little farther away, saw a car backing out of a driveway. He turned his head and looked toward the end of the street where the fields began.

Mia came up alongside him, her cell phone in hand.

"I've finally gotten a hold of Lina Engström."

"What did she say?"

"She wasn't completely sure, but she thought Philip had been home the night Katarina was murdered. She couldn't say about Johan, and I think she was difficult to talk to. She sounded upset, almost confused."

"Do you think we need to send someone over to her house?"

Mia shook her head.

"She had a friend there."

"Good. Should we…" he began, but then fell silent when he saw a woman in her sixties walk across the street. She was wearing a red down vest, dark jeans and rubber boots with polka dots. Her ash-blond hair was cut in a pageboy, and her bangs reached past her eyebrows. She stopped when she saw the police tape and then continued up the gravel path that led to the large house next door.

"I'm just going to…" Henrik said to Mia, gesturing toward the woman.

"Should I come, too?"

"No, I'll do it myself."

Henrik left Erika's house, went through the gate and walked with long strides after the woman who was already standing at her front door.

"Hello!" he called. "Please wait."

The woman turned around and looked at him with a questioning gaze.

"I'd like to ask you a few questions," he said.

"What about? What's happened?"

"It's about Erika Sandell, your neighbor."

Henrik pulled out his badge, introduced himself and asked if he could come in for a moment.

"It will only take a few minutes," he said.

"Then we might as well stand out here," she said.

"You have a lovely home," Henrik said.

"Yes, I hear that a lot," she said.

"Are you married?"

"What do you mean?"

"I'm just asking."

"There's a man in my life, if that's what you mean."

She pushed a lock of hair behind her ear.

"How long have you been living next to Erika Sandell?"

"Let me see. I moved here thirteen, maybe fourteen years ago."

"When did you last see her?"

"Oh, a long time ago."

"And you don't think that's strange?"

"No, why would I? She's probably abroad most of the time. She has…an injury."

"Why would she be abroad?"

The woman looked at him as if she were embarrassed by the question.

"If she's not home, where else would she be?"

She put her hand on her hip.

"Erika was found dead in her home today."

"She's dead?" The woman looked at him again, this time with an empty stare as if she were having a hard time understanding the meaning of what Henrik had just said.

"What happened?" she said.

"I can't disclose details," Henrik said, "but I'd like to know if you, her closest neighbor, have seen or heard anything that could be helpful to us? Have you, for example, seen anyone going to or from the house lately?"

She shook her head.

"I see her daughter now and then."

"Her daughter?"

"Yes."

"But from what I understand, Erika Sandell doesn't have a daughter."

"Oh yes, she does."

"Do you know her name?"

"No, we usually just say hi, and I've just talked to her only a few times, but she's a very pleasant and pretty young woman, with eyes like emeralds. It's so nice that she's taken care of her mother all these years, but I've always thought she should have a life of her own with a handsome man and some children."

"Have you seen her recently?"

"Yes, of course. She lives there."

Lina tried to stand up, but the effort nearly made her vomit. She held her hands to her mouth and swallowed multiple times before looking at Sandra again.

"What was that about?" Sandra said.

Lina took a deep breath before answering.

"It was the police," she answered as if she almost didn't want to form the words.

"What did they say?"

She put both hands over her face and shook her head.

"I can't. I just want to lie in bed and cry when I think about…"

"We don't have time to cry right now," Sandra said. "Tell me what they said!"

"They asked if I could give him an alibi."

"Alibi for what?"

"For the night when Katarina was murdered…and that doctor…"

"Did they say anything else?"

Lina wrapped her arms around herself and sat still, her eyes fixed on the floor.

"They said that they'd taken him into custody, that he's suspected of murder."

"Good," Sandra said.

Lina blinked a few times and looked at Sandra.

"What?"

Sandra stood, picked up her backpack and left the room.

"What's good about that?" Lina asked, but the only answer was the sound of the bathroom door closing.

With the feeling that everything was going to return to normal, Jana left her apartment and stepped into the elevator. It descended slowly, the steel cables squeaking.

Her legs felt relaxed as she walked through the long hallway that led to the garage.

To avoid the risk of being seen with him, of meeting anyone while they were together, she had gone first and taken the elevator. He was going to take the stairs.

She felt her pulse quickening in her temples as she approached her parking space. She stopped between two cars. She saw herself in the side window of the car next to her. But then she caught sight of another familiar face.

"I see you," she said.

"That was the point," Danilo said.

"There could be cameras here," she said, mostly to stress the risk of what they were doing.

"No, there aren't," he said, grinning.

He began to walk toward her, going around a car to draw it out. He was ten steps from her, five, three, two, one…

She was just about to unlock the car when the door from the basement swung open, and to her horror, her neighbor came out with a bag in her hand and headed in her direction.

Danilo grabbed her. He pressed his face against hers, and she felt his skin against her cheek.

"What are you doing?" she whispered.

"Pretend I'm kissing you. And be quiet now, or I'll do it for real. With tongue and everything."

She didn't breathe, tried to release the air she had in her lungs, but she couldn't.

They stood silently, pushed against each other, until the neighbor had started her car and disappeared through the garage door.

As soon as it had closed, she pushed him off her.

"Don't you dare look at me," she said harshly.

When he didn't look away, it overflowed in her, all of the adrenaline and hatred. It overwhelmed her, making her heart pound hard. She looked down, meeting her reflection in the car window again. She could see the tension in her face and told herself to calm down. And breathe.

"But there isn't one single piece of information that indicates Erika had a daughter," Ola Söderström said.

"Look again," Henrik said.

He stood outside the house in Fiskeby with his cell phone pressed to his ear.

"But where else should I look?" Ola said. "Do you not trust me?"

"Of course I trust you," Henrik said, rubbing his hand over his face. "And Erika was never married?"

"No."

"But she must have lived with someone, then…?"

"Maybe so, but live-in partners aren't registered anywhere, as you know."

"I know. I know! But call me if you find anything."

"But…"

Henrik hung up with a sigh.

"No luck?" Mia said, looking at him with raised eyebrows.

"Nope," he said, turning his gaze to the house again. He wanted to stop his thoughts, structure them and gain clarity about everything that had happened.

It was impossible for Erika to have a biological daughter. But the neighbor had been sure that a younger woman lived in the house and that the woman herself had claimed to be Erika's daughter.

So who was that young woman? he thought, again focusing his gaze on the wooden star hanging in one of the windows. At the same moment, Anneli Lindgren appeared at the front door.

"Henrik! Mia!" she said. "You should probably come back into the basement."

Henrik nodded and walked back to the house, closely followed by Mia. The musty smell hit him again, but he tried to ignore it as he went down the basement stairs.

"I think you're going to want to see this," Anneli said, walking toward the drapes that hung behind the dead woman. Dust whirled up as she pulled it farther to the side, revealing a desk behind which hung a bulletin board. Henrik was looking directly into the pale blue eyes of Katarina Vinston, who stared back from a photograph. Where her mouth should have been was instead a black hole. He looked away, took a step back and surveyed the other photographs that had been pinned to the bulletin board.

"Shirin Norberg," he said in a low voice. "And Johan Rehn, and...who is this?"

He pointed to a crossed-out face he didn't recognize.

"That must be Annikke," Mia said, "the nurse anesthetist. But it's hard to say when you can't really see her face. And those must be Joe and Anders."

Mia pointed to two other crossed-out faces.

"So what we have before us are pictures of the surgery team?" he said.

"Yes," Mia said, "and how that sick bastard probably planned to kill all of them."

Henrik felt his heart pounding hard in his chest when he looked at Shirin's missing hands and Johan's missing legs. Far to the right hung a picture of Philip Engström, hanging all by itself, far from the others.

He glanced down at the desk and saw several black notebooks closed with thick cords. He picked up the top one, loosened the cord and began flipping through. Mia stood close to him, reading over his shoulder.

March 3

Dear Diary,

I've turned on the light and am looking at the pictures on the wall. Looking at the faces that look so irritatingly happy and simultaneously unaware of any evil. So full of expectations, as if it were obvious that their lives lay before them. As if they had the right to live.

Today is ten years since your operation, Mom, ten years since they destroyed our lives, ten years ago. How have they been? Have they lived life? As if the operation was just a bagatelle, a parenthesis in their lives, a bad morning. Nothing more.

For us, it's been hell. Since then.

I know who did what at the hospital. You've talked about it so many times.

I can't give you your life back, but I can punish the ones who took it from you. You will get your revenge now, Mom. I'll take the hands of the surgery nurse who stood at a loss in the operating room; I'll take the tongue from the paramedic who forgot,

FORGOT! to say that they'd turned the helicopter around. And I'll take the legs from the surgeon who handed the operation over to a medical student. TO A MEDICAL STUDENT! How the hell could he justify that?

I truly hate Philip. I hate his cocky attitude, hate him because he doesn't understand what he did, hate him because he doesn't know that I hate him. Because he only lives in his own world as if nothing were wrong.

I'm going to turn off the lamp now, because it's time to begin.

And I know exactly how I'll do it. I have everything figured out. My plan is ready.

They won't get away from this, Mom. They destroyed your life. They destroyed my life. I'm going to destroy theirs.

That's what the voices in my head are saying.

And that's how simple it is.

The truth.

Henrik looked up and met Mia's gaze.

"Who the hell wrote this?"

Henrik looked at her for a long time before closing the notebook and putting it back on the desk.

"What is it, Henrik? Where are you going?"

He heard Mia's questions, but he didn't have time to answer, instead running back up the basement stairs. He rushed into the living room, stood in the middle of the room and looked at the wooden star hanging in the window.

He went closer, feeling a chill as he reached out his hand. The star was made from wooden pieces glued tightly to each other. He unhooked it and turned it over.

It looked like the sort of star you made in art class in school. He had come home from school himself with one figure after another, and among all of the things he had brought home, there'd been a similar star. If this star had been made at school, it should also be marked with a name.

Henrik continued turning it between his hands. Then he stopped. He held the star closer to his face. The paint had faded, but he could still see the name that stood there.

S, he read. *Sa*...and then a number.

He squinted again. And then he saw it.

It said, "Sandra, class 9A."

CHAPTER
TWENTY-NINE

JANA BERZELIUS CAST A GLANCE IN THE REARVIEW mirror and saw that Danilo was still lying down in the back-seat. She returned her gaze to the road and thought how they were finally on their way north, toward Nyköping, Vagnhärad and Södertälje.

Toward freedom.

For a moment she considered flooring the gas pedal, but she forced herself to calm down. She couldn't risk being caught for speeding now, so she remained at the exact speed limit, forty-five miles per hour.

They were approaching an uncontrolled railroad crossing when her phone rang. She didn't let it ring for more than a few seconds before she answered.

She heard a scraping sound before her father's voice came through.

"It's done," he said.

Jana felt her heart beginning to pound and had a hard time subduing her eagerness.

"Have you gotten the DNA result?" she said.

"Yes."

Maybe she misunderstood his tone, but she thought that there was something wary in his voice—to the extent that it was possible to sense anything in his abrupt answer.

Danilo looked at her. She felt his eyes on her but didn't look back.

"So you have a match?" she said.

The phone was quiet for a number of seconds, which didn't necessarily mean anything other than that her father was thinking. She waited for an answer, but there was nothing. He was silent for so long that she wondered if they'd been cut off. Maybe Elin was within earshot?

"Tell me," she said.

"Not on phone."

"I can't come to your house," she said. "You have to tell me now. Whose DNA was it under Mother's fingernail?"

She slowed down as she drove over a stream and saw that dense brush concealed a small promontory that stuck out into a lake. She thought that his breath sounded closer, as if he were holding the phone as close to his mouth as he could.

"The reslt said tht…tht…"

He was struggling with the words.

"Yes?" Jana said.

"The result showed that the DNA came from… Frm Sandr Gustfsson."

She felt her body tense as she listened to the sound of the engine.

"And that's definite?"

"Yes," he said. "It's defnit. But who's tha?"

★ ★ ★

"I have a few follow-up questions that I need answers to," Henrik Levin said when he was let into the cell where Philip Engström sat. "And I need answers quickly."

"Okay…?" Philip said, rubbing his hand over his neck.

"Did you see Erika after the operation?"

Philip swallowed and looked down at the floor.

"Yes," he said. "I did, I told you about it. I visited her at the hospital a few weeks after the operation."

"Did she ever say anything about having a daughter?"

"No, why would she say that to me? You have to understand that she hated me. She truly hated me."

"Yes, you said that," Henrik said. "So you've never been to Erika Sandell's house?"

"Is that her last name? Sandell?"

"Yes, but answer my question now. Have you ever been to her house?"

Philip stared at him quietly.

"But you're not listening to what I'm saying," he said, his voice rising almost to a falsetto. "I don't know her. I've never had anything to do with her after the operation."

"So you've never been to Leonardsbergsvägen in Fiskeby?"

"What? No," he said, looking suddenly upset. "Does she live there?"

"Yes, and we were at her house today," Henrik said.

"In Fiskeby? What did she say?"

Philip looked at him.

"She didn't say anything," Henrik said. "She was dead, had been for many years."

"What?"

"But it seems that she had a daughter," Henrik continued, "but I don't know if that's true."

"What?" Philip said again.

"A daughter, and we have reason to believe that her name is Sandra."

"Sandra?" Philip repeated, putting his hands to his mouth. He looked at Henrik with a terrified expression. "You mean my colleague Sandra Gustafsson?"

"I don't know," Henrik said uneasily. "Do I?"

"Sandra Gustafsson's mom lives in Fiskeby. She told me so. But I never met her mother…never been to her house…but how could she…"

Henrik looked at the man in front of him, who suddenly turned pale as a sheet.

"No!" he screamed. "Sandra is with…"

He threw himself toward the cell door, screaming at the top of his lungs: "Lina!"

What was Sandra doing? She'd been locked in the bathroom for a very long time now. Lina had heard the door close and lock, but she hadn't heard it open again. Why had she been in there for so long?

She closed her eyelids and felt her eyes burn. She was exhausted.

"Sandra?" she called.

When she didn't hear an answer, she got up slowly and walked toward the bathroom. She put her hand to her stomach unconsciously. It was hard to take in the fact that there was a life in there. She knew it would be a long time before she could feel a bump, but she found herself already longing for it.

The hallway was dark, and she was just about to turn on the light when she saw that the door to the bathroom was open.

"Sandra?" she called again, looking around. But still there was no answer.

She heard popping sounds ahead of her, and Lina Engström turned her gaze toward the living room before continuing farther into the hallway. The door to the kitchen was closed, and when she opened it she could feel how her heart was pounding in her chest.

Sandra stood at the kitchen counter and was picking something up.

Lina raised her eyebrows in confusion when she saw that it was a syringe.

"What are you going to do?"

"Don't be scared," Sandra said, turning around with the syringe in her hand.

"What are you doing?" she said, thinking that she should raise her arm to defend herself, but her muscles didn't react as quickly as her brain did.

She stumbled backward, right into the white wall.

"Stop," she panted.

"Calm down!" Sandra said.

She saw the syringe and tried to escape by throwing herself to the side, but it just caused her to bump into a lamp that fell to the floor.

"Stop, please stop!" she screamed, tripping on the rug. Her body yielded, and she tumbled over, hitting her head on the floor. She got up on all fours and tried to crawl toward the front door, but she knew she wouldn't be able to escape.

Sandra went around her, crouched down, tilted her head to the side and looked at her. The syringe was close now, right next to her neck.

She felt the needle push through the skin and then pull back out.

Lina raised her trembling hand to her neck, stroked a number of times over the point of entry and saw the small droplets of blood on her fingertips.

She tried to say something, but her tongue felt strangely

numb. She slowly looked up at Sandra, but it was hard to fix her gaze on anything. It felt like the floor was swaying.

She reached her hand out toward the door handle and got a hold of it, but her hand slipped. She tried to call for help.

A warm wave rushed through her body.

Her vision went black as she lost consciousness.

Henrik Levin ran through the hallway of the police station with his cell phone in hand. He tried to get a hold of Mia, and while it rang, he thought about Johan Rehn, who had been responsible for Erika Sandell's operation. If he had performed it himself, the mistake presumably wouldn't have been made—and three people would still be alive. But he hadn't been the one who performed it. It had been the young Philip Engström instead.

Henrik thought about Sandra Gustafsson, the paramedic. Didn't she have green eyes, emerald green?

When he came to the first step in the stairwell, Mia answered with a "Yep."

"You sound out of breath," she said.

"Yes. I have big news."

"What? What's happened?"

"If I believe Philip, Sandra Gustafsson's mom lives on Leonardsbergsvägen in Fiskeby."

"I don't follow."

"Erika Sandell's daughter is the paramedic Sandra Gustafsson."

"What the hell are you saying?" Mia said.

"Yes, what the hell *am* I saying?"

"So we'll bring her in immediately, right?"

"Absolutely, but here's the bad news. She's at Philip's house with his wife, alone. Can you have a patrol unit sent to their house right away?"

"Of course."

"And can you check with Ola so that he gathers any and all information about Sandra Gustafsson? Then meet me down in the garage."

Henrik hung up and kept running.

CHAPTER
THIRTY

SANDRA GUSTAFSSON!

Jana Berzelius could hardly breathe. She had hoped for an answer, but now that she knew it was Sandra's DNA that Mother had had under her fingernails, she didn't know quite what to do with that information. Everything was spinning, and she had to keep both hands on the wheel to steer straight ahead.

Paramedic Sandra Gustafsson had smothered her mother by placing her hand or hands over her nose and mouth. That much she understood. What she didn't understand was the motive. Why had Sandra murdered her mother? It was incomprehensible.

The aggression made her neck itch, and her arms, her legs, everywhere. She wished more than anything that the woman were standing before her right now so she could force answers out of her using every method she knew before finally...

Her cell phone rang again. She grabbed it from her lap, saw that it was Henrik Levin's number and answered.

"Jana speaking."

"It's not Erika," Henrik Levin said. "We think it's Sandra Gustafsson who…"

"Wait, wait a minute," she interrupted. "What are you talking about?"

"Erika Silver, or Sandell as we now know is her name, is dead," he said. "We found her dead in her residence today. I thought Gunnar had told you."

"And now you're saying that it's Sandra who…"

"Sandra Gustafsson," he said. "Philip Engström's colleague."

"Yes, I know who you're talking about," Jana said. "So she's guilty of the murders, you mean?"

A thousand thoughts spun through her head.

"Yes!" Henrik said vehemently.

"So have you brought her in?"

"We think she's at Philip Engström's house."

"Okay, so where is that?"

She tried to keep calm.

"At Jordbrogatan 209 in Skarphagen."

"Are you completely certain that's where she is?"

"Not completely," he said.

"That's why you're calling me," Jana said. "You need a search warrant to break down the door, if necessary?"

"That's right," Henrik said. "So I have your approval?"

"Yes," Jana said. "That should be fine."

"Good," Henrik said. "We're leaving for there now."

"Call me when you've found her," she said.

She waited to hear Henrik confirm before she hung up and let her hand sink back into her lap.

Sandra Gustafsson, she thought again.

She focused her gaze through the windshield and felt her

muscles tense up. She knew that she should force herself to regain control, regulate her breath and manage the strong emotions that were welling up inside her.

A plan had begun to take shape in her head that was different from driving Danilo straight to Södertälje.

She looked at the clock and knew that the police were already on their way to Engström's residence. But she could get there first.

With her heart pounding, she turned the wheel, tires squealing as she forced the car into a sharp U-turn.

"Where the hell are we going?" said Danilo, sitting up in the backseat.

"I have to take care of something first," she said.

Philip Engström paced back and forth in his cell. He'd tried to convince the guard to open the cell door and had pounded on it until his hands were bruised and broken, but no one had cared, and the panic he felt was on the verge of crushing all of his hopes.

His head was throbbing with pain, and he sank to the floor, searching with his hand over his clothes after a pill to take. He pulled and fumbled at the fabric of his pockets in a sort of desperate hope to find something that could subdue his angst. But there was none to be found.

A string of saliva hung from his lip to his chin, and he wiped it away with the sleeve of his shirt.

Sandra, he thought. Could it really be true? The person who'd sat beside him in the ambulance so many times? Was she Erika Sandell's daughter? His thoughts whirled around in his head.

When they had gone to help Shirin, she had already known what awaited them. When they'd gone to Johan's, too. She had been there earlier, had tied them up, mutilated them, left them to bleed to death. And then, in cold blood, had acted like she knew nothing about it.

She'd just stood there and looked on.

How was that possible?

And how long had she been planning to avenge her mother? Many years? She'd searched for him, become his coworker, gotten to know him, gotten to know Lina; all of this with one goal in mind.

Revenge—for something she hadn't even been a part of.

She had to be disturbed, deeply disturbed. There was no other explanation. Deeply disturbed, and he hadn't had a clue.

She had even taken his wedding ring and put it at Katarina's, but why? To frame him, place him at the scene? *She must have taken it when I was asleep in the ambulance*, he thought.

And now, she was with Lina at their house.

His heart began pounding harder in his chest, and the panic reared its ugly head again. He had begun thinking of the child in Lina's belly. Just think if Sandra had done something to Lina, hurt her, or even...

He didn't dare finish the thought.

Jana Berzelius crossed through the heavily trafficked highway toward Norrköping again. Ten minutes later, she reduced her speed as she arrived at Jordbrogatan in Skarphagen.

She quickly checked the street number for Philip Engström's house and soon afterward caught sight of the house she was looking for.

"What the hell are we doing here?" Danilo said.

"Lie down," she said with a harsh voice, "or you'll never make it to Södertälje."

Danilo lay down again, and she checked down the street for police cruisers and, more importantly, unmarked police cars. But it didn't seem they had arrived yet. A guy with a stroller sat on a park bench down the street, but otherwise the area was empty.

A white Volvo was parked in the driveway of the house.

Carefully, she opened the glove compartment, took out the knife and felt Danilo's burning gaze on her as she placed it at the small of her back.

She was just about to get out of the car when the front door of the house opened and a woman with light hair came out.

She presumed it was Sandra.

She walked with her back straight but was constantly looking around as if she were ready for someone to jump out at her.

Jana sank down in the seat, and although Sandra seemed to be on guard, she didn't notice the woman in the black car who was spying on her.

What had happened?

Was Lina Engström still in the house?

Sandra went to the white Volvo, got in, started the engine and began backing out of the driveway.

Jana sat thinking for a moment before she slowly put her own car in motion and followed.

Henrik Levin gripped the steering wheel hard as he cursed the traffic heading out of town. It seemed as if miles and miles of Norrköping were now only comprised of one thing. Traffic. And traffic meant delays.

Next to him sat Mia, her cell phone to her ear.

"She's not answering," she said. "I've called four times now."

"That's not good," Henrik said, wishing he could go even faster.

They went past the center of the Skarphagen neighborhood, turned into the residential area and drove past glassed-in balconies with wicker furniture, large trampolines and parked cars.

Henrik felt like it had grown warmer in the car. With his right hand, he tried to pull down the zipper of his jacket, but it wouldn't budge. It had gotten caught, and the thought of not being able to cool off made him sweat even more.

"We're almost there," he said as if to himself.

Dusk had begun to fall when he turned in toward a garage and stopped. He left the car idling while he checked the area. A man was sitting on a park bench, rocking a stroller back and forth and looking at them with curiosity, and at the end of the street two kids around ten years old were kicking a soccer ball back and forth.

Four heavily armed officers were already in place: two in front of the house, two behind.

Henrik and Mia stepped out of the car and, crouching, approached Engström's house. Both were ready with their service weapons when the officers got in position outside the front door.

Henrik saw Mia biting her thumbnail as she followed the situation.

Three muffled tones sounded when one of the officers rang the black doorbell. He pulled out his weapon, rang again and waited.

"Go in now," said a voice. "Quickly, quickly, quickly."

Mia stopped biting her nail.

The door opened.

Henrik saw the first officer gesture to the other to follow him and secure the line of fire to the right. The officer waited a few seconds, looked in quickly, then made the sign for countdown: three, two, one.

Then they stormed into the house.

Henrik listened as they moved quickly through the rooms and prepared himself for going in.

She knew that she didn't have much choice now. Considering the situation, she was walking a very fine line. Yet Jana

Berzelius had chosen to follow Sandra Gustafsson with Danilo Peña in the backseat. What's more was the huge risk of having the police on her tail.

"Where the hell are we going?" Danilo said again. "Can't you answer me?"

His voice was harsh, his eyes dark. But he couldn't do anything other than lie in the backseat.

"I'm going to miss the meeting," he said, "and I hope you understand what that means."

"We have time," she said. "But first I have to take care of something."

Sandra had sped along the E22 toward Söderköping and forced Jana to run a red light at the crossing over the Göta Canal. After the crest of a hill, Sandra had quickly turned off, and now they were driving along a small gravel road straight into the forest.

She didn't see the white Volvo anymore, and she slowed down and considered the road. It was narrow.

Following someone on small, deserted roads was risky. The risk of being seen was obviously much greater than on a well-traveled road. Sandra may already have seen her, parked behind a hill or other cover, and was now standing there, waiting for her.

Or she was already far into the forest.

But I can't lose her now, she thought, increasing her speed.

Henrik Levin and Mia Bolander looked into the house. They saw the ball caps and scarves hanging in the same place in the hallway and glanced around the sofa, books and computer in the living room.

The officers had secured the rooms.

The house was empty.

A broken lamp was on the floor. Bloody fingerprints were

visible on the frame of the front door and around the lock, as if someone had fumbled for the handle.

Mia stepped out of the house again. Henrik followed her out and felt the sweat on his back. This time it wasn't because of the warmth of the clothes or protective vest, but because neither Sandra nor Lina had been in the house.

He walked slowly to the car, sat down and pondered.

The blood on the door handle bothered him.

What had happened to Lina Engström?

He picked up his cell phone and called Gunnar.

"What's going on?" Gunnar asked.

"Everything and nothing."

"What do you mean, nothing? Was the house empty?"

"Yes, and it seems that Sandra has taken Lina somewhere. But in order to know where she's gone, I have to know more about her."

"I bet Ola has a whole lot to tell you."

"Good," Henrik said. "Make sure he calls me."

CHAPTER
THIRTY-ONE

LINA ENGSTRÖM WOKE UP. HER BODY TENSED IN panic when she felt the tape covering her mouth.

She breathed heavily through her nose when she realized she was in the backseat of a car. Carefully she moved her fingers, wanting to use her hands to take the tape off, but then she realized her wrists were tied tight behind her back with a zip tie.

With her eyes wide, she let her gaze travel to the driver's seat and saw Sandra sitting there.

Where were they going? How long had they been driving?

She tried to figure out where they were, but how would she be able to do that? She had no idea if they had gone north or south. The only thing she knew was that they were now driving on a bumpy gravel road. She had hardly any doubt that they were traveling on a deserted road through the forest. She hadn't heard any traffic.

She looked at Sandra again and tried to say something, but through the tape, it only sounded like short grunts.

Henrik Levin let his gaze rest on the park bench where the man with the stroller had been sitting. The man had now stood up to talk to Mia. Where he'd been sitting, someone had written "I was here" in ink. Henrik looked at the words while he listened to Ola Söderström's voice through the speaker of his cell phone.

"Sandra Gustafsson is in her early twenties, and hasn't had an easy life. Her biological mother died when she was two years old. Her father had sole custody and suffered from severe alcohol addiction. Two reports to Child Protective Services when Sandra was three years old. One case stated that she'd been found outside her home at three o'clock one Saturday morning wearing only underwear. Her dad was there, too, but inside the apartment, sleeping on the kitchen floor. The other case was about an injury. Her preschool had noticed a wound behind her ear, and she was reported to have said: 'Ow, Daddy!' about the injury. But both investigations were closed."

"So Sandra grew up with only her dad?" Henrik said.

"Yes, partly," Ola said.

Henrik again observed the park bench, thinking that her childhood must have left its mark on her.

"But how does Erika fit into the picture?"

"So Erika Sandell," Ola said, "grew up in a house just outside Söderköping. She finished school with low grades. There's evidence that she suffered from obesity and that she sought help for it."

"But no other problems in the family?" Henrik said.

"No," Ola said. "Doesn't seem so. She'd lived at a few different addresses in Norrköping and bought the house on

Leonardsbergsvägen over twenty years ago. But, hold on now, that exact address is in one of Sandra's journal entries."

"So Sandra and her father could have lived with Erika?"

"For sure. But there's no indication that Erika adopted Sandra or anything like that."

"But it's possible that Sandra saw her as her mother anyway, like a stepmother or godmother."

"Yes," Ola said. "Her father drank himself to death, so she likely only had Erika in the end. And then the whole situation with the operation happened when Sandra was a teenager."

They fell silent for a moment.

"Sandra is registered at an address in Karlstad," Ola continued. "But because she works in Norrköping, it seems unlikely that she lives there."

"Ask our colleagues there to check that address anyway," he said. "Doesn't she have any connections to other properties?"

"I've checked every database," Ola said. "She doesn't own anything, doesn't have any land or a summer cottage. The only thing I found was a post office box here in Norrköping."

Henrik sighed and turned quiet. All he could hear was the sound of a soccer ball being kicked against a brick wall.

Jana Berzelius stopped the car. The road had split, and she leaned forward, scanning the gravel and trying to see if there were fresh tire tracks that would reveal which way Sandra had chosen. But the road was far too dry.

It was a fifty-fifty chance.

The road to the right was a bit wider, she thought, and decided in the end to go that way.

"I have no idea what you're about to do," Danilo said, who was now sitting up in the backseat, "but it seems to be a huge mistake."

Jana looked at him, just for a second, but long enough to

understand that he was right. She was risking everything for this mission. But right now, she had no other choice than to finish what she'd started. She stepped on the gas and drove on, farther into the forest.

The sun had almost set. Henrik Levin was still sitting in the car in Skarphagen with his cell phone in his hand, sweeping his gaze over the surrounding houses. Everything was still, and he saw lights had been turned on in many of the homes.

He repeated to himself that right now, with great probability, Sandra was on the way to a place that she had planned in advance—and that they had to find it quickly, before it was too late.

He shuddered when he thought how thoroughly planned everything had been. How she had steered the suspicions toward Philip with small, effective elements, letting them think that he was guilty. How she had placed the wedding ring at Katarina Vinston's house to lay the blame on him. Her slow, methodical movements had almost been invisible. She had slowly approached Philip, sought the job as a paramedic, become his colleague, become friends with his wife. She had even been with him at the crime scenes—for two of them, at least. She was so coldhearted, or was she just desensitized?

Mia knocked on the window and waved as if to ask if it was okay to open the car door. Before he'd had the chance to answer, she'd opened it.

"Wait a moment, Ola," Henrik said, dropping the cell phone to his chest.

"I talked with the guy over there," Mia said, pointing to the man with the stroller. "His name is Jonas Ekberg and he lives at 207. He says he saw a white Volvo outside Engström's house just a little bit ago. A young woman was driving it…"

"Which direction?"

"Toward the on-ramp to E22."

Henrik raised the phone again.

"Ola?" he said. "Did you hear that?"

"Yep, heard it from the speaker. But it doesn't seem like she owns a car. There's a car registered to Erika, though, a Volvo."

"Put out a BOLO on it," Henrik said.

Henrik looked at Mia, thinking how in one direction, E22 led to the wide E4 highway, which in turn led to Stockholm or Helsingborg. In the other direction, it led to Söderköping and continued on toward Kalmar.

A thought returned that had previously only flickered through his mind.

"Are you still there, Ola?"

"Yep."

"You said that Erika Sandell grew up in a house just outside Söderköping."

"Exactly," Ola said.

"Do you have an address to give me?"

"You think that…"

"Check if there is one."

"I'm checking, I'm checking."

Henrik shifted impatiently in the seat while he searched for the car key in his pants pocket.

"I think I might have found a house, but it seems like…"

"The address, Ola!"

"It's on Lilla Ladumossen."

She smelled a strong moldy odor. Lina Engström was breathing rapidly through her nose, and her eyes were wide as she attempted to understand what she was seeing.

Sandra had pushed her into a house comprised of two rooms and a kitchen, its windows boarded up. In one room, a chair had been placed in the middle of the floor. A naked light bulb surrounded by a small steel cage illuminated the room and the chair with a sharp yellow light. The walls and ceiling were made of old pine planks, and on the floor, some of the planks had begun to warp.

In the other room was a bed, a twin bed frame of rusty metal without a mattress, which resembled more of a camping cot or a prison bed. The wallpaper had come loose from the wall and hung like a withered flower petal above the bed.

Lina turned her head in the other direction and saw a kitchen. Flies buzzed above a wooden table. A narrow staircase led to the floor above.

Sandra's eyes shone, and her gaze looked calm and innocent. "Walk," she said.

But Lina couldn't move. Her muscles were loose and tired, probably because of whatever had been in the syringe. She fought to get enough oxygen into her lungs. She struggled with the disgusting stench of mold and with the pain in her head.

Sandra took her under the arms and dragged her over the floor toward the room with the chair. Lina felt completely powerless as her feet dragged along the floor.

She hardly reacted when Sandra used a knife to release the zip ties around her wrists.

"Sit down," she said.

She fell down onto the chair, thinking she might as well do what she was told.

"Arms on the armrests."

Lina placed her arms on the armrests and watched Sandra as she fastened them with new zip ties. She thought she saw a smile in the corner of Sandra's mouth.

She suddenly remembered the first time they'd met. It was at a party, the ambulance station's yearly staff party. She and

Philip had had an argument, and she'd sat in the bathroom for over an hour, exhausted and upset. Sandra had also been there.

Philip had been looking for her, and Sandra had offered to help. She'd come into the ladies' room, convinced Lina to open the door, and they'd talked for a long time.

Sandra had been funny and understanding. She had listened and asked questions. Her eyes had radiated happiness and energy.

Now she stood here with an expression that was difficult to interpret—she wasn't the same person.

Sandra leaned over her and folded up her sweater, revealing her belly.

Lina shook her head and started to move her legs, trying to make noise, trying to make Sandra stop, but Sandra didn't even look at her. It was as if she didn't hear her, as if she were deaf—or in her own world.

Only when she began to cry did Sandra look down at her. "Calm down," she said. "I haven't even started yet."

She turned right and went up a small hill, then continued along a straight road and finally made a left turn. Then she came to a complete halt.

Jana Berzelius glimpsed the white Volvo between the trees. It was standing still in a little glade, parked in front of a dilapidated wooden two-story house.

She backed up a few yards, then steered onto the edge of the road and turned off the ignition. She rolled down the window, watching, listening, and knew there was a risk they were being observed at that very moment, that Sandra had heard the car approaching.

She jerked when her cell phone vibrated in her lap. It was Henrik Levin again. She rolled the window back up and took a deep breath before answering. She tried to sound calm and professional.

"Sandra wasn't at Engström's house," he said, sounding upset.

"No?" she said in false surprise.

"No, but we're afraid she's taken Lina. We're on our way to Söderköping. We...that Erika...grew up...Lilla..."

Jana gripped the steering wheel harder.

"Where are you now? Hello, Henrik, where are you now?"

"We...have...Norrköping...will be there in...minutes."

"I can hardly hear you, Henrik. Can you repeat that?"

"We...there..."

The conversation ended. Jana looked at her phone and saw she had no signal. She swore aloud, closed her eyes and hit the steering wheel a few times.

"Let's take it easy, take it fucking easy," Danilo said. "Who were you talking to? Who is Henrik?"

"The police," Jana said. "They seem to be on their way here."

"Here? Here, where we are now?"

"Yes."

"What the hell? What did you say to them?"

"Nothing!"

"I don't have time for this!" Danilo screamed. "Just tell me what you said to them!"

"I didn't say anything..."

"You're going to turn me in, aren't you? How could you be so fucking..."

She heard him move and reacted immediately by leaning forward, but it was still too late. A muscled arm wrapped around her neck, and she was pressed backward in the seat with brutal force. Danilo's grip on her neck was so tight that her vision almost went black.

"How could you be so fucking stupid?" he screamed into her ear.

She gasped for air and made a weak attempt to twist out of his grip.

Then she felt the knife scrape against the small of her back. She pushed her hand in behind her as far as she could, but she only grazed the knife with her fingertips. It seemed impossible, yet she tried again. She twisted in the seat, curving her back, and finally got hold of the knife. She quickly pulled it out and brought the piercingly sharp blade toward his arm. But he reacted instinctively—*too* instinctively. He pushed the knife back far too quickly and with too much force.

It went straight into her thigh.

She screamed in pain and felt him immediately release his grip on her.

It took a second for her to understand what had happened. With trembling hands, she pulled the knife out and dropped it on the passenger seat. She pressed her palms against her pants and saw the blood oozing through her fingers.

"What the hell are you doing?" she said, meeting his gaze in the rearview mirror. She looked at him, his dark hair, the color of his skin, his panting breaths...

"Drive," he said.

"No," she said, shaking her head. "I have to meet someone first."

She lifted her hand and swore when she realized how deeply the knife had pierced her thigh.

She gripped the knife again. She cut one sleeve from her top and grimaced in pain as she tied the piece of fabric over the open wound.

She replaced the knife at the small of her back.

"Who?" he said. "Who is it you're risking so damn much for?"

She slowly pulled the key from the ignition, put it in her pocket and said: "For the woman who murdered my mother."

Then she counted down, turned her gaze toward the dilapidated house and stepped out of the car.

The tears ran down her cheeks. Lina Engström cried quietly where she sat alone on the chair in the empty room. When she opened her eyes, she had lost all sense of time. She didn't know if a second had passed or a minute.

She turned her head in all directions. She felt her hair sticking to her face. She tried to move her arms and moaned when the zip ties cut into her skin. She leaned her head to the side and tried in vain to get the tape from her mouth by rubbing it against her shoulder. It was stuck tight, but then it did begin to loosen. She leaned her head to the side again, this time against the other shoulder, and pressed as hard as she could. Half of her mouth was now free. A bit of tape fluttered when she took a deep breath.

She heard footsteps behind her, a door opening, and then even, calm breathing. Sandra was back, now with her backpack, which she placed on the floor in front of her.

"Oh, did you take the tape off?" she said, opening her backpack and taking out a sharp object. A scalpel.

Lina's eyes widened, and she began sniffling again.

"No, no, no," she said.

"You might as well relax, Lina. You're not going to be leaving this house."

"What…what…what are you going to do?" she said.

Sandra's lips parted, and she showed her teeth in a wide smile.

"You have great superficial vessels," she said, rolling up the arm of Lina's sweater.

Lina shook her head.

"Yes, you do. But we'll try going a little farther into your stomach than that."

"No!"

Something in her desperate scream made Sandra stop. She looked deep into Lina's eyes, drew the scalpel toward her naked belly and watched her squirm.

"Not my belly, please, not my belly."

"No?" Sandra said, drawing the scalpel toward her belly again.

"No! Stop, please, Sandra, stop," she said. "I'm pregnant."

"What? You're pregnant?"

Sandra started laughing.

"I can see it now. You look different. How many weeks?"

She laid her cold palm against Lina's stomach. Lina squirmed like a worm in the chair, trying to get away.

"But that's no excuse," she said. "You're still going to die, just not with Philip's child inside you."

She raised the scalpel.

Lina screamed at the top of her lungs as the blade sliced through her skin. Her fingers spread in all directions.

Sandra crouched before her. "Do you know what?" she said, giggling. "You know, I truly hate Philip. I don't understand how you've been able to stand being with such a wretched, weak jerk. You should be thanking me because today I'll be saving you from a really shitty life."

Then she got up, opened the door and left the room.

Lina was hyperventilating. The last thing she saw was the blood running from her belly down to her thighs, and in the next second everything went black.

She limped fifty yards before stopping. Another fifty yards from her stood the white Volvo, empty and dark.

Jana Berzelius ensured that the strip of fabric was fastened securely around her thigh before slowly continuing toward the ramshackle house. She came to a door at the back of the house and pressed herself tightly to the wall, feeling the cracked, rotted boards against her back. She laid her ear against the facade and listened tensely.

Out of the corner of her eye, she saw a light shining from what she thought might be the kitchen and crouched down. A light, maybe a table lamp, had been turned on. She saw a shadow flutter and sweep over the windowpane.

Sandra.

She cast a glance toward the door and felt the handle, but it was locked.

Crouched down, she continued around the house. The soft grass muffled the sound of her movements.

She crept along the front of the house and listened again, but now she heard absolutely nothing.

She carefully laid her hand on the door handle, loosened the knife from the small of her back and opened the door. A dusty, lit floor lamp was in the corner of the entryway, and she was met by the smell of damp wood and mold.

Besides the kitchen, there seemed to be two rooms on the lower level. The door to one was open. She looked in, but there was nothing there.

Then she limped toward the other, listening for sounds before she gripped the door handle and opened the door. In the middle of the floor, she saw a woman sitting on a chair, her head hanging and a loose piece of tape over her mouth. Blood was oozing from her stomach, down the chair and to the floor. The scene reminded her of the photos she'd seen of the ongoing murder investigation. A person bound to a chair, sitting in a sea of blood.

She assumed the woman was Lina Engström, but that was

as far as her mind had gotten when she heard a sound from upstairs.

She stepped in, turned around and closed the door cautiously, leaving it open a crack so she would maintain a view of the hallway and front door.

Then she took a step backward into the room and waited for Sandra Gustafsson.

CHAPTER
THIRTY-TWO

HENRIK LEVIN AND MIA BOLANDER HAD TURNED OFF
E22 and found themselves deep within the dark forest. They
had driven a few miles on the gravel road. Henrik kept a
white-knuckled grip on the steering wheel, came quickly out
of a curve, and increased his speed when the road straightened
out in front of them.

The ground was hard, rocky and dry.

The car bumped and trembled.

In the beams of the headlights, he saw the holes and dips
in the hard-packed earth, but he didn't do anything to avoid
them. He was fully focused on driving as fast as possible.

After another half mile, he had no other choice but to stop.

The road split.

"According to the GPS, it doesn't matter which we take,"
Mia said. "Both lead to Lilla Ladumossen."

"Are you sure?" Henrik said.

"Yes," Mia said. "So which way do we go?"

"This way," he said, turning the wheel to the left and starting down the narrower road.

She heard steps. First on the stairs, then in the hallway, and finally coming toward the room she was standing in, the room with the unconscious woman.

Jana Berzelius lowered her chin, watching as the door slowly opened.

Sandra stared at her for a brief moment. Her upper lip twitched.

"Who are you?"

"I've been wanting to talk to you," Jana said in a controlled tone. She felt the rage rumbling inside her, felt how it was almost impossible to hold it back.

"What do you want to talk about?" Sandra said.

"I want to talk about a call you were on…"

"You're that prosecutor, right?" Sandra smiled. "I thought we were done with that. It was incredibly naive of you to come here."

"I'm the naive one?" Jana said. "You killed my mother. Did you think you were going to get away with it?"

"She died of a heart attack."

"No," Jana said, "she didn't die of a heart attack. She died because she was smothered…"

Sandra stared at her and smiled again. "You've done your homework," she said. "And I'm really sorry. I know myself how it feels to lose a mother. But I had no choice. She'd seen too much…"

"What do you mean, seen too much?"

"Well, what can I say? She woke up just as I was pulling the ring from Philip's finger. I assume you know who that is. She was going to destroy my plan, she could have sabotaged everything with her damn curious eyes…she should have kept them closed—"

"You're sick," Jana said.

"—but she stared at me," Sandra continued, sneering. "I saw the panic in her eyes when she couldn't breathe. She tried to get free, but she couldn't."

Jana couldn't contain her rage any longer. She distributed her weight evenly, ignoring the pain in her thigh, and threw herself at Sandra. She put her entire weight behind the attack, heaving herself against Sandra and making her fall.

They tumbled backward, and Sandra twisted her body to the side, rolling around and coming to her feet again. She grabbed Jana, kicking at her injured thigh. Jana howled in pain but struck back, connecting with her stomach. Sandra gasped, struggling for breath, took a few steps back, and disappeared out of the room, through the hallway and up the stairs.

Jana got up to run after her, but her wounded thigh slowed her down. She limped into the hallway and looked up the stairs.

It was completely silent and still.

She gripped the railing, hopping on one leg yet continuing upward.

Just as she was about to take the last step, Sandra appeared, her teeth bared and her neck strained, and gave her a powerful kick.

Jana didn't stand a chance. She fell backward down the stairs, hitting her head, her arms, her back—hard. She landed on her injured thigh and lay still on the floor, breathless.

When she looked up, Sandra was coming slowly down the stairs toward her with a superior look.

Jana reached for the knife she always kept at the small of her back, but she didn't feel it there. When she turned her head, she saw it lying on the floor six feet from the front door.

"Is this what you're looking for?" Sandra said, pointing to the knife. "Where did you want it? In your throat? Between your ribs?"

She picked it up, weighing it in her hand, but just as it looked like she was going to raise it, something made her turn around.

It sounded like the front door exploded. Danilo had thrown himself at it with all of his weight. Two hundred pounds of pure anger against a rotting door. Splinters of wood whirled around; the old planks split into pieces.

The door hit Sandra, who screamed and was flung backward. The knife went spinning over the floor. When she didn't get up, he went over to her.

"Get up," he said. "I like a challenge. Makes it more interesting for me."

Sandra staggered up and he let her approach.

"Come on," he said. "Do something. Just give me a reason."

Spitting with rage, she aimed her fist, but he parried. She struck again, this time toward his crotch, and he didn't delay. He grabbed her, putting his left arm around her neck, grabbed his pistol from the waistband of his pants, pressed the muzzle against her temple and shot.

She was dead before she hit the floorboards.

Danilo wiped his pistol on his sweatshirt, placed it in Sandra's hand and pressed her fingers against the steel multiple times. Then he laid the pistol near her body.

"Are we done?" he said, turning to Jana. Her hands trembling, she felt her thigh. She tried to get up, but the pain stopped her. Just then, she heard the sound of an engine far down the gravel road.

"We have to go," she said, noticing that Danilo was also conscious of what was going to happen.

She tried to get up again, but the pain was unbearable. She

doubled over and felt Danilo's hands around her waist, felt her body being lifted into the air.

Her first thought was to stop him, to tell him she could walk by herself, but she knew it would take far too long for her to get back to the car. She breathed with her mouth pressed against his sweatshirt as he carried her all the way to the car.

He carefully let her sink down into the driver's seat. They let go of each other, and he sat down in the backseat. Then they sat quietly and stared into the darkness.

It was less than thirty seconds before they saw the headlights of cars dancing through the trees. She raised her eyes, looked at him in the rearview mirror and saw him nod. It was a slight movement, almost imperceptible.

She nodded back, just as subtly.

Then she started the car, turned the wheel and drove back down the same road.

Henrik Levin picked up the binoculars and aimed them toward the white Volvo and the dilapidated house. The GPS coordinates had led them here, and now three units were in place. Two officers to the east, behind the house. Two to the northwest, in front of it.

"What the hell's going on?" Mia said from the passenger seat.

"We wait until we've gotten the all clear," Henrik said.

"But the car is just sitting there," Mia said impatiently. "What are they waiting for?"

"Everyone has to be in position first."

"Give me the binoculars," she said, holding out her hand. "Give them to me."

Henrik handed them over.

"Hard to see any movement in the fucking dark," she said.

"True," Henrik replied.

"But look, the front door?" she said, staring at him.

He took the binoculars and tried to zoom in as close as he could.

"It hardly looks like there is one," Henrik said.

Mia crossed her arms over her chest, sighing.

"Nope," she said. "There's nothing to wait for."

"Calm down now," he said, casting a glance down the road.

Mia pulled out her service weapon and checked the magazine.

"She's in there," she said. "Sandra Gustafsson. I can feel it."

"We have to assess the situation."

"But does it have to take a hundred years?"

Henrik gave her an irritated look.

"Can you stop getting so worked up?"

"But she's in there, and I'm sure she has Philip's wife, too. Who knows what she's doing to her this very moment?"

Henrik didn't answer, instead raising the binoculars again and looking toward the car.

"Screw it," Mia said, opening her car door and stepping out.

She ran with quick steps through the grass. It was noticeably chillier in the glade, and her short breaths were made visible with fog.

She saw the men signal to each other. They checked their weapons quickly, followed her toward the house and got in position outside the door opening.

One of them, the one with long hair under his helmet, held up his hand. On the signal, they went in.

Mia waited impatiently outside until she heard the calls that the place was secured. Henrik was right behind her when she stepped into the hallway. The first thing they saw was a woman lying on the floor, her mouth open and eyes empty. A pistol lay next to her body. Henrik felt her pulse and looked up at Mia.

"It's Sandra," he said. "She's dead."

The long-haired officer approached them.

"The upstairs is secure, but we found this," he said, pointing a flashlight into one of the rooms. Mia and Henrik left Sandra's body and went into the adjoining room.

Mia's heart skipped a beat when she saw the woman sitting in the chair. Her stomach was dark with blood, and her head hung over her chest.

In the dull light of the flashlight, she saw the traces of violence. The floor under Lina was covered in blood. Mia took a step forward, reached out and felt for her pulse with her fingers.

"Lina?" she said, but there was no answer.

She held her breath, pressing again on Lina's neck.

"She's alive," she said. "Cut her loose!"

They cut the zip ties and placed her carefully on the floor. Henrik ripped off his jacket and pressed it against her stomach.

Mia took her cell phone out of her pocket and dialed 911 while Henrik continued talking to Lina. Mia heard him repeating the same words over and over and over.

"Everything will be okay," he said. "I promise. Everything will be okay."

A strange silence filled the car. Jana Berzelius and Danilo Peña were staring out the windshield, focused on registering any possible movements. The engine was idling, and the high beams cast long shadows between the dark buildings and the tall fences. Beyond the industrial district, Södertälje hummed.

Seconds passed, but nothing happened.

She was just about to check the time when she caught sight of a black Mercedes driving slowly toward them. She squinted in the headlights and could make out a vague silhouette of a lone driver keeping his head low over the dashboard.

The car stopped fifty yards away.

They were the only cars in the vicinity, and they were directly facing each other with their headlights on.

"And the boxes?" she said. "When do I get them back?"

She didn't get an answer. She heard the car door behind her open and close and knew he had gotten out. When she turned her head, she saw him. He had stopped outside her window with his bag over his arm. The wind tousled his hair, casting it back and forth. He looked at her for a long time, and a slight grin crept over his face.

Then he began walking.

She followed him with her eyes. She shut out the rest of the world, shut out the dark industrial buildings and the tall fences, shut out the hum of the engine, shut out the pain in her leg, shut out everything that didn't have to do with him and the blinding headlights of the other car.

Then she couldn't see him any longer. Instead she heard the muffled slam of a car door and the crackling of the gravel as the car backed away.

She felt her heart pounding as it disappeared.

She slowly looked up into the rearview mirror again. The backseat was empty. He wasn't there anymore; he was gone.

At last.

CHAPTER
THIRTY-THREE

Friday

SHE SAT ON THE BED WITH HER HANDS BEHIND HER back and fastened the top button on her black dress. Jana Berzelius let her hand slide down to the next button and buttoned all five, one after another, slowly and methodically.

She looked at the dust dancing in the sunlight.

The door to her bedroom was open. The apartment was silent. No footsteps, no movements.

She looked at the clock and knew she was going to have to stand up now, and she got up on one leg with some difficulty. The bandage, hidden by her dress, was wrapped tightly around her thigh.

She gripped the edge of a dresser and supported herself against it for a brief moment before limping over the floor. Her thigh was throbbing, but she ignored it, had to move unencumbered. She absolutely didn't want to call attention to herself or invite questions.

Her black hat lay to the left on the shelf in the hall. She pulled it carefully over her hair. Then she took the flower that lay wrapped in paper, held it to her chest and gently embraced it.

"Where do you want this box?" Mia Bolander called as she stepped into the yellow single-family home in Smedby wearing her shoes and jacket.

"What does it say?" she heard Henrik answer from one of the rooms.

"Nothing," she said.

"Put it wherever you find room."

Mia looked around, observing the impressive staircase and the airy kitchen. She walked through a hallway and into a living room that opened out onto a balcony.

Tall, paned windows looked out onto a yard where Emma was pushing the stroller in front of her. Felix was kicking a soccer ball.

The living room was spacious. Right now, though, it contained a crib and an old-fashioned bed with a tall headboard and footboard, and a white nightstand, a secretary-style desk, a swivel armchair, a rolled-up rug and lots of boxes.

There was a parquet floor and a tile stove.

Indeed.

Henrik came into the room with Vilma close behind him and a floor lamp in his hand. His hair was messy, and his forehead was sweaty.

He put the lamp down and walked toward her. Vilma stayed close behind him.

"How does it feel to move a few hundred yards down the street?" Mia said, putting the box down on the floor.

"We couldn't find any better option."

"This is a pretty cool place."

"You know it's my mother-in-law's," he said.

"So you threw her out?"

"Threw out Grandma?" Vilma asked, her eyes wide.

"No," Henrik said, ruffling her hair. "We didn't throw Grandma out. She lives in an apartment now, remember?"

Vilma blushed.

"Nothing wrong with an apartment," Mia said, smiling at her. "Fewer rooms to clean."

"Hey," Henrik said. "Thanks again for helping with the move."

"No problem. You promised beer, right?"

"Of course. But I know there's been a lot going on lately at work and such, and I just want to say that it was really nice of you to take the time."

"But we took care of it," Mia said.

"The move?"

"That, too, but I was thinking of work. Or, at least we were able to save Lina and the baby."

She was also about to say something about Sandra Gustafsson, but she didn't feel like talking about her anymore.

They had had a whole day of heated discussions over whether she had actually taken her own life, or what else might have happened there in the abandoned house in the half hour before they'd arrived. Anneli had been absolutely certain, no doubt about it, Sandra had been shot by someone else. Yes, maybe, but there weren't many suspects to point to in the middle of the forest. Either way, it had to wait until Monday, a new week, a new life.

"Right," Henrik said, "but it's a real downer that we haven't found Danilo Peña yet."

"No more talking shop now," Mia said, opening her jacket pocket. "I have a housewarming present for you."

She handed him a plastic bag.

"But you shouldn't..."

"I know."

Henrik looked down into the bag.

"A Russian nesting doll?"

"Yes! And there are lots of smaller dolls inside. I thought it could be cool for the kids. Right, Vilma? Isn't it kind of cool?"

Vilma nodded, took it from Henrik and immediately began playing with it.

"See, it's really cool," Mia said.

"Thanks," Henrik said.

"You're welcome," she said, lifting the box again with an exaggerated groan. "It's heavy, where should I...?"

"Let me take it," he said, reaching out. She let go of the box before he was ready. He tried to parry the weight to the right but was unsuccessful. The box slipped out of his hands and onto the floor, landing on his foot.

His face turned red, and it looked like he was going to begin screaming any moment.

Vilma looked at him and said: "Daddy?"

"Mmm-hmm?"

"Is now the right time to say that ugly word?"

The sky was clear blue and the air was chilly when she arrived at the summerhouse in Arkösund. The wind blew the peony she was holding in her hand as she slowly approached the funeral gathering.

After exchanging glances with some of the funeral guests, she saw her father in a dark suit and tie. Elin brushed off the lapel of his jacket—not because anything was there, just a gesture. A thoughtful gesture. Then she saw the officiant with his long beard, clasped hands and distant gaze.

Father pulled his sleeve over his watch.

Were they going to begin now? she thought. What were they waiting for?

Elin stopped brushing and Father coughed. Two quick coughs and then a tremble in his chin.

Jana wondered if she would see him upset, see him cry again.

She walked slowly through the grass, looking at the urn that stood at the far end of a table and the wreaths of flowers that had been laid around it, and sat in the chair next to her father.

The seat was cold.

She shivered and, just as the officiant cleared his throat to begin, thought that she should have dressed more warmly.

Mother was now going to her final resting place. It was time to say farewell.

"When a loved one passes away, we often try to find a comparison in nature, where everything is mortal. We make ourselves conscious that death is a natural element of the eternal circle of life. Therefore I would like to say to you who are gathered here today, fear not…"

She closed her eyes and thought that she had never feared death. Death was the final end point and the dissolution of existence. It was nothing. It was just the end.

She had met death so many times. She'd both escaped it and caused it.

When the violinist began to play, she opened her eyes, stood and picked up the urn.

CHAPTER
THIRTY-FOUR

IT WAS TIME TO DRIVE ON BOARD THE FERRY FROM Nynäshamn, Sweden, to Gdansk, Poland. Behavioral scientist Christoffer Bohm from Mjölby let his car window roll up and looked at the bearded man waving the cars onto the boat. He was wearing blue pants and a yellow vest. Christoffer was directed to a space in the row on the right, behind a Volkswagen bus. He released the brake and let his Volvo roll forward to the indicated space.

"Can we meet in the duty-free shop in a bit?" he said to his partner, Sanna, as he turned off the engine. "I just want to make sure the car is properly locked."

"Oh, just say it, dear," she said, looking at him with an amused gaze. "You want to rest for a bit?"

"Yes, it's a little tiring to drive three hours in a row," he said, yawning.

"I can drive when we get there, if you want."

"No, I'll drive. But I'd rather nap than walk around staring at things in the tax-free shop."

She smiled at him and stroked his cheek before picking up her purse and stepping out of the car.

"See you up there," she said, closing the door.

When she was out of sight, Christoffer reclined his seat and leaned back. He closed his eyes and heard the thuds as smaller cars rolled over the edge onto the car deck. He heard car doors slamming shut and the echo of voices as passengers left their vehicles. The silence between sounds and movements increased, and finally they stopped.

"Hello?"

He awoke from a knocking on the window. When he looked up, he saw the bearded man standing outside his car door.

"You can't stay on the car deck during the trip," he called through the window, pointing to a sign. "You have to leave your car."

"Okay, okay."

Christoffer nodded and let out a grunting sound as he stretched his body in the seat.

The ferry was rocking from the waves as he stepped out of the car and began walking toward the steel wall, toward what seemed to be the doorway to a stairwell. He was surrounded by cars. He couldn't even see all of them in the darkness, much less count them, but there must have been hundreds.

Right near the door to the stairwell, he noticed a movement inside a Mercedes. He stopped, looked into the car and saw something move under a blanket. Suddenly, he was looking into a face, a man with dark eyes and a hardened expression.

Christoffer stared at him—not because the man was lying in the backseat of his car while the ferry was in transit, but because he seemed familiar.

Christoffer began walking again, faster this time. By the time he arrived at the door, his pulse had increased. He ran quickly up the stairs, looking behind him the whole time as if he were afraid the man was following him.

Breathless, he stepped onto the upper deck and crossed between the people there. Some were laughing, others were already bored. Some were angry, or upset or clearly in love. Every possible emotion was represented.

His hand trembled slightly as he pulled his cell phone from his pocket. The signal was poor, but he dialed the police anyway.

"Hi, my name is Christoffer Bohm, and I'm calling in because I think I just saw a wanted criminal, I think his name is Danilo…"

The elevator doors opened with a clattering sound. She hadn't thought about the sound previously, but she also didn't use the elevator very often. She took off her black hat, stroked her hand over her hair to straighten it and walked stiffly out of the elevator.

She approached her front door slowly.

She stood there for a moment, breathing and listening, before she took her keys out of her purse and unlocked the door.

She took a step into the hallway and the door swung closed behind her. She stood still and again enjoyed the silence. It was a strange feeling to be alone again.

She set down her purse, hat and keys, went into the kitchen, looked around and continued into the living room.

She leaned against the wall, feeling her shoulders sink and her body relax.

Just then, the doorbell rang. The shrill tone cut through the silence of the apartment.

She wasn't expecting anyone, but the first thing she thought of was Danilo, that for some reason, he'd returned despite everything. That she was stuck with him in the apartment again.

She walked with limping steps to the door. A young woman with blond curls and rosy cheeks stood outside.

"Jana Berzelius?" she said.

"Yes?"

"I have some packages for you."

Seven large boxes stood outside the door, all addressed with her name but no return address.

"Sign here, please."

She held out a handheld computer, and Jana signed her name.

"There you go."

"Where do you want them?"

"In the hallway is fine."

"Okay."

The woman carried them in, one by one, and placed them right inside the door.

"That was the last one," she said.

"Thanks," Jana said, closing the door after the delivery woman.

She grabbed a knife from the kitchen and began carefully cutting the brown tape. Her heart beat quickly, pounding in her chest, as she unfolded the flaps of the first box.

It held what she had hoped it would. Her journals, notes—everything detailing who she'd been as a child.

What she had been.

Danilo had kept his word.

In the last box was a scrap of paper, written in pen.

She stood still and looked at it, at the four words.

I'll be in touch.

When she read those words, it was as if all strength ran out of her, and she sat slowly down on the parquet floor, holding her face with both hands. The sun shone with a crystalline gleam outside the window into the living room. Everything was quiet and still.

Then the silence was broken by the shrill doorbell again. And then a knock. Multiple knocks, as if someone were eager to come in.

She closed the flaps, got up, opened the door and looked directly into Per's differently colored eyes.

"Hi..." he said, looking down at the floor. "I just wanted to say that...I'm sorry. The situation with your mom. Her passing. I heard it only a couple days ago, I didn't know..."

"Things happen in life that..."

"Wait," he said, "I'm not done yet."

"But I don't want to talk about it," she said.

"Let me say what I have to say," he said.

"Do it, then."

"Jana...if you had just said something, I would have understood."

"I don't know what I'm supposed to say to that."

"You don't have to answer. I'll leave you in peace, but is it okay if I still like you?"

She didn't answer.

Per rocked from one foot to the other. He nodded slowly as if the silence were enough of an answer and then looked around as if searching for another place to go. He was going to leave. She could see it.

But instead of taking a step backward, he took a step forward, reached out his hand and touched her cheek, holding it there for a few seconds before he lowered his arm, turned around and walked away.

"Wait..." she said.

He stopped and turned around, but she didn't meet his gaze.

"Did you want something?" he said.

"Yes," she said.

She raised her eyes, looked at him and asked: "Do you want to come in?"

★ ★ ★ ★ ★

ACKNOWLEDGMENTS

FIRST AND FOREMOST, I WANT TO THANK THE PEOPLE who helped me with the story, who've read the text and given me their opinions, who answered my questions and helped me with factual details, who have given me their attention and above all their time. Above all, I want to thank my fantastic friends Elin Carlsson Malm, Lotta Fornander and Sofie Mikaelsson, who have dedicated many hours to discussing what should happen, what might happen and what probably would happen. Your opinions and professional expertise mean so much to me.

I want to say an especially warm thank-you to my sister and my parents. Dad, your joy and sense of humor have always inspired me. Mom, there's no one in the world who encourages and supports me like you do. Thank you for always telling me that you're proud of me. I love you. Enormously.

And thank you to my readers for fun meetings, wonderful conversations and many laughs. You give me all the joy in and inspiration for my writing.

As a matter of course, I should say that this story is fictional. Any similarities between the characters in the book and real persons are coincidence. Any possible mistakes that have crept into the text are mine. I may have misunderstood, forgotten to ask or invented something to fit the story better.

Finally, I would like to thank my husband, Henrik Schepp. Without you and your conviction that this would work, it never would have worked. Not with the first book, not with the second and not with the third. We are an unbeatable duo— in sickness and in health, for richer or for poorer—behind the writings of Emelie Schepp the Author. You're the best thing in my life.

Thank you.

ML   6/2018